Seahorse

Khara L. Campbell

ARCHWAY PUBLISHING

Copyright © 2019 Khara L. Campbell.

All rights reserved. No part of this book may be used or reproduced by any means, graphic, electronic, or mechanical, including photocopying, recording, taping or by any information storage retrieval system without the written permission of the author except in the case of brief quotations embodied in critical articles and reviews.

Interior art/graphics: Jaro Nemčok, Professor Laszlo Seress, Khara Campbell

Scriptures taken from the Holy Bible, New International Version®, NIV®. Copyright © 1973, 1978, 1984, 2011 by Biblica, Inc.™ Used by permission of Zondervan. All rights reserved worldwide. www.zondervan.com The "NIV" and "New International Version" are trademarks registered in the United States Patent and Trademark Office by Biblica, Inc.™

Archway Publishing books may be ordered through booksellers or by contacting:

Archway Publishing
1663 Liberty Drive
Bloomington, IN 47403
www.archwaypublishing.com
1 (888) 242-5904

Because of the dynamic nature of the Internet, any web addresses or links contained in this book may have changed since publication and may no longer be valid. The views expressed in this work are solely those of the author and do not necessarily reflect the views of the publisher, and the publisher hereby disclaims any responsibility for them.

Any people depicted in stock imagery provided by Getty Images are models, and such images are being used for illustrative purposes only. Certain stock imagery © Getty Images.

ISBN: 978-1-4808-7426-8 (sc)
ISBN: 978-1-4808-7427-5 (hc)
ISBN: 978-1-4808-7425-1 (e)

Library of Congress Control Number: 2019901712

Print information available on the last page.

Archway Publishing rev. date: 04/09/2019

For My Family

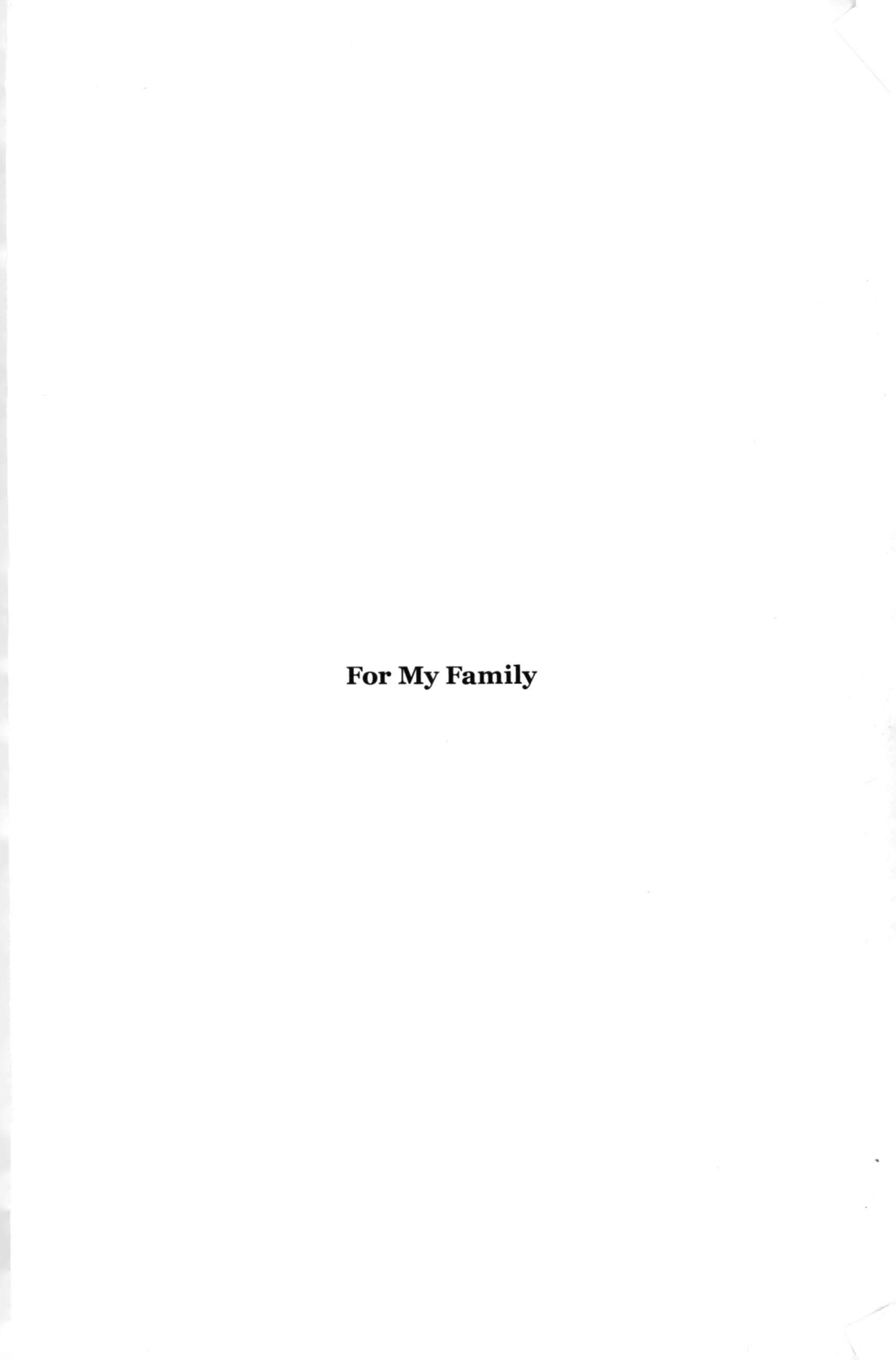

Acknowledgements

This book is dedicated to no less than three groups of invaluable people:
1. To the incredible women in my life who supported and encouraged me in this process, gave me their time, energy, thoughts, **smarts**. Annie Avlon and Sam Hanlon, this would be nothing without you. Allicia Elias – thank you for taking my calls when I had medical questions and pointing me in the right direction when it was outside your sphere. Katelyn Campbell, Robynne DeCaprio Cucinotta, Kim Walton Thomas, Anna Folwell, Kate Baldacchi Paradiso, Kirsten Giannelli, Sarah Doerrer, Julie Johnsen, Rita Colimon, Caroline Kim, Carmen Doi-Dietz, Elizabeth Ayers, Elizabeth Bohnel and of course, my editor, Roz Weisberg – your time, care, and feedback helped me get to that next "mile." Thank you. (And an honorary gold star to my friend, Dave Wedge, who supported me from the get-go)

2. To my FAMILY. Brothers, sister, parents, and inimitable extended family: you're everything to me. Ashley, I cried every time I'd write "our" scenes. You are my star and biggest support. Mom, without you this never would've happened. You made me relentless, and definitely taught

me how to fight. You made me tough *and* sensitive, and as an artist, however painful, it's a winning combination. Thank you. Dad, I love you; your work ethic and sense of humor shapes my perspective and helps me get through the tough days. To Pat and the late Connie Stone – there are few words to express the gratitude I have for you. The best I can say, is that you showed me the world and changed my life. And to my brothers – I love you so much. Thank you for making me your rough and tumble, kid sister, and for always being someone I look up to.

3. To every person affected by this senseless disease; to those who survive, to those who are in the throes of battle, and to those who were robbed of more years with their loved ones, I hope this gives you a voice. A way to be seen, heard, understood, never forgotten, never alone. To the families of those with cancer: YOU GIVE THEM SOMETHING TO LIVE FOR. I know this, because I asked. I know you are the light, the strength, the love that fuels them. To Mary Long, who shared her experiences with me, and told me to 'Keep Running' before she passed, leaving her children and loved ones behind. To Leah Fabrizio Busa – taken from her husband and children, her mother and siblings, far too soon. Thank you for sharing your feelings with me. Your voice as a wife, mother, daughter, sister, survivor, friend, *woman* with cancer came through. I felt so close to you the moment we began talking, as if it was supposed to happen. Born just 3 weeks apart, raised 15 minutes from one another, with our snide sense of humor, and our shared New England Patriots crushes, there was an element of 'mirror image' in us. I felt a sisterhood, a bond, though our lives were on

completely different paths. My life took me to California to pursue a dream, yours to your hometown to raise a family. So close, and so far away, until the Universe brought us together just 2 ½ months before you passed. We were given that tiny window, those few conversations, but it was enough. You touched my life, you passed your fighting spirit on to me.

I was told after you passed, that it was a great release for you to be able to talk to someone… If that's what I did, and it helped you, I'm humbled. If I provided one iota of relief, I'm humbled.

Family, friends, and incredible, beautiful, strong, powerful women: Thank you for giving *me* the opportunity, strength, support, and inspiration to write this, to believe, and to make sure this story was told. If it provides readers one iota of relief, I am grateful.

Preface

This book came about, quite simply, when I was on the phone with a friend. He asked me if I was living the life I wanted.

"What would you want to do if you found out you had 6 months to live?" he asked. "Hello? Hello?"

I couldn't speak. It's not that I've never heard that question before, it's just that this time, for some reason, it hit me, choked me, and the tears ran down my face. "I have so much more to do, so much more to give," I thought. To imagine *me*, with a debilitating illness that would take *me* in 6 months, I had no words. That could never be my reality. I'm a marathon runner, a more than healthy person. (Ok, I like my wine and cookies, but primarily, I'm a beast). So how could *I* ever be sick?

Because that's the way it goes sometimes. Sometimes very healthy, young people get sick. And that is tragic, and it shouldn't be this way, but it is. So I put myself in those shoes.

Finally, the words came back.

"I'd want to have a baby," I said. "I've pretty much done everything else."

We all know it takes 9 months to have a child, so I had to create the circumstances which would allow for that. But the truth is, cancer while pregnant DOES happen. And BAC, or what is now called lung adenocarcinoma, *does* happen to non-smoking, younger women. It's a rare cancer, but it happens. There are many theories as to how cancer is caused while pregnant: the hormones from pregnancy, or whether or not fertility drugs were taken. That's right, some studies suggest fertility drugs can cause cancer. We just don't know. But we do know it's happening. We can all name someone we lost to cancer far too young – but what do we *do*?

This story isn't going to cure cancer. My gift is not medicine, but I thank God for those who do practice, and for those searching for a cure, better treatment, and alternatives. I can create awareness with my stories, but awareness isn't action. Together, we have to create solutions. I had the pleasure of connecting with a young man who did just that. David Hysong, who was diagnosed with a rare form of head and neck cancer in his 20s, founded Shepherd Therapeutics by the age of 30. He makes it his mission to find treatments for rare forms of cancer – and rare cancer, by the way, is the third leading cause of death in the United States. *Third*. And if you think, once again, "Oh, cancer could never happen to me. I'm healthy, I'm young..." David was training to be a *Navy SEAL* when he was diagnosed.

It. Can. Happen. To. Anyone.

I lost people around me to diabetes and heart disease and cancer... I lost my brother when I was a little girl. Loss for me, started at a young age - some health related, some tragic – but it taught me those early lessons; to take care of my health, appreciate others, and be grateful for the moments. I know how quickly it can all go. Trite or not, life *is* a gift, and I wrote down a slice of it in the pages you're about to (hopefully) get lost in.

It was my love for life's complex and magical moments which propelled me to lose myself in these pages, too. I hope once you're finished, you'll look at your own, see the magic and wonder in it, and let the people around you know how much they color the chapters of your life.

I did my research - asking questions of medical professionals and scouring the internet — but also, *living*. I connected with people — with and without cancer. Listening to how people *feel* is a necessary ingredient to existing in this world, especially when we are buried in the momentary, superficial, digital "experience." I like my iphone, too, and Instagram and Facebook… but feeding ourselves the quick fix - 100 times a day - adds up. I hope we can all make time to listen to and connect with one another. NOTHING beats face-to-face time.

Now, get lost.

Khara Campbell
August 23, 2018
Santa Monica, CA

I always thought if you ran fast enough,
you could outrun it;
Time, age, sickness …
And for a while, you can.

-Caroline Shaughnessy, 2016

one

Caroline

Crickets. It's so quiet this time of morning, all you hear are crickets. Crickets and the sound of the ocean; even the seagulls are tucked into their winged slumber. The waves crash in, retire back, and return—nature's metronome and simultaneous affirmation that all is a cycle, something you can count on no matter what. It soothes me.

It's dark as I pull myself out of bed and tip toe toward the door. He'll be up in ten minutes anyway, but my feet respect his sleep. I turn back in the doorway to watch him, his peaceful face, his pillow-dented, spiky, brown hair, his chest rising and falling. I read that gratitude is something you should start your day with, and I'm filled with it. Two nobodies – I, from a gritty, nobody-town like Tewksbury, MA and Chris, from a much less gritty, but even more invisible Carlisle, Massachusetts – who used what we learned from the industrious rank and file to achieve the lives of the fortunate. I didn't come from much, he slightly more, but we put our heads down and carved our paths; the careers, the lifestyle, the house on the beach, and most importantly, each other. I feel nothing short of gratitude when I stop and listen to the life we always wanted.

I move through our home in the dark, padding through the hallway and down the stairs of our modern colonial, open floor plan with a shit-ton of windows and white columns, Restoration Hardware vases filled with multicolored roses and hydrangeas. Chris is incredible about getting me flowers; he knows how much a simple thing like that can make a girl smile. At the base of the stairs, a giant blue-green seahorse painting. I've always liked seahorses; they're romantics, originals, and they don't swim the same way other fish do. We could learn a lot from seahorses. I continue, passing glass light fixtures, teal rugs, plush, sand-colored couches you can sink into, coffee table art books, and finally, on an end table, my favorite "anti" picture of us. The wind blew the hair in our eyes the moment the picture was snapped, and neither of us looked at the camera, or each other. That kind. I think we got in a fight after—or wicked drunk. Maybe both. Eh. But it's that picture that encapsulates what I learned about love. Life - and love - isn't perfect.

Before Chris, I was dangerously close to losing faith that there was anyone out there for me. I was alone and overwhelmed by constant disappointment and had allowed myself to be treated poorly by quite a few men, back to back to back. I mean, wasn't that all that was out there? Had I not had so many painful experiences, though, I don't know if I would've appreciated him for the man he is. He isn't perfect— *we* aren't perfect- but in my mind, he's pretty damn close. And that helps, because I can be a total asshole. He makes me a better person, and more importantly, he makes me *want to be* a better person. That's the biggest gift love can bring – that the world gets better people in it. The quest for love is a hell of a motivator. Anyway, I dig that picture.

Our morning ritual is simple: I make coffee for us and burn off my type-A tendencies and anxieties on an aggressive 10k run, while my peaceful opposite *fishes*. Yes, all the way up to his freaking thighs. But winter, spring, summer, or fall, he's out there casting and reeling. Funny, that's how he got me, too. I fell for him hook, line, and sinker.

Chris

I snap awake. I reach to my right, my hand searches for her. Gone. My eyes adjust, and I see the sheer curtains that separate us from the windows which separate us from the waves crashing below. My panic ceases and relief sweeps over as soon I breathe in the freshly brewed coffee and faint scent of her hair. I peel out of bed and trod downstairs, hoping to catch a glimpse of her. As I pour a steamy cup, and as I lift it, I see her whisk past me in a flash of fuchsia and blue. She's on a mission.

"Bye honey," my morning voice grumbles. Slam. She must have her headphones in. "Oh well. Oh well-oh-well-oh-well," I mutter to myself as I shuffle across the cold, tile floor.

Caroline

I tighten my sneakers and Velcro my armband in place on my lean, little arm. They've always been disproportionately thin despite the bump of a bicep. My calves have always been huge, the kind you squeeze into tall boots or are strangely snug against the seams of even your roomiest jeans. Anyway, I run six miles a day at a competitive pace, and that's when I'm not training for a marathon. I like to start the day off right and run with a goal: get faster, run harder, *improve*. Our rituals are totally opposite, but they keep us sane.

I force myself out the front door and down the block of our black-paved, green-lined street. The smell of wet grass and salty air inspires a deep breath in, and although spring has sprung, the stinging air shocks me awake. For a moment, I debate heading back to the snuggled safety of my warm bed ... but it only lasts a second. The conditioned know the hardest part is always the beginning.

"If everything were easy, you'd never learn what you're made of." That's what my husband says, sometimes to remind himself, sometimes to remind me. I lunge forward, turn my music up, and leave my white, wealthy, 3.2-children-husband-works-in-finance-wifey-stays-home neighborhood in this oceanside town of Cohasset, Massachusetts. I've been here two years and I haven't been able to relate to the women here. They think those of us with careers are cold. They judge without knowing anything about you, and don't bother to consider that maybe, just maybe, you're having a hard time getting pregnant.

Come on, Caro, I tell myself. *Push.*

I stomp up the street and head to the main road, the ocean to the east, Mike's Package Store on the west. Two rugged guys in their late forties with thick, salt-and-pepper beards and cigarettes disappearing deep into them, look up and nod at me before stepping into their salty, rusted pickup truck. We see each other every morning; they're in construction or something labor intensive. Good guys. On the opposite side, near a "rustic" gift shop, there's Scowl Lady. Well dressed and probably in her thirties – but looks older - she crosses the street hurrying her two sons, roughly ages five and three. Her face wrinkles in resentment and scorn for me. I know this look. It says,

"Must be nice. Wish *I* had time for a run."

To which my squinted eyes and confrontational stare fire, "Why, yes, Scowl Lady, it is. Don't take it out on me. I wasn't the one dumping sperm in you."

"Classy as ever," she says.

"Well, you do this every day."

"Do *what?*"

"That *look*. You give me that look that says, 'The saintly and blessed have children, the selfish and wicked do not.'"

"If the shoe fits," she snorts, followed by the ever-vicious, "No wonder you don't have kids." And she grabs her sons and storms off.

Okay, that never happened. But that's what I *would* say. Imaginary conversations can get me through many miles, it passes the time. Sometimes nasty conversations are better than none, especially when the only person you have to talk to is yourself. I used to run with my friends when we lived in the city, but we all moved away from the fun and excitement of Boston a few years ago. We're all in different parts of the country now, and that transition from lots of friends to none has been harder than I think a lot of women mention. Or maybe, a lot of women are on the same life schedule; marriage, kids, etc, as their friends. I've always been a late bloomer, and somehow, that tardiness has resulted in being left behind.

I trample onto the path. The woman's voice on my app tells me I hit four miles and that my pace is 8:05. To come in around eight minutes per mile, that'd be a good morning. Some people are born runners. Not me. It takes a lot of work for me to be fast, and even though I've run a few marathons, my pace isn't fast enough to qualify for Boston. That's one of my life's great failures—being too slow for Boston—but you can run it for charity, and that's a nice way in.

Chris

The sunrise leaves a perfect pink and orange aura over a deep, dark sea. It's April —ankle-numbingly cold in the Atlantic, but then again, it's always ankle-numbingly cold in the Atlantic.

I cast my line. The loud plunk is music to my ears, the expanding ripples, a masterpiece in motion. I reel in, stand, wait… The water *might* hit sixty-six degrees at the peak of summer, but not likely. Low sixties is all we ever get, unless you go down the Vineyard, where it's a generous seventy degrees. We're not far from the Cape and the islands, but far enough to freeze our balls off. I cherish my morning ritual - solitary, tranquil, filled with possibility, and the perfect way to start my day. I cast my line.

Plunk!

Ah, a symphony! Reel in, stand, wait. I check my watch, to see if she's there. 6:48. Nope, not yet.

"Five more minutes, Legs. Four or five more, depending on the morning."

I lift a cigarette to my mouth. I quit a few years back and even then I only smoked at the bar, but sometimes it's nice to have a leisurely smoke. It's morning, it's beautiful, and I'm free to do what I like. I strike the match, bring it toward my mouth, and suddenly realize: it's morning, it's beautiful. I bend the butt in half and put it back in my pocket – don't want to give the fish cancer.

"Some things we're meant to quit," I say. My wife said that to me when I was trying to.

My wife, she's a force. A beauty. A beast. And if I told you the things she overcame, you wouldn't believe she turned out the way she did. She will never, ever complain, and she will take more shit than she'd ever give out - often to her detriment - but she is a survivor. Somehow, she came out believing in the Good - in others, in dreams, and in ourselves. I didn't just fall in love with her because she's beautiful, I fell in love with her because of who she is. She is the kind of person who makes me want to protect her – and while my marathon-running-tough-as-nails-warrior-wife doesn't much need it – I still want to. If anything ever happened to her...

My eyes dart right, but I don't turn. See, I *know* she's not there yet, so I'm not wasting a look. We have this thing down to a science, this fun, little game we play. I can't look back toward the windows until I know she's there, till I can *feel* her there. I know it sounds nuts, but that's why it's fun. And because we've gotten really good at it. There's something about a look, you know? A look you share with someone that no one else understands.

Most guys won't tell you this, but there are two moments in a man's life when he looks at the woman he loves with tears in his eyes. She glided triumphantly toward me—her white smile to match her white dress; squinted, sparkly eyes, and rose-tinted lips. She never believed it was going to happen for her—not just getting married, but marrying the love of her life. She was waiting for the real thing – I guess I was, too. Sometimes what you really want takes longer to get there. Anyway, that hot September day, she was radiant, stunning - and I was a blubbering mess. You could swim in the pools of my eyeballs. But that was it, that was the moment I knew everything I'd done to that point was for *this*.

It's getting to be that time. I imagine her rounding the bend and getting closer. A smile cracks across my wind-chilled face at the thought. In a matter of seconds she'll be standing there, waving to me from the other side of the glass. Five, Four, Three, Two…

Caroline

The voice on my app tells me I hit six miles. I round the bend toward my street, Wellfleet Circle, and I can see our home. I pick up the pace, power through with everything I've got, almost there, closer, closer, I've got more in me, I've got to make eight minutes flat.

"Come on, Caro, *push.*" I speed up for the last few steps, all the way up the driveway. I have to go the full 6.2; 6.1 isn't the same. As I reach the end, I've hit it: 6.2 miles. I check my pace: 7:59/mile. Boom!

I'm a dripping pool of salty sweat after my abusive, cardio beat-down, and I feel great. *I'm gonna crush today! Shower, have a healthy breakfast, and crush it! I am unstoppable!* But first …

I stroll up to our French doors, a hundred yards from the water and stand there, watching him. *That face.*

"Damn, did I get lucky."

I wait for him to turn back - it's a matter of seconds before he senses me. He looks back, meets my gaze, and we wave. Perfect, simple, and the only way to start my day.

🐚

My black Mercedes - or 'the Panther,' known for her sleek body and breakneck speed - pulls into the garage of Dionysus Ad Agency in Boston, aptly named after the Greek god of epiphany. Dionysus was also the God of theatre, wine, and fertility, and was described as a sensuous, androgynous type. Womanly, or "man-womanish," and his thiasus, or retained followers, were crazy, drunk chicks and satyrs with hard-ons. I'm not even joking. I walk through the main lobby past the towering sculpture of a Greek satyr. Yes, that *is* a pipe case HANGING from his giant erection. The Greeks liked to fuck and drink ... so do my coworkers.

Anyway, as Creative Director, I'm the female version of Don Draper - minus the excessive booze, philandering, and cigarette smoke. I've been at this hip, somewhat progressive company for eight years and am one of only two women to hold that position in Boston. Competition is the name of the ad game, and to never, ever rest on your laurels.

"Once you rest, you're dead," a twenty-eight-year-old hotshot repeats to me, standing over my desk.

"That's right, Kevin," I say, sighing over a shoddy storyboard he's thrown together. "It looks to me like you're Rip Van Winkle. What *is* this?" I point to the perfectly wrong couple for this ad. "Aspirational and inspirational? Please."

"The couple is consumer-friendly," as he points to their pajama-inspired wardrobe.

"Those two? You're right, you didn't alienate the consumer with a Brad Pitt look-alike and a twenty-year-old waif, but does flannel and a Dad-bod inspire you? *Sophistication*, Kevin! This is *BMW*!" I stand and pace a bit, hoping to walk it off.

"I know."

"I know you know! I don't want to take you off this, Kev, but I will if I have to. Your two minions, Dim and Dimmer, would kill for an account like this. What's going on?"

"I – I hit it pretty hard last night."

"That's your answer. Hammered at the Seaport with the rest of the degenerates. *That's* your excuse for sloppy work on a multimillion-dollar account?" His head hangs in silence. "This is due in two days, Kevin! I could fire you for this shit -"

"Jen broke up with me – it's over."

"Arghhh." My unfiltered shock spilled out of me like hot oil across a desk, so I tried to cover it up ... I'm sure I failed. "She broke off the engagement?"

"Yeah. Three weeks before the wedding. That's why I was ... out. I haven't even told my parents yet. You're the first." A tear escaped from his eye, but he caught it and swiped right with the swiftness of a Tinder decision.

I felt bad, but *obvious* sympathy would make him feel worse, and I didn't want to do that. At the same time, Kevin can be such an arrogant asshole ... but in moments like these, I know it's a cover. I sit back down at my desk and look him in the eye.

"Do you *want* the account?" I ask. His glance meets mine with a mixture of hope and heartbroken uncertainty. "Can you handle it right now?" I continue, trying to read him, "Tell me the truth." I look at him straight, no judgement.

"I need it."

I pause, "Ok. Pour yourself into it, distract yourself with it, but if I give this to you and you fuck it up, I'll kill you myself. So you have to get it right. Stop drinking, go for a round of golf, strip club, whatever. Get clear of it. Got it?"

"Yeah."

"And I'm sorry about Jen, I am. Cliché as it sounds, this will pass."

"Thanks boss." He turns to leave, eyes glassy.

"Kev - if you need anything – call me. Here or at home."

Weepy, but hopeful, "Thanks Caroline."

I stand up and stare out my floor-to-ceiling windows, at the buildings above and the city below, feeling his pain but trying not to, wondering if I did the right thing – for me, for him, for the company? I like Kevin, and I do feel for him, but if I show too much concern, the patriarch will tell me I'm a weak leader because I'm *emotional*, but if I don't show any, then I'm an unnatural, unsavory woman.

My intercom goes off – it's my assistant, Abby: "Caroline, just reminding you about your 9:30 in the conference room."

"Thanks Abby."

I walk into the glass-walled conference room where a dozen colleagues stand, ceremoniously clapping. My boss and Dionysus partner number one, Mick Tillerson - a sixty-something, Nantucket home-owning, NSFW kink-fiend - holds a bottle of Dom, struggling to pop it. When he finally does, cheers erupt.

"Our Woman of the Hour!" says Mick.

The clapping continues as he hands me a champagne flute and passes the bottle to his assistant to take over. The other partner, Rick Manning stands next to Mick. Yeah, that's right, Mick and Rick. Rick used to go by Dick until he realized it was off-putting. They're not bad guys, most of the time.

Rick picks up where Mick left off. "Caroline!" He lifts his flute into the air. "We want to thank you and celebrate your Sephora deal – a huge account, and your third this month!"

"Third!" Mick echoes.

"It's been a great month," I say, "But I couldn't do it without the work of the team, so this toast is to you!" We raise our glasses and yell "Hey, hey or hear, hear," whatever noise we can muster at this hour. Some of us have been up since dawn; the youngest of the group *got home* at dawn after entertaining clients. Thank God those years are behind me, I gratefully passed the baton.

I take a mini-sip of champagne and leave it in the conference room. I can't be in party mode now – there's too much work. If anything, I need a coffee – or water – I need to hydrate.

I make the turn toward our well-stocked, grass-fed, sustainably organic kitchen, and suddenly hear my name whispered inside, followed by laughter. I lean up against the outside wall and pretend to check emails in case a passerby notices my clandestine eavesdrop. I hear three men:

"She's a ball buster, but I'd still fuck the shit out of her," says one.

"Slap that attitude right out of her mouth. Cook me dinner!" says another. More encouraging laughter.

I listen harder, trying to make out their voices.

"Well, you'd have to pull her away from her *brilliant* husband."

"Please. A *professor* at a *Women's College*? He's soft."

"Bet he's banging six of 'em – if he had the balls." I recognize the voice. It's Kevin.

Mick and Rick trot toward the kitchen – I turn away so they don't see me. They barely look up.

"Heyyy gentlemen!" Mick says. The other three gratuitously cheer and mumble something unintelligible. Mick and Rick pass me without noticing, their sugar-free Red Bulls in hand.

The three voices laugh anxiously and wait – and I wait. Finally, I hear Kevin again:

"You know she makes more money than he does. What a fucking pussy."

I turn the corner and wait. I stare and they stare. And I wait. "You guys done?" I say. I'm pretty sure Kevin pissed his pants.

"Ah, hey boss," Kevin stammers, "Done with …?"

I hold another beat and stare *through* them, as if to say, "you know, and I know." Their mouths were agape, their eyes wide and bulging, I felt like I caught three ten-year-old boys with Dad's dirty magazine. Finally, "With BMW. You guys done?"

"Oh!" he laughs, relieved. "Right, of course. Yeah, almost."

"Almost? You know what Dionysus says about *almost*."

"Almost is the first loser," Kevin grumbles.

"We do. We do say that. Right guys?"

"Yep, totally," the other two agree.

"Great." My heels click across the floor as I open the fridge, grab my water, close the fridge - all while hearing their uncomfortable shifting and ramblings. I turn around to face them, studying their eyes as if they'd reveal a shred of character. Foiled again. "Gentlemen," I begin, "We need to hold ourselves to the highest standards, *embody* the kinds of messages we're selling, otherwise they're a bunch of cheap, empty words. As my dad always says, 'No one wants to be full of shit.' Right Kevin?" He shifts uncomfortably. "We're not just a great agency because we say great things, we're exceptional because we *live up to them*." My clicking shoes cue my exit, but I stop with one more thing: "Ten ideas on my desk by lunch."

"You got it, Caroline!" Kevin shouts after me.

two

Chris

I bounce along in my '77 International Scout II, vintage red, sans roof. It's fifty-five degrees out, and after a long winter, that's summer weather. The hunter green gates of Wells University are equal parts welcoming and elitist – the portal to an all-women's school known for its prominent alumnae, from Supreme Court Justices to astronauts, to screenwriters and scientists and activists. The list goes on and on, but includes no one who looks like me. I didn't choose this university, it chose me, seven years ago, in fact. I was intimidated at first, wondering why they would ever choose a man to teach here. Didn't they want all-women professors at their all-women's school? The answer was no. For whatever reason, they wanted me, and I take that responsibility seriously – probably even more than I would at a co-ed school. I learn as much from these young women as they learn from me, and it's an honor to be tenured here.

My Intro to Moral Philosophy normally has about twenty students, unless it's Friday, in which case, twelve deeply committed–or disturbed–pupils attend.

"So our discussion continues, what makes one a good Man?" Sighs and grumbles ensue from the students. "*Woman*, my apologies. Clearly, Aristotle wasn't thinking about our progressive university when he asked the question. That sexist pig." The grunts turn to veiled chuckles. "But that is the question – what makes someone Good? To answer that, we have to ask, what is the *function* of a human? I mean, what the hell are we doing here? Kim?" I look over at Kim, a purple-haired Korean with funky glasses and a Star Wars t-shirt. She doesn't look up.

"Kim is…texting. Makaela?"

A black, British Makaela taps on her phone without looking up, "I'm Instagramming."

"Sepideh?" I follow the sounds of her long, red nails tap-tap-tapping on her phone

"Sorry," she replies. "Snapchat."

"Excellent. Anybody *not* on social media right now? Taylor?"

"I'm pondering the virtues of mac and cheese," Taylor, head resting in hands, replies.

"Much better. With or without bacon?"

"Duh. Far more virtuous without. I'm a vegetarian. And a good Jew."

"Great. So far our function here as humans is crystal clear." More laughter. "Ah laughter, you're awake. So! The function of the ear is to hear. If you can hear, then you have good ears. But what then for human beings? What makes a man or woman *Good*? Think about that. Aristotle said the only thing that separates us from the other animals is that we think, which is then externalized by speaking. Speech is a sign of reason, of rational thought. He concluded to perform rational thought *well* is the human virtue and if you possess this virtue, you are a *good* human being."

"It seems oversimplified, Professor," Taylor says.

"I agree. Ted Bundy was a terrific communicator, but not a good man. He thought, he spoke– he performed the *function* of being a human."

"And to him, what he did made perfect sense. To him, it was rational," says Makaela.

"Exactly– which means one thing."

"What?" Sepideh asks.

"What makes someone good or bad is not so cut and dry. And I'll bet you're only wondering one thing right now."

"Why did I wake up on a Friday to come to class?" offers Kim.

"Bingo," I say. "And the answer to that is, it most certainly makes you a good *student*. So, for those of you who showed, your homework is to have a safe and virtuous weekend."

"Woo!" They cheer.

The class spills out and I notice the time. "Oh shit!"

I run down the hall for my monthly "sync up". This is the kind of meeting where I feel less "synced" and more like I'm standing in a circle of women who wield many pebbles and fling them at my genitalia, while I stand there protecting my manhood. Yeah, I'd say that describes my zeal for this. Anyway, it's *supposed* to be a meeting where we discuss upcoming events, comments, and concerns.

Mary Carter, Head of the Department presides. She's fifty-one, African-American, tough, and fair. The other three are awful. I hear them competing the moment I get in the door.

"You don't say," says Yvonne in her thick French accent. "Well, *my* dissertation was on the nature of moral judgment in France in the fifteenth and sixteenth centuries," Her nose is pointy and she's thin-lipped.

"How interesting. *My* current research is on the methodology of the Eudemian Ethics vis-à-vis the Nicomachean Ethics," boasts Zoe. Her sweater is outdated on purpose.

Gia offers something about the Magna Moralia. Gia is the warmest of the three; she merely avoids eye contact.

"Chris. Please, join us," says Mary.

"Sorry, my class just let out."

The three force a half-grin.

"No problem," Mary says. "Let's get right to it. Questions, comments, concerns?"

"Well I have one," Yvonne chimes in. "The students are complaining our classes aren't as 'fun' as Mr. Shaughnessy's."

"And that's a problem?" I ask.

"I don't think Ethics should be fun," says Yvonne.

"Ah. Would it be *unethical*?" I can't help but laugh at my own joke...but they can. "Ok, I teach my classes the way I teach them – meaning, I make the content accessible. I don't try to intimidate or exclude them by using language that turns them off to an already dying field of study."

"You dumb it down," says Gia.

"I don't dumb it down. I keep them interested. It's about them, not our highfalutin accolades."

"Are you mansplaining?" asks Zoe.

"What? I said *accessible*. Mansplaining? Don't throw that around. That doesn't even make sense."

"There you go again," Zoe fires back.

"Chris, let's step into the hall," says Mary.

Mary and I get far enough out of earshot, and I can't hold my breath, "Mary, every month it gets worse."

"Chris, you're a great professor. We know it, the students know it – they love you. Yvonne and the others...they're leaning into you because...it's like it's their *turn*."

"Mary, that's reverse sexism, and that's not what we teach here."

"I know."

"Poor behavior is poor behavior."

"I know. And I'll talk to them. Look, keep doing what you're doing. I'll talk to the bulldogs."

"Can a woman call another woman a bulldog?"

"I'll say whatever the hell I want." I follow her back into the room. "Ladies, this meeting is adjourned. Quite frankly, I like it when our judgements and insecurities *don't* get the best of us. When your house is confidently in order, it doesn't matter what's going on at the neighbors'. Mind your *own* houses. Most importantly, let's remember we're on the same team here, and the priority is our students."

I grabbed my notebooks and book bag and hurried out as quickly as I came in, but not before hearing a few final whispers. Guess it's going to take longer than I thought to be on the "same team."

Caroline

When I pull into the driveway, I see my husband lumber out of his car, spill papers that need grading, scrape them up, and adjust his glasses with heavy shoulders. His kindness and work ethic is such a turn on. I hurry out of my car to intercept.

"Anything I can do to help?" I ask, with a flirty smile. He's either not in the mood or is absolutely not picking up the hint.

So I make it clear when we get inside, and peel those professorial duds right off him. He never knows where my seemingly unprovoked gratitude is coming from, but if he knew what the guys in my office were like, he would. I am *so glad* he's not like them.

We go at it on the couch, and I make sure every last inch of his body is tended to. I know he's upset about work, but we're home now. Nothing can touch us. When we're through, we lay around naked and entwined, pillows everywhere. My fingertips trace his sculpted forearm all the way to his pouty lips, prickled by a month's worth of facial hair – the beard makes him look a little older and it keeps him warm in the colder months. He'll go from beard to scruff once the summer hits. He traces my jutting hip bone, an unusual hybrid of my mother's hourglass genetics and the athletic form I've created. His masculine hands pull me in once more to kiss my face and run his mouth down my neck. It's heaven, our little world.

"I needed that," he says.

"Me too," I smile. "My back hurts, though." I rub my lower back.

"You used to like it rough," he teases, pulling me in.

"No babe!" I laugh, "It's my new heels, they were clearly designed for sitting."

"Why don't you call Jimmy and have him come over? I'm sure he could be here in a couple hours."

"On a Friday?"

"Legs, just call him."

Chris was right. Our massage therapist, Jimmy, is there by 8, setting up his table in our great room. We open our French doors to let the ocean air blow our sheers around. The moon bounces off the sea, and the lights inside create a flickering, golden glow. Scotch-immersed cubes clank in Chris's glass as he rests it on the piano, and soulfully begins Debussy's *Clair de Lune* – achy and beautiful. His hands slide down the keys as if in a dance while Jimmy's move down my body, pulling and patting each oiled muscle, from back to bicep, forearm to lower back, glutes to hamstrings, calf muscles and down to my Achilles.

The human body - 206 bones, 600 muscles, 100,000 miles of blood vessels, and 37.2 trillion cells - is an unparalleled instrument. The things it's capable of: physically– whether sprinting 100 yards or balancing on pointe, regenerating blood, creating new pathways in the brain, warming you up, or cooling you off. Emotionally– the depth and nuance of anger, rage, love, sadness, fear. Intellectually- the thoughts we create, ideas that begin in our brains as a *maybe*, and grow outside our heads into reality, into buildings, music, films, thriving businesses, or world-changing technology. Our *body* is a masterpiece, a marvel.

Jimmy's hands heal my lower back before he glides up to my traps and pushes hard, harder, it hurts so good. Chris continues to play, both routines hit a crescendo until the tension releases and spills out of both of us; we all have different ways of letting go. When I look up and see Chris, everything else fades away. I'm here with my best friend, overcome with joy, my eyes tear up. I've been emotional lately – not sure why.

Maybe it's…something *has* been weighing on me - us - mostly me. I know we have everything. We do. Except for one, teensy weensy, itty bitty, minor, little thing…

3.1

Caroline

Her hair is dark, her eyes are blue, and she's about the most heartbreakingly beautiful child you've ever seen. I imagine my daughter might be like this – *hope*, is more like it. My four-year old niece, Sara, smiles at you when you talk to her, but is intermittently interrupted by moments of shyness – I guess it's her age. Happiness, innocence, sensitivity and wonder abound in her eyes. It's nice to be reminded of those feelings every now and again, they're so absent in adults. Every few months, a day opens up in my or my sister, Katie's calendar allowing us to get together.

I leave work early to pick up Sara from daycare and bring her back to my sister's in Peabody, MA. The North Shore has a different vibe than the South Shore – both are speckled with wealthy towns amid tough, lower-middle class towns inhabited by Irish-Italian Catholics who love to work hard, drink, shout, make jokes on your behalf, and do it all over again the next day. The residents of, let's say, Marblehead, do a lot less yelling, and their drinking is gentrified- wine over beer – but our roots are the same. Peabody is somewhere in the middle, socioeconomically speaking. They can still rough you up, but they probably shop at the Gap. Marblehead is Michael Kors to Louis Vuitton. I think the real difference between the North and South Shore is the latter's proximity to the Cape – South Shore loves their popped collars and boat shoes. They're just a little preppier there. Even a bulky, 6'4" goombah out of Weymouth will sport a pink Polo with a popped collar and feel right at home. He'll crush your skull, but he'll do it in style. Anyway, with Katie and her husband, George, working full-time, they occasionally need a hand, and it's about time I give it. I don't see my niece as often as I'd like. I barely saw her the first two years of her life –you know, work. Besides, I didn't have the baby gene the way others do, so I wasn't exactly dropping everything to catch her every new move. I've *always* been a late bloomer; a little bit alpha, and more comfortable with my achievement side versus my nurturing side. While my friends from college planned their weddings and baby showers by age twenty-seven, I was planning world domination…in ad sales, anyway. I wanted to win first, have fun first, make love first, and when I slowed down around thirty-five or so, have a kid. I'm thirty-eight, and that plan hasn't gone accordingly.

I gaze adoringly as Sara sits in the grass, playing with her dolls. The setting April sun turns the night damp, but that doesn't deter Sara. Suddenly, she leaps toward her swing.

"Auntie Caro! Can you push me?!"

"Yup!" Sara hops up and awkwardly lifts her leg onto the swing, determined to get up by herself. "Can I help?" I ask.

"I can do it!" She struggles more, and suddenly looks up at me with perfectly desperate eyes.

"I got you." I lift her up and place her in the swing. She doesn't say a word, her tiny-toothed grin says it all. I gently push her.

"One…two…three…four!" She sings as her feet extend to and fro. "Auntie, when is Mumma gonna be home?"

"In a few minutes, sweetie. She's grocery shopping and Daddy's working late."

"Oh-kayyyy. A-B-C-D-E-F-G…L-M-N-O-P."

I smile to myself. "That's pretty good, but I think you missed a couple."

"Meh, that's ok."

I break out in laughter. "Really? It's ok, huh?"

"Yeah. Why we gonna stress about it? There will be another day. Try again tomorrow."

"You're too much." I kiss her head. "Want me to push you some more?"

"Nah, I'm good. Let's go in and get a snack."

I lift her out of the swing as my sister pulls into the driveway. Katie is three years younger than me, lighter hair, more traditional, and kind of a saint. Outside of my husband, she is my best friend in the world. Of course, with busy lives, I also don't get to see *her* as much as I'd like, but we text a few times a week.

"Mum-mmmyyy!" Sara screams as she runs, arms wide open.

"Hi baby girl!" Katie scoops her up. "Hey sis." She kisses my cheek.

"Hi OK-atie!" I say, as I throw my arms around her.

"Thanks for watching her."

"No problem. It's been a while." Katie puts Sara down, and opens the trunk to grab groceries. Sara runs to help.

"Only a little one, Sar, just a light one. Here." Katie hands her a bag with bread and cereal. I grab a couple, and we walk toward the dark gray split-level.

"Yeah, we've been running around like crazy with work, and Sara's dance lessons and daycare... we barely get time to ourselves, let alone to see family. Same with you, I saw on Facebook – you and Chris seem pretty busy."

"Yeah, if it's not work, it's work events, University charities, rugby – you name it."

"Well, I'm glad you could peel away tonight."

"Peel away? That sounds pointed."

"No, no. We're both busy, I just wish I saw more of you." We get inside and stand at the platform between the upstairs and downstairs.

"You can always come down to Cohasset."

"I know, we will." She grabs the bags from me and drops them ten feet away in the kitchen, Sara hops up and down, spilling the bread.

"Yeah Mumma, let's go to Auntie's at the beach!"

"When it gets warmer, honey." Katie picks up the bread and sets Sara's bag on the table.

"Or sooner. We don't have to go to the beach to spend time at my place, we can sit inside, have a glass of wine, play Barbies – right Sara?" Katie leads us outside again.

"She doesn't have Barbie, yet."

"Mommy says next year, when I'm five."

"Oh," I say.

There's a brief silence as everyone recalibrates. Katie grabs the last bag and shuts the SUV, and stops in front of me. Sara holds my hand.

"Listen, I'm sorry," Katie says. "I've been go-go-go with work this week, and we have to enroll Sara in a new daycare tomorrow because she knows all the kids and all the songs and stories, so she's bored and wants a new school."

"Sounds like a lot of drama." I say.

"Oh, you get used to it." We exchange an awkward glance. "You will," my sister reminds me. "You will."

My eyes fill up, so I try to mask it with an even bigger smile, "Ok, well, I'm gonna hit the road." I give her a hug, and squat down to Sara, who throws her arms around me.

"I love you, Auntie," she says, a glint in her eyes. Her unwavering sincerity gives me pause.

"I love you, too, Beautiful Girl."

"Bye," she takes her mama's hand as they walk inside. I look over my shoulder once more, Sara does the same, and with her big, bright smile, waves excitedly, "Bye Auntie!! Till next time!"

I wait in my car for a second, delighting in Sara's spirit, her lit-up face. I never wanted kids the way other women do, with that *need* - I'm a New England aberration. Everyone from the southern tip of Rhode Island to the top of Maine seems to have been committed to a life of kids right out of college. Ok, grad school. "Later," I figured, "I'll have them later." It's different now.

I make the hour drive down Route 1 from Peabody to Cohasset – North Shore to South - lined with chain restaurants, car dealerships, gas stations, and liquor stores. Route 1 is more interesting to look at than, say 93 or 95 – problem is, the speed limit is slower on Route 1 because of all the intersections and stop lights. You can't drive as fast, it's far too dangerous. Mom would drive this way sometimes when we were kids, to drop Dad off for his shift at Filene's Basement, while we looked at the neon lights of the tacky restaurants. Dad worked a lot, Mom raised us, sometimes resented us, and always resented him. I wished he was home more often – so did Mom - but you wouldn't know it by the way she spoke to him, and the truth is, *somebody* had to work two low-paying jobs to put food on the table.

One night when I was about seven and Katie was almost four, we rode in Mom's Pontiac station wagon to drop Dad off at work. Katie's foot kept coming over to my side.

"Katie!" I yelled. "Stay on your own side! Stop kicking me!"

"I'm not!" she shouted back.

"Liar!"

"Would you two knock it off!" Mom screamed as she eyed us in her rear view. "Enough is enough!"

"But Mom!" I yelled. "She won't stop doing it, and then she lies and says she's not!"

"I'm NOT lying!"

"Oh my God, YES YOU ARE!" I took her foot and twisted it until she yelped in pain which turned into her screaming bloody murder. Phony.

"Goddammit, you two! Caroline! Are you hurting your sister?"

"Mom! I told you, she's not listening to me. Why don't YOU tell her to stop?!"

"Because I'm driving! You want me to hurt us? Huh?! You want me to hurt you?" Mom stepped on the gas, and the car picked up speed.

She seemed mad, like she was trying to scare us, but I knew she'd slow down in a second. She often did that kind of thing. Instead, the car went faster.

"Is this what you want?" We passed car after car, one swerved out of our way, and I heard honking. I leaned to the side, peering around Mom's seat to see how fast we were going. The dial moved past 70mph, toward 80mph, and it didn't seem like she was going to slow down.

"Mommy!" I yelled. "Slow DOWN!"

"Oh, you want me to slow down?!" She pushed the pedal even more. The car's engine roared. She looked me dead in the eye from that rearview and with no emotion, "How about I keep going and kill us all? I'll kill us all, goddammit!"

"Mommy, STOP IT! This is dangerous!" Katie started to cry and reached for me. I put my arms around her. "It's ok, Katie, it's ok." Katie unclicked her seat belt and slid next to me so she could get closer. I held her as tight as I could. "Mommy, you knock this off, right now! You're going to hurt us and crash the car. You want that?! You're being dangerous!!"

I could see Mom's eyes in the mirror. They were crazed and angry, but I knew that look: *she's sad again*. She kept going faster, till the cars and restaurant lights were a blur. A stop light ahead turned from yellow to red. She didn't stop and there were cars coming.

"It's ok, Katie," I whispered. "It's ok." I held her and kissed her head. I looked at Mom in the mirror, my eyes begged. She saw me and her face changed. Fear, conscience, I don't know. Suddenly, she slammed on the brakes, barely missing a stopped car. We came to a stop, she was breathing fast and hard, like she couldn't catch her breath. She pulled to the side, got out of the car, and fell into the grass, as tears streamed down her face. Her body shook while she cried.

"What's wrong with Mommy?" Katie asked.

"She's sad. About TJ," I said.

"TJ?"

"Our brother. You probably don't remember him, you were little. Let's get your seat belt back on." I slid her over and buckled her up. "It was a year ago, but that's a lot to a little kid."

"I'm sorry about kicking you, Care bear."

"I know. It's ok-atie.

I continue along Route 1. Our brother was fifteen when he died. Heroin. I was almost six. I don't remember everything, but I remember. Those years in that house, they shaped me, for better or worse.

🐚

I lift the oddly shaped, white stick to my eyes – it resembles a digital thermometer, the more I think about it. The kind that sat by my bed each morning for eight months while I tried to check my basal temperature until I realized an ovulation test works a lot better, especially for someone who is not exactly regular. I stare at the little window on the stick. The first line slowly emerges, and I pray for that second line. Waiting and staring, as if staring harder will make it true. Chris wants kids, and I want him to have everything he's ever wanted. The truth is, the more I see what kind of father he'll be and how much I love him, I really want them, too. I want a family with *him*. I just turned thirty-eight, he'll be thirty-six next month. For as healthy as I am, and as young as people *think* I am, I'm running out of time.

"Come on, two lines. Two!"

I have a good feeling about this month; it's getting warmer, I feel strong and healthy, – I haven't even seen many of those dastardly gray hairs popping out of my center part… and side part… But after a few more minutes, the single "Not Pregnant" line remains. I chuck it across the bathroom. This is the sixth month in a row– before that, it was even worse. I slam the drawer in frustration and the tears break free.

"Caro!" I hear Chris yell from down the hall. "Are you ok?"

The truth stares back at me. *No, I'm not, Chris. I'm letting you down– I love you more than anything, and I'm a failure, but I can't tell you that. Please don't leave me.*

"I'm fine, baby," I say. I pull myself together, stand up tall, and open the door. We'll try again this month.

My lilac, silk dress flows with every step I take, as I sashay down our stairs. I may not feel like much, but as long as the outside is held together, I have a fighting chance with the inside. This lilac number is one of my favorites, although it feels snug. I typically bring salad to work to trim some of that notorious winter weight, but when the office orders takeout– or any sugary carb– my will power goes to shit. No more of that, it's go time!

"Morning!" Chris chirps as he thuds down the stairs.

He dons a button-up shirt and a Mr. Rogers-style cardigan that makes him look older than he is - but ridiculously enough - sexy as hell. His tortoise shell glasses only add to it. As a college professor, he tries to minimize his sex appeal and maximize his credibility. *Nice try, Chris, you're still a smoke show. Wait, are those chinos? Ok, that may have lowered your score.*

I stand at the counter with my back to him, chopping away. He notices my salad and grimaces.

"Ugh, that's just sad," he says.

"I'm trying to get back on track. I'm keeping the temple pristine." I slice peppers and cucumbers and tomatoes while my mind tumbles with to-dos. "I was supposed to join this Cohasset Facebook page Patty told me about.."

"Well, did you?"

"Nah. I looked at it. It seems like money is *everything* to these people."

"Because it is."

"It's *one* thing, not *every*thing."

"I know." He pops grapes in his mouth, steals a cucumber.

"I mean, if you identify yourself by how much money you have, who are you if it's gone?"

"That's a stimulating question. Maybe I can use it for today's discussion."

I shoot him a look. "You're making fun."

"What? I'm not kidding." He pops more grapes, stares into the fridge for the dream of something exciting - the reality disappoints.

"I ate my weight in muffins last week. Someone brought them to a work meeting, and I couldn't help myself…six times."

"That's my girl. Go big or go home. Did you leave any for anyone else?"

With guilt and shame, "No."

He laughs and pokes my relatively firm side. "You'll run it off, hon," he reassures, "You always do." He pulls away, but returns, suddenly circling like a hungry lion.

"I'd need a ten-miler for this one," as I slice into a carrot. He pauses, and I feel him eyeing me.

"Still look good to me, Legs." He puts his head in the back of mine, breathes me in. "Smell good, too." He gives my hips a squeeze and lingers there a second. I feel his muscular torso lean into mine, and with outstretched fingers, he pulls my hipbone toward him. I smell his cologne – it makes me crazy. I want to breathe him in from my insides and put my hands all over him as soon as I catch a hint of it – but it's morning, and we have to go to work.

"Baby... we have work."

He pulls the hair away from my neck and kisses my bare skin. "I know." But he doesn't relent.

I smile like a schoolgirl, lifting my shoulder to ward off his tickle. My slippery, silk dress comes down in a V, exposing more skin and does little to help me play defense. His hands move down it.

"Mmm." He grunts in his masculine way.

I can smell him, feel him against me. While he may be a deep thinker, and even high on the sensitivity and emotional intelligence scale, he's all man. Six feet tall, a chest you want to hold onto and never let go. I look to my right at the forearm propping him up, the veins running down to show a life of discipline. His arms and shoulders are beautiful rolling hills of curves and lines, each defined muscle your fingers cry to trace. The jawline of a Hollywood actor – he could've been one if he weren't such an academic. Most people, after years of being together, lose interest in their sex life, in their partner. Crazy. To look at him, know he's mine – that kind of excitement *still* makes me want to fuck him.

He spins me around and puts his face on mine. "I have… ten minutes. You?"

"Mmhmm."

With one swoop, he pushes everything off the kitchen table – utensils, a fruit bowl, a pint of milk - all crash to the floor. His glasses come off, my dress, I'm ripping off his belt. He lifts me up and my ass hits the cold, hard, cherry wood table. Uncomfortable, but who cares– though I'm pretty sure that's Special K stuck to my thigh. I get his pants off. My once neatly styled hair is a tousled mess.

My hands move down his chest, his abs, I kiss his neck, his collar bone, and back up – my hands are everywhere. He grabs my wrists and pushes them to my sides to let me know who's in charge. He gets on top of me, kisses me, I melt into it. He moves fast, and deftly pushes into me. It's familiar, but never old. The table chafes my back. Battle wounds, worth it.

"Are you ok?" he asks, breathily.

"Yeah" I say. "Although… yeah."

I flip on top of him. I'm much smaller than him, but I'm no slouch. As I move, it's my knees that chafe, but who cares? I stare down at him, look him in the eyes, we smile at each other for a moment. I lean down to kiss him. He knows I'm about to go. I move against him, my whole body tightens, every single muscle. He moves into me at the right time, the roller coaster of my orgasm climbs up the track, rising steady, closer, closer…. He knows. He's close, too. My breath gets heavier; my body squeezes tighter.

"Oh my god," I whisper.

I move one last time and feel the burst. I let out a yelp, and the roller coaster rushes down the track, my body releases. I'm sweaty and exhausted, he grabs my hips, pushing me up and down a few more times, ready for his. Hard and aggressive, he grunts in release. It was intense for him too, I know by the sound he makes.

I drop my body on his, both of us panting and glowing. I roll off and lie down next to him.

"Mmmm." We both say at the same time.

We turn and look at each other with a smile, laugh. We do this kitchen table thing once in a while because we *can*. No kids, no worries, why not?

"I fucking love you," he says.

"I fucking love you," I say.

SMACK! We give each other a high-five and roll off the table leaving evidence all over the floor and a napkin stuck to his ass. I peel it off him as we get dressed and head for the door. I internally apologize to my cleaning lady for the mess she's about to walk into, but while it may be grudgingly, she gets us. We should've thought better about the milk, though.

On second thought, I grab a notepad and scribble my apologies.

Dear Theresa – I'm really sorry for the mess. Please forgive us.

I slap the note and $100 extra on our fridge.

"Is an extra hundred enough?"

"We'll add more at the end of the week," he says.

I struggle with my shoe and stumble out the door as my husband reaches for my hand.

And *that* is everything.

Later in the office, I sit lost in thought, twirling my hair through my fingers, rewatching the movie of our morning play. Hands, hair, touch, mouth, skin. Intoxicating. I dial him.

"Yel-low!" he says. *Fucking nerd*.

"Hi baby," I smile into the phone.

"Heyyy. What's up?"

"Let's try IVF again. I don't care about the money."

"Honey, you know it's not about the money. It's the time and stress on you."

"I don't care. I can handle it."

"Of course you can, but… also I heard something unsettling about the drugs. The added hormones – I read there could be a weird correlation to cancer."

"Oh come on, that's ridiculous. God, they say everything causes cancer these days."

"I know. But, let's keep trying the old-fashioned way. I kinda dig it."

"Yeah. Me too." We laugh. I hear him smile into the phone.

"We'll get there, baby, we'll get there."

"Ok. I love you."

"I love you, too."

The seahorse is a majestic creature unlike any other. The head of a horse, the body of a serpent. Its Greek name, *Hippocampus* literally means horse – sea monster. There are 54 different species of seahorses in the genus, hippocampus, and they range in size from .6 inches to 14 inches. Most are found in shallow, tropical to temperate waters throughout the world.

four

Caroline

Every weekend, Chris plays rugby in the neighboring town of Hingham. We pull into the parking lot of the rugby fields and it looks like a Beverly Hills valet: Range Rover, Range Rover, BMW, Mercedes, Escalade, Range Rover, Audi. Where I grew up, it was Honda, Toyota, Chevy, Subaru, Ford – and they were *used*. But we're not in Tewksbury anymore. Chris and I jump out of his car; Chris grabs his bag which reeks of sweaty shirts, socks and dirt-clinging cleats, while I assemble my spectator gear: a lawn chair and thermos o'mimosa.

Jay and Lola Harrington – born and raised Hinghamites - disembark from their new Tesla SUV. Their darting glances reveal they want to avoid us as much as we want to avoid them. But timing's a bitch.

"Heyyy Professor Progressive!" a tall, bulky Jay yells. "How's it goin?"

"Jay, Lola, how are you?" Chris says.

"We're great!" tweets Lola. "We became members at The Country Club. And I don't mean Cohasset, I mean *The* Country Club – it doesn't even need a descriptor. Tom Brady and Gisele are members, and I mean, *everybody*. Just everybody who's anybody. We've been on the wait list for *six years*, but Jay went to Exeter with the VP of Membership and cleared him of his tax evasion charges, so we're in!"

"Lola!" Jay says.

"Oh – keep that between us," as she waves an unusually tanned, diamond-weighted hand, and at least four David Yurman bracelets. Her shoulder-length, brown hair curls at the bottom á la Gena Rowlands circa – forever – and it bounces as she walks. "Did you know it was the first golf club in the country ever? It is *so* exclusive. Are you guys going to join?"

"Max of 1300 members nationwide?" says Chris. "I don't think we'll make that cut."

"Yeah," Lola adds, "It's expensive. *We* can barely afford it."

"Where are the kids today?" I ask.

"With my mother, thank God. How's uh, work?"

"Oh, thanks for asking. I landed a huge deal with-"

"Hey Jay, did you pay the gardener?" Lola asks. "I left for tennis before I could write him a check."

"No."

"Our gardener, Emmanuel – we forget to pay him sometimes. E-manual Labor, I call him. Man, Caroline, that figure of yours," She eyes me up and down with equal parts admiration and contempt. "I wish I had time to focus on myself."

Chris kisses me and grabs my hand. "Hey guys," he chimes in, "I'm gonna do a couple laps before warm-up begins. Catch you later." His grip goes from loving hand-hold to tow rope as he picks up the pace - he always knows when to rescue us. I was dangerously close to smacking her.

Behind me, Lola carries on – she doesn't even try to whisper, it's an audible snicker, "If it hasn't happened by now… I mean, *late 30s*? That poor guy. Who knows, maybe he'll leave her if she can't give him kids. What a shame, he's such a catch." I hear Lola greet another local and her two kids. "Heather! Maggie, Joaquin!

So, great to see you again!" The sounds get further away as I sprint with Chris. I pray that's my last encounter. Chris joins his teammates while I set up my chair on the sidelines and hide from anyone else who might want to chat. Thankfully, the others keep to their corners, but I overhear them discuss the club, their yachts and trips to Dubai.

I take a sizable swig of my mimosa and long for escape...

Fall 2011

Bom bom bom bom, bom bom bom bom – that's the sound of our sneakers as they hit the sidewalk along the Charles River, this crisp October morning. A golden glow bounces off the ripples while Harvard rowers, local kayakers, and sailboats zip past us to our left. It's 8am, and we've already run seven-and-a-half miles. Our sweaty, diamond-shaped four-pack of women stay tight so we can hear each other.

"No way," says my dark-haired, warrior friend, Allicia. Aleesh, a dumb nickname I gave her when we were fifteen, morphed into an even dumber one, Leash. Leash is my rock and I've known her since the sixth grade.

"Yep." I say.

"Come on, he *still* didn't give you the promotion? Cock sucker."

"Mick says he wants me to prove myself –*more*. Says he'll re-evaluate in six months."

"Six months? What an asshole." says a soft-voiced, strong-spirited, Anna. I met her at a run club last year and we became fast friends.

"I mean, I've been there three years, and while I want everything yesterday, I'm sure there's more I need to learn."

"How to take it in the ass, apparently," chimes in a red-headed McKenna. We met at a bar, nicknamed her, Mack.

"How's our pace?" Leash pipes up from behind.

I check my watch. "About 8:40, Leash. You good?"

"Great. Even though we're only halfway there. Those pancakes are calling my name."

"Bloody Mary's calling mine," says Anna.

We laugh. Mack, the furthest back, pulls to the side and pukes.

"Ohh shit!" we pull over to wait for her. I pause my watch.

A cyclist swerves out of the way, "Get out of the fucking way, runners!"

"Oh don't work too hard on that bike! They created the wheel for a reason – *it makes work easier*!" Mack yells, still keeled over. The cyclist gives us the finger and shakes his head as if to say, *I fucking hate runners*.

"I fucking hate cyclists," I say.

"You alright, Mack?" asks Anna.

"Yeah," as she looks up at us with bloodshot eyes. "I drank last night, one too many. Should have stopped at six." She heaves one more time.

"Trooper!" Allicia says, handing off her water bottle. Mack washes her mouth out and spits.

"Ah, to be twenty-four again." I say.

"I'm twenty-five," says Mack.

"And still able to boot and rally," says twenty-eight-years-young Anna. "You good?"

"One more swig." She sloshes it around in her mouth, spits, then douses her head with the freezing cold water. "Woo! I'm up! Let's go, motherfuckers."

"I like your style, kid." I say.

Mack moves to the front of the diamond, pushing me to the middle. I resume my watch.

Anna turns to me, "Mack is insane."

"Yeah. I like it."

We move along the Charles past the Hatch Shell and cut over to Berkeley Street for a couple blocks to take in the tree-canopied Comm Ave, which soon drops us off at the Boston Public Garden. We gallop past the George Washington statue and the picturesque swan boats. We march through the evergreen Boston Common until we reach the end, and take a left onto Park Street, with the hubbub of shoppers and construction workers of Downtown Crossing to our backs and the shiny, gold-domed State House to our chests. We take a lap around the State House until it dumps us onto Beacon Street, down past the Commons again - now to our left - and the iconic *Cheers* bar from the 80s TV show to our right. A left onto Arlington and finally, a right onto the famous Newbury Street.

"That's it guys," I say, as we slow to a stop. We all lean over, resting our hands on our knees or hips, shaking our muscles out, catching our breaths.

"Fifteen?" Anna pants.

"Yup," I say.

"How's our time?" asks Leash.

"Two hours fourteen minutes, seven seconds. Just under a nine-minute mile. Not bad, guys."

"No, not bad" says McKenna. "We won't be winning any races, but…."

Anna stares in amazement at her phone. "You know the *winner* of Boston will get close to a 2:14? *Twenty six point two miles* in the time it took us to do fifteen."

"No dude," says Mack. "This year's winner broke the record with a 2:03. His *marathon* is *faster* than our fifteen."

"What's that pace?" Leash asks.

"Hang on," Mack says, as she bangs on her phone. "Holy shit, 4:41 per mile."

"No!" We shout.

"We suck," says Anna.

"Yeah, let's go grab a beer." Leash says, as we turn to rejoin normal humanity.

"I couldn't do ONE 4:41 if you held a gun to my head. In my life. Ever." I say.

"Me neither," says Anna.

"Guy's a fucking machine," says Mack.

And with shirts and hair so wet it looks like we showered in them, we hobble down Newbury.

"Stephanie's?" Mack asks.

"They won't let us in there. We're nasty!" says Anna.

"Whatever," says Leash, "See what *they* look like after fifteen miles."

"Welp! First toast is to not giving a shit." I say.

"Here here." we yell.

The whistle blows and I'm yanked from my memory. All eyes focus on the rugby field as the pummeling begins; a sea of multi-colored Polo and Vineyard Vines ensnare, going from pristine to filthy in a matter of seconds. The suburban husband's escape; a few hours of freedom from their wives and kids, a memory of a lost time when the rough and tumble was enough, when survival of the fittest was about the physical not fiscal, when competition was gritty, dirty, honest. The bruises and broken shoulders give them something *visible* to complain about – complaining about life, well that's for wussies, isn't it?

Half of these poor souls are out of shape and overweight and they accept it. Some men take better care of their cars than their own bodies. It's silly. You get a new car every four or five years, but a new body? Not unless you're a Kardashian.

Suddenly, chatty Patty rolls up, who proudly hails from neighboring Weymouth. I know this not just because of her thick accent, but because she's told me no less than 400 times.

"Hi Caroline," Patty says, as she sets her lawn chair next to mine. "Howaya?"

When I was a senior in high school, a friend of a friend invited me to a couple parties with pristine, privileged, private school girls from Cohasset who referred to their "lowly" neighbors from Weymouth as "Sweaties." I don't know why, maybe it meant they were greasy, poor, or their parents were blue collar laborers who worked so hard they sweat. These girls didn't know it, but I was dating a guy from Weymouth. Either way, it was snotty and ignorant - it's funny how some people can get into Ivy League schools and still be fucking idiots. Anyway, Patty is a "Sweaty," and I do like her, but she could talk the balls off a horse.

"Good, Patty, how are you?"

"Good, good. OMG – ah you ready fuh this? Me and Bobby take Michael to registuh for little league, and my youngah one wants to play, but the age cut off is Novembuh first, and he was born the eighth, so I go and talk to them and I'm like 'Come on, one week? What's he gonna do, break his leg because he's a week too young? Don't be ridiculous.' But they're like 'the rules ah the rules, lady.' And so, Bobby's all pissed off and wants to punch the guy in the face, and of course he might, because he had one too many Sam Adams at the Burns's cookout. Did you go to that? I didn't see ya."

"We couldn't make it."

"Right, so anyway, I'm tryna get in Bobby's eyeline because he's got that crazy look on his face, you know, crazy eyes – you know, how he does, like this." Patty squeezes her mouth to try to make her eyes look evil – she's concentrating *really hard*– it's

Seahorse

amazing, but I can't look at her or I'll laugh, and I don't think she thinks this face is a joke.

"Ah. Yep."

"So anyway, you gonna go down the Cape this summah?"

"Huh?" I say, as my eyes connect with my husband's. They're in a timeout, and he's staring in my direction with this proud look. Suddenly, he gets the ball and takes off, moving down the field avoiding this guy and that, swerving, side-stepping, dancing on his toes. No one can catch him. Suddenly – BOOM.

Ooohs of sympathy explode from the crowd. A 220-pound beast pounds him; Chris is tough, but that looked bad.

"That one hurt," says a wildly observant Patty.

Chris doesn't move, but I don't stand up from my chair, all dramatic. I keep my eyes on him, willing him to get up, because I know he will. I know he's ok. He's down a moment longer. Inside, the worry kicks up, but I hush that voice, because he's ok. I know he's ok. *Chris get up. Come on baby, you got this, quit messing around. Come on, honey, let's go.*

A second feels like an eternity. And then he lifts his head. People cheer. He drops it back down. I'm almost terrified, but not. *You're ok, right, Chrissy?* I stand up.

Then, Chris takes a big, deep breath, and hops up, still holding the ball. He looks me in the eye, winks – I smile back – and he's off to the races. That's my baby, that's my Chris.

"So when ah you gonna have kids?" says Patty. "You're my age, aren't ya? Thirty-six?"

"Something like that," I say.

"Oldah? Don't get me wrong, you look 28, but you gotta get going. Ah you guys tryin?" I conveniently look away. We're silent for a beat…and then she has to fill it. "Well, I guess it's not fuh everybody," she explains, "Some people ah married to their careers."

"I'm married to a man."

"Right, well, mothah to their careers."

And that's the upper cut that drops me to the floor. TKO. No matter what I've done in my life, the career, the accomplishments, no matter what I look like, no matter the meaningful bond and successful marriage I have with my husband, this is the moment I feel less than a woman. That something is wrong with me and I couldn't possibly understand womanhood if I haven't experienced motherhood. "Mother to my career." A strange and unfeeling, useless creature.

Perfectly timed, Sandy Moore, mother of two, arrives. Her kids run over to Patty's boys, and the women squeal and squawk, exchanging the typical niceties and whatever high pitch nonsense they can sputter.

I remove myself, walk toward the parking lot, and close myself in the car, where the tears can roll down without admittance or shame in my private room of sorry and not enough.

Back at home that afternoon, Chris sits on the edge of our ottoman while I dab a cotton ball on his dirt-embedded scrapes. His knees are bloody and grass-stained.

"You ok?" he asks.

"Yeah."

He pulls me onto his lap. "What's up?"

"Nothing."

"Caroline."

"What?"

"Talk."

"I took another pregnancy test."

"And?" I shake my head. "Well, that's ok," he says. "We'll try again. We can try right now. I love trying." He goofs around with my blouse.

"Chris, come on, stop it. Stop!" I stand up and walk in circles. "I mean, should we look into adoption? I want one of our own, but…"

"Then we'll have one of our own. You're healthy, I'm healthy. Some things are worth waiting for. We'll keep trying. And IF we have to, in another six months, we'll look into other options."

"Chris, it's been two *years*. Two years, two pregnancies, two miscarriages. Even the IVF didn't work."

"So we *keep trying*. I don't like the IVF thing, but – look, six more months. We keep at it, do whatever it takes, but we aren't giving up. I'll never give up on you, don't give up on me. Remember?"

"I remember." I sit back down with him, he pulls me on top of him and lets me talk. "I miss my friends."

"I know. Anna?"

"San Francisco."

"Mack?"

"Chicago."

"Leash?"

"Busy with her third."

"Child or marriage?"

I smile, "Yes."

He smiles back, "Busy lady."

"Yeah," I pause. "The women here –"

"Are annoying." Chris answers.

"Yeah."

"I know. Don't hang out with the annoying ones."

I lay there in his arms for a minute, frustrated and defeated until my eyes catch a glimpse of something bright in the next room.

"Are those what I think they are?"

I step into the foyer and there a dozen fresh, orange and yellow roses are perched on the table in full bloom... and at the base of our stairs... and as I look over my shoulder, in the kitchen. I don't know when he managed to get them or set them in vases— but he did.

"How?" I turn to him.

He shrugs his shoulders, "Magic."

While the seahorse is unique in its appearance, it's perhaps most admirable for its depth of character. Several seahorse species *mate for life*, a rarity in the animal kingdom. One such monogamous species is the *lined* seahorse.

five

Caroline

Memorial Day. It's one of those perfect, 80-degree days. Chris is at the helm, grilling, with a cigar in his mouth, and a silly red, white and blue skimmer hat on his head. Thank God he's goofy; those uptight, self-serious academics are a drag. *I'm* probably a drag to him. Maybe that's just the mood I'm in today. I take another gulp of wine.

My mother, Gloria, is here. Her shoulder-length hair is colored blonde, she dons a tailored, beige sport coat, her nails professionally done, and she wears quite a bit of jewelry. She really cleaned up after divorcing Dad seventeen years ago. "Oil and water," was the excuse I'd give my friends for their demise, but truly, it was about money. When they finally divorced, I was twenty. It was a long time coming and not a moment too soon. I think they were waiting for us to be out of the house, but the truth is, they should've done it long before that. We could've at least cleared the air of the toxins that were spewed on the regular. There was never enough money in Mom's eyes, and she reminded our father, liberally, that it was all his fault. His two jobs a day just weren't cutting it.

I remember the bill collectors coming to our door and calling nonstop when we were kids. Dad would be at work, but it was us at home hiding beneath the front windows or letting the machine take the call, constantly hiding from the truth. Her words of wisdom to me were,

"Marry rich, Caroline."

Even as a twelve-year-old kid, I had a feeling money didn't solve all your problems. I found I was right. Years later, when my grandfather died and left $100,000 to my mother, it was gone a year after that. And during those twelve months, life wasn't all smiles and sunshine. In fact, there were just as many tears and more fights. A decade later, I learned it was actually $300,000. Imagine that. No, I didn't get any of the inheritance and I didn't care. I've never been one to complain about what I don't have, about what someone "never gave me." If you want something, go get it, and I figured, if the bill collectors stopped calling, good for her. Anyway, staring across at her, all decked out on my patio furniture, I'm fairly certain someone else died– a favorite aunt, a mystery uncle? Or she's dating some guy she's taking for everything he's got, because she's looking and dressing like she grew up in Cohasset.

Grill Master Chris dances over chicken, burgers, and the Fresh Prince's *Summertime*, while Mom and I sit side-by-side on the chaise lounges. I hang on to my glass of wine for dear life.

"You drink too much," Mother says. "You're never going to get pregnant if…."

"Mom! You drank *during* your pregnancy."

"Well. You work too much. And you run too much – you need some fat on that body to carry a child. You're never going to get pregnant if…."

"Mom stop. I get this on all sides. It's hard enough without you shining a light on it."

"Well, you need to be worried about this."

"Jesus Christ, you wonder why I don't visit you. Because you make me feel like shit."

"Well I don't know why you waited so long. You're not getting any younger!"

"Because I was waiting for the right guy! Unlike you, who'd take anyone's seed. You hated Dad. I didn't want that."

"Well, now what have you got?"

"The love of my life, what have you got?"

She says nothing for a long, beautiful second. Sweet relief.

"Having children is a wonderful thing," she presses. "Have you checked him out? It could be him."

"Yes, we are both fine. Everything comes up roses."

"Well, maybe you should practice more."

I look at her like she's crazy. "We should fuck more?"

"Caroline!" says my appalled mother.

"Hey honey!" I shout to Chris. "Mom says we should fuck more!"

"Woo! Thanks, Gloria!" Chris waves a victorious spatula.

"Mom," I ever so calmly set down my wine glass. "That would be virtually impossible."

"You can always make time."

She still doesn't get it. I drop my sunglasses to look her in the eye and let her know how off-base she is about the rabbit-level of fuck frequency going on at our house.

"Oh."

She casually ducks her eyes - she's officially uncomfortable. Yessss!

My in-laws, John and Paula Shaughnessy, arrive. They're blonde'ish, which I always find funny because so many people from the Boston-area are dark-haired Italians. And even John and Paula have a little Italian in them. Ok, I'm sure Paula really just colors her hair, same as my mom. And John is actually quite gray. I think it's their lightness of spirit that influences how I see them. Their warm smiles, accepting eyes, and unbridled cheer always comforts me. They're calmer, and drama-free compared to mine - or at least, it seems that way – and welcomed me into their family with open arms. Paula was a school teacher and volunteered for an after-school program for abused girls in Carlisle – a predominantly wealthy town, but even wealthy towns have a middle-class. That was the Shaughnessys. She taught Chris at a young age that girls were as strong as boys, and to challenge stereotypes. It's no wonder he ended up at a women's college. His father, John, was an electrician, hardworking, who took up the trade as a teenager to help support his mom after his father died in a tragic accident when John was sixteen. Paula and John are the salt of the earth who made an honest living, and somehow managed to love each other in a way my parents couldn't. I often admire their interactions, seeking solace in the proof that love can last - forty-three years and counting, in fact.

And then of course, there's Chris's older brother, Pete. An oddity. Pete is darker than Chris, over forty, bearded, and more guarded. I've always liked him, but I don't understand him, though I've tried. I don't know if he's ever warmed to *me* either. Pete's a Duck Tour driver. The Duck Tours are touristy rides through Boston on these little boat/trucks – DUKW amphibious vehicles, originally used in the military, specifically on Normandy Beach during WWII, and the Korean War. The tour bounces down Boylston Street one minute, drops into the Charles River the next. I've lived in or around Boston my whole life, and I have to tell you, they're not just for tourists, they're a blast. And the funnier the conductor, the better the ride. Which brings us back to Pete. Pete is a stoic guy – until you get him on the Duck Tour mic. He is the fastest talking, wittiest, "r" dropping townie out there. He has everyone in stitches. I don't even recognize him, because with us, he's...strange.

Welcome hugs are exchanged with Paula, John and I, but with Pete, an awkward side-hug and a...*Was that a curtsy*? The look he gives my mother is even more antisocial. I'd consider his half-nod *almost* cordial, if he wasn't sucking on a fully-loaded toothpick. Yes, I'm serious. Chia seeds and raisins.

Finally, my sister, Katie arrives, with husband George, and sweet Sara in tow. Katie leans down to kiss me on the cheek.

"Sorry we're late, sis. Traffic on 93 was a nightmare."

"It's ok. Mom and I were just finishing a terrible conversation."

"Great!" Katie says, grabbing some tortilla chips, and tossing them in her mouth. "Hi Mom, she gobbles. More kisses exchanged.

"Hi darling. Hi George." says Mother. "And who's this perfect little munchkin?"

My niece smiles brightly, "Me! Hi Grandma!" Sara dives in for a big hug. If she only knew.

"Sara, say hi to your Auntie," Mom prods her.

Sara turns her back to me and gives me the side glance behind clasped hands: "Hi Aunt Caro." Ah yes, the shy start, but once she warms up, we'll be the best of friends. She spies my bracelet and suddenly hops onto my lap.

"What's that?" she asks, pointing to my Alex & Ani charm bracelet; a limited edition, royal blue and teal seahorse – my favorite. Chris gave it to me the night before our wedding, "something blue" he said. I was shocked he knew that tradition, but then again, he always surprises me.

"It's a seahorse," I tell her.

"Why?"

"Well, legend says they mate for life. Isn't that nice?"

"No. Sea otters," George chimes in, tossing almonds into his mouth. "Sea *otters* mate for life."

I give him the evil eye and continue: "But what's also cool about the seahorse, is that the male carries the baby. Cool, huh?"

"Huh?" Sara snaps her confused head up at me, wrinkling her nose.

"Yes, they're very special," I tell her.

"Come on Sara, let Mommy put your sunblock on." Katie says. Sara jumps off and hurries away.

Mother looks at me. "If only." she says, full of woe.

I take another hearty sip. Something's got to get me through today.

After the bounty of meat, potato salad, strawberry shortcake and wine finds a safe harbor in our bellies, Katie and I force ourselves to move. We land in the kitchen, assigning ourselves to dish duty. As always, my sister and glimmering opposite, with a much slower ignition switch, has something to "share."

"You know, once I stopped thinking about it, it happened."

"Katie...."

"I know, you don't want to talk about it. But I also know it's going to happen for you, and I know *you* think it's not.... Which is part of the reason it hasn't. The mind is a powerful thing."

"Katie...."

"Listen for a second. I don't agree with any of Mom's 'you work too much, run too much' crap. It's all ridiculous made-up shit. Live your life. But you *do* need to stop obsessing over every little comment. Let it go. Once I stopped trying..."

"How can I stop trying?" I throw the fork I into the dry stack.

"You're right, it would be pretty hard for you two," she laughs.

"That's not what I mean."

"I know what you meant. I'm saying, don't let it consume you. You have to relax about it."

"How can I relax?" I toss the ladle. "He wants a baby, and I can't give it to him. And *every single person* I talk to brings it up, so I can't stop thinking about it even if I try. He deserves everything, Katie. *Everything.* I would give my life for that man." A rogue tear escapes. "I want to give him the life he wants, he's given that to me."

"And you will," she rests her hand on mine.. "He already has the life he wants. He has *you.*"

"He wants a baby." I yank it away. "He wanted one for years before we started trying, and I slowed him down. And now...I can't...."

"Yes you can." She grabs my arms and turns me, "Yes you can. If you wanted to travel to Italy, would you book a flight to China?"

"Huh?"

"If you wanted to go to Italy, would you book a flight to China?"

"What the hell...."

"If you want to go to Italy, you research hotels and restaurants in Venice and Rome, book a flight on Alitalia, and *go to Italy*. You wouldn't say 'Italy seems nice, China here I come.' If you want a baby and you choose to believe 'it's not going to happen for me,' you're booking a trip to China."

"This is really dumb. And not helping."

"Well, then stop thinking about it. Go to yoga."

"Oh my God, yoga! Of course! How could I have been so blind? Yoga's the solution for everything!"

"I'm not saying that. I just know it helped me. Quieting my mind. And of all people, *you* would benefit. No offense."

After tossing – and nearly breaking – the last dish onto the pile, I throw in the towel. "None taken." I put my hands on my hips and let out an exasperated sigh. "I love you." I throw my arms around her.

"I love you, too." She holds me for a good, strong moment, and then a little more. "Here." She grabs a wrapped gift from her bag and hands it to me. Inside, this small, teal and yellow book titled *Letters To My Baby.*. "Your first exercise in believing first, seeing second."

I look through it - it's a time capsule of sorts. A bunch of heavy duty, decorated pages folded into the shape of an envelope, for the Mother-to-be to write to her future child. You write inside, fold it up, and mail it. Each page is labeled differently:

On the day you were born….
I laugh when you….
My first impressions of you were….

The front side of the envelopes say cute things, too. In the top left corner where the return address would be it simply says, *From Me*. And in the middle, it says, *To the Future You*. At the end of the book, there are a couple envelopes with no headings…guess I can customize those.

I smile, "Thank you."

"You're welcome." She squeezed me tight, and finally, pulled away to look me in the eyes. "For the love of God, go to yoga."

6.2

Caroline

The yoga studio in town is on an upper crust New England street, lined with inoffensive trees, hip, local coffee shops *as well as* a Starbucks, an organic dry cleaner, and an overpriced boutique that sells the kind of designer jewelry that every woman in town wears to match their Lilly Pulitzer dresses, Jack Rogers sandals, Tiffany rings and David Yurman bracelets.

The one other time I switched up my routine and gave yoga a shot (I had an injury), I learned the studio holds classes in their courtyard when weather cooperates. Since today is sunny and 75-degrees out, I hope our class will be held there. When I arrive, however, I learn there's already a class going on outside. Ugh, I should go home.

"Are you taking the 9am?" a bright, twenty-something chirps from behind the desk.

"Oh. Um, yeah."

"Great, if you could sign in here. Feel free to grab some tea while you wait."

I head over to the corner for my tea, and hide there, taking in the room. You know how when you're looking to buy a new car – in hunter green, for example – you suddenly see hunter green cars *everywhere*? Outside the studio, a woman in a striped, stretchy top and swinging ponytail walks past, pushing a stroller: pregnant. Another woman walks in who looks forty-five - *she's* pregnant. I finish my tea and set up my mat. The instructor finishes a conversation and turns around, *she* is pregnant with a huge, round belly.

"Come the fuck on," I mutter under my breath.

The woman next to me chuckles. I see her out of the corner of my eye, her torso bounces up and down with laughter. I look over – she's fucking pregnant. I'm not kidding.

"Did I sign up for the wrong class?" I ask.

"I know, it seems like everyone is pregnant," she says. Her pig-tails wave side-to-side and remind me of kindergarten. "That's how I felt five months ago. And then – BAM." She gestures at her belly. "Susie, by the way." We shake hands.

"Caroline."

"Nice to meet you Caroline."

Susie and I are passive-aggressively shushed, ushering the start of class.

Our instructor, Han, spiritual and doe-like, tells us to lay back. "Take deep, slow breaths. Get present, be with your body. Quiet your mind."

Are you fucking kidding me? There's nothing quiet about my mind, Han, get serious. I lay there as images and memories flash through: Mom stressed out, angry and overwhelmed at my sixth birthday, and my ninth, and Christmas, and New Year's… I decided back then that I wanted more, that powerful and impressive looked like a woman with a briefcase and heels and her own job. *Happiness* was someone who made something of herself – because anyone could get pregnant… Funny. *Anyone*. A tear escapes out of the corner of my eye and rolls down my cheek. Little bastard, where did you come from?

Han lullabies further, "...and not wanting, realizing that right now, you have everything. *You already have everything.* Where you are in this moment is perfect. Breathe in, breathe out."

I listen to her calming voice, and everything drifts away – my worries, the people next to me, the ticking clock. Despite my resistance, I settle down. She's a miracle worker, that Han, a ray of light. My eyes get heavy and I let them close. I couldn't fight any longer.

🐚

Click clock, click clock, click clock.

My red heels pound heavily from the outdoor set of the Maybelline commercial I'm overseeing. Hauling ass, I leave behind the twenty-foot, white silks suspended in the air to achieve the perfect light, the enormous lights in front to balance it, the three black cameras below to catch every angle of our beauty queen - and toward the awaiting Lincoln Town Car to whisk me the fuck out of there and to LAX. Maybelline's inexperienced and overpaid rep, Benji, a twenty-six-year old in a sweater vest, tie, glasses and wiry fingers, trails me.

"As I mentioned, I'm sorry my bosses couldn't be here," Benji says, "But I sent them take-by-take, what we were filming."

"Oh, I was there. I recall."

"I know it took a really long time, but, they do trust you, promise. And the producer. And at least talent was on time!"

"6AM call time and she shows up at 8:15?"

"Well, for her."

"You know Benji, I can deal with the late start. But can't she be pretty *and* nice? Oh! *And know her lines*! You want to sell a product, *my job* is to sell your product, her job is to say the fucking tagline!"

"I know, I know. The last girl was better. But she got a Michael Bay film."

"So she can't act either." Benji chuckles overenthusiastically. "Just kidding, I really liked-" I throw my cell phone waving hand in the air to pull the movie title out of it, "Transformers, or, whatever."

"Yeah," he smiles. And again, with the excessive passion in my face, "Which one?"

I stop my speed walking, and face him, "Benji, I'm exhausted. That model was a total nightmare, and I guess I would be, too, if I hadn't eaten in a decade." A shrill laugh explodes out of him. "I need a burger. Is there a McDonald's drive-thru around?"

"Hit up In n Out, it's world famous."

"That place you're all obsessed with because of the soggy fries? No. What about a Dunkin Donuts?"

"We're supposed to get one, in like, September of 2014."

"I'm sorry, where the fuck am I? Who doesn't have Dunkin Donuts?" I look at my driver, who patiently stands in front of the car. "What's your name?"

A handsome, salt and peppering, African American with a bellowing voice answers, "Sam."

"Sam, LAX please. I need to get back to the land of Dunks." Benji opens my door and I slide into the black leather seat.

Before I can shut it, Benji pokes his head in. "How do you eat that shit?"

"I run." I shut the door and let out a breath I've been holding for twelve hours. I look at my phone to check emails, then wise up and toss it on the seat.

Sam glances at me from his rearview, "You ok, Miss?"

"I will be. Just – argh!"

"Tough work day?"

"Yes. But I'm sure you have your share of asshole stories, too."

"Naw, Miss."

"Oh, come on. Don't lie, Sam."

He laughs. "I remain mum."

"That's good of you. Sorry if I was an asshole just now."

"No ma'am, you're east coast. It's good, ya'll say what you mean. In LA, we never know where we stand. People are nice to your face, stab you in the back."

"Yeah, I see that."

"Don't worry, I'll get you back to – what was it – the land of Dunks?"

I laugh. "Yeah," I say, and in an overexaggerated Boston accent, "Get this classy broad a French vanilla and a crullah!" My cell rings, it's Chris. "Hey, baby…Yeah, we just finished, I'm on my way… Love you, too."

I toss my phone again, move my black briefcase to the floor and kick off my heels. What a fucking day.

When I finally board, I find my happy aisle seat and cozy up to my pillow, ready for a long, six-hour nap. Until the woman next to me in beige pants and Keds, starts talking:

"Live here?" She asks.

"Nope. You?"

"Visiting. What were you doing here?"

"We were filming. A commercial," I say.

"That sounds *so* glamorous!"

I guffaw. "Until you're on set for fourteen hours with a diva director, or a no-show actor, or budgets that were estimated to cover the worst-case scenario, yet somehow leave you two scenes short and 30% over budget. Not sexy at all."

"Oh come on, everyone's in awe of the beautiful people."

"You're lied to, Madame Consumer! The movies, TV, *advertising*, we all sell you the idea that *this* is who you want to be – beautiful, skinny, powerful, rich, skinny, young, skinny – we make perfection and the life of the haves so much more alluring than the have nots, so you'll *buy* the product! And we make *working in the industry* look glamorous, but let me tell you, those shoots are the longest, most fucking boring things on the planet. Most people would never get into the business if they knew what a day on set entailed – they wouldn't have the patience for the hurry-up-and-wait of it all."

"Well, aren't you a kill joy."

"Yes ma'am." I lift the cup I've been concealing and salute her.

"Is that a cup of wine? Where'd you get that?"

"Road soda. Was at the airport bar. Asked for a to go cup."

"Wow." She said, clearly unimpressed.

It wasn't intentional, but she definitely won't be disrupting my nap.

An hour or two later, I'm jolted from my slumber. And then again. The plane bounces up and down vigorously.

DING. The seatbelt sign is activated.

The plane *drops*. A lot.

A woman standing in line for the bathroom screams and falls into the row of passengers next to me.

"Please go back to your seat, ma'am," the flight attendant urges her. The woman wobbles to her seat, hanging onto the chair backs with all her might.

I rub the St. Christopher bracelet Katie gave me. She told me he's the Patron Saint of Travel, and since Katie has always been much closer to the saints than I, I wear it every time I travel. My heart races, and with another huge bump, my arms snap to the sides to squeeze the armrests - my seat mate does the same. We don't let go. *When the fuck is the captain coming on to say something like, "hey, sorry, we're experiencing some real bad turbulence?"* I wait, my eyes dart left and right. Everyone hangs on in silence, but you can *hear* the worry and discomfort in the sighs and gasps, the hushed terror. *Where's the fucking captain?* I close my eyes, try to remain calm, breathe, tell myself everything will be alright. But I'm scared. I don't want to die. I desperately don't want to die.

"Please God, keep us safe," I pray, with eyes shut and clenched fists.

The plane continues to bounce up and down, and suddenly, the nose points downward. *Downward?* It does that only when we're about to land! The sound of air rushing past the new tilt of the plane hollows out my insides. Tears escape from my pinched lids. I wipe them away, but they keep coming. I'm so afraid, I'm so afraid, picturing terrible things in my mind. Had I told everyone what I want them to know? What would I do if…? Would I make a last phone call? Or be with myself in those last moments of horror?

"Please God, don't take me this way. I have so much more to give."

I thought back to a poem Mom taped in our kitchen cabinet after TJ died, about how we only get flowers at our funeral. The poem encouraged us to "give flowers" now, while we're alive, to appreciate life and those in it, and *tell them* right now. I remember reading it when I was eight or nine, deciding *I* would tell people how I felt about them, always. But did I? Did I live it?

"Please." I pushed my head into the back of my seat, squeezed my eyes shut, and touched my bracelet.

The bumping lessens. The choppiness subsides, and the nose of the plane slowly levels out. My eyes open and remain glued to the seat in front of me. Shuttered breaths bounce from my constricted chest, and a tear moves down my cheek. The captain never came on, that sadist prick.

My seat mate looks in my direction, and lightheartedly says, "*That* was awful."

I can't look at her, I'm not ready to make light. My eyes are red and watery, and I just can't say words. I nod, shakily. Barely above a whisper, "Yeah." I clear my throat and snap out of it – a little. "I'm going to call my mom as soon as we touch down. Tell her I love her."

"That's a good idea. Me, too."

Several minutes later, when the plane is stable and the seatbelt sign turns off, a flight attendant with long, dark hair passes by. I stop her, I have to know.

"Was that the worst turbulence you guys have had in a while?"

She shakes her head, clearly affected. "No. It was the worst ever." She turns and continues on, back to work she goes.

"Wow," my seat mate in beige, says. "Don't forget to call your mother."

"Yeah."

I'm awake. I rub my eyes, *Where the hell am I?* My focus goes from foggy to clear and I see a shiny, wooden floor and orchids. The yoga studio… *I missed the whole class*? As the other yogis pack up, my eyes meet with Han's, and she gives me a knowing glance; she *chose* not to wake me. She knew I needed it. I like Han. Normally, I'd be pissed I paid for something I didn't get. *I want a refund*, I'd protest. But not this time. That Han, she may have magical powers; I think she put a spell on me.

As I walk to the door, the bright, twenty-something yells after me: "Ma'am! We're refunding your class! Han told me you didn't get to participate."

"No, thank you, that won't be necessary." The girl looks puzzled. "I'll see you next week!"

🐚

The following Saturday I went to yoga again, but since I normally go for long runs - eight to ten miles - on Saturdays, I put my running gear on first. All that sitting and stretching at yoga – it's not the same intensity.

"You're going running AND to yoga?" Chris catches me at the door.

"Well maybe just a four miler." I see the concern on his brow. "Or three?"

"Why don't you *just* do yoga?"

"I mean…"

He grabs my shoulders and stares at me, melodramatically, we both laugh: "You're enough, Caroline, you're enough," he teases.

"Don't psychoanalyze me." I laugh and push him away. This time, he doesn't let go.

He waits until I look him in the eye and says it again. "You're enough."

"Ok babe, I get it." I push him away and trot off.

He yells after me, "Seriously?"

"I'll only do three! I *like* running." *Or four*, I smile to myself.

I went to yoga after that, and the next day, and two days after that. Yoga was becoming a habit, it was good for my soul.

🐚

Suddenly it's Saturday again. I decide to skip my "pre-run," not feel guilty about it, and head straight to yoga. Susie isn't here today, but I see some women from the rugby field. I notice they kept their David Yurman bracelets on to exercise. I hear the women talking – complaining – about their kids and their husbands;

always with the disclaimer "Don't get me wrong, I love them *to death, but...*" Having conversations like these here, has the effect of cigarette smoke in fresh mountain air.

Didn't they come here to get away from all that? Isn't that what this spiritual practice is all about? Wait, didn't *I* come here to get away from all that?

"Ah, that's right," I remind myself with a smile.

I lay down in that beautiful courtyard and stare at the blue sky, the clouds move fast overhead. I watch them go by, and I'm no longer me - the me who has a million things to do, thoughts and fears racing through my mind. I'm someone *else*. I quiet the thoughts and focus on my breath. Han asks us to think to ourselves about three things we're grateful for, and meditate on them: My husband, my health, my job... and my sister. Yes, I chose four. Then slowly and non-competitively, our practice begins.

By the end of it, I'm sweating and my muscles shake. As we lay there in our shavasanas, she asks us to recall our three things.

"I can guarantee you," Han begins, "Of those three, someone chose one thing the same as you, someone chose something you've never even thought of, and someone chose something the exact opposite of you, but it's true for that person. Just because you may disagree, it doesn't make it any less true for that person. This reminds us to have perspective. We can all be here, extending love to ourselves, to others, to our practice, and have different points of view."

As we roll onto our sides into the fetal position and slowly pull ourselves up for our final Namaste, Han announces there will be a Mommy and Me yoga class starting next week, and that mothers of children from six-months to age three would be welcome; there is another for pre-K to first grade. I hear a flutter of excitement, I gather my things. I pass by the women who appear to look me up and down, and I give them a large, loving smile -which is actually liberating. I glide toward the tea station, where I see a familiar face.

"Hey Stranger!" Susie says, with a friend trailing her.

"Susie, you're here! How are you?"

"Can't complain. This is Madeline."

"Hi Madeline, nice to meet you." Madeline, a tall, hearty woman with sandy, short hair extends her hand.

"Likewise. Are you new to town?" asks Madeline.

"I've been here over two years."

"Really? I feel like Susie and I know everyone."

"Not everyone, honey," Susie flirts as she pulls Madeline close, and Madeline rubs her belly.

"Oh," I say. Friends? Partners? "How long have you two been friends?"

"Oh no, we're *huge* lesbos," Madeline assures.

I laugh out loud. "Oh my God, I didn't know Cohasset let lesbians in here."

"We arm wrestled our way in," says Susie.

"Well, I'm glad you did. You've quickly become my two favorite people."

"You're queer, too?" says Madeline.

"Maddie!" Susie shushes her.

I guffaw. "Straight as it gets, but I know how it feels to be different. Anyway, I appreciate your lack of filter."

"Me too," says Madeline.

"Let's switch numbers!" I say.

Susie grabs my phone and types in her number, "Here's mine. Call me."

"I mean, maybe we can go running sometime. Do you guys run?"

"Oh," says Susie. "Not since I got pregnant."

"Suze is lucky she gets me to this class." Madeline looks at Susie and laughs like a hyena.

"Oh, yeah, I understand. It must be hard to run when you're pregnant." I take back my phone and see a new number in it. Two, actually. I think my eyes well up, but I look away *fast*. "Ok, well, it was nice to meet you Madeline, good to see you, Susie."

"Bring it in for the real thing, Crazy!" Madeline bear hugs me. Susie does, too. I hang on longer than normal – these two are the only friends I've hugged since moving here.

Chris

I see Caroline pull up. She's different. Relaxed. I don't know what happens at yoga, but I like it.

seven

Caroline

It's seventy-eight and sunny this lovely June morning. Chris is out of school, and it's busier in town, not so much with tourists, but people passing through *on their way* to the Cape. A perfect morning for a run.

I take off. My music thumps and Scowl Lady *almost* smiles at me. Almost. My two scruffy convenience store buddies manage to wave as opposed to nod. I turn the bend to hit the trail, and I stumble, but find my footing and keep going. Not today, tree stump, not today. I feel strong, and my run seems to go by way faster than usual. I must've really zoned out. I break out of the woods and speed back to my place. I see my driveway, and my husband, and I pick up the pace…6.1 miles…6.2 miles, and DONE! I drop to my knee, huffing and puffing. After a minute or so, I can't seem to catch my breath. I try to slow it down, but it's so bad I have to put my hand on the ground to keep from falling. Damn, I must've gotten a personal record today. I look at my pace: 9:33 per mile?

"What?" I blurt out.

"What's the matter?" asks Chris, "Are you ok?"

"I'm…" I try to speak and breathe. "My pace is ninety seconds slower, and I'm more out of breath than ever." I can't stop huffing and puffing.

"Well, doesn't that happen sometimes? I read in one of your running magazines that you can have an amazing six-miler one day, and the worst three-miler you've ever had another."

"Yeah…" I take another breath. "It does happen. I don't know, it's weird. Goddamn it, I think yoga slowed me down!"

"You're psychotic." He kisses my head. "Ick, so sweaty!" Chris walks away.

I remain crouched down, messing with my app – maybe something went wrong there? After a few minutes of tinkering, I realize nothing went wrong technically, and I accept that I'm not myself.

🐚

"Comfortably" tied into my hospital gown, my feet dangle from the table as I wait. I've always trusted my doctors implicitly, looking up to them as All-Knowing Gods. But after a few stress fractures and other minor maladies, I'm a little more paranoid. Maybe it has to do with getting older, and hearing stories of your friend's neighbor who had a massive heart attack at thirty-six; "healthy as an ox, happened out of the blue." These stories and others like it cause me more anxiety than I care to admit.

The silence in a hospital room is deafening, as you sit and wait for the Truth, the result, the prognosis. No matter how large your family, how many friends, no matter how loving your husband - when you're in a waiting room, or getting an X-ray, MRI, or ultrasound, it's you and the Truth – *your truth*, no one else's. Your news that you'll be down with an injury for 8-10 weeks, your news you couldn't carry your baby to term, your news that after thirty-five, you're less fertile, and you'd better hurry up and worry about it. You and the Truth. No one else's.

Doctor Syed walks in, a lovely thirty-something Indian woman. My GP has known me longer than Chris has. I see her twice a year – double the amount most normal adults go – but I mean, we go to the dentist twice a year, six-month cleanings, why not see our doctor? This *might* be the third time she's seen me since January, but whatever, I'm paying for it.

"How's my dear patient?" Doctor Syed asks, donning a hot, red lip.

"Hi Doc, I've been better. Love the lip."

"Thanks, just got it. What's up?"

"Well, for the last several months, my times have been fast. But today, I was more than a minute-and-a-half slower. And I was out of breath."

Doc stares at me. No words. "I'm waiting for you to tell me the real reason, Caroline, because I know I didn't hear that right."

"You did."

"You're here because of ninety *seconds*? You realize I'm not an athletic trainer, your coach, a physical therapist, mental therapist. I'm your good ol' Primary Care Physician." She listens to my heart and mumbles under her breath. "Runners… hypochondriacs. One little thing goes wrong, and poof, you're at the doctor."

"I was panting."

"Maybe you were having a bad day. That happens you know."

"Not to me."

She glares at me with a look that once again lets me know I'm ridiculous. She asks me a litany of questions that seem to have nothing to do with anything. Then we get to the relevant ones:

"Have you been sleeping well? Have you been under any stress? Have you been eating well?"

"Yeah." I respond to that one enthusiastically. "Better than ever, actually. I've been eating a ton of fruit. I've never been a fruit person, but lately, I've been all about it."

"Craving fruit."

"Yeah. I figure it's summer, sort of the season for it."

"Ok. How about stress? Have you been under any additional stress?"

"Actually Doc, I've been doing yoga, and even some meditation. I feel pretty relaxed. I haven't obsessed about anything… well, ok, except my time today."

"Date of your last period?"

"Ummm." I take out my phone and check the calendar. "Oh, May 1st."

She looks up at me. "You mean June 1st?"

"No, May."

"Caroline, it's June 20th."

"Oh yeah, I'm not real regular – sometimes it's twenty-eight days, sometimes it's thirty-five."

"Yeah, you're beyond that. Get up."

"Oh. I guess I wasn't thinking about it." Well played, yoga, well played.

"Come on Caroline," Doc says, as she hands me the plastic pee container. "Down the hall, to the left."

A few minutes later, I'm back in the room, my legs hang over the table - again. I look around; there's never anything to look at except those really gross medical pictures or magazines you don't care about.

I'm sure I'm not pregnant. I don't feel pregnant – I'd know. But what if I am? That would be the best news ever. Could I be?

No. Of course not, don't think about it. Another baby heartbreak would be beyond devastating. I look down – I'm not showing or anything... most women don't show until month four or five, especially with their first kid. I look down again, touch my belly. Could there be something in there? *Someone*? A boy or a girl that Chris and I made?

Stop, Caroline.

I haven't had any morning sickness or anything. And even if I am pregnant, I could miscarry again. *Stop thinking about it.* The door opens.

"Congratulations," Doctor Syed says, "You're pregnant."

"I am?"

"Yes."

"No I'm not."

"Yes. You are."

"Nope. I think you should check again, Dr. Syed."

"Caroline, it's a standard test, I can assure you."

My look turns, and I suddenly fill with rage.

Dr. Syed changes her tone, "Caroline. There's no question." I burst out crying. She put her arms around me. "Caroline, are you ok, honey? Are these happy tears?"

"You know we've had trouble, and then I had two miscarriages, so I never thought it was going to happen."

"Of course it would. It's normal for women over thirty-five to miscarry, but you know, it's a numbers game, and practice makes perfect."

"I thought something was wrong with me. I ...what if this one dies, too? What if I kill this one, too?"

"You didn't kill any of them, Caroline."

"Yes I did. I waited, and I gave them weak eggs, and that's why they died. Because I wasn't meant to carry a baby, because I'm not womanly enough."

"What are you talking about? Where is this coming from?"

"I don't know. Maybe it's been building."

"Do you hear how ridiculous it sounds?"

"No. Maybe some women aren't meant to carry a child. Maybe some are too cold to be a mother. Maybe that's me. Maybe I don't have those instincts."

"Do you think that's true?"

I think for a second. "No? Maybe? I don't know."

"What I know of you, is that you're incredibly loving and conscientious – sometimes *too* conscientious. You and Chris will be incredible parents."

"Thank you."

"You know, there are twenty-four-year-old-women who come in here, who have trouble getting pregnant. And forty-year-olds who get pregnant on their first try. It's not an age thing, or a temperament thing. You just never know."

"But the 'after thirty-five' thing…."

"Yes, statistically it's harder. But every case is different. Like I said, some forty-year-olds are more fertile than some twenty-year-olds. Stop focusing on it. Enjoy the ride."

"Ok. Thank you."

"Of course. So, based on your last cycle, you're seven weeks. You need to make an appointment with your OB."

"I'm not telling him yet."

"Your OB?"

"No. Chris. I don't want to get his hopes up. If I miscarry, I'll go through it on my own."

"Caroline…"

"I can't. I can't disappoint him again. I'll tell him later, after the first trimester."

"Twelve weeks? Caroline, yes, you can miscarry at any time, but the most common is week six or seven. You're there. You'll be past it next week."

"I can't. I'll tell him when it's safer."

Dr. Syed shakes her head. "Well, you'll know the sex of the child week ten. Maybe you'll want to share the news then."

"Maybe."

"Congratulations," she hugs me. "I'm not mad at you for coming in anymore. You were out of breath because your lungs are working overtime. You're creating a life."

And she leaves the room, and it's me, my thoughts, and my... baby...I'm creating a life? It's actively *living*? I touch my stomach again, squish it a little – carefully. I can't believe there's something in there. I drank last week, and the week before that. *God, I hope I didn't give it fetal alcohol syndrome. Oh my God, how much do you have to drink for it to be dangerous?* Wait, it wasn't a lot, I had a little cold, so I went easy.

One thing's for sure, I won't be drinking anymore. Wow, that'll be an adjustment, and hard to hide from Chris. I'll have to pour cranberry juice in a wine glass and pretend. Five more weeks. Damn, I hope I don't show much.

I put my hand back on my belly. It's the same size it always is – maybe bloated. I can't believe it.... But also, I don't want to. If something happens...

"Please God, don't let anything happen this time. Please God, let this baby be healthy."

The door creaks open. It scares the living daylights out of me. People zip by in the hallway, and I realize it must've been the motion of the passersby that caused it. I hop up to shut it – that could've been embarrassing. Either way, it was freaky. I scramble to get my clothes on and get the hell out of there.

The next few days were a tightrope walk of bliss and fear. I'd be over the moon one minute, falling back to earth with a mind full of tragic premonitions the next. Did you know that a pregnancy over the age of thirty-five is called a *geriatric pregnancy*? Are you fucking kidding me? The name alone doesn't bode well. A *geriatric* could never carry a kid to term, and the awareness of how quickly this life could be stripped from me sent me into a world of self-doubt again. But…

I knew stressing about it and thinking negative thoughts wouldn't do me any good, so I made a vow: I'd be positive. I'd *believe*, even when I was scared. At least then, I'd know I gave it my all. There was no real reason to believe we were never going to have a child. We would, of course we would. *Calm down Caroline. It's all going to work out.*

Days turned into weeks, weeks turned into months. But before the highly anticipated week twelve, there was week ten, the week "geriatric mothers" get the CVS test for any problems with the fetus and learn the sex of the baby. Unfortunately, the test carries some risks.

I lay there in the hospital bed with my OB, Dr. Bliss, an African American woman with a giant smile and contagious laugh, by my side. She's been with me through a lot – mostly heartbreak. She holds a *huge* needle in front of her.

"Are you sure I should do this, Dr. Bliss?"

"Caroline, it's totally up to you. You can get up and walk out the door right now, no questions asked."

"But it's normal for geriatric pregnancies?"

"*Mothers of an advanced maternal age!*" She laughs and kicks her head back. "I told you! Stop using that outdated term! And yes, it's normal."

"But it carries a risk of miscarriage?"

"Some. But that's why we're doing it transabdominally. Miscarriage rates are slightly higher when done through the cervix."

"And it tests for Down syndrome?"

"Chorionic villus sampling tests for Down syndrome, cystic fibrosis, sickle cell anemia and Tay-Sachs. It can also tell the sex of the baby. We take an extraction of cells from your placenta – so, as I mentioned, it's not going to be comfortable. Are you sure you don't want Chris here?"

My eyes glance sideways as I send the thought up to my brain. "No. I can't, Doc. Just us. How can things go bad when I've got bliss?"

She laughs again. "You want some ham with that cheese?"

We both laugh. "Good one." Once the laughter subsides, a worried sigh escapes.

"Caroline, you're not supposed to drive home after this, and you have to take it easy for the next few days. *No running.*"

"I know," I say.

"So, do you have a ride home?"

"Yes."

"And you're sure?"

"Take a test to find out if my baby has a dangerous disease?"

"Yes."

"And terminate, if so?"

Dr. Bliss's bright eyes turn solemn. "Some people just want to know."

I'm normally so adept at making decisions given the facts, but my eyes wander with fear. "I wish Chris were here."

"You can call him right now. I'll wait."

I scan the room. The syringes and cotton, glass jars, white cabinets and white counter tops, the abrupt, red HAZARDOUS WASTE sign on a trash barrel. Do I put my baby in jeopardy? What if he or she already is? Is a plagued baby better than no baby at all?

"What is the actual statistic, Doctor? What is the risk of miscarriage after CVS?"

"It's .5 to 1%."

"Oh," I say, relieved.

"That's one out of two hundred at .5%. One out of one hundred at 1%."

"Oh," I say, my eyes drop. "One out of one hundred isn't so small."

She puts the needle down, and tugs at her gloves. "Call Chris, Caroline."

I sit there in silence, evaluating, measuring pros against cons. Dr. Bliss steps toward the door.

"No," I say. "I'm not having another miscarriage. I'm not. And I trust you, Dr. Bliss. And *if* my baby has a disease, Chris and I will decide what to do from there. We don't *have* to terminate."

"That's correct."

"Ok." I nod with equal parts fear and certainty. "Let's go."

It was a painful, crampy, procedure, but it was over quickly. About an hour later, I shuffled outside to the parking lot, where my ride was waiting in an orange Volkswagen Tiguan. I asked them not to come in, I don't need to inconvenience anyone more than I have. And it's a habit, this doing as much as possible by myself - been like that since I was little. I slide in, and her pale green eyes and bushy eyebrows peer up at me.

"How ya feelin, kid?" Madeline says.

"Thanks for coming Madeline." Susie, straddling the backseat like a kid, and wearing an oversized, stocking cap, pipes up.

"We wouldn't let you down," said Susie.

"Thanks, Susie."

"You haven't told him?" Susie asks.

"Is he not the real father?" asks Madeline.

"Jesus, no! I mean...yes, he is, but that's not why I didn't."

"You straighties are fuckin backwards," Madeline says.

Susie laughs, shaking her head.

"Just keep it between us, ok. As long as I don't miscarry in the next few days, I'm going to tell him." They can hear my whole history in my voice.

"Oh," Susie says.

"Oh," says Madeline. She stops at the intersection, hits her blinker left, and her hands turn the wheel accordingly. "You're gonna be alright, kid. You'll be alright."

"I hope so."

I look in the rearview and see an effervescent smile spilling across Susie's face. She love-taps my shoulder and bounces back into her spot behind us.

A week and a half later, I get the call. I can hear Bliss's megawatt grin over the phone.

"Your tests are negative. Your baby is healthy and developing right on schedule."

"Oh thank God," I say. "Thank you, Dr. Bliss."

"And...do you want to know," she paused, "what you're having?"

I waited a moment, but I'd already decided. "Yes, please."

"It's a girl! You're having a baby girl."

Tears break free. I'm having a girl. Chris and I are having a girl!

The lined seahorse, aka the northern seahorse, spotted seahorse, or its scientific name, *Hippocampus erectus*, can be found in the Atlantic Ocean as far north as Nova Scotia or as far south as Venezuela, and all along the east coast of the United States. They grow about 6 inches long during their one to four-year lifespan, and can be a variety of colors, ranging from gray to black, to orange, red or green.

eight

Caroline

God, I want to tell Chris! One more week! Eleven weeks pregnant, and there's only a little pooch which Chris hasn't noticed, or at least, hasn't said anything. My first trimester wasn't so bad. I did have morning sickness, like, twice, but it was on my way to work, and I pulled over and puked. Gross. That part sucked. The fruit cravings have continued, but he didn't notice that. I still find it weird that deli meat can be harmful for the baby, but I do what I'm told. I had to make excuses twice in the last few weeks about why I didn't want sushi. If he asks again, he *will* know something is up. He knows I love sushi. My boobs *kill*. They're so sore to the touch, and there were a couple times he grabbed for them during sex - I thought I was going to *die*. Having sex with that kind of pain makes it impossible to enjoy.

And of course, the sleep. I can never get enough sleep.

Twelve weeks, it's here! Chris sits on the couch, reading: focused eyes, concentrated brow, his index finger presses on his cheek. His hands flip the page– no Kindle. There's something so palpable about the feel of a story on your fingertips, the sound of paper peeling from one to the next, the stack of pages you've finished, and those to come. Measurable, quantifiable – it's so much better than sliding your finger over a touch screen, having no idea where you are. Best of all, the battery never dies on a book.

"Honey," I say from the dining room, "Could you come here? I need your help with something."

Begrudgingly, he gets up. This is going to be good.

"What can I do for ya?" he asks, staring with insouciance at the layout of pink baby dresses.

"Well, I like this one." I lift a ruffled, gingham number to my chest, as if I were to wear it.

"For?" he asks, his eyebrows lift and furrow.

"You don't like it?"

"It's fine, Legs, I just don't know what you're talking about."

"Ah right, you don't like gingham. How about polka dots?" I hold up another one.

"Caroline, what is this for?"

"You're right, maybe stripes are better." I fuss with a purple striped jumper.

"Is Katie pregnant? Patty? The woman from work?"

"Ok, I get it, the one with the seashell. Yeah, I like that one, too."

"Caro, I'm going back to my book. Have fun." He turns around and heads back to his spot.

"They're for her." This time, I hold the dress to my belly. He turns around and his eyes move from my stomach to my eyes.

"What?"

"I'm three months pregnant. We're having a girl!"

His face lights up. "Caroline? Oh, my–Holy sh– Congratulations!" He throws his arms around me, even jumps up and down.

"To *us*. We did it!"

"Yes! To both of us! Oh, my God, I'm…" He pulls away to look at me. "So, it's for real? I mean, could anything go wrong…"

"We're pretty much past the scary place. It can happen at any time, obviously, but I doubled that time to tell you, and all the doctor visits have confirmed she's developing right on schedule." I step toward him with glistening eyes, "Everything looks perfect."

He throws his arms around me again, "This is the best news! I can't believe it, I mean…" He pulls me away to look me up and down. "I mean… what do we do now? Do I call my parents? Your parents? My brother? Your sister, what? My buddies? I kind of want a cigar. And a scotch – a big scotch! I'm a Dad! Did you tell your family? Who knows? Wait, they better not know before me."

"Of course they don't know. Just me, you, and the doctor." I felt the lie slip out. Madeline and Susie…

"Not even Katie? How could you keep it a secret for so long? I mean…" He goes to grab for my belly. "It's not big or anything," he pushes and pokes."

"Stop that!" I swat him away, laughing. He doesn't stop.

"I mean, maybe it's bigger, but I thought it was all the summer parties, a couple extra margaritas. Wait! You've been drinking!"

"No – I stopped."

"No you didn't, I saw you. Last week, and the party at the O'Leary's."

"Cranberry juice at the O'Leary's and cranberry juice at home."

"You, sneaky little devil."

"I'm a professional."

"I can't believe you kept it from me all this time."

"I'm sorry. I didn't want to disappoint you if something went wrong."

"Caro. If anything went wrong, I'd never want you to go through it alone. Ever."

"I couldn't get your hopes up again."

"Honey, if it hurts you, it hurts me. So, from now on, no matter what, you have to tell me - *all of it*."

"Even the hemorrhoids?"

"Ick, you get those?"

"I could. Happens to tons of women when they're preggers."

"Maybe keep that one to yourself."

"*There's* the truth!"

"Come on, if it's a real problem, you know I'm there."

"Yeah, yeah, yeah." We smile.

"But I'm so f'ing pumped about this. You're going to be an awesome Mom."

"Way to refrain from the f-bomb already."

"You like that? I'm so glad she's ok, and you're ok. – We're HAVING A BABY!" He lifts me up from my legs and parades around. It scares the hell out of me.

"Chris! Chris!"

"What? Oh yeah, the baby." He sets me down.

"Yes. The baby." I stare at him. He can't control himself.

"The BABYYYYY!!"

He grabs his phone, takes a selfie of himself smiling and pointing to my belly. Then, he takes one of him with a cigar in his mouth, giving the thumbs up.

Then, he takes a video:

"My boys can swim." He assures, with a nod, and the cigar still in his mouth. "Yup! My guys, they can a-swim! Right honey?"

"Right Chris." I shake my head. I'm not the selfie co-star he's looking for right now.

"Hang on babe, let's FaceTime my parents."

"Ok honey." I'm not going to ruin his moment. This one's his. Sometimes the truth not only hurts, it sucks.

First, we FaceTime with his parents, then Katie, George, and Sara, and then my mother – who, awkwardly enough, has a well-dressed older man in the background. She's thrilled for me, but definitely distracted.

Chris and I sort of look at each other after that one. Then his eyes focus and I see the lightbulb go off.

"Pete?" he suggests.

"Your brother."

"No, Pete the Dragon. Of course my brother, numbnuts."

"If we weren't such good friends, I'd kick your ass for that."

"Gotta get all my insults in before the little one comes, because you know I won't be doing that in front of her," he pokes. I scan his face, his deep blue eyes, sharp nose, kissable lips - he *is* such a handsome man - but it's remarks like this that won me. That he will never belittle me in front of our child – or anyone else – and he can expect the same from me. That we will teach her love *by example*. "Welp," he jumps up, "Time for me to have a cocktail. Do you want– oh. Right." I shoot him a murderous glare. "Well, only six more months," he attempts to console.

"Noooo, because then I'm breastfeeding and I can't get our kid all liquored up."

"Oh my God, you'd be like, a tap. If you were drinking, and I put my mouth on you, you'd be like a beer tap – beer goes in, beer comes out your boobies. You'd be a hit at college parties."

"Did I mention I hate you right now?"

"Let's try it!" He squats near me.

I swat him. "I will stab you in the face."

"Oh yeah, that's right, no booze going in cuz it'll affect the kid. I should coin that – Booze boobs: a man's best friend." At that point, I just stare at him. "Mm. Yeah, scotch." He heads to the kitchen, and yells, "Sorry honey!"

I draw in a deep breath. No sushi, no coffee, no fucking turkey sandwiches, hemorrhoids, and no goddamn, fucking wine. But…

I'm having a baby.

nine

Caroline

The next several weeks are bliss. I'm out of the dreaded first trimester, and no longer keeping my pregnancy a secret. Chris and I do all the standard - but fun – baby shopping: We pick out her white crib together, and the singing mobile with a pink moon and blue stars that goes above her while she sleeps; an Octopus clock, we buy pink and yellow and blue outfits and booties, and those silly little flower headbands. We look in the baby name books together. We buy this beautiful, white rocking chair to place under the window in her room, where I can feed and rock her back to sleep in the wee hours of the morning, or where I can sing to her as the afternoon sun spills over us. I can't wait. I can't wait to be a mother. And the funny thing is… I'm starting to feel like I already am.

Oh my gosh, I almost forgot! My most exciting, top-of-the-mountain purchase, the one that assures me I've arrived: the running stroller. The Baby Jogger Summit X3 in all black, with air-filled rubber tires and remote wheel lock would provide Mommy and Baby their first bonding ritual. I imagine the different stages of her life - three months, six months, one year, two years – with me running behind her. We'd run together from the time she's born until it's time for her to run by my side. I used to hate to be tied down, slowed down by anyone that would hinder my performance in any arena of my life. Now, I welcome it.

I touch my belly – sixteen weeks. My baby is the size of an avocado but my "bump" looks more like a whoopee cushion, soggy and misshaped. I admit I enjoy eating for two, even though I'm not supposed to have more than 300 additional calories per day. That's it? That's like, a bagel. Whatever, it's fun not to care for a minute – gimme them pancakes and French toast and sugary breakfast foods!

Sitting at work with my cheek mashed in my hand, I daydream. What will we call her? Will she start off with blonde hair like Chris did? Or dark curly hair like me? I'm not sure I'll ever be ok with her riding a bike – I mean, I can't protect her from other cars. How do people do this?

Suddenly a knock, it's Abby, my twenty-five-years-young assistant. I can see her wavy, auburn hair through the glass.

"Come in!"

"Hey, boss. The new VP of marketing at Nike said he sent you an email – he's trying to get a hold of you for their next campaign."

"I know. I saw it. Just a little slow on the response time."

She nods and, with some uncertainty, turns to leave. I've trained her to be efficient with her entrances. She's very good at it, in fact, too good. "Abby, come on in. Sit down." She's timid again. "You're not in trouble," I assured her. "Do you want kids, Abby?"

She adjusts her black-rimmed glasses. She even lets out a little puff of air from her lips. "Caroline. Uh, I don't know how to answer that."

"I know this company - and myself, certainly - pushes people to be their best, no excuses, which can feel robotic, even militaristic." Her raised eyebrows tell me she's surprised by my unprompted confession. "I may, from time to time, have been the Bill Belichick of this company." Her head turns, and one eye squints toward me. "You don't know Bill Belichick? The Patriots?" She's afraid to answer. "It's ok, you're a New England anomaly, too. So am I." I get up from my desk and sit at the edge of it, across from her. My mini bump rests on my lap, my heels crossed in front.

She shifts forward, and apologetically, "My boyfriend watches…basketball? Or baseball?"

"You don't know what sport he watches?"

"I just can't remember. I don't like sports." She looks around nervously, needling the hem of her Anthropologie dress, and pushing her glasses back.

"I see that. Well, anyway, I'm sorry if I was too tough. Some of these guys need the stern bit – they need more steering than you do. I should've seen that." I look at her face: I have no idea what she's thinking. Does she hate me?"

"You weren't."

"What?"

"You're not too stern. You're specific. And it's only a person who truly cares who will take the time to tell you how to make something better. I didn't always like it, but that's where the learning comes."

I'm impressed. I smile to prepare her for what I'm about to say. "Abby, I called you in to…"

"*I* came in. To tell you about Nike."

"Jesus, you're right. Prego brain. Well, I was going to tell you I've noticed your work lately, your attention to detail, problem solving, communication, and was planning to give you a ten percent raise."

"Oh, thank you!"

"But I'm going to give you twenty percent. I normally only do that if you've been with the company for two years-"

"I will be in eight months."

"-and show exceptional loyalty and potential. You have a good head on your shoulders, are dependable, and have a great attitude - attitude is everything. So, congratulations. And thank you for your work."

Her mouth drops open. "Thank *you*!" She smiles brightly - I'd never seen her teeth. I nod. She stands, per her training. "Do you want me to email Nike back, on your behalf? With your schedule?"

"No. I'll do it, thanks Abby."

She walks confidently to the door, and then turns around. "Why did you ask? If I want kids? Would I not get the raise if I said yes?"

"You didn't say anything."

"So then why does it matter?"

"Exactly," I say.

She stares at me, smiles so slightly, I'm not entirely sure she gets it. And then, she does.

"I can barely keep my plant alive."

"You don't have to know, yet."

And she smiles brighter than the first time, turns to walk to the door, and turns back around. "I've worked at a couple agencies, and it's not just the money or the perks that makes an assistant want to stay. It's the culture. You're a great boss, Caroline, and a great leader."

"Thank you." I pause. "Bill Belichick. He's an emotionless, prick of a coach for the New England Patriots – football – I love him. Greatest coach of all time. He sees things others don't, sees talent in a person that others have overlooked. And he gets it done. Don't have to like him, but you have to respect him."

She looks at me blankly, shrugs her shoulders, her auburn waves bounce off them. Her glasses slide forward, she pushes them back. "Ok." She shuts the door behind her.

I smile and turn to my desk, but am quickly interrupted by a sharp pain in my lower back that shoots up my spine. My arm snaps back as if to prevent it.

"Jesus. Beat it, shoes." I kick them off and plop down at my desk, massaging my lumbar region with one hand, resting my face in the other.

Dr. Bliss told me some women run or do whatever is normal for them right until birth, but how am I going to run like *this*? Ugh, this baby's already messing with my running schedule. And think of the other schedules. I'll be making room to take her to the doctor and her friends' and ballet or soccer, and oh yeah, school. *Shit*. Chris and I are going to have to be coordination masters. And…

"Oh shit. Nike."

I bang on the keyboard immediately, composing an apologetic email to someone I'd normally be dying to meet. *Sorry for the delay, been crazy, etc.* Clearly, priorities and balance are already taking a hit. Double shit. I hit send on the email as the lights of Boston flip on, turning the city into a technicolor candle. Inside, my coworkers pack up, laugh, and head out for the night. Even my bosses, Mick and Rick, give me the "salute" as they stroll to the elevator. I walk to my door to see who's left. Like most modern companies, it's an open floor plan, and I see BMW Kevin walk to his standing desk, his head buried in thought. He scribbles on a notepad, then moves to his computer, revisits the notepad, and types wildly. A smile moves across his face as he secures a winning idea. I lumber back to my desk, warmed by the energetic buzz of my workplace on a Friday night. I've got just a few more emails to get to, I'll be out by 7pm, maybe 7:30. Doing it all *can* be done – it just takes longer.

There's a quiet in our home – a perfect, complete, sense of quiet. Chris and I will be doing something mundane in the kitchen. I'll go through the mail, lift each envelope, tear the opener down the flap, open or toss out, while Chris makes iced tea, filling the glass pitcher with water, cutting the lemons, stirring with a wooden spoon. The sound of ripping paper, and ice clanking and wood banging against glass are the only sounds we hear. We look up at one another in the middle of our banal tasks and smile. We don't have to say anything, we know we're exactly where we want to be, no longer hoping, but *expecting*.

I wish I could hang onto this feeling forever. I'll have to remember it when she wakes up screaming at 2am and 4am and 6 am, and I haven't had time to sleep or shower in days. I've been amply warned. But for now, it's like nothing can hurt us. I've never felt more invincible.

It's Sunday, early September. The crispness of fall is in the air even though it's summer for ten more days. That's New England for you, summer comes too late and leaves too early. It will briefly revisit us in October for Indian Summer and will return full-force to biting autumn weather. Today is beautiful "sweater weather" - fifty-two degrees in the morning, but you know the sun will be blazing on you by noon – perfect for Chris's rugby game. The leaves have turned deep red, yellow, and orange hues, and the kids are back in school. New beginnings are in the air.

I walk up the sidelines of the rugby field wearing a fitted, striped shirt. I drop my chair next to Patty, and she immediately notices the overstretched lines.

"Oh. My. God," she says, all over-pronounced and *Saturday Night Live* sounding. "When did this happen?"

I smile proudly. "Four-and-a-half months ago."

"Cut it out, no way! That's...congratulations!" Patty hugs me awkwardly over our chairs.

"Thank you," I say.

"So, no thermos wine fuh you. Damn, that's gonna be one good lookin' kid. Boy or girl? You know yet?"

"Girl."

"Jesus. Little homewreckah she's gonna be." I look at her with daggers in my eyes. "In the crawling, dragging things off the table, toys-everywhere-sense, not like, the husband stealing sense."

"Got it."

"Man," she begins, "I didn't know you wanted kids. Didn't know you were like that." Patty cracks a can of beer and lets the foam bubble on top, until she noisily sips it. Her eyes dart left and right as she slides her beer into a coozi with Tom Brady's face on it. She looks like a guilty kid at recess.

"Like what?" I ask her

"Well, you know..."

"Nurturing?"

"Well, I mean, you have this great body, great job..."

"Ah, the backhanded compliment."

"This isn't coming out right," she concedes.

My anger is diffused for a change. I'm... gentle. "Patty, I do love my job, always have, I work hard at it, and at my health, thus, the shape I'm in, or, *was*." I stop for a moment. "And I was working hard at trying to have a baby. *For two years*. It was difficult."

"I didn't know that."

"You wouldn't. Because it's not something I share with everyone. It's private."

"I'm wickid sorry." She drops her head.

"Thank you. It was a common misconception. Very...*common*."

I stand up at that moment and walk off to chat with my husband and his buddies. I look back – she *is* in shock and looks remorseful. Now I feel bad. But Patty doesn't think too much about what she says. Obliviousness is not innocence. I wish for once, someone could've *tried* to consider that I may have been having a hard time instead of jumping to a quick and easy characterization—"Mother to your career."

God, it still rings in my head. If she'd only known how I grew up, what I'd seen, maybe she'd understand why I did it the way I did it, why I waited to marry until I'd found the partner I was *in love with*, why I waited to start trying until we were stable. I wanted to be an "and" – a woman *and* a wife, a professional *and* a mother. I wish she could understand that I wanted it all. Didn't *she*? Didn't everyone? Why was it so hard to understand? Then it occurred to me, maybe she *didn't*, maybe everyone didn't. Maybe *I* was the one people didn't understand...

But why does it take my pregnant belly to be accepted, understood? Maybe I'm an idealist, but it shouldn't take pregnancy or anything else for that matter, to accept one another, to *see* one another. That's how I feel. And one thing I know, I'll never shame another woman for not having children. We're no less of a woman if we choose not to be a mother, and sometimes, it's not a choice. We're not all so lucky as to have that choice.

I absently shook hands with some of the new guys on Chris's team while these conclusions ran through my head; I couldn't remember their names to save my life because I was 100% somewhere else. The more I thought about it, the angrier and more defiant I got. "Patty *should be* better," I said to myself, "And so should every woman who judges a book by its cover, who wants to narrowly define other women and tear us down instead of build us up!" I look back at Patty, no one had taken my place. Good, she deserves it. See how it feels Patty, to be alone!

I look at her face – her eyes are set low. She's hurt, wounded. She looks around for someone to talk to but finds no one. I knew it all too well.

Patty isn't the root cause. Just because it was my last straw, doesn't mean *she* deserves all the retribution. Patty might need to be a little more tactful, but she's looking for the same thing we all are: a friend.

I return to my seat next to her, "Patty, I was too harsh. I'm sorry. The last two years have been really, *really* hard. And people aren't very sympathetic, here. Not everyone, but…most. I didn't mean to take it out on you. Quite frankly, you're the only person who ever asks me about my life, and actually cares. Also, I'm um… pretty emotional."

"Totally get it, hun," she says as she taps her rugged Boston hand on my knee. "Let me know if you need anything."

"Thank you." With an open smile, I look at her, gesturing to Chris who's on the ground with another guy on top of him trying to steal the ball away. Grunts and hollers and flailing legs abound. "Can't wait to see what bumps and bruises I'll have to play nurse to later."

She looks toward my bulging chest: "Ha, I thought those were fah nursing the baby."

"Good one, Patty," We laugh. "So, you resolve the Little League thing? With your kid?"

"Oh fah the love of God, listen to this. So, Bobby is livid because *Jackie McGee* is in charge…"

🐚

Later that night, I stand at the French doors and stare at the moon shimmering on the water, a white rippling reflection. I took a photography class when I was in college and they taught us about light. Daylight and moonlight are actually blue; indoor light–known as tungsten– is yellow, and fluorescent light is green. Fluorescent light is unattractive on human skin, so don't ever take pictures in the office. Anyway, it was a fun class for me, not anything for my major, but I think it gave me an edge when it came to advertising, helped me develop a good eye for aesthetics. But tonight, I look to the beauty of the black sea at low tide, the dark blue night, and the white moon bouncing on the waves for some serenity. I'm anxious. Every time I get a cramp, or something doesn't feel right, I think I'm losing the baby. I called my OB ten times the first week, and the second, then after some scolding, I dialed it back to eight and six the third and fourth week. Eventually it tapered down to once a week, but Bliss probably cusses me out when she sees my name come up on her phone.

An errant cough interrupts my thoughts. It started a couple days ago, so I called Dr. Syed. I bet she had that red lip on again, because I could hear her sass over the phone, the same sass which reassured me it was *just a cold*, caused by *the natural temperature change*. But now I'm wondering what a cold will do to my baby? Will she get sick, too? Does this affect her development? Is there something I should take to protect her? All of it, my mind runs with it. But if it doesn't go away in a few more days – my cold, not my protective thoughts - I'm going to the doctor.

Anyway, the view helps calm me down. I'm eighteen weeks, almost halfway there, and now I've told people – a lot of people, including Patty. If something goes wrong now… The thought of having to tell all those people… I'll feel like a damaged woman who can't get it right.

She works too much. She waited too long, Her poor husband.

Remember when I vowed to think positively? Yeah, and these are the thoughts running through my mind.

"Hey!" Chris puts his arms on my hips. I shriek.

"Jesus Christ, don't do that!"

"Sorry, did I scare you?"

"Yes! Jesus."

"I'm more of a Buddha man, but nevertheless I apologize. Sorry, you must've been in it."

"Yeah."

"About?"

I pause, because I don't want to let him into the crazy world of my fears and neurosis. "Well, the cough makes me nervous."

"We talked about that – it's a cold and it's going around this time of year."

"I know. I went down a spiral…" I pull away from him. "We're so far along. I feel bad about all the stress this causes us."

"The stress it causes *you*. I know she's fine, it's her mama who's a wreck. Do we need to do some meditation and relaxation?" He grabs me and massages my temples. I want to push him away because he's being a nerd, but it feels too good. He pulls me to the couch, and rests my head in his lap, squeezing my head and neck. "This brain of yours. It works overtime. You have to shut if off sometimes, C, it's not going to change the outcome. It's there, making noise, preparing you for things that will never happen."

"Who is that?"

"Tolle, and a bunch of others."

"Well, can I ask you something?"

"Shoot."

It takes me a second to get it out. I know he's going to dismiss it. "Do you ever wonder what would've happened if you married someone younger?"

"Oh come *on*."

"It's a simple question."

"No. That's dumb. Two years older is nothing."

"Unless you're close to forty and trying to have kids."

He takes a minute to think. It comforts me and makes me nervous all at once, waiting for what he'll say. "Honey, I knew you were the *person* for me, the whole package, not a set of numbers. I married the love of my life, and *if* something happens with this baby or any other, we will figure something else out, *together*."

And that's why I love him. "Sorry I'm a neurotic mess."

"I'm used to it."

I elbow him in the gut. He kisses my face.

ten

Caroline

September 30th, officially autumn, and a cold morning. I start my run later in the fall and winter months since it stays dark until almost 7am. Chris doesn't fish in the dark either. At 6:45, I head out the door. Chris passes me with a nod and a wave on his way to assemble his gear.

"Ah damn," I say.

I squat down to tie my untied shoe, but as I stand up… I guess I must have stood up too quickly, because… woo… I'm a little…I grab hold of a bush for stability. Once I get my balance, I start a slow jog, shake off the dizziness. But as I run, I feel lightheaded. I cough. And then I cough some more; I can't stop. I can't breathe.

I fall to the ground, wheezing, gasping for air. What's happening?

"Chris!" I try to choke out.

I can't breathe. Oh, my God, I can't breathe! Help! Chris! Help!

Chris

I see Caroline 100 yards out – she isn't herself this morning, so I wait to make sure she gets out ok.

I watch her wobble and collapse. I yell, but she doesn't hear me. I've never run so fast in my life.

When I get to her, she's not breathing. I start CPR – my heart races, my adrenaline is off the charts, I'm not doing anything right. I stop for a second to get her phone – it's in her armband. It's a fucking eternity trying to get it out. Fumbling, struggling.

"Help me!"

I dial 911. Put it on speaker, pound on her chest. I felt a rib crack. I fucking broke her rib, my pregnant wife's rib! What is happening?

"Oh my God. Please Caroline. Come on baby." I pound and I breathe into her, waiting for her chest to rise, I breathe more. I speak to the lady on the emergency line. Time passed as if underwater, slow motion, echoes, but also a million miles an hour. I need air in my wife's lungs.

The EMTs arrive and take over. They push me off, and I watch them. Please God, don't let my wife die. Please God, I'll do anything.

"She's pregnant!" I manage to tell them. They hoist her onto the gurney. My brain isn't working fast enough. I need to be with her, but I can't get out the words.

One of the guys from the crew lifts me to my feet, "We got you, man. Come on."

He throws me in the back of the truck with Caroline. I touch her hand, it's like ice. The EMTs work around me, the engine roars, and the sirens blare. It's 6:55am. All that happened in seven minutes.

We arrive at the emergency room where we're met by doctors and nurses who converge on Caroline as the EMTs take off. I try to follow them.

"Waiting room, sir. Follow the signs." They push me off and turn down a corridor.

Follow the signs. Maybe the signs say we shouldn't have this baby. Look what it's doing to her. We have everything, all the luck anyone could ever have, we don't need a baby to say we fit in. The American *dream?* It's all bullshit. All of it is bullshit.

I find the hallway I'm supposed to go down and watch her wheeled across it. I can't *sit* in a *waiting* room. I force my way in through the doors, until a large security guard steps in my path, and calmly but menacingly puts his giant hand on my chest.

He looks over my head, zero eye contact, and bellows, "Waiting room."

I yell around him. "Caroline, I'm here!"

The security guard gently pushes me out to the other side of the double doors, and folds me into the chair like paper. His mammoth mitts hand me a cup of water, and it's all I can do not to cry into it.

🐚

Two hours later, I'm still in the waiting room. Head in my hands, I spy a magazine through my fingers.

"Caroline hates magazines," I blurt out to a very old man sitting next to me.

"Your wife?"

"Yes."

"I'm waiting for my wife, too. Beatrice. I hope she's out soon."

I stare at this man. The sun spots on his wrinkled forehead and bald head, the frail wrists, the love still in his eyes.

"There are a *few* she likes for their articles," I continue, "But mostly, she hates them. She doesn't like gossip, so all those celebrity mags are out, and she doesn't like magazines that make you - or little girls, especially – feel bad about themselves, like they're not skinny enough or pretty enough or rich or popular enough."

"She seems like a caring person, your Caroline. I'm Arthur, by the way."

"Hi Arthur, I'm Chris." We hang on to one another's hand for just a moment longer than normal. I look him in the eye, and he sees through me. I let go. "She is." Arthur's attention stays with me, patiently silent. "She swims upstream, sometimes." I laugh a little, "We both do, always choosing the difficult thing. She's creative with integrity – in *advertising*. I teach at an all-women's school. We do *not* make things easy on ourselves." I spin the cup in my hands, tracing the lip, over and over. "She cares what she puts into the world, you know? Makes sure the message is about something deeper, something richer than what it seems at first glance. Not just selling a product. She told me that when she was a teenager, looking at magazines made her feel like she wasn't enough. So, when her girlfriends were buying Vogue, she made a decision to never buy another one, unless it built you up, cultivated the mind, body or soul. Then she got into advertising, so she could be sure of it. There's a reason all these companies want to work with her. She's got something a lot of people lost."

Arthur reached over and pulled the cup from my hands, calmly placing it on the table. He looked into my eyes, rested his sun spotted hand on mine. "It sounds like she's going to be ok, then."

I broke, the tears rushed out and my hand shook. "She's my best friend, and I, I don't know what I'd do without her."

Arthur took my shaking hand. "I know, son. But she's still here, and she's going to make it. So are you. My wife and I have been to this hospital 100 times. Forty-eight years, 100 visits. Doesn't sound like much to look forward to, does it?"

"No." I smirk

"Ah, there ya go, Chris. "There's a lot of memories in those years, though. We're all building memories."

Winter, 2009
We met at a fundraiser in Boston in 2009. I was finishing up my doctorate, so I served my time as a Teaching Assistant... and dated a twenty-two-year-old student. I was twenty-nine, so it wasn't *totally* reprehensible, but it was unethical. Like I said, I didn't make the best decisions before I met Caroline. But that night, I spotted Caro from across the room. She wore a black, tight-fitting dress that showed off her shape, and her hair was up exposing her long neck and her beautiful collarbone. I've always had a thing for women's collarbones; hers was strong and delicate all at once. That's the perfect description of her – she *is* strong, but delicate, emotional, vulnerable, it's a gorgeous combination. I watched her from afar, directing people where to go, she seemed in charge. I came to find out later that she was there with the Assistant D.A., some smug asshole who was great for her on paper, but a total wuss when push came to shove.

I made my way over to her. "Hi," I said extending my hand. "I'm Chris Shaughnessy, how are you?" I felt nervous, but knew she had to be mine.

She apprehensively took my hand and looked at me as if to say, *What do **you** want?* "Caroline McCafferty, what can I do for you?"

"Well, I noticed you directing people, so I was wondering if you knew when we're going to eat?"

"It's drinks only. Tray-passed hors d'oeuvres, but no seated dinner. It was on the invite."

"Ah, I never read those things. What do you do Caroline McCafferty?"

She looked me up and down, wondering why I'd gone from business to personal. "I'm in advertising."

"So, how are you involved with the fundraiser?"

"My boyfriend is running for Assistant D.A. We go to a lot of these fundraisers."

"Sounds like fun." She picked up on my sarcasm and shot me a look.

"He cares about education," she said.

"That's good."

"Yes, it is."

"So do I." My twenty-two-year-old blonde popped up with a scotch on the rocks for me and a glass of champagne for herself.

All perky, she said, "Hi!"

Caroline stared *through* her. And then shot a laser beam from her eyes into my heart and lit it on fire.

"Marny, this is Caroline. Caroline, this is Marny."

"Drinking age is twenty-one," Caroline said.

"Oh God, I've been twenty-one for *ages*. I'm twenty-two-and-a-half!"

Caroline glared at me. "So Chris, you care about education."

"Of course. I'm getting my doctorate in two months."

"Your doctorate."

"Yes, in philosophy. I've got two job offers to be a professor at universities here in Boston."

"*You?*"

"Why do you say it like that?" I asked her.

Her eyes immediately moved to Marny.

"He's a great teacher. He's been my TA for two semesters. He's taught me... a lot." She gives me a flirty hip-check. I cringe.

"I'm sure he has," Caroline's tone leveled me. "Chris, Marny, it was lovely to meet you."

I watched her walk away and immediately knew I was out of my league. *That* was a woman, *this* is a girl which makes *me* a boy. I was a twenty-nine-year-old boy. *Fuck.*

And then I saw that smug dipshit in a suit that was created thread-by-thread *for* dipshits, sashay up to my girl and kiss her neck. She was taller than him in heels, by the way. Not me, though, I towered over her. Anyway, I didn't like him from far away, let alone up close. I could tell he was full of shit from twenty feet, and definitely messed around with other women. I know, because I know what lying looks like. I mean, I didn't *lie* to the women I dated, I omitted the truth. Ok, that sounds awful. I wasn't in *committed* relationships with these girls, I was *dating* them and there's a big difference between dating and being in an exclusive relationship. I guarantee a woman like Caroline wouldn't give anyone the time of day unless it's in a committed relationship. And while I was out there being a bachelor, this guy, no doubt, told Caroline they were exclusive while banging young secretaries on Beacon Hill.

I watched their interaction and there was something about Caroline and Dipshit's chemistry that was off – not on his side, but hers. She wasn't crazy about him, and I could see it. I could *see* she didn't love him.

Dipshit finished showing Caroline off to his apologists, and stepped away to schmooze with another politico, leaving her alone. I had to get Marny to take a walk.

"Marn, can you grab us a plate of appetizers, I'm starving."

"I didn't see anything."

"I think there's a table near where we came in."

"Oh. Okay!" She smiled and skipped off.

I'm an asshole, I know.

I marched over to Caroline. "You don't love him." I have no idea what brass balls I grew to blurt that out, but I did.

"I'm sorry?"

"I can see it. I'm perceptive."

"Yeah," she said, "I see that. You see the unaware, unassuming target you can benefit from, and go right for it, because she's the kind of girl who'll never catch on to what kind of cad you really are."

"Ouch."

"Please."

"No, that does hurt," I said.

"You'd have to have feelings for that to hurt."

"Wow, you keep firing. Someone must've done a real number on you."

"Don't psychoanalyze me, asshole. You wouldn't know love if it bit you in the face."

"Sounds kinky."

She *actually* cracked a smile and I got to see her in that moment, her big, bright, beautiful smile, and her sense of humor. She's serious, but she kind of digs that stupid, middle school charm.

She quickly recovered, "I'd like to think that the people who are shaping the minds of the next wave of young people in the workplace have some integrity. Why would you sleep with your student?"

"Who says I'm sleeping with her?"

"You're telling me you're not?" I couldn't lie to her, and my raised eyebrows confirmed it. "Exactly," she said. "What's wrong with you?"

"Oh Caroline, I don't think we have that kind of time."

She smiled again. "You're ridiculous," she reminded me.

"Maybe." I don't know what compelled me at this moment, but I stepped closer to her. A lot closer. "Can I buy you a drink?"

She didn't move, our faces were close. My confidence intimidated her; it was awesome. "The drinks are free." She said, out of breath.

We didn't move. "I was making sure you were paying attention." I stepped back at that point.

"You know," she tried to gain her composure, "It feels like you're hitting on me."

"Is that so hard to believe?" I asked.

"Yeah. Since I just met your girlfriend."

"Exactly. *Girlfriend*. She's just some girl." Oops, that line did me worse than I thought. "We're not married."

Her wall went right back up: "At this rate, you never will be."

She walked off. I watched her little waist and hips sway side-to-side, like a model on the catwalk. I couldn't take my eyes away.

"Wanna bet?" I said.

She didn't hear me. I took a swig of my scotch to douse the flames and looked around the room. Marny must've been searching for that table - I didn't see her for twenty more minutes. Poor kid.

"Mr. Shaugnessy," a nurse interrupted. "You can see your wife now."

Arthur's face was all aglow. His light eyes followed me from seated to standing, and looked like they were still in my story, or at least, hopeful. I could use some hope.

"Thank you, Arthur," I shook his hand. "Send my best to Beatrice."

His eyes smiled. "Thank you."

Caroline

Laying in my bed, listening. This is not the ocean or seagulls. No. The beeps and ticks of the machines make me hyper-aware that I'm in a hospital. I shouldn't be here. I'm healthy – everyone knows that. Caroline Shaughnessy is a healthy human being - so what am I doing here? Suddenly…

"Chris!" I hug him so tight, I never want to let go. "Ow! Jesus," I howl. Excruciating pain of a cracked rib. I start to cry. I can't hold it in. I'm in pain, but I'm alive, and my husband is here. I can smell him, breathe him in. In a world of sterilized everything, he is a respite to my olfactory.

I wrap my arms around him, hold him as close as comfort will allow, rest my head on his shoulder so my cheek touches his. I need him. And I knew it then and there. When we married, I held myself to a standard which demanded I'd never need anyone for my survival, that no matter what, I'd stay an individual, have my own identity, finances, self-sufficiency. And for the six years we've been married, I've held to that. He is my lover, my best friend, and my soulmate – but he does not put a roof over my head. *We* do that, we are equals. But in this moment, broken and weak, I realize: *I need him*. A terrifying revelation, loaded with feelings of desperation and vulnerability – two feelings I abhor.

"Are you ok, Chris asks? What the hell happened?"

The Doctor walks in; a tall, dark haired man in his late thirties. "Hi Mr. and Mrs. Shaughnessy. I'm Doctor Stalling, your ER surgeon."

"Is my baby ok?" I ask.

"What happened?" Chris asks.

"Caroline's lungs had fluid in them, which prevented her from breathing. We were able to extract the fluid and stabilize her."

"Is my baby ok?"

"Your baby is fine," he smiles. He takes a pause and continues. "I don't want to cause alarm, but Mrs. Shaughnessy, we found a small mass in your lung."

The word hung in the air, echoing and banging around in my brain. *What did he say?*

"A what?" Chris asked.

"What do you mean, a mass? What kind of mass?" I said.

"We don't know. We sent the fluid to the lab for tests."

"Well, what *could* it be, if you had to speculate?" I asked.

"It would be irresponsible to speculate until we get the results back."

"Isn't that what speculation is?"

"She's an athlete." Chris interrupted, "The bill of health."

"I know." He said.

"Like, a tumor?" I asked.

"Look, Mr. and Mrs. Shaughnessy, I know this whole thing has been traumatic. The point is not to jump to conclusions. Easier said than done, of course, but…."

"Not all tumors are malignant, baby. And Caroline, it's not. It could be a million things, right Doc?"

"Exactly. Mrs. Shaughnessy, with your age and history, it would be highly unlikely it's anything to worry about. I hear you've run Boston."

"Yeah."

"Well, young, non-smoking women who are competitively healthy don't have to worry much about cancerous tumors in their lungs."

"I'm not that young."

"With regard to cancer, you are."

"I have a geriatric pregnancy, but I'm young? Assholes," I say, without realizing or caring. *Oops.* "Listen Doc, I worry about everything, especially now," resting my hand on my belly, "So the sooner we get those results and put my raging anxieties to rest, the better."

"I understand completely." he says.

"But you're sure my baby's ok?"

"She's perfect. Mr. and Mrs. Shaughnessy, get some rest. Have a drink, or a sip, try to relax. We'll have the labs in a few days." He turns on his heels to exit, leaving Chris and I in the loaded silence.

I'm released from the hospital the next day. The silence in the car on the ride home was palpable. Our thoughts, and that word, tumbled around in our brains, our ears.

Mass. *Tumor.*

I look at my husband driving the Panther, his focused eyes behind glasses because he's too tired for contacts - *How did we get here?*

January 2009

I was attracted to Chris the moment I met him. I didn't want to be, but I was. See, I'd stopped letting the pretty boys get my attention, realizing their looks were the attributes that got me in trouble. I'd fall for their face, then their lies, and one or two shattered years later, I'd find myself single, yet again. After three broken relationships in six years and thirty-one years on the planet, I told myself "Never again." I declared it was time for me to tip the scales: date someone less GQ and more IQ. Instead of dating a ten on the outside, and a four on the inside, I'd look for an eight, inside and out. Someone I could count on, a man of his word, who would love me, be my friend, and my rock. And I'd be all those things to him. I looked forward to my "eight." Boyfriends in the past had gotten away with less, but my *husband* was going to be someone as attractive on the outside as he was on the inside. That is the only kind of person I would marry. I promised myself that.

I didn't think Chris would be that guy. He was way too good looking. And worse, he was *charming* – completely terrifying because we all know charm is almost always a cover for being a liar. This kind of guy was my Achilles heel, so I stood firm, "Not this time," I vowed. Besides, I had a boyfriend who was smart, ambitious, political, and we made a great couple.

Ok, no we didn't. Full disclosure: I wasn't in love with him. In fact, he was kind of an asshole. A big asshole, a sloppy cheater and a terrible liar. For such an educated man, he was so dumb when it came to covering his tracks. If you're going to be something, at least be good at it, even if that thing is cheating. At least that way I can respect you. Anyway, he was slime, but I had let him keep me company for a year.

I saw Chris walk in with this young girl whom he had no business being with. She looked about nineteen, but everyone looks nineteen once I turned thirty.

I was busy directing people to Andy's whereabouts; Andy was my boyfriend, the City Councilman who was running for Assistant D.A. He was "important." I'm talking and gesturing, and I see Chris enter – his strong build, jawline, piercing eyes behind scholarly glasses, and his smile - a perfect, glorious smile which rose across his mouth in slow motion – I'm not kidding, it felt that way. *Fuck. I'm toast.* It hit me like a tidal wave. I didn't even know him, but I knew guys like him, he'd knock me off my game, and I'd abandon all the smart, safe things I was committed to.

"*No Caroline,*" my wiser self said. "It's another twelve rounds of disappointment and heartbreak headed straight for you. He's trouble. Player alert. Player alert! PLAYER ALERT!!"

And then his smile-at-large turned to me, our eyes met, and he smiled *at* me.

Hook, line, and sinker.

🐚

I stare at him as he drives – he is rattled, I know this. He's remaining positive, but he has to work for it. We're both scared. Then, he turns and smiles at me.

"I don't have a tumor. I'm pregnant. You don't get tumors when you're pregnant, you get swollen ankles and baby showers and gift cards to Amazon. I'm carrying a child, creating a life. I don't have a tumor."

"That's right, Legs. You had a scare, and we don't know what it is, but we'll find out, and move forward, correct whatever it is, and move on with having this baby. You're fine. You always are."

"It's benign. That's why they're calling it a mass. How could it not be? I don't smoke, I don't inhale toxic substances. I've had no symptoms. I exercise six days a week. I'm healthy and low stress…most of the time. I check all the boxes! Any doctor would see that."

"Exactly," he says. "There's nothing to worry about."

Chris is right. It's all fine. I don't have cancer. Why would I even *say* that? Me and that word in the same sentence don't go together – like Jessica Simpson and Billy Corgan. I'm jumping to the worst. *Jesus, why do I do that?*

"It's probably a cyst, fluid from some buildup, some lingering bronchial infection or something, but nothing serious. It's going to be ok," I say.

"Bill of health, C."

It's all about the baby and Chris, and the life we're creating together. Our home, and the future we're building. I can't wait to have this baby. She's going to be beautiful, smart, and loving. I hope she likes me, because I already love her. I hope she has all ten fingers and ten toes. I hope she doesn't act in a way the school kids will make fun of. Kids can be so mean sometimes. My mother used to say it's because "they're jealous", but even as a nine-year-old, I felt that was a cop-out for the truth. I don't know.

Why did that happen with my lungs, though?

"Are you hungry?" Chris asks. "We could stop for lunch."

"Are you?"

"No," he shakes his head.

"Me either."

🐚

Four hippocampus species are found in the Pacific, from North to South America; three species live in the Mediterranean Sea; some have been found in European waters such as the Thames Estuary, where the North Sea meets the River Thames outside London. The dwarf seahorse, the slowest fish in the world, clocks in at a whopping 5 feet per hour, and can be found in the Bahamas.

🐚

eleven

Caroline

I wake up the next morning without an alarm clock. Flat on my back my eyes snap open before 6 am. I listen for a moment: the waves are here, Chris is here, sleeping next to me. Something bad happened yesterday. *Was it real or a dream?* I look at my wrist and see the medical band, feel the pain in my rib. A nightmare. I carefully roll to my good side and put my arms around my husband who stirs, and quickly pulls me in, kissing my forehead.

"I love you," he says.

Normally, I'd say it right back, but my eyes are too wide with shock, fear, uncertainty. The words won't come out. I hide under his arm. *Please protect me, please protect me from everything out there. I don't want a mass. I want to go back to before 6am yesterday. Maybe if I hadn't run, I wouldn't have stirred it up. Maybe I would've quieted the beast, and I wouldn't know.* Ignorance is bliss.

"Can you call in sick, Chris?"

"Yeah."

We don't get up for our daily routines that day. He didn't fish, I didn't run. We put on our robes, turn on some music, sit in our kitchen and just sort of... pause. It's cold out. The heat clicks on and Chris shuffles to the thermostat, bypasses it, and heads to our fireplace instead. Seconds later our home is warm and cozy. We sit holding our warm mugs, talking to one another in the kitchen until we move to the living room where we cuddle up and hold one another on the couch.

"Chris?"

"Yeah?"

I pause, the weight of the question hangs in the air, like a heavy fog, surrounded by darkness. "Should we paint her room pink? I know that's so obvious and generic, but, I actually like pale pink. But I'd probably never paint anything pink in the house, you know, if it weren't for her, so I figure maybe we use this opportunity to paint the walls pink."

"Sure. Whatever you want."

"Really? No opinion on the matter?"

"Really."

A big pause and a breath, followed by silence. Both of us – heavily silent. "And like, the carpet, or wall hangings. I was thinking ballet slippers, or something super girly, you know?"

"Supergirl? Like, Superman's sister? Red boots and a cape?"

"Fucking nerd." I half-laugh and bury my face in his chest. He kisses my forehead. "I love you, Chris."

"I love you, Caroline."

I want to hide under the blanket of my husband's arms for the rest of my life.

🐚

In bed that night, I lay on Chris's chest with my eyes wide as two golf balls. *What if it's bad?* I can't get the thoughts out of my mind.

"What if it's bad?" I blurt out.

His quick response reveals he isn't alseep either. "What do you mean?"

"I have – we have – a day, maybe two, before we find out."

"So?"

"Aren't you worried?"

"No."

"Why?"

"Because, there's nothing to worry about. You heard the doctor. You're fine."

"Well, he didn't say that. He said it's *unlikely*...."

"See. And unlikely for *you*, is like, no fucking way. There's no way it's anything, Legs. For once, don't think the worst, huh? You make yourself sick thinking things aren't going to work out."

"That's not fair."

"No shit it's not fair. It's not fair to you. So please, for the love of God – please, please think positively."

"Thinking positively isn't going to change the results."

"Jesus Christ, Caroline!" He throws the sheets off and stomps out of bed. "What is wrong with you?! Stop it! You don't have it!"

"What? Cancer? See, you're afraid, too."

"No! It's – a tumor. Cancer isn't even on the table. Why would you think that? You have a mass, an innocuous, benign mass."

"We don't know that, and you need to consider…"

"YOU DON'T HAVE IT!"

He looks me dead in the eye. His calm, handle-anything demeanor dissipates, and this is what's behind the mask. He's angry. I've never seen him like this.

I look away.

He sits down on the bed, placing his hand on me. "I'm sorry, honey, I'm sorry. It's going to be fine, ok? I promise. You're scared, I'm scared, too. Seeing you down on the ground like that, not breathing, and I couldn't save you." He takes a long moment to register his thoughts, "I've never felt more helpless in my life. I thought I was about to lose you. I didn't even think about the baby, and I'm sorry about that. I'm so sorry. All I could think about was how that might be the last time I saw you, last time I spoke to you. I couldn't make you breathe. I'm sorry, baby. I'm so sorry." He cries. My heart breaks wide open.

I hold him for a long time. We never come apart in front of each other. I guess we never want to be less than a tower of strength for one other, never show real fear, real weakness… what a load of shit.

"Thank you for trying." I say. He looks at me perplexed, and kind of laughs. "I don't know, what do you *say* to that? 'Better luck next time?' 'If only your revival skills were as good as your rib cracking skills? I mean, what? It's CPR."

"Ok, Caroline -"

It hits me again, *What the fuck was I doing getting CPR?* The shock spreads across my face.

"Honey…" He says.

I look up at him, "Thank you for saving my life. I'm making jokes– my defense mechanism, clearly- but you did, you saved my life. I'm sorry for being sarcastic." A collective breath followed. "Let's promise to never keep anything from each other, ok? Tell the truth always, even if it's hard - and never hide our feelings, ok?"

"Promise. You have my word."

"All I've ever wanted."

🐚

It's a perfect, football-Sunday morning. We aren't watching yet, because the Pats weren't playing until 1pm, so we decide to get out and do some easy yardwork. A gray day, interspersed with glints of light breaking through the clouds. The orange and yellow and brown leaves are wet with dew. By 11am, we'd been doing chores for a couple hours, raking and preparing for the upcoming winter – and looking forward to watching Tom Brady and Julian Edelman crush the Jets. I pull my gardening gloves off to wipe the sweat from my brow, as Chris slips inside to get us some water, when I hear the phone ring. Every time the phone rang that weekend, a bolt of lightning coursed through my spine.

"Caroline!" Chris yells. I stand up. Terror fills my entire body.

Unable to conceal my shaking hands, I receive the phone from Chris, "This is Caroline."

A woman's voice replies: "Hi Mrs. Shaughnessy, this is Dr. Ryan."

On a Sunday. Do you believe they call on a Sunday? "Hi Doctor," my voice cracks.

I look up at Chris, who was looking back at me with hope.

"We got back your test results," she continues, "We'll need you to come in tomorrow to discuss them."

"Well what did you find?"

"I'm afraid I don't discuss results over the phone, but we can meet tomorrow, if you're available."

"What?" Chris asks, "What Caroline? Say something!"

"Hang on, Chris."

"Doctor Ryan, what kind of a doctor are you?"

"I'm sorry?"

"What field of medicine?"

"Oncology." I hang my head in silence. She continues, "The nurse will call you and set up a time."

"I'm pregnant."

A long pause on the other end, and a draw of breath. "I know," she says, "I'll see you tomorrow, Mrs. Shaughnessy." She hangs up. I don't move.

"Caro? Baby? Caroline, what's wrong? Talk to me. Please!" Chris crouches down so I have no other choice but to face him.

"We have to go in tomorrow to discuss the results," I say.

"Well, that doesn't mean anything..."

"She's an Oncologist. If it was good news, she could tell me over the phone."

"It could be anything. Could be a benign tumor that you have to remove, and they want to discuss it with you. Any surgery is a big surgery while you're pregnant, so of course they want to discuss it with you."

"What if it isn't, Chris? What if there's something wrong with the baby? Or what if ... what if it's fucking *cancer*?"

"It's not."

"STOP SAYING THAT!"

"NO! You don't know what it is. Neither of us do. And people get second opinions all the time. You don't get to give up because you're scared. We said that, didn't we? So why would you assume the worst?"

"I don't *want* to think I have cancer! But I'd rather mentally prepare as if I do."

"Mentally *prepare*? We don't know. There's no use making yourself miserable anticipating what we DON'T KNOW! And I'm sure it's nothing. Look at you – you're the picture of health. People don't get cancer while they're pregnant, and especially women like you. We need to drop this whole thing and get back to our normal lives."

"Normal lives? Chris, this isn't normal. We have to deal with it. She's a *cancer* doctor, for God's sake."

"It's nothing. You're stressed because of the hormones."

"I'm sorry, what? *I'm* being irrational? I collapse because of a tumor in my lungs, and my fears are *irrational*? Because I'm *pregnant*?" I step toward him with my arms gesticulating.

"Caroline, let's calm down."

"DON'T tell me to calm down! Are you kidding me? Are you out of your fucking mind?"

"*You're* out of your fucking mind. Look at you."

"FUCK YOU!"

"FUCK YOU!" He peels away. "I'm sleeping on the couch tonight."

"Good, you prick."

He looks at me with fire in his eyes, and finally walks away.

I hate me, too. And I hate this tumor. I have a *baby, and* a *tumor.*

It's 2:30am and I can't sleep. I'm imagining all the cells in my body. *What are they doing? Creating or destroying? Multiplying or dividing? Why? Why me?* I hear the waves, but they're more anxiety-inducing than tranquil. My anger from our earlier fight has dissipated into sadness and I want my husband. I lay in bed, staring at the ceiling, and a memory rushes across my mind...

June 2011

I stare at the ceiling, waiting to get up. I quietly turn my head to make sure Chris is sleeping; perfect, he is! The sun shines through our Boston brownstone, and it's time for him to get up. He's thirty-two today and I've got something special planned, no *choreographed*. I push the button to my alarm and the bouncing, obnoxiously cheerful (but awesome) beats of Wham's 1986 hit, *I'm Your Man* begins. Chris's eyes open and turn toward me, confused, groggy, pissed? I smile this HUGE cheesy grin, bopping my head to the beat.

I leap out of bed. I've timed it out, and at the fifteen-second instrumental part, I sexily strut to our closet door. I open it dramatically, and there's a strategically placed suit hanging - his pants, white shirt and tie, and a stylish fedora. I run my hand along the tie, as my hips sway side-to-side and I mouth the words, "Call me good, Call me bad". I proceed to step into the pants–while I continue dancing–which is a terrible idea. THUMP. Down I go.

"You ok?" he's 90% laughing, 10% concerned

I wave him off and spring up. Still laughing. Perfect.

I strut some more, sliding my arms into the white shirt – not enough time to button buttons. The tie goes over my neck and I grind down and shake my booty, continuing the lip sync: "I'll make you happy with the one thing that you never had." Run back to the closet for the final touch: his fedora. He props himself up against the headboard to get comfortable for the show.

"Why are you putting clothes *on*?" he laughs.

I fling the hat at him to hush him up; he deftly catches it. I'm prancing around the room, now taking my clothes *off*, dropping them one-by-one on the floor, and giving him these ridiculous fuck-me eyes, all while singing, "Baby, I'm your man. If you're gonna do it, do it right, do it with me." Booty shake, shoulder lift to the beat (I *might* look like I have Tourette's), my hips gyrate round and round till my butt hits the ground, and then I come up with an arched back…or try anyway. I'm crawling toward him like a tiger… he's getting a litttttle excited. He reaches for me – and I JUMP away.

"Ba-by, I'MMM your MANNNN!" I sing. "If you're gonna do it, do it right, do it with me. If you're gonna do it, do it right…."

I run out of the room for the big surprise finale; a tray of stacked pancakes, eggs, bacon, and coffee. In the middle of his super stack are lit candles, "32".

He's out of his mind psyched! YESSS! VICTORY IS MINE!

He blows out the candles, carefully places the tray on his bedside and GRABS me, tossing me underneath him and covering my face with kisses.

"That. Was the best freaking birthday present EVER."

"I'm not done just yet," I smile. I kiss him, and we get to work on them birthday suits.

I throw the covers off and tip toe downstairs. There he is, crunched up sideways on the couch. I carefully lift my leg over the back of the couch – cringing from the lingering pain of my rib – and slide in behind him, hugging him in. I whisper in his ear:

"I'm sorry, Chrissy. I don't want to fight."

He pulls my arms around him, "I'm sorry, too." He turns around to face me and kisses me.

"I love you," I say.

He throws the blanket over me, as we hold onto one another in our best attempt to sleep.

The next morning, I stare in my closet. It's bitter out, and all I want to wear is something warm and comforting. I have this beautiful taupe cowl neck sweater that seems perfect for how I *need* to feel - protected, insulated. I adore this sweater, it's a favorite. Will I forever remember it as the sweater I found out I had cancer in - "the cancer sweater" – every time I wear it? Or maybe I'll never wear it again, I'll give it away. Maybe I should wear something expendable – a ratty old t-shirt I can throw out after.

But it won't make the cancer untrue.

Maybe Chris is right. Maybe it's benign, but they still have to operate. The ER doctor agreed that not all tumors are malignant. This one is benign and causing some weird breathing issues. That can happen. Why would I have a malignant tumor? That's got to be impossible for someone like me.

"What's the matter, honey?" Chris asks.

"I don't know what to wear."

"Throw something on. We have to go."

"It's not like that," I mumble. "I'm trying." I want to feel good, but I don't want to lose my favorite sweater. I want to *not* have a malignant tumor. Is there an outfit I can wear to prevent *that*? I grab for a long, black sweater, my black leather jacket, and a pair of maternity jeans. I probably won't need these for a couple more years.

Wait.

Would I be able to have another baby? What about *this* baby? Will I be able to get pregnant again if I have a tumor, or a tumor removed? Jesus, what if I have to have chemo? I heard chemo makes you infertile… Infertile – are you kidding me? I barely got pregnant this time, and now? Is this our only baby? Oh my God – what if….

The thought knocks me to the floor.

Chris hears the thud and yells up from downstairs. "Caroline?" Panic courses through me. Chris hurries in. "Caro – what is it? Come on." He lifts me to the bed.

"What if this tumor takes *her*? I'm five *months*…What's happening, Chris?"

"Shhh, it's ok." He holds me and rubs my back. "It's ok. We're going to listen and hear what they have to say, and do everything we're supposed to, one step at a time, ok? I'm here. You're not alone. I'm here."

He helps me into my jeans. He pulls out a pair of socks, and my favorite boots, he puts them on one by one. I look up at him, holding each foot in his hand, sliding them into my boots, calmly, patiently.

"You're going to be an incredible father," I say, "Because you're an incredible husband." He smiles and puts his head down, still working with my boots.

And in that moment, I'm so grateful. I stare at him and thank God for him.

twelve

Caroline

Usually when I'm at the doctor, I'm in the examining room with crappy magazines, some sort of computer, a sink, and a bunch of posters with cautionary facts screaming at you. I'm also alone. Today, Chris and I sit together, on one side of a *desk*, waiting for Dr. Ryan. Two chairs for the "guests", for news so bad it's more than one person can take. I sat wondering how many hearts have broken in these chairs, how many tears have fallen, how many lives have been cut wide open. *Think positive, Caroline.*

I stared at the pictures and degrees in this room. Boston has some of the best universities in the world, best hospitals in the world, and Brigham and Women's has some of the best doctors in the world.

"I'm in good hands," I smile at Chris. He smiles, too.

I notice one of the framed pictures on the desk – Dr. Ryan is a pretty woman, her husband looks older than her, but is an attractive man. They're holding their little boy who looks about four. A nice-looking family.

Dr. Ryan enters. She has an olive complexion and long, black hair, maybe Lebanese or Armenian – she reminds me of Leash. And I notice something else, her white coat can't hide it; she's pregnant, almost as far along as I am.

"Hi Mr. and Mrs. Shaughnessy, I'm Dr. Ryan." Chris and I apprehensively shake her hand.

"How far along are you?" I ask.

"Seventeen weeks."

"Congratulations," I say.

She smiles briefly. "Thank you." She settles in, "I'm sure you're excited about your little one. How far along are you? Five months?"

"Twenty-one weeks. We're due early February."

"That's great. Your first?"

Chris and I look at each other in agreement, and smile, "Yeah, it's our first."

"That's wonderful," she says, taking a long time to say anything else.

Chris breaks the silence, "So Doctor, what are we doing here?"

Good energy and positive thoughts, Caroline. Without hope, we have nothing.

Dr. Ryan takes a breath and her tone shifts. "We got Caroline's cytology and pathology back. As you recall, the X-ray in the ER shows a mass in your lung." She turns her computer monitor around to show the X-ray images of my lungs, exposing a marble-sized white ball on the black backdrop of my lungs. "There is a tumor in your right lung, here."

I look and see this scary blob. This can't be me.

"Can we get it out?" I ask.

"I'm afraid it's inoperable."

"Why?" Chris blurts out.

Another breath by the doctor. "I'm afraid the cancer has spread to other parts of the lung. Same lung, no metastasis — which is good."

"No what?" Chris asks.

She said it. Cancer.

"Movement to other regions in the body," she answers.

I grab her trash can and puke into it. Chris puts his hand on me.

"What did you say?" he asks.

"Water," I say.

The doctor pushes a button on her phone and a nurse hurries in. Dr. Ryan hands off the trash barrel and asks for water.

The nurse runs out and returns with a Dixie cup of water. Chris helps me with a Kleenex, but his focus is outward. The water is handed to me. The nurse runs out carrying the trash. My watery, red eyes look up at the doctor for more blows.

"Normally radiation would be administered to shrink the tumors for advanced lung cancer.

"Advanced?" Chris asks. Dr. Ryan drops her eyes and nods. "No, she doesn't have that." he says. "There would have been signs, symptoms."

"Often there aren't any until the advanced stages. Sometimes there's back pain, coughing, trouble breathing, but they can be minor, almost unnoticeable, especially while pregnant… and especially with what she has."

"Which is?" I ask.

"It's called BAC or Bronchioloalveolar Carcinoma, though that's an outdated term. It's a lung cancer affecting non-smokers. Many of the symptoms go unnoticed, sometimes until Stage 4. Fortunately, she's not Stage 4. Based on certain factors, Caroline, you're Stage 3B. However, to treat this the most aggressively and extend your life…

"*Extend*?" I stop her.

Dr. Ryan looks at me, sits up straight, and closes her eyes. "It's treatable, but not curable."

"No." I hear Chris argue. "That's not true. She's young and healthy. You must have someone else's chart. Run the test again."

"Mr. Shaughnessy…."

"RUN THE FUCKING TESTS AGAIN!"

I look up at my husband, standing over the desk, pointing his finger at her. This is not my Chris, not the one I've ever known. Sweat beads on his brow. He yells something else, but I don't know what. I'm watching him, but I can't hear the words, I see the slow motion of his pointing and yelling like it's a dream.

She remains calm: "We can do that. But I want to walk you through a treatment plan in the event the tests come back the same."

"They won't. We'll get a second opinion, Doctor."

"We encourage that. But we have to…"

"No! We're not talking through…"

"It's urgent, Mr. Shaughnessy." This time, I could hear the unwavering tone in the her voice. I look up at her, she's immovable, "Normally, we'd administer chemo *and* radiation to treat the patient, but we can't perform radiation while she's pregnant. The most effective course of treatment would require us to terminate the pregnancy."

"What?" I ask.

"Caroline, the best-case scenario for *your* health, is to contain the cancer, and terminate the pregnancy. Legally, that must be done before week twenty-four. We cannot perform the procedure after twenty-four weeks. So, you need to make this decision right away."

"I'm not killing my child," I said.

"Wait a minute," began Chris.

"No. I'm twenty-one weeks, my baby is five months old, how could…"

"It's not five months old. *Patient* is five months *pregnant*" Dr. Ryan interrupts, "and it's our job to protect the patient."

"I have three weeks to decide… me or my baby?"

The doctor peers up at me from lowered eyes. She doesn't answer, wanting the truth to be something else.

It's me or my unborn child. This can't be real.

"No," Chris orders, "Run the tests again. This is a hack. There is no way she has cancer. Look at her! Does she look sick to you? Does she look weak to you? She's pregnant and tired, not sick and dying. She's…"

I look up at him with weary eyes, it stops him.

"I advise you to get the second opinion right away," Doctor Ryan says. "There are excellent oncologists and high-risk obstetricians all over the city. I'm happy to refer you to any of them, let me know. But don't wait."

The doctor gets up, leaving the two of us alone, I hunch over, Chris stands, ready for war.

Chris

June, 2009

Damon's was a piano bar in Boston – Ok, Somerville - it was too slummy for Boston proper. But I'd play there a few nights a week to make extra cash until my full-time job kicked in. It was June and the school year had finished, and so had my days as a Teacher's Assistant. In September, I'd become a full-time professor at Wells, the illustrious women's college just outside the city. I was a thirty-year-old Doctor– a *PhD*– and feeling pretty damn proud. My student loans sucked, but the salary was decent enough, and would help chip away at my debt.

I loved playing the piano there, I loved the crowd, the night life. When I first started playing there – maybe 2003, the rooms had this smoky haze to them. But by '09, the smell of the walls held only the history of a once cigarette infested joint. Billow-free, some of the charm was extinguished, too. Before they changed the laws, those rooms made your clothes smell, even if you weren't smoking – and though I didn't (much), it did feel something was lost when the laws abolished smoking indoors. The encouraged debauchery, the bluesy vibe, the effusive sadness – all that is now trapped under the visage we decide to show the world. Those feelings still exist and will come out eventually. It's just a matter of how and when.

Anyway, I was sitting there playing my heart out, and I was a couple scotches deep, so I thought I sounded better than I did. Oh, I sang, too. Good piano player, mediocre singer. I'd asked Caroline to come half a dozen times, but she was always busy; "work's running late," have a "client meeting," whatever. Tonight, she assured me she'd make it, we'd been dating six months.

It didn't take much to steal her away from that snake – here's how it happened. At the end of the fundraiser that night, while everyone received their coats from the coat check, she put her purse down on a chair. What's-his-name was somewhat helping her into her coat but left her hanging half-way through – it was awkward. I grabbed her purse and quickly took her wallet. I know what you're thinking, hang on.

The next day, I called her to let her know she "dropped" her wallet and that I found it. I suggested we meet up for a drink, and I'd return it to her. After a typical amount of resistance, she agreed.

We met at a dark, little bar in the North End. She was relieved I had it, because even though she'd already canceled all her credit cards, there was a special necklace in the zippered part she was anxious to get back. It was a necklace she wore every day, but had only taken it off to wear a fancier piece to the fundraiser. The necklace, a diamond "C", was from her grandmother who had passed when Caroline was nineteen. I never would've taken the wallet had I known I'd cause her this much anguish. She was nearly in tears when I handed her the wallet, but the overwhelming relief on her face when she pulled out the necklace, her heartstopping smile when I offered to help her put it on, what it *meant* to her...the feeling hit me like a Mack truck: I was in great danger of falling for this woman.

I remember every moment. The way she'd look down, think, and look up, smiling, how she'd carefully touch my hand when she agreed with me, or touch her face when she was pensive, kick her head back when she'd laugh. How her eyes would widen with wonder, or squint when she was focused and trying to understand. She's not closed off at all. She's wide open like a child, vulnerable as they come. The shield, the armor, was created out of necessity.

I realized about thirty minutes in, that I'd do anything to stay around her, and then I kissed her, mid-sentence. Shock moved across her face, and she produced no words, so I blurted out:

"I want you to know I've been listening to every word you said, and I'm totally interested in what you're saying, but I had to kiss you. You're the most electrifying person I've ever met."

She didn't say anything. It was a slow and cruel four seconds.

And then she grabbed me and kissed me with the hunger of a starved animal. It was the best kiss of my life.

She broke up with him the next day, and we were inseparable the day after that. Being inseparable, however, doesn't mean without bumps. I was becoming a new me, for sure, but there was residual crap from my past relationships, and from hers as well, that would set us off. Basically, she knew I was a super flirt – *prior* to meeting her – and I knew she had some trust issues. She hated to feel foolish, or like the wool was pulled over her eyes. Sometimes that created a hyperawareness, a search for the "truth." Really, it created a hyper-skeptic, and would get in the way of us having anything real. I tried to explain that to her. She told me to fuck off. She was kidding. Mostly.

So there we were, six months later, and I wanted her to see me in my element, holding court. I got a lot of attention at Damon's, I was impressive, and I wanted to impress her, too. I'd been very unsuccessful in getting her there.

One time, I said, "Caroline, come see me play. Piano players have sex appeal which I'm quickly losing each day I spend as a TA."

Know what she said?

"I don't trust musicians. Emotional. Unstable. And they fuck everyone."

That's my girl. My diplomatic, unopinionated, easygoing Caroline.

But that night, she finally showed. I'd finished my crowd pleasing *Hey Jude* when she shuffled through the crowd and found a spot against the side wall. She looked hurried, like she'd gone through a lot to get here. I was thrilled, and I said so on the mic.

"Ah, my girl is here. She didn't want to come until I told her this was a side gig." Laughter from the crowd. "Yeah," I continued, "Teacher's Assistants don't make as much as big, fancy ad execs. She's had more time, though, she's older." The crowd laughs and even gasps at my lack of discretion.

"It's only two years, asshole." Caroline playfully chimes in. More laughter from the crowd.

"I love a girl you can take home to Mother!" I fire back. I hit the keys and shift gears for a warmup intro. "Let's see how you do with this one. It's a little-known ballad from a well-known pop band. Don't judge it by its cover." I pause – no one laughs.

"Not a comedian," some biker-dude type yells.

"Clearly," I laugh. The crowd laughs with me. "A wannabe musician. But you know, it's too bad that once a lot of people like your music, you lose credibility. Do me a favor, do *yourself* a favor, and give this one a chance."

I began the piano chords and my eyes glance over to Caroline, who waits on my words with excited anticipation. I breathe them into the mic and let a smile move across my face, but not for long because it's a somber song about the pain of love and the desperation of wanting to get back with your lover after a breakup. The powerless addiction of it.

"Every time I wind up, back at your door..."

It's a great song, and women love it, but this time, I'm only singing it for her. The trouble is, the tipsy blonde in front is pretty sure it's for *her*; the fuck-me-eyes she's giving are intense. I avoid her for a while, but as a musician, you *have* to flirt a little. I smile at her for a *second* and continue to perform the song. I bang on the keys for the finale, and when I look up, Caroline is gone.

Where had she gone? The ladies room? In the middle of the song? She couldn't stay for *one* song? I hoped she didn't take a call. If she took a work call at 10 at night and couldn't even stay for one full song...I look back at the girl in the front row, who is now smiling *and* blowing me kisses. I look up at the door - Caro stares straight at me. She shakes her head in disgust and walks out. Is she *jealous*? *Caroline*?

That's it, she's jealous! She thinks I'm interested in this woman. She's being irrational and immature, but I'm thrilled she cares enough to be jealous. Honored even. One problem: *she's* pissed, and about to write our relationship obituary.

"Oh shit," I accidentally say out loud, on the mic. "Hey everyone, I forgot to plug my meter." I push the piano bench back and pop up.

"They're off at 6!" Biker-dude yells.

I pretend not to hear him and run after Caroline. I look outside – she's gone. I speed off in my little VW Golf – a car I'd had for years as a student, a car I planned to get rid of as soon as I began my new life as a working professional, as a grown up, as a man who would one day be a family man. I hadn't ever wanted to be locked down, but I stopped thinking about it that way once I met someone *I* wanted to lock down. I figured I had more time, but this rainy, June night, it was clear I'd have to put it all on the table. True, I hadn't done anything wrong, but that wasn't the point. She was going to quit on us, based on fear. She let me see how much she cares and I can't let her blow up what we have. We both would've lost something that night.

I pull up to her little rental condo in Allston. The light on the stoop is off, but the lights inside are on. I bang on the old Victorian door.

"Caroline! Caroline, come on!"

She opens it enough to say, "Go away!" And quickly slams it.

I shove my foot in the door to stop her, but she pushes back. "Jesus, you're strong," I say.

"Exactly, so fuck off!"

A dog barks, and the neighbor's lights flip on. "Hey!" shouts the neighbor.

"It's ok," I say, "A lovers' quarrel."

"NO!" Caroline says. "NO love. None!"

"Yes there is!"

"Bullshit!" She pushes the door back hard - it splits my lip.

"Ow! Jesus." I cover my lip, her eyes soften, and she steps forward. Thank God she injured me. She never would've come out.

"Well. You deserved it," she says, trying to defend her righteousness with crossed arms.

"No I didn't. I know what you think."

"What I think? What I *know* is that you left your girlfriend for me, and now you're eye-fucking the shit out of Titty Tuesday over there."

"What?"

"It's Tuesday. She had big tits, it worked."

"Nice." I reach for her hand.

She slaps it. "No. You left your last girl, you're a piano player, YOU are a player, and I can't trust you."

"I'm a professor."

"No…" She raised a finger to correct me, and step backwards from my advancing steps.

"…Yes. I'm a professor, who starts in two months at Wells University. I have a real job, I got it yesterday, but you've been so busy, I haven't been able to tell you. I was going to tell you tonight after the show, but you took off."

"Well," she began, temper cooling, "I'm happy for you. Congratulations."

"Thank you." I step closer.

"But it still doesn't excuse the fuck-me eyes you were giving to the first row!"

"I don't have fuck-me eyes. They're eyes." And then as cheesy as can be, I sang "And I only have eyes forrrr youuuu."

She's amused... but still tries to shut the door. Gently, at least, but this time, I overpower her, and take her hand.

"Hey." She pulls it away.

I become even more gentle in my tone and approach. "Caroline," I say.

"If you cheat on me, I'll kill you," she says.

"Oh I know."

"Dead. Murdered. But not like dead fast, dead slow, torture."

"Wow, Lorena Bobbitt."

"Lorena Bobbitt was a pussy. She shoulda finished the job."

Her words choke my brain, but I follow her inside anyway. Her vicious creativity half-terrifies/half-impresses me. "Marry me."

"What?"

"You heard me."

"No. I didn't."

"Yes you did."

"*No. I didn't.*" My gaze doesn't change. "Are you CRAZY? We've been dating like, five months."

"Six, if you count the night we met, not our first date."

"I don't."

"Well you should. Listen, I dated *a lot* of women."

"Great selling point."

"And when you know, you know."

"Cliché."

"Will you shut up and listen to me?" I take her hand and get down on one knee. She blinks several times quickly – that's what she does when she's shocked. "I know what I want. I haven't wanted to be with anyone the way I want to be with you, and I don't think that's ever going to change. Will you marry me, Sweet Caroline?"

She was dumbfounded but left her hand in mine. "You don't even have a ring," she stammered.

"Can I get some credit for spontaneity?"

"You can't propose without a ring."

"Fine." I reach over her shoulder and pull a hair out of her head.

"Ew!" She shrieks.

"Sorry," I struggle to tie the "ring" around her finger.

"You're not wrapping a hair around my finger and calling it an engagement ring."

"Fine." I rip it off and kiss the place a real ring would be. "It's the thought that counts," I smiled sheepishly. "Say yes to the thought."

"You crazy son of a bitch."

"Is that a yes?" I asked.

She took a deep breath in. What was that breath? Disappointment? Impending bad news? Then she smiled.

"Yes. It's a yes."

"REALLY?" I jump off my knee and scoop her into the air.

"I can't believe I said yes to a kissed engagement ring."

"You said yes to happily ever after."

"Do you believe in that?" she asks.

"Yes I do," I kiss her nose, "Yes I do."

Three months later, in front of a small group of our closest friends and family, we said "I do" at the Black Dog Tavern in Martha's Vineyard.

The seahorse is a unique fish, swimming upright as opposed to horizontal, and possesses a prehensile tail, which allows it to anchor itself to seagrass, coral or even manmade objects. It has a bony crown-like structure on its head, aptly named the coronet which is as distinct to each organism as the fingerprint is to every human.

13.1

Caroline

I want to skip work again, but I've missed so many days already, I force myself to go. It's as if I'm not there, anyway. I sit in my office with the door locked and stare out the window at the world moving below. As soon as the clock strikes 3 P.M., I sneak out, tell them I have a client dinner.

I get home and do more sitting and staring out our windows. I watch a runner on the beach, her ponytail swaying, arms pumping. The seagulls dance and swoop around her, the waves crash in close, then far, close, far, but never touch her. She's good, she knows exactly where to step to avoid the water. She's probably about thirty, and in good shape from what I can see. She wears warmup pants, her form is good – which happens less often than you'd think. If your form is bad you expend valuable energy, so it's important to work on it, be efficient. I watch her get farther and farther away from me.

Running has been something of a savior for me. I've used it when I need to get away; from the hurt, the disappointment, the loss, from insecurities and doubts, from overeating or overdrinking – to get myself back on track. To forget, to remember, to recreate and renew, to dream and scheme, to believe again. The fresh air and open road always does something to me, changes my chemical and emotional make up. I'd run after an argument, a breakup, a lost job, a lost New England Patriots game, a lost diamond earring...whenever I felt lost, I found running, and it found me. It made me stronger, happier, and more self-assured than the self-doubting girl who began the run in the first place. Without it, I don't know who I'd be.

It may be an addiction, but luckily, the open landscape and the sound of my sneakers hitting the pavement is my drug of choice. I've been all over the world on these feet. I've run over the Golden Gate bridge, and admired it from the cliffside trails of Land's End; I've run through Central Park in the foliage-speckled fall and over the snow-covered hills in Park City, Utah, as my teeth chattered in January; I ran through the lava rocks and dense humidity of Kona, Hawaii soaked with sweat in June, traversed through downtown Atlanta in the spring and Chicago in the fall, beneath and through that windy-city architecture. I trotted down the quaint, back roads of wine country in California, and farmland in New Hampshire; through the kindhearted, residential neighborhoods of Indiana, and the exclusive, mansion-lined seaside of Newport, Rhode Island. I watched the sun go down in the southern-most tip of Key West, and the western-most tip of Santa Monica. I even ran through crowds of debauchery in Vegas, and through the Brits in Piccadilly Circus. I trotted past the Louvre, leaving Mona Lisa in my dust, and it was my feet making the thunder from down under. I stomped through ten miles of puddles in the pouring rain, winds at my front, winds at my back, winds at my side, helping or hurting my pace. It was running that put me at one with nature, with fellow warriors, sometimes strangers, and always with myself. There are so many more places I'd like to visit and run. Running over the land acquaints me with a city and its neighborhoods; we're not close and don't understand one another until I run over it, and it's not until then do I truly see a city. No, when I truly *feel* a city - we're old friends once that ritual is complete.

In saying all this, I realize I don't often let people in. I may keep to myself sometimes, I've needed the quiet. I don't share my pain, my hurt, or the crummy things that happened as a kid after my brother died. A mother's pain when that happens, losing a child, she's inconsolable. Her sadness, depression, anger and hatred… it can't be fixed. No one can fix it. Her pain exists only in her – she thinks. But it isn't trapped inside, no. It travels, no matter how hard she tries to prevent it. And sometimes, hers is so big, it invalidates all of yours…

It's complicated, though. How do you blame someone who has suffered so much? Someone who has cared for you your entire life, someone you owe a great debt to. How do you blame her? The answer is, you don't. I went away to college and that's when I began running. Watching movies as a little kid and running as an adult-- my momentary lapses of escape.

🐚

We schedule the second opinion for a few days later. Dr. Ryan gave us a list of doctors for us to talk to, and I felt so guilty. How could she be so nice to us after the way we treated her? What must it be like to deliver news like that…

By the end of the week, we have a second, third, and fourth opinion. All of them the same: BAC – a term no longer used, and is now reclassified as lung adenocarcinoma - is the most common form of lung cancer in women, Asians, and people under the age of forty-five. In fact, the rate of lung adenocarcinoma is *increasing* in young, nonsmoking women. Also unfortunate is the fact there's little research into *how* any of us non-smokers contracted it. The stigma that lung cancer is a smoker's disease has stymied further investigation into possible causes. That's helpful. Anyway, I've got advanced lung adenocarcinoma, "will not perform radiation with a fetus". "Cancer while Pregnant" is what they call it, that's an actual thing. Cancer while pregnant. Did you know that happens? That you could be pregnant *and* have cancer? How fucked up is that? And it happens more than you'd think, but typically the type of cancer is breast, melanoma, or ovarian, triggered by the hormones of pregnancy. Those cancers are treatable while pregnant, and are often not terminal. No doctor will perform radiation while pregnant, however, there are chemotherapy medications that can be taken, *they say*, which will not harm the baby. I don't care what "they say". How can they *know*? They're putting chemicals in you that kill cancer cells – how can something so destructive be "safe" for a growing baby?

"Caroline," Chris says to me as we're lying in bed, that night, staring at the ceiling.

"Yeah."

"You want to… terminate, right?"

I don't move or say anything for a minute. "Chris…"

He turns his head to me: "Your health is the most important thing to me. You're here, she's not. She's a half-formed blob of…"

"Don't talk like that. She's not a blob of anything."

He props himself up on his side, staring at me. "Well I don't know what else to call it."

"Her."

"I'm having as much trouble as you."

"I don't know about that."

"Caroline, I'm trying here. I don't know anything. I don't know what to do, what to say. I– I don't know how to do this."

"Neither do I, Chris." I feel heated, and immediately force myself into diplomacy.

"How ever long this road is, I need us to be unified – I can't do this without you."

"Don't talk like that, you're going to be here for a long-

"Let's go to bed, try again tomorrow," I cut him off.

"Ok."

He kisses me on the cheek, and it's weird and awkward. *We're* weird and awkward lately. I don't blame him. This is a fucking nightmare.

I schedule an appointment with Dr. Ryan and I. Since I've got the cancer, I decide I want to be the one making decisions, or at least, let the information tumble around in my brain and let me think about it without anyone else's influence. Selfish? Maybe. Selfish if I decide to kill his baby without consulting him– definitely. But is it selfish if I choose to kill me? Let me rephrase, if I *prioritize* the baby's life? Isn't that what we do the second we find out we're pregnant? No wine, no sushi, no deli meat. This is more of that.

It's not that simple, of course. And Dr. Ryan is the one I want to talk to about it, even though we saw three other doctors. She was right all along, and the truth is, I trust her.

I enter her office, and she stands and hugs me. I get the impression she doesn't do this often.

"Hi Dr." I say.

"Please sit down. Would you like something? Water? Tea?"

"No, thank you."

"I can't offer you coffee unless it's decaf," she reminds me.

"I thought we could have a cup a day, can't we?"

"I mean, some studies say yes," Dr. Ryan rubs her pregnant belly, "it upsets my stomach. He doesn't seem to like it."

"A boy, huh?

"Yeah. We were hoping for a girl this time, but, it's ok."

"Well, maybe next time."

"I think this is it." A silence washes over us. We have that in common, too. "So, Caroline, you wanted to talk about your options."

"Yes. I know I have a couple more weeks before the week twenty-four deadline, but, I'm not sure that's going to be a consideration for me. Some of the reading I've been doing..."

"Good, you're self-educating, you should. A lot of times, if a problem isn't communicated to us, we don't see it right away. You're your own best advocate. But also, make sure it's a reliable source. Don't go believing everything you read on the internet."

"Ok. So, for women - who have a higher survival rate than men - the number for Stage 3B lung cancer patients who survive five years is less than 9%?"

Dr. Ryan waits a brief beat, "Roughly."

"So I have a 91% chance of dying before my daughter's first day of Kindergarten."

Another long pause. "The numbers vary from person to person."

"But," I interrupt.

"...Yes, those statistics are accurate."

"Good, that whole 'watch her get on the school bus for the first time' seems like murder anyway." I laugh. The doctor doesn't know what to do, but her observant eyes soften. She's with me, not watching me. "Doc, I – I've lived a great life. That expression that everyone dies, but not everyone lives, I have. I don't want to die. I don't want to leave my husband, the life we have. I don't want to miss those moments with my little girl, those moments *you'll* get to see of your kids." My eyes glance over at the family of three on her desk. "Her first steps, first words, carving a pumpkin with her, watching her ride a bike, seeing her with her friends, who she becomes. It's all gone. One little word took it all away." I look her in the eyes – dark brown and attentive. "My dream to have a baby is shattered, but his isn't. Terminating my child's life might give me a couple years *at best*. A bunch of radiation, chemo, hair loss, throwing up – whether vomit or blood. And that's not the quality of life that *I'm* after. I want her to have a full, healthy, happy, *long* life. I had my chance here. I wish I could have more time, but it looks like my number is up. So, I won't be terminating my pregnancy, and I won't be seeking any treatment."

"Caroline, there are chemo medications that are safe for the baby."

"Doc, if *coffee* isn't safe, there's no way I'm putting cancer-destroying drugs in my body."

"Being pregnant alone is exhausting. You need a tremendous amount of health and energy to carry this baby to term."

"Well, luckily you're dealing with a distance runner so stamina is my forte."

"You won't be running anymore."

That one stopped me. "What?"

"It's not safe."

"I was told I could run well into my pregnancy, that I didn't have to give up exercise that was normal to me, and some women exercise right up until labor."

"You cannot deplete your strength or your immune system."

"It's who I AM!" I stood up and lunged forward.

Unmoved, she continued, "And you cannot overwork your lungs. They're incapable of any kind of strain."

I lean over her, locked and loaded, armed with my right hand to point and yell and tell her there's no fucking way I'm stopping my normal life… and sure as shit, I start to cough, a loud, heaving cough. Guess I strained my lungs. Fucking shit, are you kidding me? "Fuck you."

Dr. Ryan looks at me with raised eyebrows.

🐚

When I was young, and after Mom had put my sister down for a nap at the other end of the house, she'd crawl into the corner of the living room and bawl over the loss of TJ. It was loud and deep, the moans of an animal at the side of the road standing over her dying young. Mom would rock back and forth, the sounds coming out of her... to this day, I've never heard anything like it. If Katie ever woke up, we never heard her. I didn't know what to do except just lie there, staring up at the ceiling. Anytime I'd tried to help her before, she yelled at me. Mom got mad so easily. So all I could do was disappear into the dream world of my mind. Sometimes, I'd make up stories, fantasies, anything to escape what was real. I loved movies. I'd get lost in the triumphant tales where the hero wins - Superman, Luke Skywalker, Perseus – the hero saved the day, and justice was restored. I loved that feeling, craved it.

I want to fight like them, be a hero, save the day, but it looks like the only one needing saving is me. This can't be true. I'll reason around it, outsmart, prove wrong, get my way, I'll...

But now I have cancer, and I'm dying. And I can't run.

"Where's my husband? I want my husband!"

"He's at work, you said." Dr. Ryan says.

"No! Get my husband, I want him! You can't keep him from me! WHERE IS MY HUSBAND?" I slide my hands across her desk, throwing files and X-rays and picture frames to the floor. "Chris? Chrissy, help! Come get me! Help! Help me, Chris!" I feel a nurse's arm come over me, and a pill is offered. I slap it away and keep yelling. A male nurse retrieves it and forces it in my mouth. "I'm not gonna swallow it. You can't make me swallow it."

Doctor Ryan strides over to me, cradling the broken frame of her family. "Caroline, we can do this in other ways, you know. Swallow it, or we'll be forced to inject it."

"No! No drugs. You know, Doc, NO drugs!" My eyes plead.

The nurses look to Dr. Ryan for direction.

"Let her go. Go ahead, Caroline, spit it out. But if there's one more outburst, they're injecting you with a sedative immediately, got it?"

I nod and cough again. "There's that fucking strain on my lungs, huh?" Dr. Ryan nods. "I'm sorry about your picture frame."

"It's ok."

I slide back into the chair. I'm so tired. The sadness washes over. I hunch over, head between my legs, my body heaves, and suddenly words I've never uttered come out.

"Why? Why me?" I cry into my hands, bouncing and shaking. I feel the doctor's hand as she rubs my back. "Why? It's not fair. It's not fair." I cry harder and harder until I can't breathe. She stands by my side and doesn't say a word, but her hand never leaves my back.

🐚

I twist the white paper coffee cup in my hand – black and bitter. I hate black coffee. But it was nice they offered it to me. I wonder if it's decaf… I hate decaf even more, it's useless, like non-alcoholic beer or avocado ice cream. Fucking fuck. What is happening? It's not a dream.

I stare down at the cars below from the doctor's office– turning, stopping, going, and doing it all over again. It's a rhythm, a boring, monotonous rhythm. The pedestrians bury their faces in their wool jackets. I can't see their breath, but in a few hours when the sun goes down, I will. There aren't many trees around but of the ones I can see, they're bare - the trees are bare and gray and dying.

Dr. Ryan's heels click toward me in the long, reverberating hallway, and she touches my shoulder. "Are you ready to come back? There's a few more things I want to talk to you about." I look up at her with red, strained eyes. "We don't have to today," she continues.

"Now's as good a time as any, right?" I wobble to stand as she ushers me back down the hall. "This coffee tastes like ass. No offense. On the other hand, it's probably better you didn't put that non-dairy borax in there. That's an affront. Granulated 'creamer'? You fucking kidding me? It's like dry-frozen spooge."

We arrive back in her office.

Dr. Ryan sits down in her chair, "Your OB will likely suggest bed rest. If not now, soon. We'll write you a doctor's note to your employer so they'll give you disability."

Disability. She can't be talking about me. "How long would I have to be in bed?"

"Until you have the baby."

"No. I can't lie in bed all day, I'll go fucking mad. Figure something else out. There has to be another way." She stares at me. No words. "You can't name one good thing? One silver lining in any of this? Tell me something good, dammit! One thing, there MUST be something."

"You'll have a daughter." It stops me in my tracks. I look into her soul-penetrating eyes. She doesn't flinch, doesn't back down. "It's only until the baby is born," she says. And once that happens, we'll be able to treat you."

I search her face, desperate. "How did I get this? How? I don't smoke, I take care of myself…"

"There's no real way of knowing. There could have been radon in the house you grew up in."

"Then my mom or sister would have it."

"Not necessarily. We all have different predispositions, something in the DNA. What affects one person in a similar situation may not affect the other. Family history… But right now, we're focused on what's next for *you*, and your treatment plan once the baby is born. Treatment is taxing – but after the chemo cycle is over, you will feel better. The silver lining, Caroline, is *you*."

"What do you mean?"

"You have a healthy lifestyle, you took care of your body, you may be one of the survivors who lives longer than five years; a small percentage lives ten years or more. You could be one of them. Belief is an unmeasurably powerful force, Caroline, and I want to encourage *that*."

"Don't ever give up."

"Exactly."

"My husband and I, we say that to each other. It was part of our wedding vows. We remind each other of it when we're… going through something."

Doctor Ryan gives me a side-smile. "Try to keep stress levels low; lots of rest, meditation or light yoga, or there are certain prescriptions for mood."

"No. No prescriptions. Nothing in my body until the baby's born. And no bed rest until I absolutely have to. I'll go fuckin insane."

"We'll talk to Dr. Sylver."

I can't concentrate on anything she's saying anymore.

What is happening? I was King of the World, two seconds ago. I fired on all cylinders, the epitome of alive. Now I'm "incapable, disabled, with cancer?"

"Pregnancy is exhausting for anyone – for a woman with lung cancer, it's nearly impossible. But something tells me you can do it." She smiles warmly. For a moment, I feel honored. Her way, her soothing, nurturing way calms me down.

"Doc? What would you do if you were me?" She shifts in her chair. "Knowing what you know, would you extend your life, spend more time with your husband and little boy, and kill your unborn, and the ability to ever have another one? Or do whatever you can to protect the life of your baby?"

"I can't speak to personal decisions. As your doctor, it's my job…"

"I'm not asking you as my doctor."

I hold my gaze on her. She does the same. I know she's uncomfortable. She leans closer and almost inaudibly says, "I'd do the same as you."

I stand up, she stands up, and we're mirror images of one another. Two women, both about five months pregnant, both in our thirties. The only difference is one of us has cancer, but you can't tell by looking at us. That's the hardest part – and the fact she'll see *her* children grow up.

I stand there awkwardly – wanting to hug her, but not knowing how. I hold out my hand, "Thank you, Dr. Ryan."

She pauses, and pulls me in, holding me tight. I stare over her shoulder like a dazed stuffed animal. She lets go first. "I've scheduled a meeting tomorrow morning, with a high-risk OB. His name is Dr. Sylver. Will that work for you and Chris?"

"Um…It's just a lot all at once, and I have work, but.. I'll be here."

"You'll have a team of multidisciplinary doctors consulting on your case. I'll talk to Dr. Sylver about your bed rest concerns. I understand how devastating inactivity is for you, but at a certain point, we must do what's safest for you and your baby. I want you to know, we're going to do everything we can to keep you comfortable and strong for your term."

Interesting word, *term*. Terminally ill, while carrying to term. "I'm *dying* to have a child." The darker my sarcasm, the more I want to cry. She doesn't dignify that one. I shrug and head for the door.

"We're all rooting for you, Caroline," she says. It stops me in my tracks. I read her eyes -there's hope, support, and encouragement in them.

fourteen

Caroline

In a marathon, you experience every emotion. Joy, fear, strength, pride, defeat, love, exhaustion, anger - like on mile twenty when you're beat to shit and someone will not get the fuck out of your way, and you *know* it's because he's tired too, and simply CANNOT go any faster, or muster the one-third of energy it takes to step to the right one step to make space for you. And if you yourself had the energy to do it, you wouldn't be so annoyed – but you don't. You're fucking tired, and over this race, and wondering when the next water stop is – or better, Gatorade, because some electrolytes would save your life right now. You look at your watch and see that you've slowed your pace and that makes you even more upset. You're by yourself, and you have SIX miles left. Fucking Six. Two would be totally manageable, but six? Six is so far away. Loneliness. That's when it kicks in - loneliness and doubt – and that's the hardest part of the race.

"How am I going to do this?" My inner defeatist, cries. "I'm all by myself. I don't even *want* to do this. All the training I did will be for naught because I don't have the will, and if I don't have the will, I certainly won't have the speed, so my finishing time is going to suck, and then I will have failed. I started out so well. I'm blowing it, I'm blowing it right now."

That's the despair talking. Loneliness and despair can happen at any moment. You hope it's later in the race, and not early, because if you're giving up on yourself early, it's going to be a long fucking race.

"One foot in front of the other, Caroline. Keep moving," something inside me would say.

So, I would. And full of piss and vinegar, I reach mile twenty-one. Five miles left sucks, too. It's at this point that I let go of the race time I'm trying to beat–which was likely too ambitious anyway, and let go of the pressure I put on myself – it's too much to carry. I settle for a slower time. I don't like it, but I simply don't have the strength to argue with myself. Slowly but surely, I make it to twenty-two.

"Four miles left," I tell myself. Four is good – four is an easy day, but I wish it was three – three miles left would be great. Two would be even better. "One foot in front of the other."

Maybe if I commit to running these next three minutes and take a one-minute walk break, I'll get closer. So, I do that for a mile and sure enough, I'm at twenty-three-and-a-half. I ask myself if I can run the last 2.7 miles, or do I want to take walk breaks for another half-mile and get to twenty-four. I know I can blaze through the last 2.2 – I want to, I want to do those last two miles *fast*, at a pace I'm proud of. Finishing strong is my thing, so I decide to take it slow with walk breaks, until I hit mile twenty-four.

And then it's go time. I'm tired, *exhausted*, but I'm alive. It's mile twenty-four, and I'm about to finish my *seventh marathon*, I remind myself. The impending finish puts pep in my step. Pride. Pride and excitement come over me. I'm strong and I can hear the people cheering. They're there, supporting me and the other warriors, willing us to go on. I may have tuned them out and tuned in to my music for the bulk of the race, but this is when I let them in. I see myself passing other runners, I see them beaten down, because that's what a marathon does – it beats the living shit out of you mentally, physically, and emotionally – man or woman, young or old. I pass hot shot men who went out too hard in the beginning because they don't know the strategy of endurance running, and I've been lapped by a sixty-five-year-old man. I ate *his* dust. That's when humility comes in. Those moments you realize age is a state of mind, and that you can do anything you put your mind to. Humility and inspiration. I'm inspired by the people I see in races each time – wheelchairs or bare feet or soldiers in full combat suits and boots, sometimes carrying a giant flag. It reminds me how much harder some people have it. That I'm there struggling, in comfortable running sneakers and the perfect amount of clothing, my music to get me through, a water bottle, and enough snacks to fuel me – and this guy is carrying a flag and running in combat boots for *26.2 miles*. Toughness, mental toughness. The military guys have so much of it. Then there are the jokesters in Elvis suits and Elvis wigs- also terribly uncomfortable "running gear." Man, those guys have a great sense of humor. You experience that on the course, too, especially when a spectator holds a sign that says "Worst Parade Ever" or "Who are you running from?" Humor can get you through a race.

There are runners on the course who have a picture of a loved one on the back of their shirts. When you're running behind them, you can't help but be inspired. They've lost, and they're out there, using the opportunity to gain something back, to accomplish, to turn loss into something won. And they're raising money for a cause. So many times, they're running for someone who died of cancer. I never realized that one of those people would be me.

The finish is near. I can see it. The street becomes heavily lined with fans, and they're loud now. I've got a half-mile left. Everything hurts – quads, hips, even my arms are heavy. I pick up the pace hard core now, even though it kills. I pass person after person. I want that finish line, and I want it now, so I pump my arms and keep moving. Elation. I'm almost there. Unstoppable. I turn my music up –U2's *Where The Streets Have No Name* can erase any pain I've got. I go. Faster. Thirty yards, twenty yards, ten yards, ten feet… I cross the orange finish line with a smile as wide as the street I'm running down. Cameras flash. I throw my arms up.

"I did it. Another one, I did it!"

Sometimes, I'm so happy, I start to cry. But my lungs are so fatigued, they can't handle it. One time, I nearly started to hyperventilate, so I immediately stopped.

"Ok, you can't cry." I told myself. "Or you're going to pass out." Survival mode beat out emotion.

And that's it. That's marathoning. Every emotion.

I suddenly realize that these doctors are going to be the ones to get me through – they'll be the coaches and security, the volunteers handing out water and Gatorade and finisher medals, the fans cheering me on. "We're all rooting for you," she said. This pregnancy – this carrying a life while losing my own – is going to be the marathon of my life. I hope there's beer at the end.

I return to the long, hollow corridor, past all the infirm knowing one day I'll be one of them, that *I'll* be the sickest. It had only been two weeks since we got the diagnosis. They say belief is the most powerful thing there is, so if I don't believe I have cancer, maybe I don't. Maybe it won't spread. Maybe if I keep acting healthy, practicing positive thinking, meditation, maybe I can make it go away. Shamans can do that.

I walk into Dr. Ryan's office, and standing next to her is a tall, white-haired man with a beard and wire-rimmed glasses.

"How do you do," he says as he gently shakes my hand, "I'm Dr. Sylver, your OB." He takes a seat next to Dr. Ryan.

"I'm told you're my 'team' of specialists," I say.

"This is half of us," Dr. Sylver corrected.

"Couldn't you guys be a team of manicurists and pedicurists? Or how about all those personal shoppers from *Pretty Woman*?"

Dr. Ryan smiles at Dr. Sylver as if to say I told you so. They launch into a serious-sounding speech, but I'm stuck in my imagination, sitting in a big, bougie chair just like Julia Roberts, surrounded by Beverly Hills employees as they present me with dresses, hats, *and* pizza, oh my! The medical jargon grows louder, and suddenly my daydream pops like a balloon, snagging me from Rodeo Drive and dumping me at Brigham and Women's. Reality is for losers. Fuck.

I want to ignore this reality. Chris is going to be furious I came without him. He'll be furious, he'll be hurt. I don't want to hurt him... But, it's going to be me and only me who's six feet under, so why shouldn't *I* decide? These are going to be the biggest decisions of my life, and I want to be clear-minded and informed; I can't handle anyone else's emotions right now. I need to know what *I* think, how *I* feel.

So here we go – death prediction 2016, bring it on!

The more I listen– or fade out of listening - I wish he was here to catch the information I drop.

"Survival rates are *statistics*, not people," they remind me. "There are some long-term survivors of advanced lung cancer."

Somewhere in the conversation, I hear "six months." I could have six *months* left? My listening gets hazy and I want to puke or cry. I actually did. I start to cry and I can't speak.

"You'll have the baby, but you will probably be too weak to hold her the first two months," Dr. Sylver says.

"And with your six-month prognosis, I'll be dead shortly after."

"I didn't say that, I said as short as six months," Dr. Ryan says.

"At least I won't die on the table during birth," I say.

"Labor alone will be taxing," says Dr. Sylver. "And it can be dangerous to your health. So, we strongly recommend a C-section."

"And give up my chance to join the ranks of natural childbirth and earn my official Women's Badge of Honor? I hear there's an induction ceremony and everything."

"That's impractical," says Dr. Sylver.

"I was joking," I say.

"Oh good," says Dr. Sylver.

"About the induction ceremony. They don't have that."

"A natural birth leaves too much to chance – if there are complications and we have to resort to an emergency C-section, it creates further risk for you and the child. We need to *schedule* it, not push it to an emergency, based on your condition," adds Sylver.

"I can do it," I say.

"It's not a matter of can or can't," Dr. Sylver says. "It's senseless. It's out of the question, Mrs. Shaughnessy."

"I prefer Warrior Princess." His thin lips don't even purse. He doesn't have Dr. Ryan's sense of humor. "Ok, can we keep phrases like 'out of the question' out of our conversations? I'd like to keep everything regarding the birth plan an *option*. If I am, as you say, an individual and not a statistic, I want to be treated like one. At this time, I feel good, I'd like to at least be considered for natural child birth. It's something I've always wanted."

Under her breath, "Certifiably insane," says Dr. Ryan.

"Oh, and when I say 'natural' that refers to my lady parts, because epidural, hell yes. I'm not fucking crazy."

"As you wish. Warrior Princess," says Dr. Sylver.

"I like you, Sylver. I didn't think I was going to, but here we are."

We discuss their *original* birth plan - a C-section six weeks prior to term. I tell them I'd consider nothing more than *three* weeks prior to term, and reiterate that I'd like to hold off on scheduling anything, and see how I'm holding up in a couple months.

"We'll see," Dr. Sylver says.

"The sooner the baby is out, the sooner your treatment begins," says Dr. Ryan. "But I'd like you to consider..." Dr. Ryan says.

"Treatment begins after she's born. Stop telling me some chemo is safe for the baby. Please. Safe for a baby with three heads and fourteen toes, and that sounds like way more backtalk and socks than Chris is prepared for."

"I understand, Caroline. But know we will address this on a week-to-week basis. Things can escalate quickly – certain symptoms, metastasis. Or, they can stay the same for months. We don't know. We do know the placenta protects the baby from the chemo."

Dr. Ryan tells me I could live anywhere from six months to five years – five if I'm lucky, but that percentage is roughly 3% *if* I receive treatment. Not receiving treatment until after the baby is born puts me in great jeopardy of only living a few months.

"How come it doesn't protect the baby from coffee?" They didn't have an answer for that.

Then there actually is a silver lining, the type of cancer I have – BAC or lung adenocarcinoma - spreads at a much slower rate than other lung cancers. So, on the one hand, it shouldn't spread rapidly, on the other, it's advanced, and it's not a quick operation to remove the tumor or part of my lung. If they'd found it during the early stages, I could've had the tumor removed, and my five year-survival rate would be 100%. One. Hundred. Percent.

But I'm late stage. That's the thing about this kind of cancer, the early symptoms are so minimal – fatigue, soreness in the back – barely noticeable. I've had aches and pains as a runner since I can remember – pain is part of the gig. How would I ever know the pain I was experiencing was early cancer? I couldn't. I could never know that, and now it's killing me. Now add the new aches of pregnancy, the exhaustion and unfamiliar *weirdness* that goes with it and it's a double whammy of WTF.

My head swirls; weighing one thing over another, variable after variable; survival rates for this stage for this kind of lung cancer, based on treatment versus none. I don't even have time to feel, to digest what's happening to me or think about what *I'm* losing because I'm dealing with a series of numbers, statistics and what's going to be right for my baby and husband – my survivors. Ok, the doctors don't refer to them that way, but I do. I may as well attack it head on – I certainly know that's how an insurance company would see them, or an attorney, or financial advisor. If we're going to talk about death, let's talk about it.

Funny, the doctors are strangely optimistic – not that I'll live - but that my timeline may be longer than the statistics because I'm such a "fighter." I'll let them be optimistic, I need to sleep. No idea if it's from pregnancy, cancer, stress, or all of the above.

I excuse myself, tell them I'm done with today's meeting and I'll catch them another day. I find my car in the parking lot and take a two-hour nap before I can think about meeting Chris for dinner. Tired doesn't even begin to describe it.

fifteen

Caroline

How did I get here? I rub my eyebrows, my eyelids. How did I get here? It seems like this is somebody else's life. Did I get dealt the worst possible hand? Me or my baby. This has to be a joke, a cruel, humorless joke. I keep waiting for someone to yell "April Fools!" But it's October.

I sit across from Chris at one of our favorite restaurants, Stephanie's on Newbury Street. The big green awning and twinkle lights wrapped around the trees have always been so charming to me. It's chilly – two weeks from Halloween – but thankfully, the patio is still open. The heat lamps turn an otherwise intolerable situation into one that feels cozy, even romantic – or wishing to. The street is lit up with even more twinkle lights and shoppers on the iconic brick-lined promenade which has always been a great place to people-watch the wealthy.

Chris and I haven't said much since I got here. To say we're not ourselves is a gross understatement. I'd like to tell him I didn't go to work the last two days, but then I'd have to explain that I went to the doctor without him. I *had* planned to go into the office for a couple hours, but it's funny how once you know you're going to die, finishing a killer ad campaign for Nike doesn't have the same appeal.

I take a swooping dive with my chip into Stephanie's signature lobster guacamole and pile drive it into my mouth. I know I should be devastated, but I'm fucking starving. Cancer 0, Baby 1.

Chris is tense. I'm not sure if it's work, or the last ten days of doctor appointments and the second, third, and fourth opinions.

"Are you ok, hon?" I lean forward and touch his hand.

He grabs for his wine, takes a swig. "Fine."

"You seem – preoccupied."

"I think that's a fair assessment. Why are you so calm?"

"I'm not sure. Maybe it's because there's no other choice," I say.

"No other choice than to be calm? Or because you think they're right about you?"

"I mean, four different doctors. I think it's safe to say I have cancer."

He slams his glass down. Diners look over. "Well, it doesn't mean it's not curable," he adds. "My cousin had breast cancer, and…"

"This isn't breast cancer."

"Well we can explore more options."

"I met with Dr. Ryan today."

"Without me?"

"I needed to hear the facts on my own, get a clear perspective."

"Without me."

"I needed to hear my own thoughts."

He lifts the wine bottle from the table, fills his glass and takes an even bigger swig. "This isn't just about you, Caroline."

"I know it isn't. It's about all three of us, and I need to think carefully about what to do."

"This is an *us* decision, something *we* come to. Not Caroline McCafferty, Caroline *and* Chris *Shaughnessy*. You don't decide this on your own!"

"Chris, lower your voice."

"Don't tell me what to do!"

Chris gets up and hurries down the sidewalk. I follow him and I see he's lighting a cigarette.

"Are you CRAZY!?" I snap it out of his mouth and stomp it under my foot. "We don't want our kid to lose *two* parents to cancer. What is wrong with you?"

"How can you be so calm? We have *ten* days to decide whether to have an abortion or let cancer spread through your body, while I sit idly by, doing nothing! My best friend. My best fucking friend in the world. You want me to watch that? I won't."

"Chris, she'll be the living memory of us."

"That's darkly poetic, but no." He takes another cigarette out and studies my face. With the cigarette now dangling from his mouth: "Did you make *our* decision, Miss. McCafferty?"

"I..." I reach toward him.

"No," he steps away. "Don't touch me."

"Chris?"

"Caroline, if you did this without me... This is your life we're talking about-"

"That's right, MY life!"

"OURS! Our life! Please tell me you haven't made this decision without me – this isn't like picking out a new couch or paint for the bathroom. This is EVERYTHING! Every promise, every word I've ever given you, every word you've ever given me. Tell me I'm wrong."

"Chris..."

"I'm waiting."

"I had to."

He looks me dead in the eye. "Had to what?"

"I had to decide. Chris..." I reach for him again.

He pushes me away. "Fuck you."

"Chris. I'm going to die anyway." I reach again. "Please Chris…"

"Yeah, because I'm going to kill you right here." I laugh, but he's not smiling. "I don't want a baby without you, how about that? I want you! And if it means no baby, but I get you for one more *hour*, that's what I want."

"Chris."

"I *don't* want a baby without you." He stares me deep in the eye. It knocks the wind out of me.

"Chris. I can't kill something we created. It took us so long just to get here!"

"Yes you can."

"No I can't. I can't do it. It's our last chance, you understand that? This is it, baby. This is IT."

"Stop saying that, it's not! There are people out there who *survive*; a small percentage, but it's there - I read it, people who make it *ten* years. Ten! You know what we could do with ten more years? We can adopt if you still want to be a mother. I want you. *You*. We can go to Europe, a safari in Africa, fuck, a sailboat from Greece to Morocco, adopt five babies, put the Jolie-Pitts to shame! The sky's the limit. Please, I'm begging you. Don't leave me."

"Chrissy, please-"

He steps back again. "Don't leave me. You're one of those, I know it. A small percentage. You've never been less than extraordinary to me."

He disarms me, renders the prolifically verbose, speechless. I take him in, his beautiful pleading eyes, his strong posture weakened by despair, his fighting spirit fueled by hope. I will never leave you, Chris. Never. And this is why you need to hear me.

"Chris, I don't want you to be alone. When I'm gone, she'll be here. If I do this, terminate our baby, and die in six months, you'll have no one."

"*Six months?* Where the hell did you get that?"

"It's possible."

"So is ten years!" His face reddens with emotion. "So that's it, you've made this decision on your own. Fuck me, or anything I want, right, Caroline? Couldn't think about anyone but yourself? Selfish. I knew that about you. I just thought I could break you of it."

He lights up another cigarette and walks away. And I'm there, with nothing.

August, 2009

I gaze proudly at my engagement ring; it was shiny, not huge, but ornate, Estate jewelry. He knew better than to get me a Tiffany ring which would look like everyone else's Tiffany ring, and be overpriced. I wanted something unique. He had it designed for me: the setting is beautiful - everywhere there could be a diamond, there is one, and inside, he had it inscribed. I can't tell you what it says, because that part is for us. But I'm proud of it, of him. This ring will last forever. I'll wear it for the next fifty years of my life, so I think that three months-salary limit is fine. Makes me feel like I'm worth it, and I'll make him a happy man for the rest of his life.

Every time I see his dirty socks – again – where I told him not to put them, fine. I'll look at that shiny ring and remember "Oh yeah, he loves me, I'm worth it." Stayed at the strip club for his cousin's bachelor party one too many dances long? I'll get over it. Look at that ring! Forget our anniversary or one birthday? Yes, just one. You get ONE get out of jail free card for this. I'm saying, Fellas, don't skimp on this. DON'T. SKIMP. It's the only one you'll ever get her, so make it right. Make it MORE than right – make it more than she expected. You do that, those benefits will come back in spades. The engagement ring: the gift that keeps on giving – to BOTH of you.

We drive to Cape Cod to check out the venue once more – we'd decided to get married at the Black Dog Tavern in Martha's Vineyard, a place from our childhood. I didn't know him and he didn't know me back then, but it's fun to think we may have crossed paths with our families twenty-five years ago. It's a place that meant something to both of us. My favorite auntie used to bring me there, and Chris's favorite uncle brought him – we both went to the Vineyard with relatives that had more dough than our parents. I'd spend a week with Auntie Peg and Uncle John, and Chris would do a day trip, but we both always loved to go to the Black Dog. Maybe it's that iconic pooch that appealed to us as kids – how could it not? We wanted our wedding small and intimate, full of charm, and very New England, and so it had to be the Black Dog.

But this car ride is tense. Chris is kind of out of it. He went to his college roommate's bachelor party the night before, and it seems he had a rough night. It's gray and starting to sprinkle outside, and the dirty windshield wipers make it messier and hard to see.

"Are you gonna be ok to drive, hon?" I ask. "The visibility is bad and you seem kinda tired."

"I'm fine." He says curtly.

I frown. "Ok, let me know if you change your mind. I'm perfectly happy to drive." He says nothing, wipes at his nose a few times, sniffs hard. "You ok?"

"Yup." He sniffs hard again, and I automatically hand him a tissue. He takes it without a word, puts it to his nose, but when he pulls it away, there's blood on it.

"Oh Jesus, you're bleeding!"

He swerves quickly, almost hitting a car. "Jesus Christ, Caroline! Don't yell like that. You scared the fuck out of me." He pulls over to the side of the street and grabs the tissue, putting his head back. The blood drips on his shirt.

"Honey. I'm sorry. I didn't mean to startle you." I reach to touch him and he swats me away. "Chris, *what* is wrong?"

He tends to his nose. "We had a bit of a late night last night. I didn't sleep."

"What are you, college kids? Why wouldn't you go to bed? Even a few hours?" He gives me a look that said "Figure it out". "I don't know what you're trying to tell me, Chris."

"What drug makes you stay up all night?"

"*Drug?*"

"Yes, Caroline. White powder."

"Coke?" *Why would he take coke? Everything about me is health, everything about him is health.* "*Why* would you do coke?"

"Because we were partying."

"You can party without coke! Do you know how easy it is to overdose on that? Do you know how often it's laced with other shit that could kill you?"

"Oh come on, Caroline. Don't be such a nun."

"A nun? How could you do that when you know my brother died from an overdose?"

"I'm not your brother. I can handle it."

"Yeah, I'm sure he said the same thing right before they carted him away on a stretcher." I yank the car door handle and storm out. I can hear Chris before I slam the door.

"Where are you -?" he says, reaching for me.

I plod down the street. The rain comes down hard, but I don't care. I stand on the sidewalk as a river of rain flows down the street, picking up leaves and debris, dropping them in drains.

Chris runs after me. "Why are you making such a big deal about this? It was one night."

"Really? You haven't done it before last night? Since we met? Because I didn't notice, but maybe that's because I never imagined you'd do something like that. Maybe I just thought you were in a good mood."

"There may have been one other time – two, two times since we met. They were parties, nothing crazy."

"You're thirty-years old, Chris, you're not a kid. I'm about to share my life with you, have a family. If something ever happened to you, and I had to explain to your Mom or my Mom, or our kid, that Daddy's gone because a party got out of hand…"

"Jesus Caroline, it was ONE night."

"That's all it took for my brother! And then I had to say goodbye. I'm not looking to do that with you."

"Well, I think you're being ridiculous."

"Ridiculous? You're right." I begin to pull the ring off my finger and lift it in the air. "I was ridiculous to say yes to you." I throw it at him.

"No!" He immediately drops to his knees, feeling around in the moving water. He searches desperately, patting the ground, the street, the sidewalk. And then he sees the drain. Gone.

Brokenhearted and destroyed, his head falls. I'd never seen him so low in his life.

With all the energy he has left, he mutters, "How could you do that? Everything I had was in that ring. I would give you everything I have, Caroline." He throws his hands up, and turns around, aimlessly pacing, searching for something – words, explanation, hope.

I wait a second, watching him, wondering what to say. *Do I really want to marry this guy? It happened so fast, do I really know him?* I see the desperation in his face. He cares, I know he really cares.

"All I want is your word. It's the most important thing to me."

"My word that what?"

"Your word you'll never EVER put your life in jeopardy again. I love you. And I'm not willing to lose you." I open up my hand, and there is my ring.

About nineteen emotions run across his face in a split second, "You had it the whole time?"

"Yes."

"I'm so sorry," he gasps, hugging me hard and whispering in my ear. "I'll never do it again."

"Good, because I don't want to live in a world without you."

I remember his Uncle pronouncing us Man and Wife, Mr. and Mrs. Chris Shaughnessy one month later. It was the day I'd been waiting for my entire life.

Their courtship begins with what is known as a "predawn dance;" they may change color, swim side-by-side holding tails, or link up to the same strand of seagrass. Once it's confirmed their interest is mutual, the real bonding begins through *sound*.

A bony structure resembling a crown, called the *coronet*, rests at the edge of the skull. As the seahorse lifts and bows its head, the coronet shifts back and forth against the skull, producing a clicking sound. Mating seahorses swim slowly together, alternating their clicking sounds. Once the male and female embrace, their sounds unify, becoming indistinguishable from one another. This creates a loud, singular sound, and solidifies their bond.

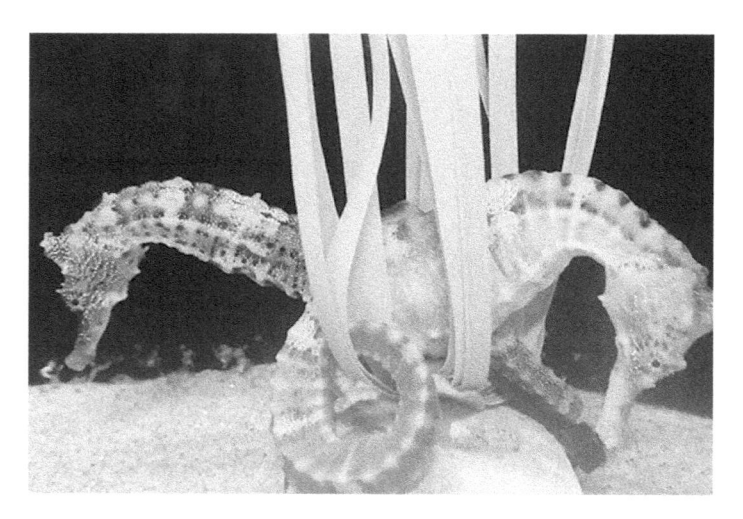

sixteen

Caroline

Being in a fight with Chris is one of the emptiest feelings I can stomach. It feels like half of me is missing, and it's definitely the better half. Add to it that I can't run, and you've got the makings of a listless hole of despair. Laying alone in our bed, watching the clock tick past 6am then 7am then 8am reminds me I am disabled, incapable, with cancer. Identity is such an elusive thing. I pull myself up and shuffle downstairs so I can steal a glimpse of Chris from our French doors.

Look back, I will him, *Look back, Chris*.

He doesn't. He doesn't look up at all. I don't know how we're going to do this divided. For the first time since we moved here, I walk away without meeting his glance.

The next day, I stand over a boiling pot of pasta. I'm making his favorite dish, farfalle with chicken, peppers, and mushrooms in arrabbiata sauce, served with fresh Italian bread, extra virgin olive oil and parmesan cheese. And, his favorite bottle of Montepulciano. It's a pathetic attempt, I know, but a man has to eat. He walks into the kitchen without looking at me, opens the refrigerator.

"Hi." I say. He says nothing. "I'm making farfalle con pollo with arrabbiata." He doesn't acknowledge me and leaves as quickly as he entered. I shout after him. "You know arrabbiata means *angry* in Italian! Just kidding babe." *Shit.* "Farfalle means butterflies… which I get every time I see y… never mind." *God, my tactics suck.*

That night, as I rub lotion on my hands before bed, I see Chris in the reflection of our mirror, taking his pillow off our bed, apparently to sleep downstairs. We catch each other in the reflection, his dead eyes reveal disappointment. He puts his head down and continues downstairs. I follow him and stop at the top of the stairs, watching him below as he curls into fetal position on our couch. I don't dare walk down this time, I can't take another rejection.

The next morning, trudging to my bathroom to brush my teeth, I stub my toe on the toilet. It hurts like a son of a bitch, but it isn't the physical pain that unleashes the tears. There I sit, on the cold toilet seat, clutching my foot as I weep. He startles and rushes to me, his natural, protective instinct. He stands in the doorway for a moment, only long enough to make sure it's not serious. And then, he's gone. I only see peripherally, I didn't bother to look up. Watching him walk away is harder than assuming he did.

I go back to bed and don't get up the rest of the day, or the day after that. He only comes in to get clothes for work. I pretend to be asleep later that night when he comes in for a t-shirt. He doesn't turn on the light, only creeps in and out thirty-three footsteps, and he's gone. I didn't sleep at all that night as my heart swelled with pain. I want to call my sister and ask for advice – but that would mean having to tell her I have cancer, and I'm just not ready, yet. I need Chris so bad it hurts. I cry myself to sleep sometime around 5am.

I sleep the entire day. I make my way downstairs around 8pm for a peanut butter and jelly sandwich, hoping he's home. He isn't. *Where could he be?* Out, starting a new life without me? Moving on, finding someone else already? A beautiful, young co-ed, vibrant and healthy? A doctoral student in her late twenties with her whole life ahead of her, her vitality, fertility, smarts. Chris always liked smart women. I've never been more insecure as I am in this moment, and the house has never felt so dark and empty. All I hear is a ticking clock and the ocean. I stand in the middle of my kitchen with all the lights off except for one, in my sweat-smelling bathrobe, eating alone. Even pregnant, the heartache over Chris murders my appetite and the dry peanut butter won't go down. I drop the sandwich in the trash and lumber upstairs, only to notice the vase of roses are dried up and dead. Any other day, I'd toss them out, but I don't have it in me.

The next morning, I wake up with a horrible stomach ache. I need to eat, so I go downstairs for some cereal and fruit. I crave fruit again and need something tart to stimulate my taste buds. As I pour the cereal and fruit and milk into my bowl, I look out the window, and there he is, casting and reeling, his breath creating a visible plume. He doesn't look back.

Is this it? The beginning of the end? My illness is going to kill us *now*? I touch my belly. There's a life in there, but do I risk our marriage for her? Spend my last days in a fight with the one person who means the most to me, with him hating me, maybe divorcing me, just so we can have a child? I thought he *wanted* a family. Our marriage is crumbling because of her.

No, because of cancer.

No, because of me. My decisions, my handling of it. *I'm* the guilty party. He isn't going to divorce an unborn child, or divorce cancer, he'll leave *me*. Maybe that sounds extreme, but this is how it starts, when something irreversible happens and nothing is ever the same. Have I ruined us?

I look down at the cantaloupe-size ball attached to me - I'm five-and-a-half months pregnant today, also known as three days left to decide whether or not to legally abort our child. Three days left to choose me or our baby; choose Chris or our baby. I'm going to die anyway, but I can save her.

But am I really ready to say goodbye to life?

I look out at the waves crashing in, the light bouncing off the water, creating a glimmer in his eye. *Please talk to me.*

I wait for him to come in. When he enters through the glass door in the corner of the room, he strips off layer after layer of gear. His nose is red, but the rest of his face is white, even his lips, and he blows into his hands to warm up. I stand idly, waiting for him to notice me.

He looks up, and gives me a restrained, "Hey."

"Cold out, huh?"

"Brutal. It's fucking brutal out there."

"Stayed out longer than usual."

"Yeah."

It's strange when you've been with someone for seven years and suddenly, are afraid to talk to him, to begin a sentence. It's as if I don't know him at all. But I do. It's that we've never been through *this*.

"Chrissy...."

"Caroline. Do whatever you want."

My face drops. He doesn't care – I've pushed too hard, he doesn't care anymore.

"I can't imagine what it's like being you right now - giving life to one but knowing every minute yours is slipping away. And you haven't for a second had a chance to think about what *you're* losing, how you feel. And I added to that. For me to call you selfish was unforgivable, and I'm sorry." His face cracks and he struggles to get the words out. "I…don't want to be in a world without you."

I hug him hard and speak over his shoulder: "I'm sorry. I love you so much."

"Please don't say sorry to me."

"I don't want to leave you, and I'm sorry for going there without you. And for everything I said."

"You did what you needed to do. I'm in no position to judge."

We pull away and take turns kissing our teary faces, wiping them off, smiling.

"I have had a chance to think about what I'm losing, Chris." I move the hat-mashed hair out of his face, "I want to live, I want to be here with you. I want more time." I lay my forehead on his, "I don't want to give up… but on who?"

To give up and leave Chris doesn't make sense. The trouble is, I'm not just a wife anymore.

🐚

Chris and I meet with Dr. Ryan and Dr. Sylver. They go over everything again. I hear them in slow-motion and sound bites.

"Statistics…Six-months… Five years… Remain positive… Chemo is safe for the baby, radiation is not… Need both… Scheduled c-section… Warrior Princess…."

"Are you ok, Caroline?" Dr. Ryan asks.

"What?" I say. I didn't realize my mouth was wide open as if I were catching flies and my gaze glued to the window.

"Are you ok," she repeats.

"Yeah," I straighten out my sport jacket and sit up straight. When I can speak like a human and not a zombie, I say, "I'm sorry to make you go through this all again. I should've just brought Chris the first time."

"It's a lot to take in. We do it all the time," Dr. Ryan says with a graceful smile. Dr. Sylver nods in accordance.

It may be trite, but there's a reason their lab coats are white – I think they might be angels. The lab coats are the Clark Kent-cover to their white-winged alter-egos. I don't know how they do their jobs, but I'm so grateful for them.

I slouch back down and hear more information leave their lips, devastating information laced with a dash of hope, and stare out the window. A branch hits as the wind blows, back and forth, back and forth.

A minute or ten later, I look at Chris. His face is white with sickness or fear. I can't tell, but I can tell he knows less about what to do than when we arrived.

"Do you have any more questions, Mr. Shaughnessy?" Dr. Sylver asks.

Chris looks interrupted. "Huh?"

"Do you have any more questions? We're here for whatever concerns you have."

Chris turns to me, bulging, red eyes, sagging skin underneath. "Caro?" He robotically puts his hand on mine. "Do you?"

"Nope. Nope, thanks," I say, wobbling up to a standing position.

We get out of there staring outward, not saying a word. Zombies. When we finally arrive in the parking lot, he pulls me in hard, buries his face in my shoulder and breathes hard for a long time. He hangs on and doesn't let me go.

I feel the same way, Chrissy, I feel the same way.

seventeen

Caroline

I feel her kick today. Or move, I'm not quite sure. I sit in the white rocking chair, hand on my belly, waiting for her to do it again. I hope it wasn't gas. Nope, it's her tumbling! She must like the rocking chair. I want to yell for Chris so he can feel, too, but of course, she stops– tricky little bugger.

"I'll get you next time, little one," I say to her.

The pink polka-dotted Octopus clock hangs across from me on the wall. Its tentacle sways from side-to-side as it ticks. It's a loud tick, adding to my anxiety. Today's the day. *If* we were to schedule the termination, today's the day we tell them. How could I possibly? I felt her move. There's no way I'm terminating.

Tick tock tick tock, says the Octopus.

But she's not even here, there's nothing for her to lose. I've got everything to lose and I'm giving up even the *chance* to fight for my life? Maybe I'll just call, schedule it and I can change my mind, I can cancel. But I should schedule it, just to be safe. I pick up my phone and dial.

Scheduling the termination of my child is "safe?" Making sure we're "on the calendar" to put an end to something we fought so hard for is the safe choice? I hang up.

If I don't seek treatment, I may not live six months. I may not make it to the delivery room. I pick the phone up. *I have to seek treatment.*

But how do I feel? Do I *feel* like I'm going to die in six months? Well – my ankles are swollen, that's from the pregnancy. I've gained about fifteen pounds, which seems to be in the normal range. My back hurts – I assume that's from the baby, but after conversations with the doctors, that can be a symptom of the lung cancer. *How would I have ever known that was cancer?* I have shortness of breath often. Again, this is a symptom of lungs working overtime when you're pregnant…except, I have lung cancer. *What the fuck?* I put the phone down. Breathe - healthy in, toxins out, positive in, negative out. Protect my child, protect me. Keep me strong for her.

Tick tock tick tock, goes the Octopus.

I pick up the phone again. I don't want to die.

I pull up Brigham and Women's in my contacts. Five more years to live. And what if it is ten? *I can make it to ten?* My finger hovers over the call button. I push it, and raise it to my ear. My heart pounds through my chest. The phone rings on the other side. I wait for them to answer.

Do I want five years knowing I'm going to die? Knowing I'll be in the hospital nonstop, that I can't run or live my life fully? Knowing the last year - or two - could be really bad?

"Brigham and Women's," a dutiful voice answers. *What will this do to my husband, my family?* "Hello? Brigham and Women's."

A compressed pocket of air falls out of me. "Hello. Can I, um, be connected to Dr. Ryan, please?" *Chemo renders you infertile… not that it matters.*

"Dr. Ryan, extension 1201, please hold."

A burden to my family. Seeing me as someone they never knew but will always remember – weak, needy, sick. The phone rings as I'm transferred. My life as it's always been – or as I dreamt it could be? The phone persists in its quest for an answer. *Would I want to walk away from this life knowing the only thing I hadn't done was create one?* Suddenly, the phone picks up. I hang up.

I yell downstairs, "Chris! Can you come up here?"

"Yep!" Bang bang bang bang thud thud thud. His 190-pound footsteps stomp upstairs.

"What's up?" he says, winded.

"Come here." He gets down on his knees so we're eye level. I place my hands on his. "Chris, I promise I will do everything I can to stay healthy and strong as long as I can – I never want to be a burden to you-"

He shakes his head, his eyes drop to our hands, "Caroline…"

"No, I've done everything I've ever wanted in my life– everything *except* have a baby. If I get to do it for ONE day, it will all be worth it. I just know. My dying wish: I want a baby. I'm having this baby."

He looks upset but forces a half-smile, "You're sure?" he asks.

"Yes."

He looks me in the eyes, reading my face. "Ok." He bows his head, then touches his forehead to mine. "Can you do me one favor?"

"Anything."

"Live. And consider chemo. I'm not ready."

"I told you, I don't want chemo."

"Caroline – I don't want you to go through it either, but…"

"Chris…"

"You said *anything*. I'm not ready, ok? Not to be a father, not to lose you, I'm not ready. I wanted this for so long, to have a family, but I wanted *us* to have a family."

"I know. You have my word. I will do everything I can."

"That means listening to your doctors. Exploring treatment options."

"I'll do my best."

"Do better than your best." And he walks off.

The thing about time is, it keeps going. It moves on without you, whether you're on board or not. There's a lot to do when time is limited, and I know it's time to talk to my family.

I envision Mom walking through my unfestive home, complaining there aren't any Halloween decorations, "You need to create an environment of fun when you have a child" she'll say, as she walks through the ghostly barren foyer of our home. "Children respond to fun."

"Thank you, Gloria," Chris will dutifully say, as he ushers her through the door, only known to me that it's through grinded teeth.

Chris and I make the calls to our families. We tell them to come over for dinner, but to leave little Sara with a sitter. The reason for this impromptu get-together? We give them some lame excuse, like, it'd be one of the last nights we could spend time kids-free, before the baby is born.

They roll in around 7pm, and sure enough, Mom doesn't disappoint, "You need to create an environment of fun. Would a couple jack-o-lanterns and ghosts here or there kill you? Lighten up, will ya?"

"Thank you, Gloria," says my reliably patient husband. He sits her down in the living room and pours her a glass of wine.

"Not too much, I'm driving." He heeds her request.

My sister is next. As I open the door, "Hi sweet C!" she says, arms extended.

"Hi my sister." I hug her so she won't see my eyes fill up. It's all I can do to hide it. "I love you so much." I don't let go.

"Hey!" She rubs my back. "Are you ok? I'm sorry George couldn't make it, he had to work."

"No problem." I swallow hard, wipe my eyes. "No problem." I pull away.

"Care bear, are you ok? What's wrong?"

"Long day, hormones, pregnant brain, you know."

"Yeah, I do. Come on, let's get me a glass of wine. No kids, no husband, I'm with my big sis and her big, healthy belly – it's wine o'clock!"

The tears come – it's nerves. How can I tell my sister I'm leaving her? I hide my face. "I'll be right back, help yourself." I run to my bathroom and the tears spill out uncontrollably. My hands shake as I wipe my eyes. "How can I leave her?" I cry. "How?" I blot my eyes, *try* to de-flush my skin, pull it together, but it's no use. I drop my head and let out a defeated breath.

I look in the mirror. My skin is puffy, the summer tan has faded to white, my eyes are red. I look devastated, but I do not look like I have cancer.

But I do. It isn't supposed to go this way. I'm supposed to live till I'm ninety, die of old age after my kids have gone off to college, gotten married, and have children of their own – my *grand*children. Mom and Dad aren't supposed to bury me. I'm supposed to complain about getting older, about how my kids never visit anymore. Chris and I are supposed to cave and retire to Florida the way the rest of the New England snowbirds do. That's how this was *supposed* to go. Fuck you.

I look myself in the mirror. "FUCK. YOU."

Chris knocks on the door. "Honey, my parents are here. Are you ok?"

"I'll be right out." I futilely dab concealer on my face to cover the blotchiness, fix the runny, black stains under my eyes. "Fucking useless." I toss the makeup, take a deep breath, and suddenly start coughing, it goes on for a while. Goddammit, what I wouldn't do for a drink, right now. I take another breath – it's shallow.

Today is the day I tell my family I'm dying. This is the worst day of my life.

"Oh my *God.*" My face crumbles and my hand shakes as I try to hold my mouth quiet. "I can't. I can't do this. I can't break their hearts, disappoint them. I want happy news for them…. *Jesus Christ.*" I let the tears flow until they're emptied from me, for now, at least. I squeeze the sides of the sink tight and build my strength. I *have* to do this, I tell myself. I *have to* be strong for my family. I slow my breathing, calm myself, slower, slower, slower. I wet a tissue and clean my black and beige tears, dab concealer under my eyes once more, push the sweaty hair off my face. Chest up, eyes up, big breath. I drop my tense shoulders and open the door.

"For my family," I repeat.

I enter the living room where my in-laws sit patiently in front of their glasses of wine. Their faces light up when they see me, my pregnant belly preceding me. I extend my arms before I reach them. I hope they haven't seen my eyes – but who cares, they'll know soon anyway.

"Paula, John!" I say. Paula greets me with a giant smile, rubs my belly, and throws her arms around me.

"You look amazing!" she says.

I hang on to her longer, "It's so good to see you, Paula."

I move over to John, "Great to see you, John".

"You too, Caroline."

I hug him a beat longer than normal. These are the last moments they'll know the me from before, because once those words are out, they'll never look at me the same. I'll no longer be a fortress of hope and strength. I'll be sick and weak. Admired in one breath, pitied the next.

The next guests are Chris's older brother, Pete, and my father. I hug Pete, he jokes about rubbing my "Buddha belly." Pete sits Indian style in our chair. He's in old, tattered jeans, a wrinkled flannel and a black leather jacket. Chris hands him a cold beer.

"Can I get a glass?" he asks.

"For your beer?"

"Yeah, I'm not gonna drink it out of the *bottle*. Jesus."

We all stare at him. He may very well *be* high, but as Harry said to Sally in the greatest romantic comedy of all time, "You're the worst kind. You *think* you're low maintenance, but you're high maintenance." That's Pete.

Dad's the last one to arrive. Ohh, my Dad. He wasn't in my life too much in my younger years, but he left an impression. His sense of humor, work ethic, the little things he'd do – like bringing home a can of Grape Crush or Sunkist from the vending machine from Filene's Basement. That stuff made me bonkers. I'd go nuts over those colorful cans and sugary taste. The little things.

"Hi Dad!"

"My star." He gives me a hug and kiss. I still feel like a little girl when Dad arrives. "Look at that belly!" he says, "Oh my God, are you cooking him well in there?"

"It's a her, Dad."

"Well, it's your mother's fault. She said it was boy."

"No, she definitely didn't."

"Ok you're right."

"She's here, you know."

"Great!" his fake smile is part joke, part not. Any sense of humor I have, I got from him.

I lead Dad into the living room. "Hey everyone, Dad's here!"

They smile and put their arms out for a hug. Except Pete of course, who continues to sit like a master Yogi and nods in an upward motion. That's the most we'll get out of him. Mom sits cross-legged in pale pink, her body turned away, hiding behind a sip of wine. She almost looks over her shoulder.

"Martin."

"Hello Gloria."

And that's it. Everyone is here. Eight different little balls of energy, I can hear the hostess in my head calling for our table now, "Shit show, Party of 8. Is there a Shit Show in the house?"

"Yes, Miss, that's us."

Everyone sits, except Chris and I. He rests his hand on the small of my back.

Paula shouts gleefully, "So how far along are we with our little angel?"

"Mom, Dad, everyone," Chris says, "We need to talk to you about something."

I add, "We're sorry to call you here under such cheerful pretenses, but the truth is, we've got some…difficult news."

"Is the baby ok, Caroline?" Mom asks.

I smile reassuringly, "The baby is fine."

I take a beat, my eyes fill despite wanting to be strong. Chris rubs my back, hangs his head. I start to cough, and quickly regain my composure. Their eyes are glued on us, fearful and concerned. This is the hardest moment. The tears come, I can't stop them. I hang onto Chris's arm so I won't fall over, dizzy and breathing heavily.

"There is no easy way to say this," I start. "And it's going to come as a terrible shock… but I'm sick. I'm real sick."

"What kind of sick?" Mom asks terrified.

"You don't look sick." says my always innocent sister.

I smile comfortingly, "I know Katie, but I am. We've been to four doctors."

"What do you mean?" Katie asks.

"*Four* doctors? Why?" says Mother.

"It's..." I can't get the words out. My head hangs as the tears flow. Katie jumps up next to me and puts her arm around me.

"It's ok, Care Bear, what is it?" Dad says.

I shake my head. "I can't. I can't. Chris, please."

Chris looks at me with bags under his eyes, "Everybody um, Caro... has... a rare form of...

"Of what, Chris?" My dad says.

Chris looks at my father pleading. He doesn't want to say it either. "They found a mass in her lung."

"What?" Our Moms say.

"What do you mean a mass?" says Katie, staring at me.

"I have a rare form of lung cancer."

There was an eardrum shattering silence.

"No you don't," says my mother. "That's impossible."

"No. How could that be?" says Dad.

"Four doctors, four opinions. All the same."

"No," squeaks my sister.

"Well, you don't have lung cancer. You don't smoke, you're healthy, you do everything right. How could *you*..." Mom says.

"It's a non-smokers cancer called lung adenocarcinoma," Chris helps. "Luckily, it's slow growing. But they rarely catch it in the early stages because the symptoms are so minor, and because she's young..."

"She's not that young," Mom blurts out.

He gazes at her, to let the lunacy of what she said hang in the air. "She is for cancer," Chris tells her.

"What he's trying to say is that my cancer is advanced. That's how we found it."

"How did you find it?" Mom asks.

"A few weeks ago, on a run, I…"

"A few weeks ago and we're finding out about it *now*? A run! Jesus Christ, I told you! How could you have known about this for weeks and not tell us? What kind of daughter….Do you ever think about *anyone* but yourself?"

Katie throws her arms up, "No. No!"

Her tears look exactly the way they did when we were kids – hurt and helpless. I can't make it better this time. I sit down next to her and hug her.

"And Chris!" Mom attacks, "No call? Nothing? *You* couldn't let us know?"

"What does this all mean?" my Dad asks.

"Isn't there anything they can do?" asks John.

"Well, Dad" Chris began, "Most of the treatments aren't safe for the baby, so – it has to wait until after she's born."

Pete adds "Isn't that late?"

"No," I interrupt, "It puts me at a disadvantage, but…"

"What do you mean, a *disadvantage*?" Mom asks.

"And what do you mean, *most* of the treatments aren't safe?" my Dad asks.

"In order to preserve the health of the baby, mine could decline. We're betting on minimal to no spreading of the adenocarcinoma in that time, and the placenta protects the baby from the cancer, which is an incredible phenomenon. I'll start radiation and chemo after she's born."

"In three more months?" Paula asks.

"Yes."

"Closer to four," Chris says.

"That sounds like a long time to wait for help, Care Bear," says Dad.

"I know Dad, but we had to make a choice. The treatments will render me infertile, so there's no hope for a child after. And, anyway…she's our one chance, and I have to protect her."

"You could adopt," says Katie.

"What about protecting *you*?" Dad asks.

"We're not going to kill our baby," I say firmly.

"You could adopt!" repeats Katie.

"Katie, please respect our decision." Katie's mouth drops open.

"Honey," Dad starts, preparing me for what I know is going to be a big question. He stares through me, and I use my eyes to plead with him, *please don't ask*. He continues, "Honey, lung cancer is usually…" I look at him, and all around the room. Their faces beg for good news. "Did they give you a prognosis?"

"There are many variables," Chris adds. "If she seeks treatment, treatment in the form of safe-for-the-baby chemo, she'll live longer."

"*Longer*?" Mom asks.

I give him a look. *Why is he telling them about "safe" chemo options?*

"But Caroline doesn't want to," he continues, "for the baby".

"Live *longer*?" Mom repeats.

"Yeah, Mom." I answer. She looks up at me. Her eyes fill and resemble mini-tide pools.

"Caroline. What does that *mean*?" Mom asks.

"We don't know exactly," says Chris.

"*Caroline*?" she repeats.

"We don't know, Mom. Like Chris said, there are variables, but I'd like to wait until after to start treat…"

"So it's terminal?" asks Pete.

My eyes meet his. Dad looks up, wrestles with it in his brain. I can't acknowledge that word, not to my family. Not yet.

"I – we don't like that word."

"Well it is or it isn't," says Dad. "Caro?" He stares at me. I turn away, fidgeting with my hands. I hear Mom choke on the news.

"This can't be true, Caro. This can't be true," Katie whimpers.

"How long?" asks Paula. "Because if the doctors say it's safe, why not try it?"

"Dammit Chris! We discussed this! I don't want cell-destroying drugs anywhere near my baby!"

"Well if there's cancer in your body and that doesn't touch the baby, then the meds wouldn't either" says Katie.

"We don't know that."

Mom pipes up, "Well why aren't you asking more questions, Caroline? Why aren't *you*, Chris? This is your wife!"

"Mom!" I yell. My sister does the same.

"That's enough, Gloria," Dad says.

"Why? Why is that enough? We're going to let our daughter die? Our beautiful daughter? She didn't even have a chance," she breaks down. "Here she is, finally pregnant, married to the love of her life, and she's not even going to get to enjoy it? There has to be *something* we can do." Paula moves over to Mom and comforts her. "We can't let it happen," Mom cries.

They look up at me for mercy, for an answer. I look at Chris, who averts his eyes, drops his head, and I realize, *he's with them.*

"I thought you and I were unified on this, and agreed what to do. But clearly, I was wrong."

"There are some things to consider, Caroline." Chris says.

"I thought we considered them, and ruled them out."

"*You* ruled them out," he raises his voice. The family takes pause.

"We'll discuss this privately," I say.

"No. We'll discuss it now. In front of all these people who love you. In front of your *family*, because each and every one of us has a stake in what happens to you. I feel my eyes welling up, a knot in my gut, and a pain in my heart that feels like a stab wound. I look at my family, their faces full of heartbreak, fear, compassion.

"I'm sorry," Chris continues, "but your life matters to all of us." I hear a gasp from someone, an exhale from another, the sounds of solidarity. "Those meds are palliative, they'll make you feel better, and I will not watch you suffer. There's a handful of meds that will help you and won't hurt the baby, *especially* in the third trimester which you're entering in less than two weeks. You're ready for these meds *now*. I can talk to doctors in private, too, you know."

With the last splinter of fight I have left, I mumble, "I don't want to hurt the baby."

"You won't Caroline," Katie says. "You won't. You have to believe it."

"I don't believe anything anymore."

"Well it's true," chimes in Pete. We all look up. "God has a plan. He's looking out for you." He pauses for a moment, waiting for us to hang on his every word. "He's saving you from shitty diapers." We stare at him in silence. "Come on. No one's gonna make a cancer-lady change a shitty diaper. That's a get outta jail free card, right there." He takes a swig of his beer, eerily similar to the way my neighbor with Asperger's does.

The entire room turns to him with apoplectic mouths agape.

"Are you high?" asks Chris.

"Yes," Pete says.

I smile at him. I'm actually grateful for his comic relief. I'm not sure anyone else is.

"Do you have any more?" Dad asks.

Later, when everyone else is gone, Katie and I cuddle on the couch, her arms wrap around me the way mine used to when we were kids.

"Are you going to lose your hair?" she asks.

"Only if I take the drugs."

"I think you should take them."

"What if they slow down her development, or give her down syndrome? What if she's a stillborn baby?

Katie pulls out her phone and types, "There is a risk of harm to the fetus if chemotherapy is given in the first three months of pregnancy. Chemotherapy during the first trimester carries risk of birth defects or pregnancy loss." During the second and third trimesters, doctors can give several types of chemotherapy without apparent risk to the fetus. Because the placenta acts as a barrier between the woman and the baby, some drugs cannot pass through, or they pass through in small amounts. Studies have suggested babies exposed to chemotherapy while in the mother's uterus do not show any abnormalities either after delivery, or during their future growth and development, when compared with children not exposed to chemotherapy."

"I read that."

"Well why aren't you doing anything about it?"

"Because I don't want to mess with it, ok?"

"Listen, Caro, it's ok to be afraid. It's ok to be afraid of what it'll do to you. The side effects, losing your hair."

"You think losing my *hair* is the problem? You think I'm that vain?"

"No, but I'm sure you want to feel attractive, to yourself, to your husband. He'll love you anyway."

"What the fuck are you talking about? That's not why! Jesus, give me some credit!"

"Well, why?"

"I told you why. To keep the baby safe!"

"The research shows she'd be safe."

"Research can be wrong! I did everything right. EVERYTHING. I ate right, I exercised, I drank enough red wine to be fun, yet health conscious, I drank my water, took my vitamins, I ate enough red meat to support my blood type, but not so much it harmed my cholesterol. I ate the egg whites, not the yolk, I cut out most of the breads and simple carbohydrates. I knew my blood pressure, my glucose levels, my resting heart rate, my good and bad cholesterol. I managed my stress. I did fucking yoga and even sometimes meditation. I practiced gratitude, I had enough sex to raise my endorphin levels for the rest of my life. I had a job I loved, a husband I loved, a LIFE I *LOVED*. And where in the Sam Fuck did it get me? Dead by 39? There is no God, and if he exists, he fucking hates me because I did everything right. And, it was all for nothing." I drop my head in my hands. "God dammit!" I chuck a glass against the wall, shattering it everywhere.

Chris runs in wiping his hands in a dishtowel. "Are you ok?"

Katie stares at him, knowing the only truthful answer is no. "We're ok, Chris."

He nods and leaves us. My sister says nothing else, and pulls me in.

Later, after everyone left, deafening silence. Stillness. Nothing moves or makes a sound, the whole world is on pause.

My whole family wants me to do chemo, saying that keeping me alive is just as important as the baby... Chris, too. They all disagree with my decision... I've never had that. At odds with Mom, sure, but not Mom *and* Katie *and* Dad *and* Chris. Perhaps, making this decision myself, even though it *is* my life, wasn't right. They are my life.

But if it hurts her, I will lose everything. Everything. And so will Chris, and so will my family. I believe in miracles, but I believe in science, too. And I *may* defy odds, but even that has an expiration date. My God, I so deeply want to do what's right, and not hurt my family. But if I take chemo and live, and she dies or is adversely affected, living *with myself* will be impossible.

I sit in my daughter's room in the rocking chair, and I sing the words with the hope that maybe she'll hear,

> *Lullaby and goodnight, with pink roses bedight*
> *With lilies o'erspread, is my baby's sweet head,*
> *Lay thee down now, and rest, may thy slumber be blessed.*
> *Lay thee down now, and rest, may thy slumber be blessed.*
> *Sleepy head, close your eyes, mother's right here beside you.*
> *I'll protect you from harm, you will wake in my arms*
> *Guardian angels are near, so sleep on with no fear*
> *Guardian angels are near, so sleep on with no fear.*

Chris

She doesn't know, but I stand outside the door watching her sing. My heart shatters into a million pieces. I can't take it.

I step away from the door and slide down the wall, losing my shit in our hallway, sobbing like a child. I can't handle this. I thought I could handle anything, but I can't. I don't know what to do, how to help her, or if telling her to start chemo is right. What if *she's* right? What if it hurts the baby? What if we have to wait a few more months and everything is fine for her *and* the baby? She will listen to me – eventually – I know she will. It'll all be my fault if something goes wrong, and she'll hate me.

I sniff hard, and when I look up, she's standing above me. She kneels down in front, holds my wet face in her hands, and whispers, "I love you."

"I love you," I say.

"I know." She hugs me hard, kisses my face over and over. Suddenly, "She kicked. Honey, she kicked!"

"She did? Lemme feel." I put my hand where Caroline leads. She moves it around to find the spot and BAM. "Oh my God! I felt it. I felt it."

"You felt it?"

"Yes! Ahhhh!" I hug her excitedly, and realize, that baby in there, she's determined to live, she's a fighter.

"Baby," Caroline starts, looking her big, terrified eyes into mine. "Baby, I'll call Dr. Ryan about the safest chemo option tomorrow. And Dr. Sylver. Whatever they recommend, I'll-"

I stand my wife up and scoop her into my arms, same as a bride and groom over the threshold. She gasps. "Come on, Legs, let's go to bed."

"You're gonna break your back," she giggles.

"Nah, I got you." I kiss her, and I mean it.

"Hon, you want to go at it, like *this*?"

"Absolutely. You're a MILF, and I actually get to."

"That's cute, but seriously?"

"One hundred percent."

"Well then take me to bed or lose me forever!"

So I do. And it's still as good as it always was; belly, cancer, and all.

eighteen

Caroline

The next morning, I find myself standing at our French doors, staring out at Chris again. An indescribable sense of calm washes over me - strange under the circumstances. But whatever will be, will be, won't it? My family knows, now, and even though it's terrible news, I'm not holding it in, anymore. At least we all *know* I'm going to die, at least we're forewarned. A sudden, tragic death like my brother's, is devastating. It was for my mother and the rest of us. No matter what, I think this way is better, and now I'm doing what I can to fight for more. Dr. Ryan and Dr. Sylver are thrilled I've decided to explore treatment. They're working on a plan together, and I'll begin next week.

I breathe air in, breathe air out, because right now, I can. I'm alive. I'm here. And the things I love are all around. Chris looks back, our eyes meet, and we smile and wave as we always do. What a relief to have him back.

I sink into the comfort of my couch. Outside, it's bone-chilling— so are the thoughts I had a few nights ago, visions of not making it to labor. Like maybe I pass out again, and the doctors have to perform an emergency C-section because I'm unconscious. What if it's worse than last time and I don't make it, and I'll never even know I had her? She'll know nothing about me, except that I was her house for nine months - or eight, maybe less. She'll have Chris, and he'll tell her all about me, but it'll be his side of the story. There'll be nothing from me except my genes - half of them, anyway. I want her to know me, but if I'm not around, or if I'm hooked up to machines, she never will. Chemo or not, there are always complications.

I get up and hurry to my home office, *hurrying* these days, is more like a brisk waddle. I fish around in my desk drawer for something to write on – there are things I have to tell her. I toss aside all these sketch books and magazine clippings from print ads I worked on – Sephora, Volkswagen, Addidas, Maybelline. I don't care anymore. So much of my life was spent caring about my career and that kind of success, pushing, obsessing, competing - against men, women, and mostly myself. It was an endless battle of never-enough, and bigger-better-faster-more. It's a funny thing about dying, you realize peace is the thing you want most. That restless rumble inside, that storm which signifies discord and things unsettled, we can *choose* to stop it. We're terrified, though, that our world will fall apart, that we'll have no money, no job, no life if we stop. I'm not advocating becoming a couch potato, but there is something to be said for taking a breath when you need to take one. Give yourself that moment to say, "Job Well Done." Enjoy for a second, savor it, quiet the mind, and like the Beatles said, *Let it Be*.

I see a picture of me with a Maybelline model, and a print ad with Anna Kournikova for Addidas. I push them aside, searching for what I'm after. There's so much I want to tell her.

I read Eckhart Tolle's *The Power of Now*. Yeah, exactly. Because now is all we've got. But it doesn't mean to be reckless – no, it's quite the opposite – it means be grateful. You don't realize how lucky you are to still be here until you get older. I wish we could teach that to the young, to love life, to treat it with care, because it's the only one we've got, and it could go damn fast. We can die in a car crash tomorrow, slip on ice and hit our heads and that'll be that. I guess that's what I want my daughter to know. But you can't outright say it, can you? You can't say "Hi honey, it's Mom. Life is beautiful and it's a gift, so don't be dumb. Got it? Great, thanks, bye."

No. You have to say it... differently.

I rummage past a print ad with LeBron, a watch ad with Vanessa Hudgens and... I don't even remember this person's name - my niece would - and there it is, the teal and yellow book. *Letters to My Baby*, I hold it to my chest. Where to start.

I cozy up near the fire while Chris fishes in the stinging November sea, and I write to our daughter the Story of Us. I tell her about me before her father walked into my life; who I was, who I am, and the woman I became after her father swept me off my terrified toes. That he was the best thing to happen to me, and she was the best thing to happen to *us*. That she was the result of the dots of our life.

Steve Jobs, in his 2005 commencement speech to Stanford talked about connecting the dots. He recalled how sometimes in life, you never quite know what you're doing or why you're doing it *at the time*, especially if an interest like calligraphy class with no real-world application strikes your fancy, and it isn't until many years later when that reason emerges and it all makes sense. He called that "connecting the dots." He pursued his interests, followed his passion, and it led him to the Mac – where strangely enough, that calligraphy class saw its application when it came to fonts and spacing.

Coincidentally, Jobs also talked about the power of death, "Remembering I'll be dead soon is the most important tool I've ever encountered to make the big choices in life. You are already naked. There is no reason not to follow your heart." That's an important one to tell her. He was diagnosed with cancer in 2004 and talked about it in his 2005 commencement speech at Stanford, noting he was grateful for the lessons "death" taught him. Death eventually came to Jobs in 2011, but not before he created the iPhone, and changed our world, how we relate to and communicate with one another.

We get one shot here, and we're here to create. So, my little girl, your father and I created you.

Well there they are, my first words to my daughter. *Are they good enough? Is that where I want to start? Where-to-start-where-to-start-where-to-start....* I bang my pen against the side of the book. Tap tap tap. Suddenly I drive the pen toward the page! And then... clamp the cap between my teeth, twisting it as I think. *What do I want to tell her? What is important for her to know? OMG-OMG-OMG-OMG-OMG...*

I'm hungry. I "hurry" into the kitchen. I need snacks before I dive into the most important advice I'll ever give, so I'll eat now instead of interrupting the flow once I get into it. I mean, it'll pour out of me, there's so much to tell her...

I stand at the counter, noshing on pita bread and peanut butter, scooping straight from the jar (don't tell Chris) ...staring back at that empty book. It glares back at me from its lofty perch on the couch, haunting me, taunting me, it mocks me.

Hmm, what else can I eat?

🐚

I pull up to Dionysus, and park in the subterranean garage, sitting there with both hands on the dark wood steering wheel. A deep breath fills me, and the exhale drops my already deflated shoulders. It's November 6, week twenty-seven, and since I prefer to keep the last shred of dignity I can, I'm not going to let my coworkers see me go through chemo. If my family won't be able to remember me as an unmovable force, I'd like it if my colleagues could.

I get out of my car and click my heels across the spotless light gray cement to the elevator. I'm sure this is the last day I'll be wearing anything other than slippers, so although my pregnant feet are swollen, I suck it up for the beauty of a great pair of heels – sparkles, little rhinestones all over. They're far too dressy for today, but if I'm going out, I'm going out unforgettably. There's a young woman waiting by the elevator, her strawberry blonde hair pulled neatly into a French twist – her eyes drop down to them.

"*Great* shoes," she ogles.

"Thank you," I smile. We step into the elevator and the doors close.

I arrive in the lobby on the first floor, passing that grotesque statue of the naked satyr, and the slightly regal, but also nude, Dionysus.

"Well boys," I say looking straight at their dicks because that's the awkward eyeline I'm dealing with. "I guess you're the Gods of fertility after all. Your sense of humor blows, though." I smack Dionysus on the cold, marble ass. "Put some clothes on, would ya?"

My cool heel-clicking becomes a labored lumber. I called out sick all last week, so it's been a while since I've been dressed like this.

I see the security guard standing behind his desk, a tall, dark, mustached man in his early sixties.

"Morning, Frankie," I say.

He nods at me, "Mrs. Shaughnessy," he says.

I continue up the marble stairs where I take the elevator to the eleventh floor. When I arrive, I stand outside the glass doors to my floor, eyeing the bustle inside. You see everything, that open floor plan. I breathe out. My last day.

Hold it together, Caroline.

I open the doors and glide through as if I'm in a hair commercial. Gotta use it while I still got it. I pass through the bullpen of coworkers buzzing about their desks from one colleague to another. Some look up to notice me, others are focused on their work. Kevin's mouth drops, but it turns to a smile.

"Welcome back, boss! We are so happy to have you here. Stomach bug?"

"Yeah," I say. "What's the latest?"

"The Nike execs are impossible to please. And they've been asking for you. They don't want to deal with *me*!" He laughs, but I know the frustration is just below the surface.

I put my hand on his arm to stop him. "You got this Kev… You've managed it this far without me. Right?"

His eyes fall to the floor, he thinks a minute. "I guess."

"It's hard being in charge, isn't it?"

"Hell yeah it is! But I've had the other two on it for support." He gestures over his shoulder at the two guys I refer to as Dim and Dimmer. *Lord help him.*

"Oh," I smile. "Well, some help is better than none, right?!"

"For sure," he smiles big and terrified.

"Keep it up," I pat him on the arm, and continue in the direction of my office. I hear him yell after me, with a desperate crack in his voice,

"You're back for good now, right? Till the baby comes?"

I pretend I don't hear him and greet Abby whose desk is just outside my office. Her hair is in a ponytail, and she's not wearing glasses.

"Caroline," she says, nervously. "I didn't know you were coming in today." Her quick hustle and scattered movements accentuate her lack of preparation.

"Don't worry, I'm not staying long."

"Oh," Abby says, relaxing ever so slightly. A concerned brow raises, "Are you still contagious?" She steps back a foot.

"Noo. But, I'm not feeling great, and…" The truth escaping from the lie threatens to crack my forged smile. Deep breath, smile again, "And for the baby's sake, the doctors prescribed bedrest. A stomach bug like this while pregnant, with the added stress of work, it's not good, so I'm just here to grab a few things."

"Oh," she says, reading my face. She doesn't believe me. I know, just by the way she said it. I never realized how great a bullshit detector Abby is. "Ok," she nods, moving slowly, assessing her next move. "Can I get you some coffee? Tea?"

"No thank you. Send in Mick and Rick, please. Tell them I only need five minutes. And that while I don't *think* I'm contagious, it's better I get out of here." I wink at her. "That'll light a fire under em!"

She smiles, "Will send them in right away."

"Thank you."

I enter my office and shut the door behind me. In front, the spacious, stylish office I always wanted. Function *and* form – my favorite. Cool, structural white tables with pops of bold blue and yellow; artsy coffee table books, stored *and* presented in see-through glass drawers. Function and form. Most importantly, my office holds a decade's worth of accomplishments, which actually started much earlier than that, as a kid with a dream of being somebody. Of doing something, something great. Of escaping the sadness and overhanging, dark cloud of Mom's depression - something she was never actually diagnosed with, because she never went to see anyone. But the more I thought about it, year after year, I realized that's what Mom had. I was well into my thirties when I said it out loud. When you grow up with something, it just *is*, like air, you coexist with it. Someone *else* has depression, Mom is just in a bad mood or yells a lot.

Anyway, I built this office the way I built myself – something pretty, I could escape to, that I created from the rubble. Out of nothing came something. I was proud of it.

The door opening pushes me back.

"Hey!" A pinstripe-suited Mick says. "We missed ya! He cracks open a sugar-free Redbull and takes a noisy swig. "Ahhh," he whispers out. "So what's up? You still sick? Don't get me sick, I'm headed to Nantucket this weekend."

"Kind of cold for the island right now, isn't it?"

"Brutal. But we're having new hardwood put in, so I have to go there and make sure they don't fuck it up. You know how it is." He smiles a toothy grin.

"Where's Rick?"

"Client meeting. Everything ok?"

Another deep breath – which results in a cough. I cover my mouth and pray it's just a little one.

"Oh Jesus, you are sick. Please Caroline, go home if you're not feeling well." He inches back further and covers the opening of his can. "We'll see you next week."

I recover from my hunched position, wipe my hand on my side, and smile, struggling to breathe normally. "It's not that, Mick. The cough isn't contagious – it's…" I realize it's easier to go with the lie. "Yeah, maybe I still am. Listen, I came here to tell you, that I actually have to take leave, early medical leave. I'll get a doctor's note and all that, but my blood pressure is high, the doctors are prescribing bedrest…"

"Oh Caroline. I'm so sorry." And in perfect, work-minded Mick, "I mean, we really could use you on the Nike account.

Kevin is so green, and arrogant as fuck. This could cost us a lot of money…"

I tilt my head. He resets, clears his throat.

"This must be really scary for you and Chris. Your first pregnancy – I remember our first. I watched my wife like a hawk." He moves to me, puts his hand on my arm. "You're really valuable to us, that's all I'm saying. If there's anything you need, call us – whether my wife and me, or anyone here at the office. We're here for you. And we'll see you as soon as you're better."

I look at him, pained, as if he did something wrong. He doesn't know why, and I know I better wipe it off my face immediately. I look down, so I won't cry, I bite down so hard. "You're going to make me cry, Mick."

"Well," he steps back, likely remembering my "contagious" cough, "I won't tell anyone. You're still tough as nails to me."

Nodding because I can't speak. "Thank you."

"I'll let Rick and the others know. You will be missed."

"Kevin is really working hard on Nike."

"Hard as he knows how – which is limited."

"Come on, we were young once, too. And he turned his work around with the BMW campaign. I didn't let up. He rose to the occasion."

"That's how we find em. Sink or swim," Mick toasts to me with his Redbull.

"Rise or fall." We nod and take an extended glance at each other. "Well…"

"Well. I'll see you in May, Caroline. Maternity leave is over in May, right?"

"Yup." I walk toward him to give him a hug because I can feel the tears coming. He puts his hand up.

"Sorry, Caro. Nantucket. Can't afford the sniffles right now."

"Right right. Well-" I stand with my hands on my hips and my gaze directly on him. "Ok Mick, well, this is the last time I'll see you before the holidays and you know, New Year's and a whole bunch of other holidays before May. We're expecting her in February-"

"Call as soon as she's born, we can't wait to meet her."

"We will. But… I just want to let you know, I've appreciated everything you've done for me this year, how you've supported me through the years – it's not easy being a woman in the Man's Club. But, you were fair to me, welcomed me, you celebrated my accomplishments."

"You earned it."

I smile fondly. "Take care of the place while I'm gone."

"It's just a few months, Caroline. We'll all be here when you get back," he smiles. "Ok, air hug." He lifts his arms in an awkward beach ball shape and pretends to hug me, cheek leaning to the side, and all. It's actually funny.

"You're right. Pregnancy hormones, my emotions are out of whack."

"Oh, I remember. Janice was the same." He turns on his heel, "See you in May, Caroline."

He shuts the door behind him, and I turn away so I can let the tears come out. I pinch them back after a few whimpers, because I know I have to face the others on the way to the elevator. I gaze once more out the grand windows, at the great cityscape. I've always loved tall buildings – they reach to the sky, above their potential, and make the city so damn exciting. That view five days a week – I had the best of both worlds - city life and beach life. I exhale. I had it all. And now….

Now I have to walk out of this office, with the few things I can't leave behind; some photos and awards, and a few pens. I reach for my business cards, but remember, I don't need them anymore. I grab the wedding picture of me and Chris that stared at me from my desk each day; and another one with my three best girls, Leash, Mack, and Anna in the hospital holding Leash's first baby; a picture of me after the Boston marathon, proudly showing off my medal, and one holding my niece Sara, and hugging in Katie. I drop them into my purse, put my head down, and duck out of there, quietly closing the door behind me. As I look up, Abby stands in my way.

"Caroline?"

I gasp. "Jesus, Abby, you scared me."

"I'm so sorry. Did Mick tell you, Rick was unavailable?"

"Yes, he did, thank you."

"Are you ok, boss?"

"I'm fine, just startled."

"Ok, well I'm sorry. I hope you feel better." She throws her arms around me and gives me a giant squeeze. I pat her on the back, affectionately, and pull her ponytail out of my mouth. "See you next week?" Abby asks.

"Yep," I squeak out. I duck my head again, walk through the bullpen, through the glass doors, and take the elevator all the way back down to my car.

And that was my last day of work.

The seahorse has similar characteristics to that of the chameleon, in that its eyes move independently of one another, and it can change color; however, the seahorse doesn't simply change *color* to camouflage itself, it can grow and retract spiny *appendages* to blend in with its surroundings.

nineteen

Caroline

Chemo – they say – is safe after the first trimester. I waited until the third when it seems even "safer." If the third trimester is when it's okay to have a drink here and there, I figure anything else that's potentially risky should also wait until then.

"Hi Doc," I say as I enter the chemo room.

Dr. Ryan nods hello before kindly handing me off to the chemo techs. I had the port installed earlier in the week, above my heart, below my collarbone. The port is where I'll be hooked up, like some robotic creature from a sci-fi novel. A comforting, non-creature woman and a pleasant, non-creature man connect my teleport to the magical elixir, and soon I'll be transported into a cotton-candy-pink utopian world of health and unicorns. It sounds so much nicer than connecting the metal piece above my boob to the IV so the poison can course through my veins and kill all the bad cells as well as the good– like my hair and finger nails, anything that grows.

I sit there and wait. I recently read some accounts of pregnant women with lung cancer. Some died within the first month of the baby's birth, the majority lived between three and five months after giving birth, and there was a small percentage who lived another six to eleven months, but that's it. There are accounts of women living a year or more after the child's birth, but the lung cancer had been discovered in the early stages. That's not me. Nope, I'm advanced, stage 3B. I'm not yet stage 4 since it hasn't metastasized to other regions— which is great— but every day I delay chemo, it could. So, here I sit, trying to have faith that some good will come out of this, and she won't be harmed, and that maybe it'll extend my life. That regardless of the pain, weakness, baldness, nausea and discomfort that will inevitable come, so will she, and *that* will be worth all the pain. I'll do it for her, and for my family – though I cringe at the thought of being a burden, of being *dependent* on them. The thought alone makes me uncomfortable in my own skin.

One of the techs comes to check on me, the comforting, non-creature woman, in unusually snug, pink scrubs and a thick Boston accent. I see on the picture ID clipped to her pocket, that her name is Barbara.

"Ya doin alright, hun? First time, you said?"

"Yeah," I say, "First time."

"Well yah doin great. Play ya cahds right and I'll give ya a lollipop aftah, whaddaya think?" She laughs and squeaks her Hoka One One sneakers away. Hokas are running shoes, but I notice a lot of the nurses here wearing them, since they're on their feet all day. Smart move.

I yell after her, "I like your kicks!"

She turns in her tracks. "Oh ya? Thanks, my boyfriend gut em fah me. Annaversary present. Faw yeahz."

"Congratulations."

"Thanks, hun."

Barbara goes behind a closed door and I know I'm alone again for another ten minutes – they told me I'd be there twenty minutes. I watch the liquid move from the bag to me. You know, you don't just lose the hair on your head – it's everywhere. Eyelashes, eyebrows, pubic hair – well, I guess that one's not so bad, I'll never have to shave again. I'll look like I had a Brazilian! No stubble. See, there's always a fucking bright side!

I've done a lot of reading lately, research. It's the only time I ever wished for breast cancer. Breast cancer is the most common type of cancer while pregnant, and survival rates are much higher. Many more patients live to see their kids grow up – at least five years – even if diagnosed with Stage 4. Five years is the measurement for survival – isn't that crazy? If you're alive five years after diagnosis, you survived cancer. I don't think five years is very much in the grand scheme of things. Then again, if that means you get to see five years of your *child's* life... Five years compared to a couple months.

What a measuring stick. Strange the things that occupy our thoughts when we're one person versus another. I don't *want* to think about this stuff all the time. This darkness. It's not me. But I don't really know who the hell "me" is anymore. Two days ago, I walked out of an office I spent the last nine years in, figuring out who I was *in the world*, the professional world, what I was good at, who I was in the workplace. It made me feel self-reliant, strong, accomplished, and even liked. Identity. Who am I supposed to be now? Without a place where people need me, where I can be good at something, where I can feel smart, creative, able, useful... *Who the fuck am I going to be now?*

Bald.

Guess that's not a who as much as a how. *How will I feel?* Confident? Not so much. Beautiful? Nope. Vital? Negative. And that will impact the who. Unless I can somehow stay above it, my perception of self is going to take a major nose dive. Who will even want to be around me?

Twenty minutes are up. Barbara returns and unhooks me from the time portal to the magical land.

"Is my baby gonna have three heads, Barbara?"

"Nah. Just two, but they'll be pretty ones."

"And at least her mama will have a bare bush."

"Bah-hahahahaha!" Barbara cackles, tilting her head back far enough to expose her dark fillings. "Yaw fun-ny! Jesus, who knew? Ya come in he-ah lookin all Banana Republic and Ann Tay-lah, and they-ah you ah! Townie-fabulous as the rest of us!" She walks to the room.

"Am I free to go?" I yell after her.

"Nawt yet. Don't move, hun."

I sit in the chair, annoyed that I have to wait but don't know why. I hate being idle and I really *hate* waiting. If you're waiting, you're not doing. Ugh. Barbara reappears with a round green lollipop extended in front of my nose.

"Yawz. Ya did good, hun. See ya Friday." I pull my mini-bump out of the chair. "Oh Jesus, no, lemme help."

Normally my response would be to wave her off. The old "I got this" wave. The athletic beast and career woman accepted little help. But now a pregnant, cancer patient, I think I finally earned the extra care and for once, I gladly accept. Identity, ever elusive.

Chemo is twice a week, Wednesday and Friday. I have weekly appointments with Dr. Ryan and Dr. Sylver, also. They said they would try to schedule our appointments on the same days so I won't be there four days a week, but sometimes, I will be.

Today, I meet with Dr. Sylver. He gives me an ultrasound, checks on the baby, makes sure everything is ok. Each time, I'm relieved to hear her beautiful heartbeat, see her three-pound body onscreen. She's fifteen inches now. Fifteen! It's hard to believe a few weeks ago, we had the choice to abort her. She would've been one pound and a foot long...a pound is so tiny, but a foot long? She's a real human being, now. I spent most of my adult life trying *not* to get pregnant. I had a couple scares in my mid-twenties, and believed that if something did happen, I'd have an abortion. Luckily, I never had to make that choice. Finding out the size and weight of my child during different stages of pregnancy makes it real, and I'm grateful I was never pregnant before I was ready.

A baby – it starts out as a cell; a cell that divides and splits, divides and splits, creating more cells. Cancer is a bunch of cells, too. Our bodies are capable of creating life and death. And in rare cases - 1 in 1000 - some do both at the same time. Not all will perish - some cancers while pregnant have a high survival rate. It depends on the type of cancer you have and the stage....

🐚

I've had two weeks of chemo now, and this is the time my doctors tell me I'll feel the effects– the fatigue, nausea, and hair loss. Not necessarily the full head, but chunks of hair. Knowing something is going to happen usually makes it easier to handle for me, but actually seeing a clump of hair on my pillow this morning, about two inches wide, is something so unreal no prior warning can prepare you for. It was just lying there, as if to say "No thanks," as I got out of bed to start the third round of poison. The doctors recommend cutting or shaving your hair, so the hair loss isn't as upsetting. I'm not quite sure that'll do it for me. Sucky is sucky. However, having clumps of *long* hair fall out in *front of* someone isn't ideal, sooo, do I get a pixie cut à la Peter Pan, or shave it like G.I. Jane? Shaving it reeks of "I have cancer." Maybe a wig? The doctors can write me up a prescription for a wig and some insurance companies even cover it.

I don't know. I don't want any of these questions. I have a baby coming. My will. Should I write my will? See? I go from life to death in seconds flat. Fuck. No, I'll let Chris know the few key things, but that's all I want to say about that.

I skim the floor with my feet into the chemo room, see Barb and manage a half wave.

"Not feelin so good today, huh, hun?" As she rushes over to help me into the chair.

"No Barb, not so good."

"I know. Yaw in the hahd paht, now. You'll feel crappy for a few days, and then bettah."

"Yeah, but I get it twice a week, so that means-"

"The only day ya feel good is Tuesdee."

"Yeah."

"Yaw not alone, hun." She leans down and touches my shoulder. "And I'm sorry. I'm sorry yaw not feelin good. We're doin ah best to help, ok?"

I nod. "Thanks Barb."

"You got it." She finishes hooking me up, and the chemo IV runs through my veins.

When it's over, I take my orange lollipop and go outside to meet Mom in the parking lot. I asked that my family take turns picking me up. I don't want one person to carry all the burden.

She jumps out to open the car door for me, gently hugs me.

"How are you feeling, honey?" Mom asks.

"Eh. Not so great, Mom." She helps me lower myself into the seat, touches my face once I'm in there, and carefully shuts the door. I really don't feel well.

The car ride home starts out easily enough, and Mom is warm and tender, nurturing, even. But once we start talking, it sort of erupts into a shit volcano.

"I'm glad you're wearing a hat," she says, "But where are your gloves?"

"My pocket."

"That's a good place for them."

"Mom, I don't feel well. I just wanted to get in the car."

"See, you don't feel well. That's exactly why you put them on. You need to think, Caroline! Use your head…"

At a certain point, I fade out. I'd much rather think about…

May, 2012

The time Chris and I argued – or as Chris preferred to say, "have a discussion" about whether or not to leave our sweet brownstone in the city. We rented, yes – but it was glorious. Incredible location in the Back Bay, a beautiful place –pricey as hell, but I loved it. You could walk everywhere, great restaurants, like Stephanie's, Sonsie or Joe's American Bar and Grill, shops like Newbury Comics, Trident Books, Urban Outfitters, Burberry, Starbucks, Ben & Jerry's… and the work commute was a couple of T stops for me. Chris, on the other hand, had to drive to work, and was ready for a yard and a family. I wanted to enjoy city life a little longer.

We'd been saving up since our wedding for a home. We knew we wanted to live on the water, and we'd been looking up and down the North and South Shore. We also knew how expensive that would be, but I'd recently gotten promoted to Creative Director and now we're actually be able to *afford* a home. So, I understood his compulsion to move on, but city life was so exciting! Moving to the burbs meant we'd slow down, grow old, be with a bunch of white yuppies. I wasn't ready for that. But, it did seem like I always got my way. Chris deserved to get what he wanted, too. And the houses *were* beautiful where we looked. The house in Cohasset jumped out at us. We couldn't say no.

"Caroline!" Mom shouts.

"Oh," I snap out of my memory.

"Are you listening to me?" she yells again.

"Sorry Mom, what were you saying?"

"Oh for God's sake, I'm not going to start over again. What's wrong with you?"

"A lot of things, Mom. For one, I have dry mouth from the chemo, dry eyes, dry everything. For another, I'm losing my hair at a laughable rate, but also, I feel like I have to pee all the time because of the baby. There's a whole list of other things I don't want to go into because I'll sound like a complainer, and I'd rather not be. Does that answer your question?"

She looks over at me - her normally militaristic eyes soften. She drops her head.

"I'm sorry, honey. I'm sorry." Mom spent a lifetime telling us what we were doing wrong- my illness may finally break her of it. "I don't know what to do," her tears break free. "I'm beside myself!" She sobs helplessly, throwing her arms up like a sixteen-year-old who accidentally crashed Daddy's eggshell blue Cadillac. "Why is this happening? Why? I get upset and depressed, and then I get angry, but I'm not angry at *you*! But it comes out that way." I hand her a tissue, she takes it. "And then I realize, I've been doing this my whole life; I get upset, and it comes out as anger, and then I'm mean and awful...And I'm sorry."

"Mom, pull over."

She does. I lean out of the car and vomit. It feels like blood on fire rising up my throat, but luckily, it's water and I guess a packet of saltines. I think that was the last thing I ate.

"Are you ok?" I hear Mom ask, through soft whimpers. She reaches out for my arm, I catch hers and squeeze back.

"I'm ok. Maybe a tissue, some water... a vodka tonic, maybe."

I hear her burst out laughing. Thank God. Thank God she still has a sense of humor.

She hands me a tissue. I blot my mouth, hawk phlegm (which turns Mom's stomach - she could've been a squeamish Southern belle if she weren't from here) and slide a piece of gum in my mouth. Still half out the door, I feel Mom grab my arm and pull me back in the car. I take a swig of water, swish and spit it out. Normally, she'd say something like "That's ladylike," but not today.

"What a fucking nightmare. Have I said that enough?"

"You know I don't like that word, Caroline."

"I'm sorry, Mom, but it is. I should make cancer t-shirts with that phrase on it. Anyone with cancer *and* their families would buy them. 'What a fucking nightmare.' What do you think?"

Her half-grin breaks through her resistance. "Probably." She starts the car. "They'd probably sell out. This fucking sucks."

Gloria!" I shriek. "You're going to Hell!"

"I know! I'll have to say Ten Hail Marys! Hail Mary full of Grace. The Lord is with thee. Blessed art thou amongst women..."

We laugh and stare forward a minute, not ready to drive.

"Mom. I know you were sad all those years. I'm sorry you had to go through it, it must've been painful."

She processes what I've said, her brain recalibrates. "It was. And lonely. But I'm sorry I put you through that."

"No, Mom, don't apologize."

"All I ever wanted was a better life for you girls. I was so proud to see you get it, both of you. And now... You're such a goddamn perfectionist; how is it that *you're* sick? How is it that I'm going to have to bury another child?"

And that's when I get it: her nagging, her anxieties, her quest for *our* perfection comes from being a Mom who lost a child. And in her head, probably harbored the belief it was her fault and that there was something *more* she could've done to prevent it, had she been perfect. That's the kind of mom we got after our brother died, a mom who went above and beyond to try to make us better, protect us. I understand her in this moment - *exactly*.

"I'm sorry, Mom."

"What are you sorry about?"

"That I'm sick."

"How can you be sorry? You didn't do this, it happened *to* you."

"I guess." I wait a moment to make sure I want to say what I'm about to say, forgive a lifetime of pain. "It happened to you, too. TJ. What happened with TJ happened *to* you. It wasn't your fault." She's looking down and can't face me. I watch a tear suspend from the tip of her nose and drop. "Maybe both of us should stop apologizing for something we didn't do."

Her ears point toward me, but not her eyes. She puts her hands on the wheel quietly, and listens. Having a daughter see right through you is something no parent is truly ready for. But she needs to hear it.

She clears her throat, "Thank you." She looks over her shoulder, signals appropriately, and pulls us back onto the road.

In the United States, there will be roughly 1.69 million *new* cases diagnosed this year. There will be an estimated 595,690 deaths from cancer by the end of the year. The current population of the US is 323 million people, so fortunately, only .5% of the population will be diagnosed with cancer in 2016. But again, that's *this* year. Of those new cases, 54% belong to those 65 and over, 46% belongs to those under 65, and of that, only 8% - or 141,290 - of those diagnosed will be under 45 years of age. "Just" 141,290, you say? In the grand scheme of things, it's not an alarming number out of 1.69 million new cases. Until it's you. Or your sister or brother, best friend, wife... What I've got is rare; only 1,760 cases of lung cancer for women under age forty-five this year. Rare, unusual, tragic... and it's on the rise. Non-smoker lung cancer in women is *on the rise*. Each year, more people die of lung cancer than colon, breast, and prostate cancers combined. Any way you slice it, cancer sucks - for the 5-year-old to the 65-year-old – it sucks. And it sucks for our families who have to watch us, wishing they could do more. Oh, one more fabulous fun fact: the probability of developing cancer over a lifetime for men is 1 in 2. It's better for women:1 in 3.

And you thought I was obsessed with numbers.

After driving in silent thought for twenty minutes, we pull into my driveway. I put my hand on hers, their pale whiteness expose her blue veins. Hands that look like mine, now more than ever. *My pale whiteness, my blue veins.* But I can't blame seventy-two years on the planet, or the dwindling autumn sun for the fading of my skin's color. The weight of my once healthy body is slipping away, too. The chemo makes me nauseous, and the doctors would like to administer anti-nausea drugs to take with it, but because I'm pregnant, they can't. So, I vomit. But then, I have to take weight gainer, so I can keep enough weight on for the baby. I gag when I take it. It's everything I can do to keep that shit down. It's hard to feel colorful when I'm becoming colorless.

But I have to. I have to use every minute. I never did call my mother after that flight. I look over at her - her strong, evergreen eyes.

"Mom. I know this is hard, but I have one request. Can we enjoy every last moment? I'm not going to fight with you, but can we try to keep the tears away, too? I don't want to spend my last days crying, or watching everyone else cry. I'd rather look at what we do have, than what we don't." She stares at me with watery eyes. I smile, "You know, when I was young, I thought you were so pretty."

"Oh God," she waves me off.

"I'd look up at you and think 'my Mom is *so* pretty!' And you were older than the other moms and we didn't have the money for you to go to the salon, or buy expensive clothes or makeup, but even still, you were prettier than the others. And independent. You did everything by yourself while Dad was at work; set up the cable, the VCR, you painted, carried heavy furniture– all things the other moms needed their husbands to do. Plus, you cooked, cleaned, took us to doctor appointments, softball practice, threw birthday parties – all by yourself. This can-do independence, I got that from *you*. The side of me you think is so hard, isn't. Because it's like yours - a shell that covers a protective, vulnerable heart. There are so many things I got from you. You're a great mom, and if I'm not mistaken, all any mother wants is for their kid to be happy, live a great life. Well I'm here to tell you I have, and I want you to carry that with you every day, ok?"

Nodding, whimpering, "Ok". She pulls me in. We hold each other for a long time. When we come up from sniffling, she says, "Do you want me to cut your hair?"

I think about how she'll probably do a nice job – because cutting hair is another one of her many talents– and that I'd like the pixie look, but how useless it will be, because it will all fall out eventually, too.

I smile anyway, "Sure. Thanks, Mom."

twenty

Caroline

November 20, a few days before Thanksgiving. Everything these days is a part of the cancer process: chemo, fatigue, nausea, chemo, haircut, fatigue, hair loss, nausea, weight gainer for the baby, sore back, chronic cough, chemo, sleep, sleep, sleep, try to eat, not today, four sparkling waters on my bedside table to stay hydrated, sleep, sleep, sleep. I do what the doctors tell me, go to weekly appointments – sometimes bi-weekly– with my oncologist and OB. I go through the motions. I'm so tired, I don't even care I'm having a baby anymore. I don't fucking care, and I wish it would get out of me. I have less than ten weeks to go. Being pregnant isn't fun. This is why we get the nice ring, I told you.

Oh, and the hemorrhoids – they're for real.

Mom cut my hair today. I don't cry as she cuts it, and I decide not to look in the mirror while she does. I trust her, or don't care, and I let her go about her way, only once interrupting to put my hand on hers as a silent thank you. It's actually Mom who desperately fights *not* to cry. Mom is very emotional about hair, maybe it's a mom thing. When it's done, I stand in front of our hallway mirror. Just as I hoped, it's a fabulous pixie cut, my brown "bangs" (aka, same length as the rest of my hair) sweep across my brow.

"I love it, Mom." I turn to her.

"Really?" She says.

"I wish I would've had the balls to wear it this way earlier, so I could've enjoyed it longer." My volume drops – why do I have to bring the darkness to every light moment? "I'm told it will all fall out in a matter of weeks." Mom's eyes drop to the floor, staring at the long, brown locks covering it. She bends down and picks up a strand.

"Is it weird to save it?" she asks.

A side smile creases the corner of my mouth. "No, it's not weird."

Mom heads to the kitchen to get a ziploc, and I fuss with my hair a minute, flipping it over my eyes. It's sexy, this short haircut. For a moment, I feel hopeful. This isn't so bad, it's just another part of the process. And time for a nap.

March 2009

"Happy birthday, Caro!" Anna says to me as the waitress drops off a bottle of Don Julio and four shot glasses at some noisy, obnoxious club, in the city clearly chosen by Mack.

"Gross!" I yell. "You know I don't do shots anymore."

"Well, tonight you are," encourages Mack. "Come on Grandma, you're thirty-two, you're not dead."

"We'll play a game," says Anna, as she pours. "This Chris character..."

"Who is basically stealing you from us 24/7," says Leash.

"Hey, you got me tonight," I say.

"He's at a conference." says Leash.

"Anyway," says Anna, as she slides the shots to us, "We want to know why this guy is so much better than the other ass clowns you've been with. So, we're going to ask you a series of questions. Every time Chris possesses this desirable quality more than the other dudes, you take a shot."

"This is a lose-lose situation!"

"Not for us!" Mack says. "You'll get drunk!"

"And married!" says Leash.

"Nah, it's not going there. Come on guys, he's a for now. He's hot and fun, and shows promise, but no. It's been two months, let's calm the fuck down, ok?"

"Great in bed?" says Mack.

"None of your business." I say.

Leash grabs my wrist and grinds her teeth like a rabid dog, "*Play. The. Game*!"

"Jesus! Ok, Crazy." I stare at my shot glass, negotiating with it. Then abruptly throw it back. "Gah! That's disgusting. You guys hate me."

"Don't worry, I brought Gatorade for tomorrow morning, but probably better to use it now," says Anna. She hauls a stupidly large purse onto the table with three giant bottles of Gatorade spilling out. "Here." She opens one and hands it to me.

"Ode to the Gatorade chaser," I say as I take a glorious red gulp.

"Thoughtful?" asks Leash.

"Ehh," I shake my head and think about it.

"Uh oh! That means *we* drink," says Mack.

"Hang on," I say. "He sends me good morning texts when we're not together. And he plans all our dates. And they are awesome."

"DRINK!" they say together.

"Opens the car door for you?" asks Anna.

I look at them, puzzled. They drink.

"Nice package," says Mack.

"*Absolutely* none of your business," I say adamantly. And quietly sneak a shot.

"Ohhhh!" They yell. I smile through my Gatorade sip.

"We're not gonna get drunk at all tonight," says a mopey Anna.

"Waterfall!" Mack yells. We clink our glasses and shoot.

I slam the glass down. "Ok, I'm done, guys, that's it. You *are* trying to kill me."

Later that night, I hang onto the toilet for dear life. In between barf rounds, I grab the bottle of Gatorade and take it down.

"More like *savior-ade*. Yeah yeah, not my best work. Ode to the Gatorade chaser." I wipe my mouth, curl up in fetal position, and pass out.

🐚

"Caroline!" a voice yells.

I'm snapped out of my reverie. I hear the hustle and bustle downstairs. It's nearly 3pm; my twenty-minute "power nap" turned into a four-hour drool fest. I stumble to the mirror – my face is yellow with dark circles under my eyes, and I have a tiny patch of hair missing from my pre-pubescent boy haircut. I go to cover it, and some stray hairs gather in my hand.

"Shit."

I look back at my pillow - another clump of hair rests on it – small, but noticeable. I frantically wipe it away, but it migrates to Chris's side. It's all over the bed. Why did I have to buy white sheets?

"Caroline!" Katie yells again.

I drop my futile task, and look in the mirror, patting my hair down, trying to make it look cute again.

I give my face one last glance. "Ugh." I turn for the door, "Coming," I say, slightly louder than six-inch voice.

Thanksgiving – our two families sit across our long, dining room table. I'm at the head. Chris and Mom sit on either side of me, Pete finally stops texting. We hold hands as my father-in-law says grace:

"Thank you, God, for this wonderful feast set out before us, so that we can eat and feel your abundance. Thank you, God for our health and the ..." He paused a noticeable pause, realizing the thoughtless script needed to change, but he spat it out anyway: "and the health of our family, Amen."

"Sure glad that's over," I say.

"We should go around the table and say what we're thankful for," said Mom. "Caroline, why don't you start?"

"Are you fu-"

As you can infer, I wasn't much in the mood for that tradition. I glance down at my belly – nearly seven months large - and know I ought to be grateful... But as I stare at this beautiful spread–a perfect turkey, stuffing, cranberry sauce, corn, burning red and golden candles, a pile of desserts in the next room –all I want to do is vomit. I won't be able to keep any of it down, and what's more, I don't want to. I am absolutely not hungry. Nor am I feeling thankful, nor loving, nor healthy, nor... Fucking great.

Then it occurs to me that this could be my last Thanksgiving.

Good, it's a day to get fat and drunk and stupid, anyway. Big loss there. I won't miss you, Thanksgiving. You're Christmas's trampy, illiterate stepsister. Piss up a rope, Thanksgiving.

"Your hair looks beautiful, sis; it's really flattering on you," Katie says.

I touch the brown swoop of bangs on my forehead. I forgot she hasn't seen it, yet.

"Yeah, I like it, too," says Chris.

"Yeah," the rest of the table says in agreement.

"Me too," says a late, awkward Pete.

"Mom did it. She did a nice job. She's good at that stuff."

Mom smiles, and then notices a missing patch of hair over my ear. She pulls a longer piece to cover it, gently and lovingly touching my face.

I let out a big breath. "I'm thankful for my family."

I'm underweight. I should be 150 pounds right now, and 160 by the end of my pregnancy, but I'm only 140. The weight gainer sludge, which I take as a shake, is nothing short of repulsive. So admittedly, I have skipped a few days here and there. I have to get back on track. I often drink it sitting on the floor of my bathroom, because I know it makes me sick. But I *have* to keep it down. I have to gain weight.

I tip it back and swallow.

It comes right back up. I spit it in the toilet, take it down again.

"Go DOWN you son of a bitch." I spit up again. "Jesus H. Christ."

I storm out of the bathroom in the same gray sweatsuit I've been wearing for the last three days. It's become my uniform. I thud to the kitchen, yank a spoon from the drawer, stand over the sink and pour a tiny amount of the weight gainer onto the spoon. If it takes forty-five fucking minutes to get this shit down, one spoonful at a time, I'll do it. I pause and grab a Gatorade from the fridge.

"Ode to the Gatorade chaser."

I stand over the sink, armed with spoon, sludge and Gatorade in ready position when my phone rings. It's Leash. Fuck.

"Hello," I say, trying to sound decent.

"Heyyy, mama."

"Hey. Been awhile," I say.

"It has. It has." She lets out a held breath and a long pause. "I'm sorry I haven't called in a bit."

"No, it takes two, we both…"

"Well, under the circumstances, I feel like your excuse is better than mine."

"So you heard."

"Yeah, I heard. What the fuck, Caro? Why didn't you tell me?"

Now it's my turn to pause. I bury my forehead in my hand. "Look, Aleesh, it's hard enough admitting it to myself, then my family. Telling your best friends you're going to die, it's… I just hadn't done it, yet."

Silence on the line.

"And there's no way…" She begins.

"Maybe. Maybe I'd live *longer*. But I'm here for the baby, ya know? I'm here for the baby."

"How did it happen?"

"They don't know. Nobody knows."

"It's not right. It's not fucking right. It shouldn't be you. How is it *you*?"

"But, here we are."

She waits a real long moment to speak, when I realize, she can't. She's fighting hard not to cry, to be my rock, but her silence makes it clear the tears won.

"It couldn't have happened to a better person, a better friend, and… it's like the world doesn't make sense. It's not fair. No reason for it in the whole world." I hear her sniff hard. Her voice squeaks out, "If anyone can fight this to the bitter end – in thirty or forty years – it's you."

"Ha," I say. "Yeah. Listen, I know your hands are full with the kids, and your husband."

"Same difference. I swear I'm addicted to man-boys." We laugh. "None of that is an excuse. I'm coming down to see you. You tell me when. I know there are days that aren't good, because of the chemo."

"Yeah, the chemo knocks me out for days. I literally sleep for three days, so maybe the fourth day."

"I'm there. You let me know when."

"I will."

"I love you, Caro. We all do. The girls are thinking about you. They said they called."

"Yeah I wasn't ready to talk."

"Well, they said they'd come down to see you. Whenever you're ready."

"Of course. I'd love to see all of you. That'd make my year."

"Mine too."

"I love you, Aleesh."

"Love you, C-note. Keep the faith. We're here."

I hang up the phone. I lift my spoon of sludge to my mouth, swallow, and immediately chase it with Gatorade. It stays down. I do it again, and again, and again.

🐚

This week has been tough. I was assigned a mental health therapist for the mood swings. Some days, I'm over the moon about the baby and almost forget I'm sick – other days, I want to be waited on hand and foot, and then yell at my family and husband for doing it wrong. Then I cry because I hate myself for it, then I cry because I hate the situation and the bad luck dropped on me. Then I want to smack myself in the face for blaming bad luck – weeping over "bad luck" is for the powerless and weak, and I'm not that. But then I remember, I am. I'm literally infirm. Which makes me angry, because if I had caused this by smoking, it *would* be my fault, but I didn't, it happened *to* me, so now, I'm someone who allows the words "bad luck" into my vocabulary.

I've always subscribed to the notion we make our own luck. But I see now, that isn't always true. Was I insensitive before? Was my repulsion for excuses and weakness within myself so strong that it impacted others? Did I push people away? Am I responsible for my loneliness and now, my illness? I start to cry.

It makes perfect sense, I've cried about everything else! Like the pink booties my sister brought over, the high chair I ordered online, my husband leaving his shoes in the doorway so I can trip over them and rip my ugly maternity jeans, my ugly bald head – because it's all gone now – that's a kick in the cooter. I had that cute pixie cut for two weeks, and now I look like Daddy Fucking Warbucks. The fact that Christmas is next month, and that it's probably my last one... Fuck. Fuck. I'm ugly and tragic and it fucking sucks and I hate it. I'm going back to sleep. What did I wake up for, anyway?

I don't want to sleep my life away. I don't want to sleep my life away. I don't want to sleep my life away.

My last Christmas... I can't.

🐚

December 1. I decide to get up and get dressed this morning. We need toilet paper, I'm craving gummy bears, and I need to get out of the house. So, while Mom is napping, I sneak out. She's going to be pissed if she wakes up, so I'll have to make it quick.

I pull my gray cashmere hat down to where my eyebrows would be. With a hat so low, no one knows I have cancer. My pale skin doesn't help, but it's fucking cold in New England, everyone looks like Casper. I slide into my arctic car and glance at myself in my rearview.

I'm so white, I'm translucent.

"Welp! Off to the store!"

I put my hands on the steering wheel of my beautiful, black beast; sleek, beautiful, dangerous. I remember the day I bought her: it was right after my promotion to Creative Director, the two markers of success I never thought I'd attain: a killer Mercedes, and a killer job title. There are so many things that came together in my life I never thought I'd achieve. I went toward them anyway and was always surprised when I was victorious. It took many years and a lot of work to learn I was the one sabotaging my dreams. You see, when it comes to our dreams, *we* choose whether to believe others or ourselves, we're the ones to fight or give in. Whether you come from a ton of money, tons of connections, or none at all, both roads will be strewn with obstacles. We may as well choose yes to our dreams. A lot of times, I find myself grateful that we didn't have much growing up – it taught me how to fight. Once I started believing in me, things started happening.

I push the pedal to the floor and let the Panther roar. She chokes at first—she hasn't been driven in a month— but once we get the lead out, she rumbles like she always does, all 8-cylinders firing, warning others to get the fuck out of her way. I like her so much. It's invigorating to get out and drive again, to be me, to feel powerful for a second, to remember the woman I used to be. The boss, driving to her big, powerful job, at the big, powerful agency, and bringing home the big, powerful bucks. I was a badass, I was accomplished, *and* I was good to others. Now...

Well, it's good to be driving, anyway. To get away and have some quiet from the concern and overwhelm that is my family. Being alone has become a real polarity for me - I crave it, but I'm also terrified of it. I don't want to feel weak and dependent... yet, if something happens to me while I'm alone...

I slow to a stop. *Maybe I should go back.*

I look in my rearview – home isn't far. I can turn around, tip toe upstairs, and go back to bed like nothing happened. *Yeah, I should just go back.* I pull a u-turn, and then sit there, frozen, facing the other side of the street.

"I'm still alive. I won't live in fear."

I push on the gas and speed down the street.

CVS is a one-stop-shop for the TP and candy, and within minutes, I clutch them in my white, veiny hands and hit my key fob to go home, when something across the street catches my eye. The Little Shop Across the Street is a home and gift store with crafts designed by local artists, one of those places you pass by every day. It's forgettable because it's been there the whole time. I never go in. But I wasn't ready to go home yet and something about it calls me today. Who knows how long it'll be before I can get away on my own again, if ever, and anyway, maybe I'll find some Christmas gifts in there.

I push the heavy, wooden door which creaks as I open it, and a little bell clangs. A plump woman in her fifties, looks up and smiles pleasantly. It smells of evergreen and a hint of burning cinnamon. It's warm and quaint and welcoming, with sunlight shining through the windows. The whole store isn't more than 300 square feet, and the only sound you can hear is the occasional muffled hum of the shopkeeper, and the steps of my shuffling feet.

I turn a wonky rack of one-of-a-kind postcards of Cohasset and New England life. I run my hand over the quilts of a Martha's Vineyard map, a Fenway Park design, and the Swan Boats from

Boston Public Gardens. I wish I had come here years ago. I could have filled my home with items that possess personality, history, roots - of *belonging* - as opposed to the chic, but mass produced Restoration Hardware. Or at the very least, a mixture of the two. Shame on me.

I walk over to another rack where I see magnets – a weighty, beige, square stone with a light blue whimsical font: 02025 – our zip code.

I pull it off the rack – this is what our home is missing. The bell rings suddenly, and in walks Scowl Lady from my morning runs. I drop the magnet, and quickly bend over to pick it up, but as I do, my winter hat falls off, exposing my head. I rush to put it back on, but it's too late. Scowl Lady has bent down to help.

I see her eyes react sympathetically as she sees my baldness. And as I dodder upright, the other reaction comes; not pity, but *tragic* pity.

"Oh. I'm sorry," she said, as her eyes moved from belly to head.

"Ha, thanks for recognizing the shit end of it." She looks at me, shocked. Why did I say that? "No! I'm serious. It is the shit end of the stick. I appreciate your sympathy." And that makes it *no* better. What the hell is wrong with me?

"I'm so sorry. I...I don't know what to say."

"Me neither. Clearly."

"I'm Amelia," she says extending her hand.

"Caroline. Nice to officially meet you. I used to see you in the mornings, with your little boys. I'd run past."

"That, was *you*?"

"It was."

Quickly recovering, "Oh, I don't have my glasses on."

I smile complacently, matching her courtesy. "It's ok, it was a long time ago – at least it feels that way. Anyway, it's good to meet you, Amelia." I nervously put the magnet back and head for the door.

"You, too. Oh, Caroline. Here's my card. If you ever need anything, I'm around the corner. I think there are lots of women in town who would feel the same."

Pity. Great. They can all feel good about themselves because they helped the poor, sad, broken lady. And then I look at her. Her ruffled eyebrows and wide-eyes are sincere, compassionate.

I try to push the words out, but have to hurdle the frog in my throat, "Than- thank you, Amelia."

She squeezes my hand, lovingly, "You take care."

The bell rings as I hurry out and throw myself into my car. I look down at her card: Amelia Gantz, Esq. Amelia is an attorney - a strong, smart, professional woman like I'd been. So many times I figured the snotty Mommy Clones and Stepford wives here were co-dependent, unambitious, and even a bit dim. I'd been holding something against them, squeezing them into a mold the same way they did to me. That feeling, that discovery of wrongful judgement on *my* part, humiliates and disappoints me to the core. *I* was cruel and narrow-minded.

I drive home in a state. I don't feel well. When I arrive, I soft shoe through the front door— Mom is still passed out in our oversized Restoration Hardware chair, mouth agape. I go upstairs to my room, put on my sweat-uniform, and crawl into bed. It's time for sleep.

twenty one

Caroline

September 2009

I stood there facing Chris, beaming, while his Uncle Bill officiated. I held Chris's hands as he delivered the vows we wrote: "I promise to never give up on you," Chris began, "Please never give up on me. You have my word, and-"

"PLAHBAAAAAAHHH!" the sound shook from Uncle Bill's direction.

"Whoa!" said a surprised Uncle Bill. "Sorry guys, that one slipped right out."

Yes, Uncle Bill farted. Ripped one right in the middle of our vows. It was loud and smelled beastly. It was so loud, that everyone heard it. We were dying laughing, we couldn't hold it in – apparently neither could Bill. He was mortified.

I finally caught my breath – which was tainted with scotch and chili cheese fries, and maybe…

"Is that – were those *garlic* chili cheese fries, Uncle Bill?" I asked.

When our intimate party of sixty calmed down, we resumed our vows. Chris had tears in his eyes – but I'm pretty sure it was from Bill's burning crop duster.

"Ok, guess I should get through this before he torches the whole place. It's flammable, Uncle Bill," Chris said. Bill also wiped a tear from his eye – from laughing. Chris's tone got serious, and his dark blue eyes focused on mine, "Caroline. You have my word, and that's the most important thing to me." His gravitas shifted again, as a huge smile moved across his face, "And I promise to love you till the year Three Thousand One Hundred and Eighty-Three."

The crowd chuckled, and Bill added, "Caroline, your vows please."

More composed than I thought, I set my eyes on Chris's as well, smiling and with an upward chin. "I'll never give up on you, please never give up on me. You have my word, and it's the most important thing to me, and I promise to love you till the year Three Thousand One Hundred and Eighty-Three."

Bill hurried, "Great. I pronounce you man and wife! You may kiss the bride."

Chris lifted me into his arms and kissed me proudly. Everyone cheered. Bill quickly escaped.

"You've gotta be kidding me," Chris said. We buried our faces laughing.

We embraced and turned together, and he walked me up the aisle for the first time as his Mrs.

REASONS 491 AND 492 TO LIVE: Haribo gummy bears and the New England Patriots

You know what one of the best things on the planet is? Haribo gummy bears. Those things are fucking absurd they're so good. Whatever you do, don't get the imitation, squishy, bullshit kind, no siree, get the good ones. The tough ones that don't let your teeth sink in, the ones that fight back. I can pile drive at least 100 Haribos in my mouth, nonstop for twenty minutes. Granted, I want to barf after, but what else is new? And hey, this way I'll puke a rainbow. Taste *that* rainbow, Skittles.

I bite their hands off, then their feet, and I do it in different flavor orders while we watch the Pats on TV. We're two games away from the Super Bowl - again - it would be Tom Brady's fifth and unprecedented title. No other quarterback has five wins – this isn't a 'no quarterback *alive*' situation, no, no. This is *ever*. The Pittsburgh Steelers have the most victories overall, with six Bowl wins – but not the same QB, and it looks like we're creeping on 'em! TB12 is insane – thirty-nine-years-old and better than ever. What an inspiration! I'll be thirty-nine this spring....

Green. Arms, legs, head. Anyway, he's incredible, and so is trash-talking, smoke show, Julian Edelman. He's Brady's go-to wide receiver. The thing about trash talk is, it's only cool if you can back it up. *These two can back it up.* I love watching them play – two guys you can count on. They were underdogs, like me and Chris. Yellow, legs, arms, head. Pineapple – the best one – head, arms, legs. Nice catch Edelman!!!! Red, arms, legs, head...

🐚

I stand in the wig store with Katie, staring at myself in the mirror as a platinum blonde with straight hair and bangs; a California surfer girl.

I am not a California surfer girl. I put it back on the mannequin.

The cancer is contained. I nearly said *my* cancer, but it's not mine. It'll never be my cancer, it was never invited. It's there, like a wart or saddle bags or cankles – in my body, but I don't want it. Fuck you, cancer, I hope the radiation fries your fucking balls off and you rot in hell. You hear me? I'd gouge your fucking eyes out, you worthless piece of shit. I will fucking kill you. Ahhhh, illness-inspired rage, my new best friend. I often cheat on him with illness-inspired sarcasm. Our threesome would be off the hook.

How did I house something growing inside me without knowing? A silent, insidious killer. There's got to be a better way to find this sooner, to test for it. Symptoms so innocuous, they're *missed*? Rare cancer... sure. There are 374 types of "rare" cancer and they account for 30% of all cancer diagnoses, 500,000 people per year. Rare my fucking ass. We're going about our lives, thinking everything is great – and then one day, boom. What a fucking joke. I swing my arm and a mannequin head goes crashing to the floor.

"Oh shit."

Katie turns around and notices, "Are you ok, Caro?" I struggle to bend down and pick it up – my belly is really in the way. Katie intercepts me, placing the head, and the thick, luscious hair from some lucky, kind soul, back on the shelf. She puts her arm in my arm to walk me down the aisle of real and fake hair.

My mind runs. Did I do it right? Did I live my life? Every day I can feel it, time ticking down. Every moment becomes so much bigger, because it might be the last. I want to tell everyone how much I love them, but that scares people, because they think it's goodbye – and it is –but maybe not this second. I don't want to freak people out... but I need to tell them, there's so much to say. This timeline, it's real for me. How do I stay true and honest to myself, and not freak them out? How do I do this? I squeeze my sister's arm tight, and look her straight in the face, side by side.

"I love you so much," I say.

"I know, sissy. I love you, too." She smiles and bites hard, she does her best, but we both tear up, and then laugh at our ridiculousness. "Come on, let's get you a new 'do."

I run my fingers through the Jackie O, and the crimped Madonna circa 1985's *Dress You Up*. There was "the Rachel" from *Friends*, and a Princess Di, but where is "the Me?" I want *me*, but better. Thicker, longer, more of it than I had before, but damn, they're expensive. Luckily, insurance will pay for it, and that's nice of them, but I figure they know they're kind of winning. They don't have to insure me until I'm ninety. I'm a steal.

"What do you think, Caro? See any you like?"

I throw on "the Rachel" and stare at my face and this unflattering mop. Blank stare, with my sister gazing over my shoulder. In agreement, "No."

She places it back on the mannequin head. "We'll find one."

"Since the cancer hasn't spread anywhere new, Doc has given me the green light to stop chemo for the next six to eight weeks before the baby is born."

"Is that safe?" she asks.

"They stop chemo before childbirth so my white blood cell count can rise, and I don't pass on an infection to the baby. Ridding the chemo from my system will allow me to breastfeed for a few days."

"Oh that's great! But why just a few days?"

"Because I have to start chemo again right after."

"Oh."

"Ooh! I'll have a glass of wine, then – can't feel guilty about drinking if I'm not allowed to breastfeed. Ah, there *is* a silver lining!"

"Caro, I'm sure you're not supposed to drink on chemo."

"Yeah, God forbid there's more poison in my body. Then radiation begins. Radiation to try to shrink the tumor even more. Radiation and chemo, sounds like a party."

"One day at a time. Don't overwhelm yourself with all that. You will get through it, and you will do it. You always do, sis. Ok?"

I nod and let out a big breath. "Right. Positives. Right now, no chemo, no radiation."

"Come on, how bout this one," she says, laughing, holding up this hot Jessica Rabbit wig, red and flowing.

"I mean, I have always loved red hair, and my pale skin almost goes with it. It's the dark, hollowed out circles under my eyes that don't."

"Positives!"

I put it on my head. I snap it off. "Shit. What am I going to do?"

"What?" says Katie. "If you like it, get it."

"No. I - I feel so unattractive, and - This isn't me, Kate. This isn't…" I put my hat back on. "None of this. Not the wigs, the sickness, the helplessness – this isn't *me*."

"I know," She rubs my shoulder, puts her arm around me as we walk side-by-side to the exit. "I heard there's a service that gives cancer patients…"

"Please don't call me that." I try to pull away.

She pulls me closer, "…that gives women makeovers. They take care of you for the day, give you a massage, manicure, pedicure… makeup – whatever you want. Would you like that?"

I nod and bite my lip, throw my arms around her and squeeze her hard. "Thank you," I whisper.

A relief and a rescue, my kid sister.

Chris

I grab the pail and rod from the garage. It's not sunrise, but it'll do. I don't feel comfortable leaving Caroline alone in the mornings, so I go while she's with her sister. And at least with the sun out, it's warmer.

I wade into the water, sloshing one thigh in front of the other. I get to my spot, cast out, reel in, cast out. Numbness. And it isn't the December temperatures. Casting, reeling, *waiting* doesn't feel so fulfilling when it's exactly what I've been doing in my life. People constantly tell me all I can do is love her, be there for her, give her the best life I can. But what I want is for her to have more of it. She *deserves* to be here longer. She deserves a good, long life. She tells me she has one, but I feel like I'm failing her, sitting idly by. A fucking bystander.

The worst part is, it has nothing to do with *deserving* more life. Tons of people don't deserve to die when they do. We tell ourselves that good things happen to good people, that there's some sort of reward system in life, justice, balance. Bullshit. To know that one day, not long from now, I'll look over my shoulder and she won't be there… I don't think I can do it. If I don't have Caroline – newborn or not – I don't know if I want to be here.

In addition to the idiosyncratic nature of the species, there's another extraordinary trait: the *male* carries the child, or rather children. After their ethereal courtship dance where their clicking coronet sounds become one, the mother releases her eggs into the male's external pouch called the brood sack, where he will carry the fertilized eggs until birth.

Jaro Nemčok

twenty two

Caroline

Katie picks me up for my "Cancer Spa Day" the following Sunday morning. Ok, it's just called "Spa Day", but sarcasm has become a way of life. Anyway, I didn't realize how much I *relied on* feeling beautiful BC (before cancer), how that was so much of my identity. I had hair and color in my skin. I had a nice body. I was the picture of health and style. Now, I walk around in oversized sweaters and sweatpants. I want to look better for myself and my husband, but most days, I don't have the will. I don't know how he's been able to look at me. Suddenly the baby kicks.

"Ooh! That was a big one."

"What's the matter, Care Bear?" Katie asks.

"She nailed me! Damn!"

"Oh lemme feel!"

I take my sister's hand. "Got it?"

Biggest smile I've seen in months, "Yes!! Oh my God! Hi little one!" She pulls her hand away. "She's active alright! Psyched for today."

"Me, too. I've really let myself go." I hold up the tattered gray sweatshirt.

"You have not. Jesus."

"Katie, I could've gotten a wig, put some makeup on, made an effort. At least, gotten out of these goddamn rags."

"For what? To lie in your bed?"

"I could've done *something*."

"You're growing his child."

"It's a wonder he hasn't cheated on me with some co-ed."

"He'd be the world's biggest slime if he did."

"No, I wouldn't blame him."

"And he never blames you for wearing sweats while you're pregnant *and*…"

I look at her and cut her off, "I'm glad we're doing this. I need to feel like myself again."

We enter the salon, all pink and cheerful. A tall woman greets us and introduces herself,

"Hi there, I'm Rita. Here you go, doll," she hands me a mimosa. "There's a lot more OJ than champagne in there, and you don't have to drink it if you don't want," she says as she escorts us to the pedicure station.

"Ah, what the hell." I take it and tip it back. Rita is right, it's three-quarters orange juice, but that's fine by me. I haven't tasted alcohol in seven months, and my taste buds do cartwheels.

They sit me in the chair and go to work. They start by massaging my shoulders and put my feet in the whirlpool for a pedicure, treating me like a queen. Despite my promise to myself, it's difficult not to cry, this is going to be a *happy* day.

When I'm finished getting my mani and pedi, the girls lead me to another chair. I sit facing the mirror, and Beth, the woman assigned to me with dark hair and a southern accent, turns my chair to face her. She lifts up these bountiful, beautiful lashes, and that was it, I lost it. She catches my head as I dive into her, weeping.

"It's ok, honey, let it out. We never know what's going to snap the levees, but something always does. It's usually hair – or the massage."

"I used to be pretty. I used to have these eyes…my husband would say you could see them from across the room. Now they're dry and red with no lashes, no eyebrows. I feel so ugly."

"Oh darlin, there ain't a damn thing ugly about you."

I know she's lying, but her kindness moves me and I don't want to let go of her. I suddenly feel the arms of six strangers wrap around me. I've never felt love like that in my life. Here they are, more angels.

When we walk out the door three hours later, I have a soft brown wig, color in my cheeks, thick, luscious eyelashes, eyebrows, a pink shirt that says on the belly "My Mama is My Hero", and most importantly, a smile on my face. My sister does, too.

We pull up to my house, and there are cars in the driveway, and all along the street. Chris comes out to greet us dressed in a black cashmere v-neck and sport coat.

"Why does he look so cute? I ask Katie. Chris opens my car door and takes my hand to help me out. "What is all this?"

"Wow. You look incredible. My beautiful wife," he hugs me.

"Don't make me cry again."

He whispers in my ear, "I've missed your smile so much."

I hang onto him, "I know," I say, smiling brightly. We don't want to let go. "What is all this?"

"Come in and we'll show you," Katie says.

"You knew about this?" I ask her.

"I might be the younger sister, but *I* know *everything*."

I follow them through the house and see baby shower decorations all over the foyer and into the main room. Little hanging seashells, seahorse plates, napkins, even utensils with a starfish on the handle. As they bring me through the house to the backyard, there's a big white tent, dozens of heat lamps, beach sand, a mini pool, a mermaid and a seahorse statue. I can't believe the whole thing took less than five hours to set up.

"How did you do this?" I ask Chris.

"It was Katie – and all of them."

I turn around to see Patty and the Mom-friends from the rugby games; Amelia the attorney, and a dozen other women I've seen in passing from Cohasset. Mom and Dad, Paula and John. And a very pregnant Dr. Ryan stands with the group.

Susie from yoga and her partner Madeline walk up, carrying their little boy.

"Hey stranger!" says Susie.

"Oh my God, Susie! Madeline! And who's this?"

"This is Jackson," says Madeline. "We try not to bring our two-month-old anywhere, but this isn't to be missed."

"Thanks for coming." I hug them hard.

"If we have to escape early," Susie whispers, "It's only because he's having a meltdown."

"Understood."

Suddenly, a raucous chirping sound rises behind me -it's the girls from the Beauty salon. Rita, Beth, and the rest of the team.

"I thought I should invite them, too" Katie says.

"Couldn't get enough of us, darlin'?" Beth yells, as she kisses my forehead. "Wow, is this Mr. Shaughnessy? Dayummm, girl!"

"Hi, I'm Chris."

"I'm Beth, from the salon. Doesn't she look beautiful?"

"Stunning. Thank you so much." Chris hugs Beth.

"My pleasure, sweet potato." I think she *may* have patted my husband's bum, but we'll give her a pass.

Mom runs over to me, arms stretched out, "Oh my God, you look gorgeous." She holds me tight. "I'm happy to see you looking like yourself again."

"Thanks Mom, I feel good."

Suddenly, a familiar face catches my eye. It's Leash, followed by Anna, and Mack. I nearly lose my breath. "You're here."

"We wouldn't miss it for the world," Leash says.

"You look fucking amazing," says Anna. They hug my frail shoulders hard.

"Smoke show, always a smoke show," says Mack.

The party is complete. I haven't felt this way in a long, long time. Another dozen women stand nearby- I don't know all of them.

"Hi everyone," I say. "Thank you, so much for doing this. I had *no* idea." I smile and push my wig out of my eyes. "I know I don't know all of you, but I will. I am so touched that you did this for me, a stranger. We won't be strangers anymore. You've all made my day– our day, actually. I think I can speak for Chris when I say this means a lot to him, too. It's not just me going through this." I look over at him and see in his weary face that I speak the truth. He cracks a trembling smile. "The families of those of us with cancer, in a lot of ways, I think it's worse for them. Without my husband, I would've given up already."

The women gush. I continue "This shirt might say I'm the hero, but he's mine." A muted sniffle is heard from the crowd. "My sister, too. Katie, Mom, Dad - you're everything, and I can't thank you enough. And to all of you, the kindness you've shown, I'm forever indebted. Thank you." The women nod and smile back. "Alright, let's eat."

The women converge on me, and we all move under the tent. Fifty women, half of whom I've never met before, join me. I chat with them all day. They are so open, so curious, so loving...*Why hadn't I let this in earlier?* I know why, but look what it cost me. Man, it would've been nice to have friends here.

If only I'd let them in about what was missing, about the struggle I'd had to have a child, about that loneliness, and the feeling of not being good enough— they would have understood me. They'd have been with me for the journey instead of the end, but better late than never.

A couple hours after chatting over finger sandwiches and baby shoe-shaped desserts, we sit down in a circle to open gifts. Like the women I'd watched so many times before, today it was me, finally me, in the middle of the circle. I take in all the faces staring back at me, I want to hold this image in my memory forever. Amelia walks up and places something on the gift table next to me.

"I forgot something," she says sweetly, and walks back to the circle.

It's the 02025 magnet from the Shop Across the Street. I bite down, trying hard not to cry. Katie comes up and rubs my back.

"I'm ok, I'm ok," I gain my composure and smile through the teeniest escape-artist tear. "I'm ok." I look back at the women. They're teary, too. "Ahh shit, sorry ladies." We all laugh. "I'm coming apart like a fucking faucet." We laugh more. "I might dress like a lady, but I talk…"

"Like a truck driver, we know," Katie and Chris chime in.

More laughter. Mood officially lightened.

"Ohhh-kay," I say. "I'll try to keep this tear-free." I open baby bottles and bibs, pacifiers, a bouncy chair, one of those pack-and-plays, and cute clothes. Cute everything. Little Swaddle-me things, diapers, diapers, and more diapers. "Can't wait to be surrounded by shit," I say.

"Daddy duty!" someone yells.

More laughter. Thank God. I don't want to cry anymore. The laughing is the perfect distraction for me to toss the oh-so-sexy nipple cream to the side. I don't want to break anyone's heart, but I'll never use it – nipple cream is for women who actually get to breastfeed and don't have toxins running through their mammaries.

At the end of the afternoon, we take a group photo. Me, with dozens of women who began the day as strangers but are now friends. I squeeze Amelia's hand as we snap the photo. It was she who found my sister on Facebook shortly after we met, and organized the other women. I hug every one of them before they walk out the door, and especially Amelia. She promises to keep in touch, and she invites me to her page, yet another Facebook page. This time, I wasn't so reluctant.

"If you or Chris need anything, we're a click away."

Chris, Mom, and Katie jump in, taking turns squeezing her. As I look over, I see Patty hanging back.

I bounce to her as quickly as I can, "Patty!" I say, embracing her enthusiastically.

It's the first time I've seen her wordless. She stands a few steps back, hands in her pockets.

She stammers, "I tried calling ya a few times. I figured you were busy, aw mad at me, aw…"

"Why would I be mad at you?"

"I don't know, maybe fuh some of the things I said befaw. About you not wanting to be a mothah. Aw, choosing yaw caree-ah ovuh mothahood."

"Patty, you never said that."

"Not exactly, but, sorta. I was wrong. And I'm sorry." She looks down and begins to cry. "It's so sad."

"I know, Patty."

"Why is this happening to you?"

"Shit end of the stick, I guess."

"At least." She waits a moment, "Can I take a crack at yaw husband?"

"Um… Wait till I'm dead, maybe? I whisper in her ear, "And he's totally worth it." We laugh. "Don't worry, I won't tell your husband."

"Oh, he's banging the babysittah."

"I'm sorry?"

"Yeah. It's not like she's sixteen aw anything, she's out of college. Twenty-two, perky tits, heavy eyelinah. You know the drill– he's drilling *her*."

"Patty. I am so sorry."

She chokes up a little, and I put my hand on her shoulder. "Oh, I'm not losing it, I choked on my gum is all." She tries to cover. And then she sputters and the tears come. She wraps her arms around me, burying her head in my mountainous breasts. I don't think the wetness was her tears, I'm pretty sure there was a heavy layer of snot moving into the crevice there.

"It's ok, Patty. He's an idiot. You can totally have my husband when I'm dead."

Chris hears it and shoots me a death stare. I throw my hands up, and silently mouth, "What?"

Patty moans and groans into my chest and it gets awkward. Finally, she pulls away – and no joke – wipes her nose from *side-to-side* in the *middle of my boobs* to get rid of the snot. *Serenity now, serenity now.*

Chris chuckles in the background.

"I hate you," I say to him.

Patty rises out of my chest, "Huh?"

"Nothing, I was– Listen, go home and talk to your husband. It might be a fling – it's probably a fling. She's twenty-two, what's she gonna want with your old man?"

Seahorse

"He's pretty great."

"Not really. Go home and talk to him, and you let him know… you let him know that if he doesn't pull his head out of his ass, you'll make Lorena Bobbitt look like a pansy, you hear?"

"Threats? That won't work."

"You'd be surprised."

I look back at my husband, hands in his pockets, shaking his head and smiling, as he walks inside the house.

"Patty, if you want him back, fight for him. You deserve to be happy. *Nobody* steals my friend's husband. Don't give up."

She gives me one last hug, and before she leaves, she turns. "Yaw still the most beautiful person in the room. Ready to pop, fucken cancer… yaw still the prettiest woman I know."

I stand back and look at her, "Thank you, Patty. But there are different measures for beauty, huh? And this took hours. Yours is there when you wake up in the morning. You're not lying to anyone." I squeeze her tight and kiss her cheek. "You're a really good, honest friend." She looks at me perplexed as I walk away and into my home.

Once in the kitchen, I firmly press my new magnet onto our refrigerator – 02025, right where it belongs. I turn around to see Katie and Chris cleaning up; Mom and Paula, do the same.

"Hey guys, please don't. I'll call Theresa to come in."

"You can't have your housekeeper clean up a party she was at," Katie says.

"Well, you guys are!" I put my hands on theirs. "Stop sis. Mom, Chris, stop. Let's take the night off, ok? It was a great day. I'll call a cleaning *service* in the morning."

"I'll do it," says Chris.

"You've done plenty. I can still dial the phone."

"Well, since we're here, I may as well give you my gift," he says.

"What?" I say, stopping in my tracks.

"Our babymoon," he holds my hips toward him. "The last time it's just us before the baby comes."

"Chris," Mom says, "I don't think it's a good idea."

"We're not going far, Gloria, a few days in the Vineyard."

"Yes! I love the…" I begin.

"In the wintertime?" Mom retorts, "It's freezing there. Why would you go *now*?"

Chris's face turns red, "Because *now* is when we go, now is when the baby is in and not out."

"Mom," I say.

"It's too dangerous, you have to skip it," she says.

"Mom!" I say.

"It's the only time we can go. She's free from all the doctor visits, she's not having chemo, and it's only a few days."

"But she needs a good hospital, and the *Vineyard* hospitals…"

Chris blows a gasket! "IF IT'S GOOD ENOUGH FOR PRESIDENTS SINCE ULYSSES FUCKING GRANT, IT'LL BE GOOD ENOUGH FOR US."

I think Mom pees her pants a little, I let out an accidental giggle. Mom shoots me a snarling glare.

Mom throws her hands up. "Reckless! I think it's absolutely reckless!" And she stomps into the other room. Katie rushes after to control the damage.

I smile at Chris, who is still uncharacteristically on fire. His face is red, his eyes set and jaw clenched. It's not often, but when it comes to me, man, does he yell and scream.

"I hate fighting with your mother."

"Welcome to my world, pumpkin." I take a tiny sip of leftover wine.

"I don't know how you did it."

"I cannot wait for our trip." I pull him as close as I possibly can with seven months in between us and gaze up at him. His forehead rests on mine.

"Are you sure? You're not worried about being away from your doctors and all this?"

"I think getting away from *all this* is exactly what we need. Don't you?"

"I do."

We lean toward each other and kiss a long, soft kiss. I hear my mom and sister at the doorway, about to say something, but they opt to walk away.

Before bed, I look at all the items laid out in the baby's room. I touch the soft little pajama pants and fuzzy stuffed animals, listen to the sounds of her rattle and electronic ice cream truck. I hang up the painting of a pale blue and green seahorse, gaze at the Pack N' Play everyone says they can't live without. I look back in the corner at the running stroller we bought so many months ago. I run my hand across the black leather grip, the untouched, spotless tires, clean as the day they rolled off the warehouse floor. I can feel the icy pangs of sadness descend upon me. But I put a stop to it, I'm not letting it in, not today. And there on the shelf is the teal and yellow book – I put it back when I didn't have the words.

Letters to My Baby – a Paper Time Capsule. Time *is* fascinating. Katie gave it to me back on Memorial Day, and we didn't know it, but I was already pregnant. I was so devastated about not being pregnant – but I was. And I didn't know I was sick - but I was. Seven months ago, my world was one thing, and now, anything can happen. Maybe I'll live five years, or ten, or fifty, but in case that doesn't happen, I better write these letters to her.

My wishes for you are...
The world I want to give you is...
What I want you to know about me...

twenty three

Caroline

Friday morning, Chris and I pull out of our driveway and set off for the Cape; we'll hop on the ferry and touch down in Martha's Vineyard before noon. It will be bone-chilling there, but Chris is right, now is the time. Sitting in the passenger seat as Chris drives the Panther, I watch the world go by – the colonial-style homes of Cohasset, with frost-covered lawns, gray skies and bare trees. Winter is near, death making way for new life. We turn onto the highway and it's the same route we took seven years ago when we went to check out our wedding venue. God, that fight, the ring… I rest my hand on his and smile at him. He smiles at me, and calmly puts his eyes back on the road.

We arrive at our little cottage in Oak Bluffs a few hours later. It's set back from the rocky beach; a charming, gray shingled, two-bedroom with a fireplace and huge picture windows exposing a breathtaking ocean view.

"Well, what do you want to do first?" Chris asks.

I laugh, "Sleep?"

"Oh, hell no!"

He grabs our coats and ushers me out the door. Minutes later, we pull up to a big red barn with a carved sign "Flying Horses,

America's Oldest Carousel." I loved this place as a kid, trying to go for the gold – or brass, really. Each time around, you'd grab at a little arm that dispensed silver rings and *one* brass ring. The goal was to get the brass ring. Kids got crafty – myself included– we figured out a way to pull three or four rings at a time. If we were deft, we could get five, but that was rare. In seven seasons of visiting the Vineyard, I never got the brass ring.

Almost no one is there in the winter, just us and this lovely older couple. Maybe kids are too busy on their iphones, watching YouTube or playing video games, pushing down their thumbs instead of reaching up and grabbing for something.

We chose our horses –a dark one with black hair for me, and, a white one with yellow hair for Chris. Straddling the plastic horse as a pregnant woman is a lot harder than when I was a skinny eight-year-old kid. I'm afraid they might kick me off due to weight restrictions! The carousel conductor smiles at me – a fifty-something, thin man with tortoise-rimmed glasses and a plaid button-down shirt. He knows I'm about to give my daughter her first carousel ride– special, indeed. I watch the older woman – probably eighty or so - sit down on one of the carousel benches with her husband, beaming from ear-to-ear. The carousel has been in Oak Bluffs since 1884 – 140 years of riders; if these horses could talk…

The conductor moves to the microphone in the center of the carousel, and with his weathered, New England accent, he recites his spiel,

"All small children seated on the horses must be securely strapped in. Please sit with both legs on either side of the horse – no side saddle, backwards, or standing on the horses. Your chariots are equipped with real horsehair, so please no pulling or hanging on to the manes or tails. Thank you, and please enjoy the ride."

The 1923 Wurlitzer organ starts up, and we move round and round. I'm transported back to my childhood, and I want that lucky ring.

"Chris!" I shout. "Did you ever try to get more than one?"

"What? No."

"I'll show you!"

So, as we go around again, and approach the arm, I lean out with fingers curved like a lobster's claw, and I pull, pull, pull. Three rings.

"See!" I show him.

"You're nuts."

"What?! It increases the odds!"

He smiles and shakes his head. I look back and notice the older couple isn't pulling. They're content to sit. *More for me!*

Round and round we go as I pull multiple rings. Chris continues the lackluster monotony of only pulling one. My odds of getting the win are going up and up! After all these years, today is going to be my lucky day. Today, I'll get the ring!

After a few more times, I realize how long the ride is. The endless, aimless nature of it never bothered me before, but now it becomes a bore. I stop pulling. I don't want the ring, what's it all for anyway? I'm not a kid anymore.

"Caroline," Chris yells. "What are you doing?"

"I don't need it. What do you win anyway? It doesn't matter."

He looks me dead in the eye. "Of course it matters. Keep pulling."

My heart isn't in it anymore. I know he took me here, *for me*, so I could cheer up and revisit some of my warmest childhood memories, but the current circumstances tarnish the shine. I can't change that.

He looks so sad. *Goddamn it, Caroline, get it together, pull the fucking ring for him.* So, I keep going. I pull two at a time, three at a time – still no brass. I have this sneaky suspicion Chris will end up with it. When I look back, he's stopped pulling, he is just sitting there. So, I pull faster, with more excitement.

"I'm gonna get it, Chris! I know it, I'm almost there!"

He seems to perk up or tries to.

The music slows and so does the carousel– *please no, please let me find it, please!* The music slows down, I'm a few horses from the arm, when suddenly, I see it. The brass ring is right at the edge of the arm.

I reach up. "I got it! I got it! I got the brass ring, Chris, I got the brass ring!" Chris's eyes jump from their downward stare. "I got it, honey! I've never gotten it before!"

The ride stops, and Chris runs over, throws his arms around me, and squeezes me tight.

"I'm so happy for you, baby, I'm so happy."

"Me too! Thank you, Chrissy. This was so much fun!"

He doesn't let me go. He holds on tight.

Chris

Back at the cottage, I watch her sleep, soundly, happily. I can't keep my mind from reeling, desperate and dismal, "Please don't die in your sleep." Or, "How many more times do I get to watch her sleep and *wake up*?" or "Is this the last time before her eyes close for good?" Every day that her eyes open is a good day.

There are so many things I want to tell her, but those kinds of conversations inherently say "this is the end," and I never want to say that to her. I never want to make her feel that way. Never.

Caroline

I wake up from a nap to find Chris staring at me from across the room.

"Are you ok, honey?" I ask.

"Yeah." He turns his head to stare out the window.

I slowly pull myself up, waddle over, and place my hand on his shoulder. He startles. I touch his hair lovingly, but his gaze is locked outside. When he looks up at me, his eyes are filled to the brim with tears. He tries to crack an encouraging smile but can't. His heart is breaking, too. *I know, Chrissy, I know.*

"Do you want to lay down with me?" I ask.

"Yeah."

He throws another log on the fire, brushes his hands on his pants, and flips his shoes off. I set up pillows on the floor, but he grabs a couple more to place under me so I – and the baby – will be comfortable. He wraps us in blankets, and lays behind me, with his hand resting on my belly.

"What are we going to name her?" he asks.

"I don't know, honey. I've been thinking about it a lot, and I can't come up with anything. I know that's strange, I'm usually able to make decisions."

"Oh, don't I know it."

"Well, compared to you, Mr. Indecisive."

"Not about you. I knew that."

"So romantic." I kiss his cheek and snuggle back under the covers. "Do you have a preference? For her name?"

"Nope. I mean, I always liked the name Kate, but then it seems like it's after your sister."

"Which isn't horrible."

"No, but I think if that were the case, we'd want it to be for a specific reason."

"Uh, because she's awesome."

"She is, but I don't know if we're naming our only child after her."

"Right." He squeezes me tight, knowing the word 'only' stings. "Well, let me know if you think of any."

"Sure. But you know, I won't be able to decide anyway." We laugh. He pauses a long time, "What do you want me to tell her? One day, when she's older, and…"

How did he know I'd been thinking about this, but didn't know how to bring it up?

"Tell her how we loved, that I was crazy about you, and that I'd do it all over again, a million times if you'd have me. Tell her, I wasn't so bad." I stare forward, clear my throat. "Tell her I love her more than anything, that I never gave up, and that I'm sorry."

He buries his face in my back, fighting hard not to cry. I feel the warm tears through my shirt. He nods his head firmly and repetitively into my shoulder.

🐚

I decide to wear the wig this weekend – I have to say, the one good perk about not having hair is you don't have to blow dry it – that saves a lot of time. I promised myself I'd keep up appearances, and I'm sticking to it. When I feel better about my outside, it helps my mood, even if it demands more energy. We pull up to the Black Dog – the tavern on the water where we were married. Chris helps me into the restaurant. Bustling and decorated for

Christmas, with twinkle lights and garland, wreaths and red bows a plenty, it's charming, welcoming, and the hostess is the same.

"Welcome to the Black Dog," a bright, sixteen-year-old girl says.

"Hi," says Chris, "Shaughnessy for two."

The girl smiles knowingly, "Oh, Mr. Shaughnessy. Yes, right this way."

She walks us over to a table by the window, a chilled bottle of champagne awaits our arrival. The girl gives me a slight look when she sees my belly.

"It's mostly for him," I say, gesturing to the bottle. She smiles and walks away.

Chris pulls out my chair and we sit, gazing at one another through two tall, white candles; Chris must've arranged for those, too.

"Nice touch," I say.

"Thanks. I thought you'd like them."

Tim, our waiter, introduces himself, pops the champagne, and pours it into our glasses.

"Oh," I say, using my fingers to show a tiny amount. "Just a little, please."

"Of course," said Tim.

Chris looks at me, holding up his glass, "Cheers, baby. Seven unforgettable years, and here's to 100 more."

"Cheers to that."

Our glasses clink and before I can sip it, I break into a coughing fit. Hunched over and gasping, the look on Chris's face changes to horror. I keep coughing, trying to catch my breath. Patrons turn around one-by-one to see what's wrong. I finally get a grip and catch my breath.

"It went down the wrong pipe," I tell the diners. They nod and go back to their meals. "Sorry," I say to Chris.

"Don't be sorry, are you ok? Do you want to go home? Do you feel ok?"

"I'm fine, hon, it happens sometimes. You know that. It's going to happen."

"Well if you want to go back to Cohasset, we can go right now. Whatever you're comfortable with."

"Honey. It's fine, I promise."

"Ok. Say the word," Chris says.

"The safe word? Like what you're going to need to call out tonight?"

"Mayonnaise Masturbator? Or bowling ball butt plug?" he says.

"Oooh that's a good one. Would you like one of those?"

"I mean, it's an aggressive turn, but you know, you gotta spice it up."

"Sure do, honey, sure do."

Tim breaks up our filthy banter.

"Tim! I didn't see you there!" Chris says.

"Don't worry Mr. Shaughnessy, I didn't hear anything. Ready to order?"

"I'll have the swordfish, Tim," I say, as I look over at Chris to see if he reacts. Eyes down on his menu, his twelve-year-old mind betrays him and provokes a smile. Perv.

He clears his throat. "I'll have the tuna please." He checks to see if *my* seventh grade mind does the same…this is why we married each other.

"Yes sir," Tim runs off. Poor guy didn't know what he was getting into; a pregnant woman with cancer, holding a glass of champagne, and a husband who can't *not* make fish jokes in public. Tim's definitely going to spit in our food.

"I was sure you'd get the lobster, tonight," I say to Chris.

"Nah, there's nothing immature about lobstah." Chris's ears perk up when he hears the piano chords. "Ooh, I love this song, I used to play it. But you wouldn't know that."

"Give me a break."

"Come on. Dance with me." He stands up and takes my hand.

"No, Chris, I'm huge!"

"Who cares, come on." He pulls me up, I resist. "Caroline."

"Chris." I sit down. "This isn't a dancing kind of place."

He leans in and whispers, "Let's show these fogeys what love looks like."

I protest with my eyes, but get up anyway, smiling as soon as he pulls me close. I *love* dancing with him.

He spins me around as the singer croons *Call Me Irresponsible*. No one else is dancing, and we carve out a mere four feet in between the other tables, but it's just enough. Chris steps left, then right, leading my hips to do the same – he's such a freaking showman, sidestepping and spinning, pulling me close, pushing me far and back in again, putting his palm on my cheek, singing the words. Sensual, fun, romantic.

The song comes to a close, and he spins me around, kisses my cheek, and as the awe-struck spectators look on with glee, he dips me. The crowd erupts with boisterous clapping. A few even stand and cheer.

"That's right," he says to me, "That's how it's done, son!" We walk back to our table.

"That was the best!" I say. My cough comes back beyond control. The fit lasts a few seconds, which seems like an eternity.

"Are you ok?" he jumps up

I nod, I can't speak. I take a sip of water, wave off the onlookers, and smile through it. "It was the best, Chris. Thank you for making me go."

"As long as you're ok."

"More than ok." I sip more, get my act together, kiss his cheek.

Dinner arrives and we talk and laugh and gesticulate – two "hands talkers." We're *that* couple. Dessert is a big chocolate cake, creamy and sky-high. It looks amazing, but suddenly, I don't feel well. I get up in a hurry.

"Caro, are you ok?"

I run outside - I won't make it to the bathroom - and heave into the water. *Fuck.* I'd been keeping food down for a while, putting on the weight. But the doctors told me people can get ulcers from chemo, and ulcers can make you sick. Or maybe, I shouldn't have eaten seafood? I thought I was ok as long as it was cooked.

Chris comes out and touches my back. "Honey, you're scaring me. *Please* tell me if we should go home."

"Hon, I feel better already. I don't want to go home. I can breathe, I can dance, and I don't think I can throw up anymore. I think we're good."

We go back inside, and I stare at the cake. I cautiously lift my fork and try to take a bite. Chris watches me. It's delicious.

"This is repulsive," I take a few more bites.

"All yours, all yours."

"If I could create a town, it would be made of Chocolate Cake. And that's the only thing anyone would be able to eat there. My clothes would be made of chocolate cake, my car, my bed. And if I was hungry, I'd just turn my head into my pillow of chocolate frosting and eat it."

"You had some of your magic brownies before we left, didn't you?"

"No. But that's a good idea for when we get home. They don't get you high, though."

"Too bad." He smiles and pats my arm as he moves past me.

"Where are you going?" I look over my shoulder to see he's bumping the pianist off the bench, adjusting the mic to his height. "No." I say out loud.

"Hey everybody," his silken, bassy voice fills the restaurant. "My name is Chris, that's my wife Caroline over there – we were married here just over seven years ago."

People cheer and clap.

"Yeah, I'm starting to get that seven-year itch. Look at all the weight she's put on."

There are a few uncomfortable shrieks and gasps, but more laughs from the observant ones.

"C'mon guys, she's pregnant. Keep up." Everybody laughs. "She's due in early February, with our first. We're taking suggestions for names." People throw out some names. Chris smiles. "Martha? Ah, for Vineyard. Yeah, I don't know, honey, what do you think?"

I smile and shake my head no.

"This is our babymoon. So, before that little terror kicks her way out, I figure I'll sing my incredible wife a song in front of all y'all. If that's ok with you?"

"Yeah!" The crowd screams.

"Cool. Merry Christmas."

The jazzy, romantically haunting chords of Leon Russell's "A Song For You" rise from the piano. Chris's voice is more like Michael Buble's version, smooth and soothing, but he plays the keys more like Leon.

"We're alone now, and I'm singing this song for you. I know your image of me, is what I hope to be."

I watch his face, his hands moving. He's good at freaking everything. That was one of the other reasons I fell head-over-heels for him way faster than I wanted to: he's good at the things I'm not. I couldn't play an instrument if you paid me. He hasn't played in months, but he can pick it right back up – and that's just a fraction of the list. I hope our kid has at least a quarter of his talent.

"But now I'm so much better so if my words don't come together, listen to the melody, 'cause my love's in there hiding," he sings.

He keeps it together, pouring his heart out through his voice and hands. The room is still, except for the song. No one lifts so much as a glass of water or clanks a fork against their plate. I don't even hear the creak of someone shifting in their chair. The guys in the kitchen must have stopped working to poke their heads out and watch.

"I love you in a place where there's no space or time, I love you for my life, cause you're a friend of mine. When my life is over, remember when we were together, we were alone and I was singing my song for you."

He comes to the final chords, the final words as if in a trance, as if no one else was in the room.

He looks up and stares at me, "We were alone and I was – singing my song for you." We were locked in. *Locked in*. All I could hear was my breath.

A scream, a cheer, uproarious clapping breaks the spell. These people - mostly middle-aged yuppies - go *nuts*. Chris comes out of it, stands up and waves. Someone throws a bra onto the piano. I turn around to see the guilty fifty-year-old woman and her hammered party of four cracking up. It was insane.

I rush over to hug and kiss him. "I love you." We stand there a long time, grinning from ear-to-ear. "A million times I love you."

The next morning, we wake up to the sun shining through the windows. We have breakfast at our little bar-height table in the breakfast nook, and talk and listen and laugh. We read the newspaper – that's right, news*paper*. We jump in the big, hot, bubbling bathtub opposite one another, and read some more, then walk around in robes, until we cuddle up on the couch to watch Netflix. Once the movie is done, we order pizza and listen to some music.

"Who is this Father John Misty you're obsessed with?" I ask.

He puts on this indie-folk dude, the guitar strums, and a song called "Real Love Baby" plays- it sounds like music for lovers and hippies.

"Oh, he's the best. So good, so much smarter than everyone else. Or at least he thinks he is. I dig it." Chris says.

It's actually good. We dance around the room, when I notice the album art for *Real Love*; it's a paint splattered mess, a Jackson Pollock knockoff, but like those 3D images that have images hidden and layered within, I stare into it, letting my back focus dominate.

"Come on image, come on IMAGE!"

"What the hell are you doing?" asks Chris.

"I think it's one of those paintings. Where it looks like nothing, but if you stare into it, there's something. Know what I mean?"

"Yeah. Yeah, I know what you mean. Lemme see." He takes it and stares, mouth agape. "Nah, I'm not seeing anything. Hang on. Wait a minute."

"Lemme see!" I grab it. "Is that a rabbit? Or a baby foot? Wait, it's gone. Hang on, I'm getting it back, getting it back."

He steals it from me. Stares. "Babe, there's nothing. Clearly it's, wait, hang on. It's like, is that a penguin?"

"C'mon, lemme see."

"No, no, hang on. I see something. It's a… a… it's a baby Tyrannosaurus Rex. Do you see it?"

"Oh yeah! I totally see it. It's like…" I make a claw action and roar like a dinosaur.

"No it isn't, you fibbing motherfucker, I was pulling your leg. There isn't shit there."

"Come on! There totally is – it's like, right… there." There was nothing. Absolutely nothing. "Pizza?" I ask.

"Pizza," he concurs. And we pile-drive the third helping of the day into our pie-holes.

🐚

The next morning, I open my eyes to Chris packing. He moves around quickly and with urgency.

"Hon?" I say, slowly peeling my eyes open.

"Oh, you're up. Sorry, I didn't want to wake you, but it's good you're up."

"What? Why? It's 7AM… on Sunday. Come back to bed," I reach for him.

"No babe, we should get going."

"What do you mean? I thought we were going out for breakfast and then the lighthouse and then ice cream at Mad Martha's."

"It's freezing out. You want ice cream?"

"It's tradition."

"Well then get up. We'll get it on the way out." He whips the blankets off me.

"Chris." He keeps moving. "Chris, wait! What are you doing? Why are you all anxious?"

"Because it's time to go. Hurry up." He throws a sweater and pants at me.

"Chris. Stop. STOP!" He stops moving. "Please. Sit. Talk to me."

He stands still but doesn't sit down. "Caro, I think we should get you home. Closer, where it's safe."

"Where is this coming from? My coughing? I feel better."

"No, it's everything. The coughing, the throwing up, the…" He looks over at my wig tossed on the edge of the bed.

"Oh," I quickly grab it, and frantically place it on my head. "I'm sorry. I forgot. I didn't… I'm sorry, Chris."

"Fucking…No! Don't YOU be sorry. Jesus. No… *don't* apologize. That's not what I meant." He drops down next to me, head in hands. "None of that is what I meant."

"What do you mean?"

"You don't ever need to apologize. You understand? *Ever*."

"Hon. I'd like to stay the day and leave tomorrow morning as planned. Can we do that?"

"I think we should be closer to your hospital."

"Why?"

"Because if something happens to you, I'm responsible. And if your mother-"

"Ah. I see."

"What?"

"Chris, I'm still of able mind. I can still make decisions on my own."

"That's not what-" He turns his head away.

"I'm serious. Listen." I pull his head to face me and hold it in my hands. "I need you to know this. Don't do anything just to appease my mother. Don't hurry up for her or let fear or doubt take over what you intend. When I'm gone, don't let her or anyone bulldoze your ideas or make you doubt yourself, *especially* with our daughter. You *know*, honey. You know what you're doing. Your decisions are sound and you're going to make an incredible father. Trust yourself. I do."

He looks afraid, fragile in a way I've never seen him. But he heard me.

"Ok," he nods. "Thank you."

We have breakfast, ice cream, and go to the lighthouse at Gay Head. The tagline for the historic site – "Gay Head Lighthouse: Keep on Shining"– I like that. The wind blows our hair back, and it's so cold, our faces look even more pale, our lips are dry and pink. We snap a picture of us this way, the lighthouse behind us and the hair, this time, out of our faces. At the last second, I kiss his cheek. I think that'll be a good one.

Monday morning, we take the ferry back to the mainland. I sit outside on the deck, it helps with the nausea. Of course, I'm the only one out there – December winds in New England appeal to few. Chris opens the door, struggling against the rocking of the ship and wind, holding two hot cocoas. He hands me one and sits.

"Woo!" The icy temperature constricts the muscles around his mouth, requiring extra effort to form the words. "You wanna come in, babe? *I'm* freezing, you must be dying out here," he says.

My eyebrows raise at his pun, he doesn't notice. I rest my mitten on his thigh. "It feels kind of nice today. You go ahead, I'll be a few more minutes."

"Ok," he says, "I'll be right inside the door if you need me."

He slips away, and I wrap the blanket around me tight – the wet, winter knots sting my face, my lips, my non-existent eyebrows. I barely feel my toes, but it feels good. I'm still here, and it feels good.

While several of the seahorse species are monogamous, the lined seahorse is a true romantic. The male and female seahorses choose partners they will continue to mate with for the rest of their lives. They perform ritual dances every morning to renew their bond, protect their love from growing stale, and ensure their beloved doesn't go running off with the neighbor.

twenty four

Caroline

Christmas comes and goes, followed by New Years. It's officially 2017. Hello 2017! I'm here, how are you?

I stand in front of my full-length mirror in my bathroom in my underwear. Oh boy. *Remember what I said about humor getting you through the race?* I'd love some right about now. I'm eight months pregnant and it's just *out there* - my belly, it's like BOOM - along with the stretch marks, and cottage cheese ripples on my upper thighs, YEAH! My back hurts, my ankles, hands and feet are swollen. When I look at my wedding ring, there's like, a watery, doughy sack of flesh surrounding it. Love handles of the fingers, if you will. I cough and have shortness of breath which is hard to admit, because I used to be able to run uphill and have a conversation with another runner. My kid is kicking *through* the insides of my belly, and I have constant indigestion. Huge tits, bald head, pale skin, and dark circles. Oh, and I still have no eyebrows. Hahahaha!

I pick up the stack of eyeliner pencils I bought and lean close to the mirror to start my project.

"Roy G Biv. Red. Orange…" I apply the colors to my face.

Chris and I have a doctors' appointment with Dr. Ryan and Dr. Sylver today. I pick up two more colors.

"Yellow. Green" I apply more to my face. "Blue, indigo, violet." I step away from the mirror and look at my work. "Hope they like my *rainbrows*."

Chris and I sit side-by-side at the doctors' office. Chris looks at me next to him, and shakes his head.

"You're tapped, babe." He laughs at the ridiculousness of it. "Just fucken tapped."

Dr. Sylver stares blankly at me – he is unperturbed. Dr. Ryan enters with her head buried in a folder and a belly bigger than mine.

"Hey Doc, how you feelin'?" I say.

She doesn't look up. "Can't complain," she says. Then she does a double take at my new look, but is business only. "We have your labs," she says.

"We want to move up your C-section," says Dr. Sylver.

"I thought natural birth…"

"Right away," he says.

"What's right away?" I ask.

"Monday," says Dr. Ryan.

"That's only thirty-five weeks," I say.

"Dr. Ryan and I are in agreement on this." He says.

"Two more weeks. Forty is full-term, I'd consider thirty-seven…"

"You *consider* what you're working with. You don't have the luxury to consider when you want, or how you want," Dr. Sylver says.

"I've come this far carrying her. You said she's healthy and developing right on track. If we were going to stop this close to the end, why did we even bother?"

"At this point, we can't risk further delay," Dr. Ryan chimes in. "Thirty-five weeks, for what you have is incredible."

"I want two more weeks," I say.

"Caroline!" Dr. Ryan raises her voice and her eyes bulge. "We need to protect *you*. Your cancer is spreading, and if we don't rein it in…"

I back off a step. "It's been pretty contained. It's going to spread so much in two weeks it'll kill me?"

"You've been off chemo." She stares me in the eye, dead-set. "Yes."

"What?" Chris says.

"You need to be healthy enough for a C-section," says Dr. Sylver. "Which brings us to another complication. Your white blood cell count is low, because you've only been off chemo for four weeks as opposed to eight, which means it's not where we want it to be, and puts you and the baby at risk of infection."

"But it's a risk we have to take," says Dr. Ryan. "We need to get the baby out, and the chemo and radiation in."

"But I *feel* fine!"

"No you don't," says Chris.

"Caroline." Dr. Ryan begins, "It metastasized."

"What?" I say, my lip trembles. "Where?"

She stares at me, withholding information she doesn't want to give me. "Your neck." Dr. Sylver's eyes dart to hers, and Chris's eyes dart between both of them. I can't lift my eyelids. Even though there are rainbows above them. Dr. Ryan exhales. "If you don't seek treatment immediately, it could move so fast, you're looking at weeks, not months."

"*Weeks*? That…can't be…" I whimper.

Dr. Sylver looks to Chris, pleading for help.

"Caroline," Chris says. "We need to trust our doctors. They've been with us the whole time. Please, baby, please listen. I'm begging you."

I see the anguish in his face. But...My tears come. And come and come, and I shake, and I feel like I'm three, because I can't stop.

"I... can't... Chris, please... please tell me it's not true... please. Doctor...Ry..please."

"I can't understand you, baby," Chris says. "I can't understand you. What did you say?"

I nod my head agreeably, up and down, up and down.

"Ok. Ok, ok, ok." I nod and cry. My husband throws his body around me and I can hear him sniff. When I can see again, and my chest stops heaving up and down, I look across and see even Dr. Sylver couldn't keep it together.

When I compose myself, I fold my arms, challenge them both, like a twelve-year-old being held in detention, "Do you guys like my rainbrows?"

Dr. Sylver and Dr. Ryan look at one another, exhausted.

My white blood cell count is so low Monday morning, they don't feel good about doing the C-section. They say they'll see where I am Wednesday morning. By Thursday, I have the flu, and it lasts five days. Those white blood cells, our biological body guards, are out on a smoke break or something, because *all* the disease beasts are getting in. I'm lucky I don't die of chicken pox. A few days later, I look and feel better than I have in a while. The labs show my cancer is staying put. (Credit to all the meditation and positive visualization I did the last two weeks – guess it worked.) They schedule me for Friday morning, January 20th. Thirty-six weeks and four days. She'll be born on the first day of Aquarius, my little water bearer, and she's coming out, ready or not. We still don't have a name.

I don't sleep well that night – or at all. To say I'm anxious is a gross understatement. I know I want to be as healthy as possible, and I know rest is extremely important… knowing *how* important makes it impossible to sleep. I'd be a mother for the first time and I'm excited and scared all at once. Worrying I might die of complications, never to meet her scares me more than death itself. I wish I could calm down - I'm going to give myself a panic attack if I don't. I go downstairs and stare at the ocean. I sit and stare, paralyzed by the unknown, and there, staring at me from the couch, is the book of letters I haven't finished for her.

I tear into them - I want her to know about her father and me.

To my daughter,

It's the night before your birth, and I want you to know how excited I am to meet you. Your father and I can't wait. I'm going to tell you a bunch of things I may not have the chance to tell you when you're older – it's not a full list, but they're the most important things I can think of right now.

Your father is the Love of my Life, and just like you, I had to wait a long time to meet him. And like you, it was worth the wait. Our love is one for the ages, and I hope he will share our stories with you, there are so many. He is my best friend, and my favorite face to look at before I close my eyes and when I wake up. Also, he has the nicest, most calming voice, and when I'm worried, it's the sound of his voice that heals me. You'll know what I'm talking about soon enough. I believe in true love, even when it hid from me. I hope you will, too. It is my life's greatest reward.

I also want to talk to you about what it means to be a woman. Hopefully, by the time you become one, it'll be a little easier, but here are some truths to help you along the way. There are many guidelines, or mis-guidelines, about what it means to be a woman and I'm fairly certain women had no part in creating them. Having emotions doesn't make you weak, caring about and helping others, being compassionate doesn't make you weak, being vulnerable doesn't make you weak. It makes you strong. What I think it means to be a woman, is that we are as strong as men, sometimes even stronger, but in different ways. And WHO CARES? It's not a competition. The differences are in fact, what makes us stronger as a whole. Being equal doesn't mean being the same, diluted or homogeneous. There's a bit of us in them, and a bit of them in us, but our differences create the patchwork of life.

And life, my sweet girl, is many things – choppy, messy, glorious, exciting, bumpy, colorful—there is no map or rule book, but there are tools and tokens of knowledge you can take from wise, old owls along the way. But the most important knowledge I want to impart upon you, is that the greatest gift you can give yourself is self-worth. Knowing you deserve a wonderful life – and not letting anyone take that away from you. Knowing that if someone treats you poorly, you can either walk away, or try to understand where they're coming from, but never accept it. You aren't to be treated poorly, and you mustn't treat others poorly.

Do not to wait for some boy to love you.

Love yourself. Right now; because, I do. Mommy loves you right now. And now. And again. I love you and always will. You are worthy now – not when you get to this point or that, this accomplishment or that - but RIGHT NOW. You are capable of anything you set your mind to. When you believe, you can do great things – for others, for the *world, and for yourself. Believe. Take the ball and run, create and give. Follow your soul's purpose - you'll know it when you feel it.*

Having said all that, boys – men – are wonderful. And you can totally date one the second you turn thirty. Or women, if you like. Whatever floats your boat. Still, thirty is a reasonable age to start dating. Right? Great, glad we had this talk.

The sun is coming up, my dear, but I want you to know, on this night before you were born, I wrote my little heart out so that you would know me. I don't know how much time we will have together, but I will treasure each and every second. You have changed my life forever – mine and your father's. You have the BEST father a little girl could ask for. Listen to him – he is the wisest of all owls.

And anytime you feel alone or misunderstood, read and re-read my letters – I am here with you. I am always by your side.

Love always,
Mom

Chris comes down the stairs, dressed, and rubbing his eyes – it's 7AM.

"Ready?" he asks.

Chris

At the hospital, Caroline's blood pressure is up, she's nervous. The nurses try to calm her down, I try to calm her down, but the one person who makes her feel at ease that day is Dr. Ryan. Caroline sees her, grabs her hand, and her fears subside.

"It's going to be ok, Caroline," says Dr. Ryan, gently placing a hand on Caroline's forehead. It's nurturing, loving, and then she says, "Don't be an asshole."

Caroline laughs. An inside joke, I guess, but it definitely helps. Caroline focuses on her breath, and they give her a sedative; that helps even more.

About an hour later, we are in the operating room, Caroline receives a local anesthesia– a spinal block– so she can't feel anything from her waist down, though she's awake during the procedure. They put up a sheet so she can't see what they're doing. They're supposed to begin by cutting through her lower abdomen, then a layer of fat, a thicker layer called fascia, then they'll move her bladder over, because that's in the way, and then they'll cut through her uterus and pull a baby out. They'll take the placenta out, put her bladder back in place. They'll start sewing up the uterus, then the fascia and finally, the outer incision near a woman's bikini line.

That's how it's supposed to go, but Caroline is having trouble as soon as the first incision is made. She can't feel it, but she says can "hear it." And something about it is sending her heart rate and blood pressure off the charts. The beeps and noises of the monitors and other instruments aren't making it any better.

"Doctor? Sylver!" she yells.

"What is it Caroline?" asks Dr. Ryan.

"I don't like it. I don't like it. Stop. I want to deliver naturally."

"That's not an option right now," said Dr. Sylver, instrument in hand.

"No! I gotta get out of here!" Caroline's upper body starts jolting, her lower body won't move.

"Caroline," says a phlegmatic Dr. Sylver, holding her bladder in his left hand, "I need you to calm down or we have to put you under. We don't want to do that, right? You want to see your baby, right?"

"I can't see anything! Take this sheet off! I can't move. This isn't right, I'm suffocating!"

Dr. Sylver whispers something to a nurse, who runs out and comes back within seconds. Joining her is an older man, early seventies, in a white coat. He leans over Caroline as a nurse prepares an IV.

"Caroline, I'm Dr. Bender, I'm the anesthesiologist."

"What? No!"

"We prepared in case of an emergency, your drip is ready to go."

"Emergency? No! I told you no! I want to be awake! I want to see her!" Caroline struggles, pulling her weak arms up, "This wasn't part of the plan! I want to talk to Dr. Ryan, I…"

"Caroline," Dr. Ryan leans over her, "Honey, it's ok. Go to sleep."

"No! I want to see my baby! I want…."

"I know." Dr. Ryan holds Caroline's hand, looks in her eyes. "It's ok, Caro. Go to sleep."

A nurse runs over and connects the bag to Caro's IV.

Terrified, Caroline gazes over at me. Her eyes beg for a different fate. Her eyes get heavy, but she fights back to open them, determined as ever.

"Caroline," says Dr. Ryan. "Come on, Shaughnessy, help us. Close your eyes."

She fights. I don't know what to say, I'm scared, too. What do I say? I lean over her, touch her face,

"It's ok, honey. We're almost there. It's ok."

She looks at me, her frightened eyes take refuge in my perceived calm. She *wants* to trust me. Her eyes close. *Dear God, please let her see this baby.*

Suddenly it's quiet. Caroline is out. Everyone let's out a sigh of relief. Dr. Sylver looks at me.

"Well done," he says. "You ready to have this baby?"

"Yes sir."

Doctor Sylver continues, completely composed. He places her bladder to the side and makes one incision after another. I don't look. I stay on the other side of the sheet.

"Here we go," he says.

He begins pulling my daughter out. I hear her cry. I see her slimy, red body and her face. The doctor cleans out her mouth so she can breathe. She looks like an alien, but she is beautiful. My beautiful, little alien.

"Do you want to cut the cord?" Sylver asks.

"Um. Ok." Dr. He hands me the scissors and I snip where they tell me to, causing some blood to come out.

"That's normal, right?"

"Yes," say Dr. Sylver, "Good job."

They take her back, clean her up, and swaddle her.

The nurse asks, "Do you want to hold her?"

I look at my wife. *Isn't the mother supposed to hold the child first? Isn't that an important bonding ritual? What will I take away from her, and from my daughter by holding her first?*

"It's ok," says the nurse, "You're not the first father to hold his newborn before the mother."

"Technically, I held her first," says Dr. Sylver.

"And better you than me," says the nurse.

I stare at Caroline. It feels like a betrayal, my wife lying unconscious on the table.

But my daughter is crying. I reach out and take her. Her beautiful face, I'm speechless. She doesn't look like an alien anymore, she looks like… a tiny, clean, little human, a perfect little human that somehow, Caroline and I made. She wails at the top of her lungs, and I cuddle her closer, as if I know it will work.

"Heyyyy baby girl. Welcome. Welcome to the world. Mommy is going to be so happy to meet you." I put my head on hers, kiss her, smile and laugh. I can't describe this feeling. I'm a father. I'm a father. Thank God, she's ok, I'm a father.

And then I hear the worst sound I've ever heard: it's Caroline's heart monitor.

"Nurse!" Dr. Ryan yells.

I look over at Caroline, there is a yellowish foam around her mouth.

"Obstructed airway."

They move frantically. One nurse grabs me pulling me out of the room.

"Come with me."

"No!" I stop. "What's wrong? What's wrong with my wife?"

"Mr. Shaughnessy," the nurse pulls me and the baby into the hallway, "Let them take care of your wife"

"I need to be in there."

"*They* need to. And we need to take care of your baby. Come with me."

🐚

I stand there, staring through the nursery glass, at our nameless baby in pink. Yawning and sleeping, her little arms in a flutter. She has no idea what world she's come into; neither do I. Five pounds, eleven ounces, our little girl is perfect. I pray her mother will see her soon. *You're ok, right, Caro? Sweetheart, if you can hear me, please wake up. There's so much more for you, now. Wake up, baby, wake up.*

The thoughts that race through my mind… No. We're all going home, one family, for whatever time we've got. But where the hell is the doctor? It's been hours.

I feel a hand on my shoulder, it startles me. I turn to see Dr. Sylver. The last three hours aged him ten years.

He pushes out a smile. "Congratulations," he says. "Your wife is stable and doing fine."

A sigh of relief pours from my tightened chest. I throw my arms around him. "Thank you, Doc. Thank you." I hang onto him until it feels too long, and then a moment more. I catch my breath, pull myself off him, "What happened?"

"We didn't want to put her through general anesthesia – it's always risky for someone in Caroline's condition, and with her weak lungs… There were complications. But we were able to stabilize her, she's ready to see you. Congratulations, your girls are doing great."

"Thank you, Doc." I throw my arms around him once more.

Caroline

I stare outside my window. *How can one body go through so much?*

Chris walks in – tiptoes is more like it – a giant smile on his face, and he's holding our baby, all curled up against him. I wanted to see her hours ago, immediately after she was born, placed in my arms the way every baby since the beginning of time is - not like *this*. It's my turn to meet her, love her, and be her *mother* – and I don't want to. In every movie, every book, the mother, who has been through the ringer for hours – no months – gives birth to the child, and then *holds her baby*. That bond is so important. I didn't get my moment, and I'm pissed. Maybe that's wrong, but what the fuck am I supposed to do about it? It's how I feel. He took that moment from me, and here he is, all happy-go-lucky. It's not fair, and it's not fucking right.

"Look who's here!" Chris says. "Mama's here." He walks close, leaning in to kiss me. "Hey babe, how are you feeling?" I turn away and shrug my shoulders. "Ok, well, do you want to hold your little girl?"

"No. I'm too weak. I'll drop her."

In this God-awful goo-goo ga-ga voice, "No you won't Mama, that's impossible. I'll lay her down right here."

"Chris!" I yell. "I don't want to hold her right now, ok? I'm woozy, I don't know what the fuck happened, and I almost died on the table! So no, I don't want to hold my *little girl*, ok?" He looks at me, shocked. "Take her back to the nursery. Let her… eat or sleep, or whatever the fuck she needs to do."

"Ok." He slips out.

I put my hand on my neck, squeezing it. "Fucking cancer in there, too!" I pull at the skin at my neck and squeeze and then pound my fists in my bed. Then cringe in pain because my abdomen hurts. I stop and lay there. I don't want to fucking cry anymore. I just don't want to. I stare up at the ceiling.

"Welcome to the world, Baby No Name," I say. "It fucking sucks here." I take the TV remote and threw it against the wall, shattering it into pieces.

Dr. Ryan enters. "Everything ok?"

"Sure."

"I'm glad you're feeling better. She's beautiful. Does she have a name yet?"

"Nope."

"Well, I came to say congratulations – you did a great job."

"No I didn't."

"Caroline." She sits down next to me and puts her arm around my neck.

"No!" I swat it away. "Don't Caroline me and give me some bullshit that everything's going to be ok. It's NOT ok! You get to see your kid – *kids* – grow up. I'm a fucking invalid. I'll be lucky if I can pick her up."

"I know you're angry," she says.

"You think? Yeah I'm fucking angry. You don't have to go through any of these treatments, any of these feelings, any of these…. fuck. So, don't tell *me* it's going to be ok, because it's not."

She stands up, chooses her words carefully, "Caroline – I know this is the last thing you want to hear right now, but you're going to be here a few more days."

"Fuck you."

"Before you leave, I want you to start radiation."

"Nope."

"It's a twenty-minute, painless process. You're here–

"FUCKKKK YOUUUUU!"

"–and I'd rather get it done. You shrink the one on your neck. It'll give you more time with her."

Out of breath, shaky, and ready to scream my lungs out, but instead of sound, comes uncontrollable coughing. It keeps coming, I hold my chest, lunging forward, more coughing, I struggle to breathe. Dr. Ryan, rubs my back, and hands me a sip of water. My incision hurts so much. I look down– there's blood soaking through my robe. I look up at Dr. Ryan, her eyes show alarm, but her voice remains calm.

"Apply pressure. You probably tore one of your stitches. It's ok." She helps me into bed carefully and yells over her shoulder, "Nurse! Need a nurse please!"

I lay there, while Dr. Ryan applies pressure. At least the coughing stopped.

"Fine," I say.

"I'm sorry?"

"Schedule the radiation."

"Ok." A nurse hurries in. "She may have popped one of her sutures," Dr. Ryan tells her.

The nurse rushes over and looks at my wound. She wipes away the blood. Waits a moment. "I'll keep an eye on them."

"Thank you," Dr. Ryan and I say at the same time.

The nurse nods and hustles off.

I lay there, staring out the window at the gray city below. Boston is so bitter cold and dingy in January. The snow makes everything wet and muddy. And ugly. I know Dr. Ryan is looking at me. I don't care.

"Do you want me to wheel you to the nursery?" asks Dr. Ryan.

"No. I can't even get up. It hurts too much to move."

"I'll help you."

"No." I turn to her. The blank look on her face evokes a deep guilt. I should *want* to see my baby. But I'm so angry, upset, or *something*. I don't know what the fuck I am. "You about ready to pop?"

"Next month," she says.

"That's exciting," I turn my head back to the window.

"Caroline. I'm not going to pretend I know how you feel right now, just because I'm a mother. I'm not going to pretend I know just because I see hundreds of cancer patients a year. No one can tell you what's *reasonable* right now. Only you know how you feel.

But I will tell you this; the sooner you go see your baby - what you just did, *how* you just did it - you will feel *better*." I look up at her, my eyes soften. "You did it, Caroline. Let's go see her."

"Ok," I say.

She supports my back and holds my arm as she pulls me from bed, slowly sitting me in the wheelchair. She places a blanket over my legs and tucks it in the sides, like a mother, or a best friend. She slowly wheels me down the hall, and twenty feet away, I see them: Chris beaming, holding the baby and handing her over to Katie who squeals with delight. Mom throws her arms around Chris's neck. John shakes his hand. My father does the same and hands him a cigar. They're laughing and celebrating in their own little bubble.

"Take me back."

"What?"

"Turn me around. Now! I'll go later."

She wheels me back to my quiet, little room, helps me into bed, squeezes my hand, and lets me be. I lift up my robe and see the staples holding my incision together, and my giant, sore tits, loaded with milk I probably can't use. I rub my bald head, turn out the light, roll over so my back is turned toward the door, and pull my blankets over me.

Fuck this.

APRIL 2012

The pack and I had been going strong for eighteen miles, but I was starting to feel it: the pangs of exhaustion and defeat, and I got the impression Leash and the girls were just getting warm. I could already see them inching a few steps, then yards, ahead. I can't keep up. We'll cross the finish line in eight miles, but that felt *really* far. I wanted to hang in there for as long as I could - I didn't want to quit on them, but this was their marathon, too, and I didn't want to drag them down. I tried to quiet my nerves and take in the crowds. Maybe they'd keep me going.

By mile nineteen, I was pissed. Or guilty, but it manifested as pissed. The pressure of letting them down was mounting, and *those* feelings became too heavy to carry – and they saw it. I dropped back ten feet. I look to my side and see the "Young at Heart" Johnny Kelley statue - two men holding hands in victory, a young Kelley and an old Kelley. He ran Boston sixty-one times, but the first time, he dropped out at mile twenty-one. *If he can run it sixty-one times, I can do it today.* And I kept up with Leash, Mack and Anna…until we got to the infamous Heartbreak Hill. It's not *that* steep, but it's a half-mile long, and it's at mile *20-and-a-fucking-half*.

"Fuuuuck that." I stopped abruptly and rested my hands on my knees. The girls stopped too.

"C-note, what's up," asks Leash, "Are you ok?"

"I'm not feelin' it guys. Go ahead."

"Knock it off Shaughnessy, you got this," says Mack.

"We're almost there," says Anna.

"We're not almost there! Five miles *after* this fucking hill. And I don't have it, today. I'm not slowing you guys down. Go. Run your race."

"Are you sure, Caro?" asked a skeptical Anna. "We can drop from fourth gear to third, slow down a bit and let you get your steam back."

"I'm outta fucking steam, ok? I appreciate it, but go."

"Ah come on-" says Mack.

"GO!" It startled them. "I love you guys, but I don't fucking have it today. I don't have it. I'll see you at the finish. Run your race."

"K," said Mack. "Love ya." We all exchanged hugs.

"Keep the faith, C!" yells Leash.

I watched my girls go from a diamond to a triangle… I couldn't let them down, so I had to let them go. There's nothing worse than struggling to keep up… it was debilitating, way more mental than physical. Some days, you want to be alone. I love them, those warriors, for their strength, support, friendship. But more than anything, I needed to survive… alone. My self-doubt was so loud, I wasn't sure I was going to *finish*, let alone finish well.

Chris

"Can we see her, Chris?" Katie begs from outside the nursery.

We'd just put #Baby, her temporary Instagram handle, back down for a nap.

"Katie, she's not ready for visitors. I will tell her you asked, call me tomorrow."

"Ok. Love you," she hugs me.

"Love you, too."

"You're a good man," Gloria says.

"Thanks Gloria." Gloria hugs me, my parents hug and kiss me, and drag Pete away as he yells,

"Did you keep the placenta? I hear it's loaded with nutrients! If you guys don't want it…."

"Home we go, Pete," says Dad.

I walk into Caroline's room. The lights are out, her back is to me.

I pull up a chair next to the bed and rest my arm on her back. She doesn't turn around, I can feel her back shake, she's crying. I rub her back and don't say a word.

twenty five

Caroline

The next day, the sun wakes me. It burns through my window. Poor Chris is hunched forward, his body in a chair, his head sleeping on the edge of my bed. I move the hair off his forehead to see his face.

"I'm ready to see her," I say.

"Huh?" He lifts his head from a pile of drool. "I'm up, I'm up."

"Can you take me to see her?"

"I'll do you one better." He disappears, and a few minutes later, he returns with her, and a bottle of formula. "Mommy's here," he says, placing her in my arms. "I'm gonna go get us some coffee."

He leaves us. I want to take this moment without another soul here. As the sun sparkles into the room, I look at my healthy baby's face –ten fingers and toes, a mop of dark hair, her tiny button nose, her pink little lips– and I know. Everything I've fought for was right here. She was the reason. And everything else fades away.

Her mouth opens to yawn, her little face points to the sky.

"Are you hungry, sweetheart? Are you hungry?" I give her the bottle, she takes it right away. "You made it. You're here. I felt you kicking, you wanted out! I'm so glad you're here. I'm sorry I didn't get to hold you right away, but I'm here now." I rub my hand across her tiny forehead, her pink skin, her tiny eyes looking, that suddenly focus on me. She sees me. I've never felt anything like it. "I love you, Mommy loves you so much. Forever and ever and ever. Mommy's here."

Chris

I stand outside, watching her talk to our little girl. I hear her whisper "I love you" over and over. I turn and lean by back on the wall, exhaling. That was the moment, the one we'd been waiting for, and she got it. Thank God she got it. I've never been so happy and devastated. But more than anything, I'm grateful.

Caroline

Later that day, Mom and Dad, Katie and her family, Paula and John, squeeze into my hospital room. I'm jubilant, and I don't realize how horrible I look. I feel my head again – a hairless dome- and frown. Katie sees me.

"Can I get you something, sis?"

I gesture to my head. "Yeah, actually. The Jackie O, the uh…"

"Right." She opens a little closet door and hands it to me.

I place it on my head, "Jackie O, a woman of style and class, handled tragedy with grace." I say, flipping my hair out of my face. "That's it," I look up at Chris.

"What?" he asks.

"Her name. It's by the grace of God or *some* greater power she's here. Baby Grace, that's her name."

"I like it." Chris says.

"Me, too," says Katie.

"Gracie!" little Sara says, holding her hand, staring into her face, and touching her head.

Mom, who has an opinion about everything, is uncharacteristically silent.

"Mom?" I asked. "What do you think?"

"Oh!" She snaps out of a staring trance. "Yeah. That's a really nice name. I always liked Jackie O."

Pete, staring into space, "I'm just trying to think of what nicknames can make fun of Grace. Face. Mace. Nuh, nothing good. I'll think of something."

Our nurse, Roberta, pops in.

"Hey Roberta," Chris says, "Can you tell the appropriate person we have a name for our little one?"

Roberta studies my chart, "Sure whadya come up with?"

"Grace," Chris says.

"Oh that's nice. Any middle name?"

"Not yet," I say. "We'll let you know."

Chris

I watch Roberta leave, and I step into the hallway to stop her.

"Roberta," I say. "Her middle name is Caroline."

"Oh. That's lovely. Grace Caroline Shaughnessy." She jots it down on a notepad, and looks over my shoulder to record our room number.

"A lot of boys have their Dad's name, why can't she have her mother's?"

"Good point. I'll take care of it for you."

Caroline gets her way a lot, I feel ok about getting mine.

The next two months are abysmal. I'm home with the baby while Gloria, Katie, Mom, and even Pete run Caroline to the hospital for radiation and chemo, and then she comes home and sleeps all day. I'd like to sleep, too, but with the baby, forget it. Sure, I nap an hour here or there, but it's sporadic. I go days without showering. Today, I'd forgotten how long it had been since I'd showered, until I catch my reflection in the mirror. My beard is as thick as the Red Sox's on a winning streak. The next time I put the baby down– at 11pm– I hop in the shower and shave.

I get out of the shower and towel off when Caroline pushes the bathroom door open and crawls in on her hands and knees. She leans over the toilet and pukes. Her body convulses. I lean down next to her and I rub her back. When she's finished, she pushes herself up, fills a glass of water, rinses out her mouth, and crawls back to bed. This has become routine for her.

I go downstairs to where I've been sleeping on the couch for the last two months– I want to give Caro the best night's sleep she can have and not wake her when I have to get up for Grace. Sure enough, by 3am: WAAHHHHH!

I run into the nursery.

"Whitney! Beyonce! How do they fit such enormous pipes into such a tiny human? How is this possible? I think you're more like Queen B." I pick her up and bounce her.

I put a mini-fridge *and* a microwave in Grace's room so I can warm up her bottles. She crushes that thing as soon as I give it to her– that's my nickname for her, The Crusher. It suits her. I sit down in the rocking chair to feed her. She looks up at me, and I look down at her, while she squeezes my hands and she chugs her bottle.

"Thank God this isn't beer. I'm worried about you, kid. If you chug beer like this….Know what, you're not going to college. No, that's it, too much of a liability." I crack up at my own joke, when I notice Caroline standing in the doorway. She's not watching with love, no, it's contempt. Our eyes connect, and hers burn a hole through me. She walks away.

I'm left alone to feel the pain and unfairness that is cancer. It doesn't only attack the physical body of the patient, or the mental, or the emotional… it attacks *everyone and everything* around it. It hurts *everyone* – and it makes me angry. It takes everything I have not to go in there and scream at her, point out how unfair and selfish she's being. But anything I can say to her about what I'm feeling is nothing compared to what she's feeling. I almost resent her for it.

A few months later, the baby has a particularly tough time. She's teething and screaming bloody murder. Sleep for her is pretty much non-existent, and so it goes for me.

It isn't any easier for Caroline. She lost fifty pounds in four months. She's a whopping 110 pounds, which is less than her weight prior to pregnancy. Her face is hollow and colorless and she looks awful. It's hard to say this, but one time I caught the sideview of her tiny body in the bathroom, and I didn't recognize her. She's unrecognizable in every way. The doctors tell us that it gets worse before it gets better. I hope that's true. We don't talk much. Once she learned we can't even kiss during treatment because her saliva – any of her bodily fluids – would be poison for me, too, she became a shell of who she is. We both are. Her first round of chemo was six weeks. She had a month off. We're at the end of her second six-week cycle. After this, the doctors will decide if she can have a longer break.

Tonight, I'm at my wit's end. I need sleep, and the baby has me up at 12:45, 1:30, 2:40 and 3:15 in the morning. I cradle Gracie, trying to rock her, but she won't stop screaming. By 4:30, I can't take anymore.

"Please Gracie, come on. Come on," I beg her. I try to feed her the bottle, she won't take it. "Caroline!" I yell. The baby wails over me. "Caroline! Can you help me? She needs her mother!" I bounce Gracie, struggling as the rubber nipple bends against the trapdoor of her mouth. "Caroline!"

Caroline

Staring at the ceiling, I hear Chris get up 100 times that night. I feel sorry for him, but there's not a thing I can do about it. I can't keep anything down, my throat is raw and stings and even water hurts to swallow. I feel like I'm going to die. Everything hurts. The baby cries because she's teething, and I can't think about it or I'm going to throw up .

I sprint to the bathroom covering my mouth, I'm not going to make it. But I do, barely. I rinse, gargle, which makes me gag again, and I puke mostly water everywhere, but now I have to clean it up. I grab a towel from the rack, sop up my watery bile with it, and leave it in the tub. There's no way I'm dealing with laundry tonight, even though it's all fucking toxic for Chris. I salamander-crawl back to my bed and slide in. I can see him standing in the hallway, bouncing Grace up and down to no avail while she screams.

"Caroline! Can you help me?" he yells. "She needs her mother!"

I bet she does, but I can't. I leave him standing there.

It's June and I feel a lot better. My doctors said the last two rounds of chemo took, and I get a break.

"At least a month," Dr. Ryan's replacement said, "Maybe more."

Dr. Ryan is out on maternity leave with her new baby girl. Despite what the ultrasound showed, that little trickster was giving a thumb's up, saying "Fooled You, no boy here!" I'm so happy Dr. Ryan got what she wanted. I love seeing life throw little surprises when science is sure it has the answer. Anyway, I have another appointment in two weeks to see how long before I start my next round. Hearing that it's working gives me hope. Maybe I will survive this thing, be the extraordinary case that proves science wrong. I put on ten pounds already, almost back to my pre-baby weight. Chris and I are sleeping in the same bed again. It's nice to have him back. As soon as the chemo cleared my body, I kissed him so long and hard, as if I'd never kissed him before. In a way, I hadn't. These last several months feel like a different lifetime. I *am* a different person, so is he. And I love him more now than I ever thought I could. I've been a useless sloth in my home, a black hole robbing my family of light and time. A lesser man would've left, and he'd have every right. But I married a man who practices what he teaches, I married a man of virtue.

Thank God for my therapist, Dr. Madison. These feelings, they are some complicated shit. A foul, gross understatement, but I'll give you a break from the melodrama.

And I regret to say, during treatment I barely bonded with my daughter.

I've only skimmed the surface of that level of self-loathing with Dr. Madison. But the truth is, I need to stop talking and start doing. Whether I feel I'm enough or not, it's time for me to be her mother. To do the best I can with what I've got. I'm so afraid.

※

One August morning, I wake up before dawn, no alarm, no nothing. It's quiet, dark, still. Only the sound of the ocean and my husband's breath break up the silence. I'm over the moon, because yesterday I found out I have more time. I still don't have to do chemo…yet. Dr. Ryan and I – she just got back from leave– decided that since my labs look good, spending healthy time with my daughter is the priority. Chemo flattens you. I'm not exaggerating when I say I sleep for *three days straight* after chemo, and I'm not unique. All of us undergoing chemo sleep for days on end - I found a local support group who confirms it. We commiserate and share our stories, our symptoms, our prognoses and our small victories. Connecting with people who just "get it" helps with the loneliness and isolation. It helps me feel like I'm not alone, and I help them. It feels good to be useful again. They all agree – healthy time with my family is the priority right now. I can "go back in" when it's time. The port is still in, below my collarbone above my boob. Funny, in Sci-Fi, a portal is the means by which you travel through time, a "time portal." Mine connects me to the black hole. Time. It's such an elusive thing.

But today, to wake up knowing I have good days ahead, brings a smile to my face so unbridled I can barely keep quiet.

"What a gift," I whisper, through gleaming teeth.

I throw the blankets off, kiss my sleeping husband on the forehead, stand up and pad downstairs. I make coffee. I sit on the couch, and stare out the picture windows while the sun comes up. The vibrant oranges and pinks spread over the deep blue sea. *Letters to My Baby* sits on my lap, but I have no plan. I stare at the beauty outside, alone with my thoughts, and today, they're healthy ones. God I've missed them. I mindlessly move my pen up, down, all around and back again, not looking, just moving the pen while I daydream. When I look down, I see what I've done. An infinity sign stares back at me. I was mindlessly drawing an infinity sign, my subconscious at work.

Infinity means we go on forever. When this body here on Earth ceases, *we* go on forever– into the soil, into the atmosphere, into the rain, back down to Earth, over and over. We are all made of stars. I believe our soul or energy carries on, without the confines of our physical bodies. We're all going to die - we're doing it right now, whether it's cancer, Alzheimer's, heart failure, diabetes, or old age. But we go on - through our children, through the words we write down, the pictures, the stories we pass down, the memories we share, we go on. I've been sick for longer than I knew, but it was by the grace of a greater being I got to be here long enough to meet my husband, conceive, experience great love, feel the agony of defeat, and the exuberance of victory. The grace of God kept me alive to meet Gracie, to see the fruits of my labor – quite literally. I've never been a religious person, but after seeing life *and* death, it changed me. I know in my heart and soul there's more to it, there's more out there.

I head into the laundry room to find what I'm looking for; I slide my sports bra over my lean body, avoiding the scarred skin where I had radiation on my neck. There's a slew of other sores and scars that don't heal because I've kicked the shit out of my immune system and birthed a little girl. My body may not look the way it did two years ago, but what it has been through… it's a marvel. And I can feel my power coming back. I go into Gracie's room, run my hand over the handle of the Baby Jogger Summit X3 in all black. I pick up my daughter and kiss her face obsessively.

"You ready, baby girl? You ready for our special day?"

I carry her downstairs and safely place her in her swing, handing her a favorite stuffed animal she loves to put in her mouth, while I charge upstairs for the stroller. I grab it and run back downstairs. The thumping wakes Chris.

"Caroline!" he yells. "Are you ok?"

"Yes hon!" I yell back. "Can you come down here?"

He appears immediately and doesn't look pleased to see the stroller, my running outfit, or the baby on board.

"Waaaaait a minute. No way, Caro, no way. You're not well, and…."

"Babe, I feel good today AND I want you to come with me. Just a walk. Ok?"

"A walk?" He knows me better than that, "I'm holding you to it. I'll get dressed, but you're not running. I'll go, but you're not…"

Minutes later, the three of us are outside. It's a perfect eighty-degrees out, with the sun shining on my face and the wind blowing my wig. It may not be *my* hair, but I don't care.

Seven-month-old Grace is strapped in, and I hold the rail behind her. I peek over to see her face – her mouth is open so wide, I can see all of her gums and her two bottom teeth.

"You like it out here, Gracie? Let's go!" I walk at a decent clip, I can see Chris eye me peripherally. I know he's nervous, but I *have* to do this.

I walk faster, Chris does the same. I break into a light stride, Chris keeps up. I wheeze.

"Caroline." Chris warns me.

"I'm ok." I break into a light jog, my knees shifting from straight to bent, the air under my feet going from minimum to maximum, my stride covers a little, then a lot, of ground. I watch the trees go by faster and faster, one after another. The smell of the ocean air, my outstretched legs, I feel it. I'm moving, I'm strong, I'm back, and I'm with my daughter. It's all I've dreamt of. I go faster, faster, faster.

Chris yells, but nothing can stop me. I peek my head around to see my baby again – she's giggling! Her body bounces with each bump and her eyes squint with delight. She likes it. She *loves* it! A surge of power moves through my body - I'm me again. For a second I'm free, unstoppable, unencumbered. I'm not infirm, I'm me. A woman, a wife, a runner, and a mother. I'm on fire and I'm free, my baby girl and me.

Suddenly… I'm wheezing. I stop. I can barely breathe.

"Caroline!" Chris yells. "Caroline!"

I crouch down, catch my breath. *Stay calm, Caro, you can do this, stay calm.*

"Caroline!" Chris screams, catching up to me. "What the hell are you doing? I told you to stop! Jesus Caroline… Are you ok?"

I get my bearings, take a deep breath, control the coughing. I stand up, "I'm ok. I'm good."

"You don't look good" he says.

"I know." I take a knee again, cover my mouth and cough hard, there's a spray of blood on my hand.

"Honey. *Are you ok?*" He puts his hand on my back. I quickly hide my bloody hand.

"I am baby, I'm extraordinary." I stand up too fast this time and get woozy. I grab on to him for balance.

"Let's walk home," he orders, "Slow."

"Ok."

26.2

Chris

She's remarkable the year after Grace is born - a fighter. The doctors give her a prognosis, she beats it, they give another prognosis, and she beats that, too. She's made liars and fools of them over and over– and believers, too – she's made believers of all of us.

Those first few months after the baby was born were beyond difficult, but by month six, she is on the up and up – looks better, isn't getting nauseous all the time, even gains some weight back. Despite those first few months where she and Gracie had virtually no contact, she's fallen head over heels for her. They're inseparable.

Caroline makes it to Grace's first birthday. We watch our little girl try to blow out her first birthday candle, perched in her highchair, pink frosting all over her face. She's so cute… both of them. Making it to Gracie's first is a big moment for Caroline. Later that night, she holds Gracie in the rocking chair and rocks her back and forth. She holds on and hugs her so tight, singing her to sleep. My two girls – what a lucky man am I.

It goes downhill quickly after that. A few weeks later, we are back in the hospital… Caroline has been feeling foggy, slurring her words, not making sense. The doctors call for an MRI. And as they feared, the cancer has spread to her brain. There isn't anything more they can do, and at this point, all we can do is make sure she's comfortable and prepare. We make arrangements to start hospice at our home.

🐚

Caroline

A few days after I get "the news," I set up an appointment with Dr. Ryan. I tell Chris I'd like to take this one alone, for him to wait in the waiting room. Bald, rail thin, with dark circles and sallow skin, I stare at her from across from the desk.

"Dr. Ryan," I lift an oxygen mask to my face, take a long, slow drag, rest it next to me. "I want to thank you for everything you've done for me. There were so many moments I couldn't have gotten through without you. You were an angel to me."

"Of course, Caroline. It's been my pleasure. You're a hell of a fighter."

"Mmm." I breathe from the mask again. "But you know, I came across this article in the *Times*. A woman, an author, named Louise Hay, passed a few months ago. Ninety years old. She died of natural causes."

"Oh yeah? Long life."

"Sure was. She was diagnosed with cervical cancer in 1977. Lived forty more years."

"Wow, one of those extraordinary cases."

"Yeah. She refused treatment." A long pause. I lift my phone to read, "She cured herself with a regimen that included nutrition, reflexology, and forgiveness."

"I'm sorry, Caroline, but would you want to bank your healing on that?"

"I couldn't kiss my husband, because of poison running through my veins. We put poison into our bodies that kills us. It kills the cancer, but it kills us, too."

"So this pie-in-the-sky, alternative talk is the answer? There's no conclusive evidence to support..."

"I'd say *she* is conclusive evidence. I'm not saying I have the answers." I take another long drag of oxygen. "But if this lady can believe her way out of cancer for *forty years*, I think she may be onto something. And I think you'd do well to explore new forms of this 'treatment.' So that by the time our daughters are grown up, they won't have to deal with this shit." I throw my mask to the side and pull myself up. All 100 pounds of me.

She jumps to help me up. "Caroline-"

"No, I got it." I turn and pull my tank, and shuffle to the door. I get there and turn to her. "We're all rooting for *you*."

I wobble out the door and see my husband.

He hops up. "You ready, baby?"

"I'm ready, baby."

🐚

Hippocampus, the scientific name for seahorse, is also the name of a section of the human brain named after its resemblance to this unforgettable sea creature. The hippocampus is responsible for *memory*. It belongs to the limbic system, the region responsible for emotion, and plays important roles in the consolidation of information from short-term memory to long-term memory. Neuroscientists believe the hippocampus is where memories are stored in the brain.

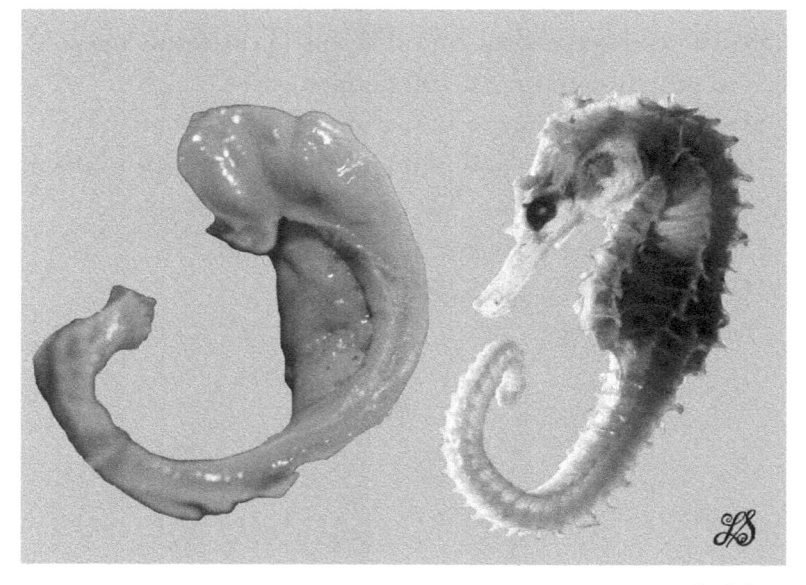

Laszlo Seress

Once upon a time, my health was the most important thing to me; now, it's my memories. They're the only things that keep me going and make me feel alive. They remind me of this life I've been given, and that I'd do nothing different. Nothing.

🐚

Chris

We arrange for hospice at our home. I set it up in her office, among her ad awards, marathon medals and photos of her family, all of her proudest moments. We added the photo with the women from the baby shower, and most importantly, her definitive, proudest moment, right in her eye-line, a picture of her, Gracie and me. I think about putting hospice in our bedroom, but I know I'll never go in there again if she passes in there. I'm glad Grace is only a baby – I'd never want her to see her mother like this. At a certain point, it stops being the Caroline you know.

I visit her amid all the beeping, sit down next to her bed. She struggles to breathe, an oxygen mask permanently resides on her face. I see her eyes recognize me, and she squeezes my hand, but that deteriorates, too. We know we are getting down to days.

Caroline

It's a bright, sunny, beautiful day. Not too hot, not too cool. I have on my running shorts, the pink ones. I'm sweaty, but the breeze makes everything all right. I think for the first time, I'm actually glowing as opposed to sweating. Yeah, definitely a first. I stop at the Gatorade station at mile nineteen. I'm tired, but I'm having a hell of a race. I feel strong, and I have a feeling I'm going to beat my best time today, I'm going to get my personal record. I take the Dixie cup of Gatorade and check my watch.

"I better get a move on." I tip back the cup and toss it in the trash. I'm going to make it.

I start running. I look over and see someone sweeping all the cups from the street— wait, is that Rita from the salon?

"Hi, Rita!" She looks up and waves back with a smile.

I continue at a decent clip, and then I see someone else from the salon. She's handing out water.

"Beth? Oh my God, hi Beth!"

"Hi darlin', you keep going now, you hear? Not too much longer!"

I run like she told me to. I'm nearly at mile twenty. I can see it in the distance. And standing there, right at the mile marker is Patty and her husband Bobby. He reaches down to kiss her on the cheek, and she looks up at him, taking his hand.

"Patty! Patty, Bobby!"

She sees me and starts jumping up and down, clapping. Amelia and her two boys are a few steps away, holding "Go Caroline" signs. She waves and blows me a kiss. A swarm of other women from town run up to the sidelines with their signs: "Worst Parade Ever", "Run Like a Zombie is Chasing You", then "Run Like Julian Edelman is Chasing You"– I smile at that one, I'd stop running if he were chasing me.

Suddenly, Julian Edelman darts out! He's got his helmet on, and is carrying a football, but I know it's him because of the "11" on his shirt. He spanks my butt and runs past me, hanging on to the football. Weird, but awesome. I must be hallucinating – which can happen at this point in the race.

I see mile twenty-one in the distance.

"Five point two miles left!" Jules yells over his shoulder, before speeding ahead.

I wish it was only four, three would be better.

"One foot in front of the other, one foot in front of the other," I tell myself.

I pass twenty-one and keep moving. Maybe I need a walk break? No, I'm getting my personal record, today. Maybe if I keep Edelman in sight, I'll be able to keep this pace. I can see him in the distance (I'd know that ass anywhere), so I keep it up. One foot in front of the other, keep going, breathe. I grab for a Gatorade at the station – my Dad hands it to me.

"Go get em kid," he says.

"Ok Dad, I love you."

I take it and keep going. I see college kids handing out mini cups of beer – we must be at mile twenty-two. Crazy kids.

"Beer?" one offers.

"Maybe after!" Damn it smells good, smells like celebration, but I'm not there, yet. Four point two left, four point two.

I see Dr. Sylver, smiling and clapping. Right next to him is my chemo tech, Barb. They're cheering.

"Keep going Caroline!" they shout.

A few moments later, I see Paula and John. "Keep pulling, Caro! Keep pulling!"

Pulling? They must mean running. Whatever, I love them. They wave and blow me kisses – I blow one back. Pete is right next to them, all in black. I don't know what he did, but it looks perverted. *Oh, Pete.* Then he blows something out of a straw – I think it's a spitball, but it unfolds and turns out to be a paper airplane that zips by me and opens up to read: mile twenty-three.

"Oh thank God I'm here." This is when I can turn it on. I keep a cool, easy pace the next half mile or so, and then after that – see ya.

I see Dr. Ryan, holding her baby girl, next to her husband and son. They wave flags at me. I look Dr. Ryan straight in the eye.

She nods, "We got this," she says.

I nod back, smiling through the sweat and tears, and I push on, pointing at her as I pass.

I see my girls, Anna, Mack and Leash – they're running in a pack.

"Ladies?" I say, as I pull up next to them.

"Hey Caro! Run your race," says Anna. "Run your race."

"You don't want me to hang here, with you guys?"

"Not today, babe, this one's yours," Leash says.

"Go get that PR!" shouts Mack.

"Ok! I love you guys!" I say.

"We love you, too!" They yell after me.

I pick up the pace and keep my eyes forward, until I see…mile twenty-four. I'm so close. Mom holds out a Dixie cup of water. I take it, and she throws her arms around me:

"I'm so proud of you. I always knew you could do it, even when it sounded like I didn't. *I believe in you.* Now go, go finish your race."

"Ok Mom, I love you." I give her a sweaty kiss on the cheek.

It's time. I hit play, and the distant church bells of my song brings serenity to my ear drums and a fire in my quads. *Where the Streets Have No Name*, let's go.

At mile twenty-five is Katie, jumping up and down, screaming louder than anyone.

"Go Caroline! Go Caroline!"

She runs out next to me, we do a cartwheel next to each other and as we come up, she holds my shoulders and looks me in the eye,

"You're the best friend I've ever had, I love you. Go get your PR."

"Ok sis, I love you."

I run *fast, faster*. As I run, I notice a boy on the sidelines – a teenage boy - he's pale, thin, and looks sick; I see track marks. He takes his hand and wipes it over his other arm, and like magic, it erases the marks, brings color to his skin. It's my brother, TJ.

"Keep going, little sister, keep going!"

"Ok TJ!"

My music blares, I pass mile twenty-six, only .2 miles to go. My feet move faster and faster, my hamstrings hurt, my quads feel like eighty-pound boulders, but it doesn't matter, my hips ache, but it doesn't matter.

Go Caroline. Go. GO!

I pass runner after runner. Young, old, strong, beaten down, man, woman – it doesn't matter, *I go*. I want that finish line and I want it now, it's mine, and so is that PR. I see the clock ticking, I'll be there in fifteen seconds, thirteen if I move.

I sprint, faster, faster, it doesn't hurt, I see the finish, it doesn't hurt. My family and friends are all there now, at the sidelines, screaming and cheering, the crowd is going nuts. Ten, nine, eight, seven…

I see my husband. He's holding our baby. Their shirts say: "You're our Hero."

Six, Five, Four… Bono wails. I'm gonna make it, I'm gonna make it.

Three… I take my last steps

Two… One more step – my husband cheers and waves me in.

One… I cross the finish line. I did it. I did it. My personal record, I did it!

I hug my husband and my baby – my soulmate and my daughter - my two favorite people in the world.

"You did it, baby," Chris says.

"We did."

He holds me tight, and I hug them in. The crowd cheers, and I start to cry - it's hard to catch my breath, but I got it.

"Don't cry Caroline, don't cry. There's nothing to cry about. Don't cry."

I hold them as close and as hard as I can. I look up and see the sun above me, it's blinding. It's so bright.

Chris

It's 11am when I sit with her. She doesn't react to my touch, she hasn't for a few days. I sit down and run my index finger down the back of her hand, all the way up her skinny arm and down again. I keep at it, drawing the sign for infinity, up and down, back and forth, circling around as the tears come from my eyes.

I don't know why, but I find myself muttering,

"It's ok, honey. You can go if you want to. It's ok."

Her fingers move, and I hold them.

Tears come from her eyes as she lay there, but she's smiling. The doctors explain any activity at this point is the body's unconscious reaction to dying, and systems shutting down.

Still I whisper, "Don't cry Caroline, don't cry. There's nothing to cry about, baby, don't cry."

I hold her hand as her body strains and jerks against the pulls of death. Her hand rips away from mine, flailing in the air, and lands back down squeezing mine for good. She pulls her last breath of air from this Earth, and then gives it back.

And she's gone.

When lined seahorses find their mate, they create harmonious clicking sounds while embracing their partner, which eventually becomes one unified sound. This seahorse is monogamous, and performs ritual dances every morning, continually reaffirming their relationship as mates.

The intensity of their bond is conveyed in how they handle the death of their partner; if either the male or female should die, the mate does not automatically replace the deceased with a new partner. Often, it fails to find a new mate in its short lifespan.

Chris

She dies on a Friday, her favorite day of the week, the day she'd get margaritas after work in her twenties, and wine at our home in her thirties. Who am I kidding, she'd have wine any day of the week. "Live life to the fullest," she'd say. And she did, she truly did.

She passes a week shy of her fortieth birthday, she never wanted to be over the hill anyway. Old age wouldn't have mattered – she could be 100 and she'd still be the most disarming woman in the room. That was my Caroline, my prize, even though she believed *she* was the lucky one. Maybe we both were. Maybe we only get so much luck in this life, but I don't want to believe that. I want to believe there's an infinite number of good things, I have to.

To say her funeral is the worst day of my life is an offensive understatement. I had to stand there and be strong while my world falls apart. The look on Katie's face, Gloria's and Martin's, on my parents', even her boss's face, her running friends, the women from town…

When a woman dies – a young, vital woman – it's the deepest of tragedies, second only, to the loss of a child. As I stand in the pew, I look over at Gloria, tears streaming down her face as she holds Gracie tight. She offered to hold Gracie, claiming I couldn't because I was a pall bearer. Of course, that isn't until the end, but I let that be my excuse anyway. I couldn't have held Gracie, I can barely hold myself up. She's a good girl though, cooing and smiling, she doesn't cry once. I think she is the only one in the whole gathering I can say that for.

Katie creeps to the podium and reads the Second Letter of St. Paul to Timothy. She does her best to get through it, her hand trembles while she holds the page, and the black of her mascara creates a straight line down her cheek.

"Beloved: I am already being poured out like a libation, and the time of my departure is at hand. I have competed well; I have finished the race; I have kept the faith. From now on the crown of righteousness awaits me, which the Lord, the judge, will award to me on that day, and not only to me, but to all who have longed for his appearing. The word of the Lord. Amen."

Katie puts on a brave face, much like her sister.

The final commendation...Father Sullivan swings the smoking censer over the casket to signal our farewell. When the incensing stops, Father Sullivan looks up at me, urging the final piece. "It's time," his eyes say. I want to disappear, be invisible so he can't see me. But instead, I nod, acknowledging our turn to push her up the aisle– my wife. I was twenty-nine when I met her, thirty when I married her, thirty-seven when I lost her.

There are two indescribable moments in a man's life when he looks at the woman he loves with tears in his eyes. This is the second, as I push her down the aisle of the church; our last walk. I gasp for air, I can't breathe.

A month or so later when I'm able to return to work, I expect everyone to hassle me over my new garb of choice. I mean, it is a progressive *women's* college, but it's still a place of work. Surely, I can find a nanny instead of bringing - no *wearing* - my child to work. But everyone is surprisingly more supportive and understanding than I ever imagined. Grace gets more wide-eyed and high-pitched hellos than she can handle; by the time I start my lecture, she's passed out. I carry her in that baby bjorn everywhere – through lectures, lunches, to the pharmacy, the barber shop, the grocery store; I wear her to the gym, walking on the treadmill. Ok, once I *tried* a light jog…she spit up. I even wear her in the restroom; although, I cover her eyes. She's s only fifteen months, she doesn't know naked parts anyway. But the looks I get from other men in the public restroom, they don't know if I'm a pervert, or worse, Mr. Mom. They don't get it. I grade papers at home while she sleeps in my lap. Sometimes I get so distracted looking at her that I lose hours.

I wouldn't change my life, or my experiences for anything. I didn't know going in that I'd be a single Dad, but you know, life doesn't always go the way we plan. But we have to keep our chin up, carry on.

The only place I don't bring Gracie is to Caro's grave. That's something even I can't get close to. Each time I go, I step closer; from a hundred yards, to fifty yards, to forty. The last time, I leaned up against a nearby tree about thirty feet away and stared at her gravestone, "Loving wife, selfless mother". I want to step closer, but stop.

"That's close enough for today," I say.

A few months later, when the warm months return, a letter arrives in the mail for me. It's in Caro's handwriting – a ghost rising from the past. It's both comforting and haunting at the same time. I open it, as it instructs me.

In it are one of those "Letters to My Baby". She'd handwritten on top of it – "You know she's not my only baby," with a smiley face.

Dear Sweetheart,

Happy birthday! At least you made it to another one, old man! Kidding. You know age is a state of mind. And speaking of minds, I want to tell you how much I love yours. Such a thinker, you were always a professor in my eyes, fancy degrees or not. A curious soul, the eternal student, and don't they make the best teachers? I think so. Your talents – from music to academics to sports – were enough to make me green with envy. But how nice it was not to admire you from afar, but to call you my own.

To associate with you was the greatest gift I've ever known; to be your wife was a dream come true. I thank you for that, sweet Chris. A beautiful mind, your face even more so, but what I love most about you, is your heart. You are, and always were, a kinder person than me. Once again, being near you elevated me, kindness by association. I was more likable, lovable, tolerable because of you. I became the person I wanted to be— compassionate, selfless, generous, brave— because of you. It is for this reason I held off on the radiation and treatments in favor of our daughter. I wanted her to have the chance to be cultivated by a perfect human being. You're as damn near perfect as I've ever known. Thank you for choosing me to share your life, to let me know you, to spend every day with you.

You filled my days with love, and I lived more in 39 years than most live in 100. I am forever grateful and complete because of you.

I love you, Chris. You are never alone. I am with you every day, watching you with our little girl, mastering the art of fatherhood, because that's what you'll do, it's who you are. I'm still there, same spot as always, loving you from behind the glass.
Until we meet again,
Caroline

I hold that letter against my chest and break down on our doorstep. I let it out in the middle of the day, in front of the trees and the grasshoppers and the birds. No one is outside to hear me, rocking back and forth, tears streaming down, crying from a guttural place. I cry so hard, sweat runs down my back. It feels good to let it out this much.

I cry until I'm out of breath, stop a beat, pant, get another image in my head, and let it out again. I cry like this for twenty, maybe thirty minutes, it's exhausting. Finally, I remember my daughter. I stand up, put one foot in front of the other, and move forward.

I had a good teacher.

Crickets. It's so quiet this time of morning, all you can hear are crickets. Crickets and the sound of the ocean. It's still dark. I tiptoe out of the bedroom to wake her up– she's gotten so big. Bright and beautiful, she looks like her mother. And she's the coolest, too. Daddy's little best bud.

I walk into her pink and purple room – she's four now – and I tap her arm gently. She rubs her blue-green eyes awake. I can see the delight when they open.

"Is it time, Daddy?"

"Sure is, we gotta hurry. The sun rises in fifteen minutes."

"Oh-kayyyy."

And she does. That perfect little kid hops out of bed, puts her pants and boots on and is ready to go.

We walk downstairs to where our fishing rods wait for us. We pet our two-year-old Golden Retriever, Gus, as we walk by– poor guy, he's barely awake himself. We walk through the great room, past the framed pictures of Grace and Caroline, the teal and yellow book, and a letter from Caroline. Gracie gets one letter each year on her birthday from age 4 to 21. Gracie has me read it to her every night, though I often sneak in something lighter – like Dr. Seuss or *Sports Illustrated*. We continue through the kitchen, past the beloved zip code magnet, and a picture of Gloria, Katie, Sara, and Grace - three generations of McCafferty girls, shining on our fridge - and through to the back doors.

"Ok, honey, let's go!"

"Yeah!"

We skip to the water and wade in, but only up to mid-calf – and that's pushing it. She's so little, I don't want her to get in too deep. When we're finally in place, we cast out, reel in, wait.

Grace looks up at me, "Daddy, this is fun."

"It sure is baby. Look at the sun. See the pink little sliver? Here it comes, Gracie, here it comes!" I slide a black pair of sunglasses over her eyes to protect her. "Don't look straight at it. If your eyes start to hurt, look away."

"Ok, Daddy."

Cast out, reel in, cast out, wait. Wait for the sun, wait for the fish, wait for life to happen. Wait for her to look. I look over my shoulder at the glass, and I see her there. I *know* she's there, watching, smiling, full of love. Forever.

"Your turn, Daddy, your turn!"

I cast again and put my arm on my daughter's back. And we're there— Grace, me, and the sea.

I didn't skimp on the ring, not at all. And I *always* brought her flowers, not just for her funeral. I got her flowers all the time. I think that's how I kept her.

-Chris Shaughnessy, 2018

Khara L. Campbell

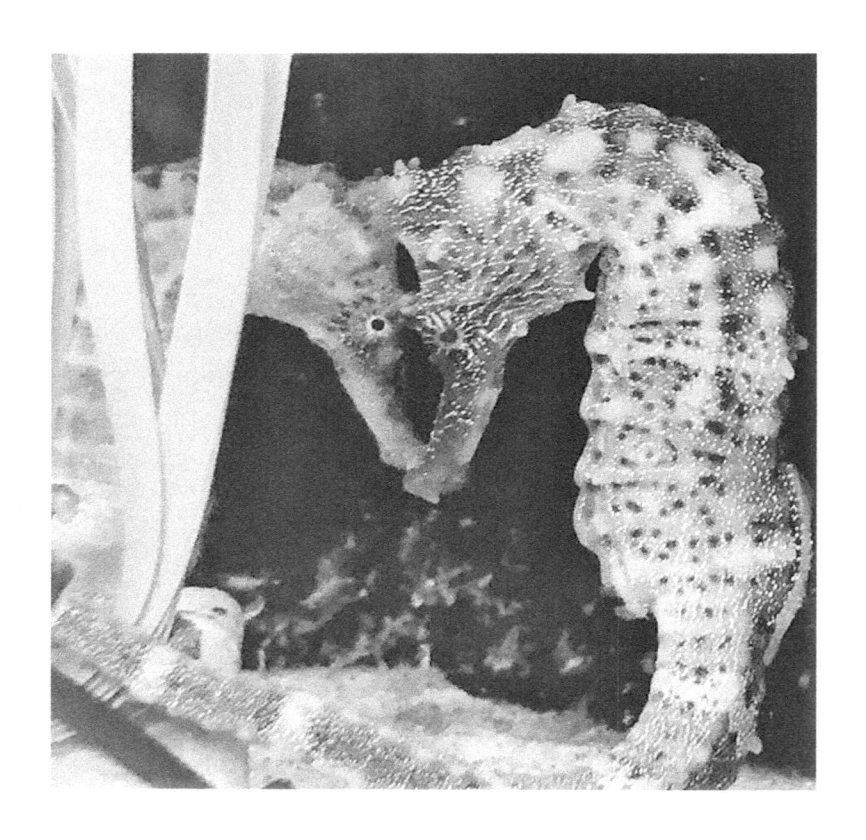